# DREAD WARRIOR

# DREAD WARRIOR

## *THE ENCHANTER'S WEB BOOK 1*

### *M. Turville Heitz*

For information address Oakland Hills at P.O. Box 531, Cambridge, WI 53523
Oaklandhillsfarm.com

Cover art and design by Ingrid Kallick https://ikallick.com/

For David who wanted to see this in print and didn't, and for Morgan who will.

# Acknowledgements

Thanks to all those who provided feedback and insight as this work took its long journey from a college writing thesis to novel. Special thanks for in-depth review by Jay Clayton, Kandis Eliott, Hal Gillam, Kathleen Massie-Ferch, Steven Rogers, Fred Schepartz and Morgan Turville-Heitz.

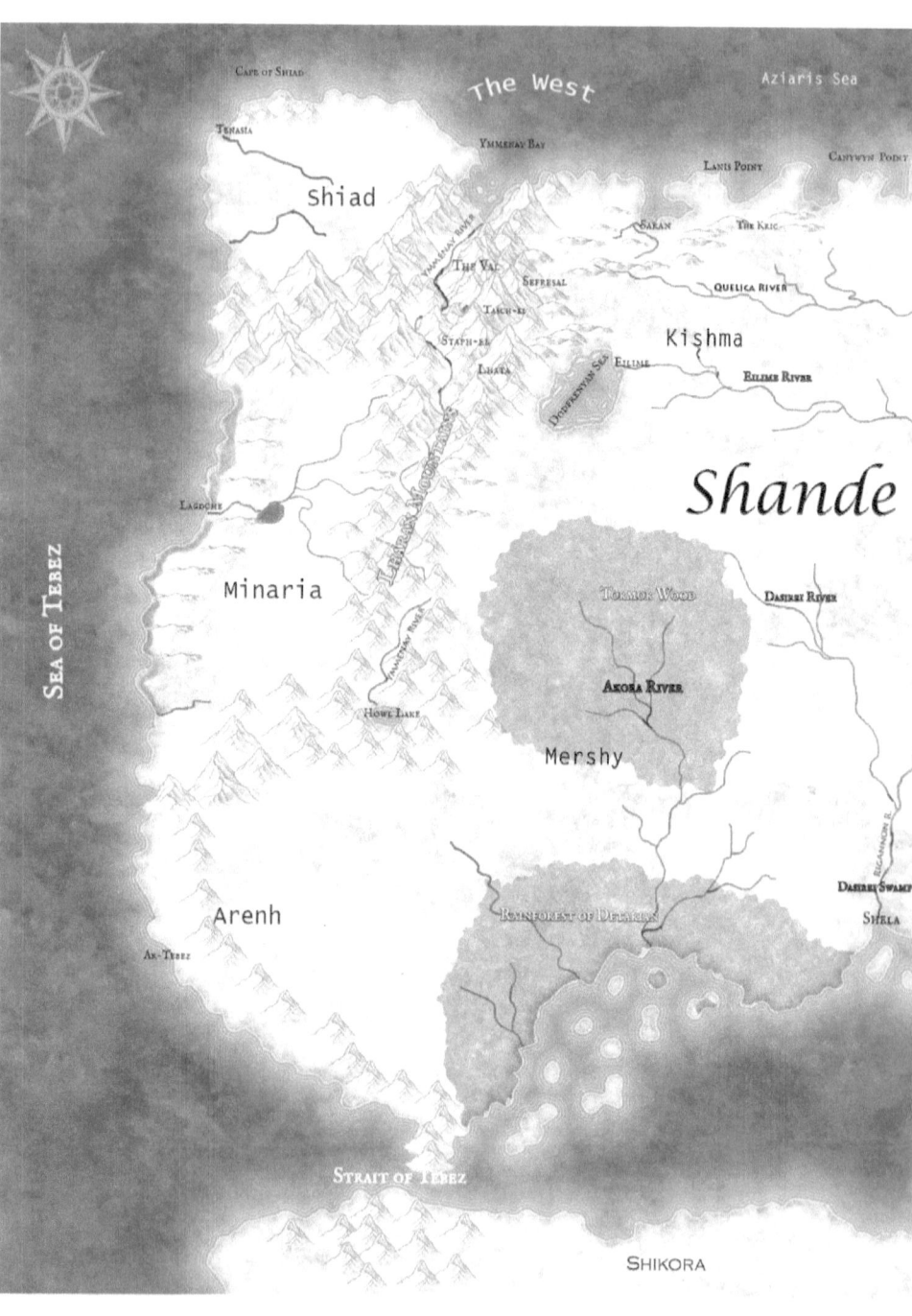

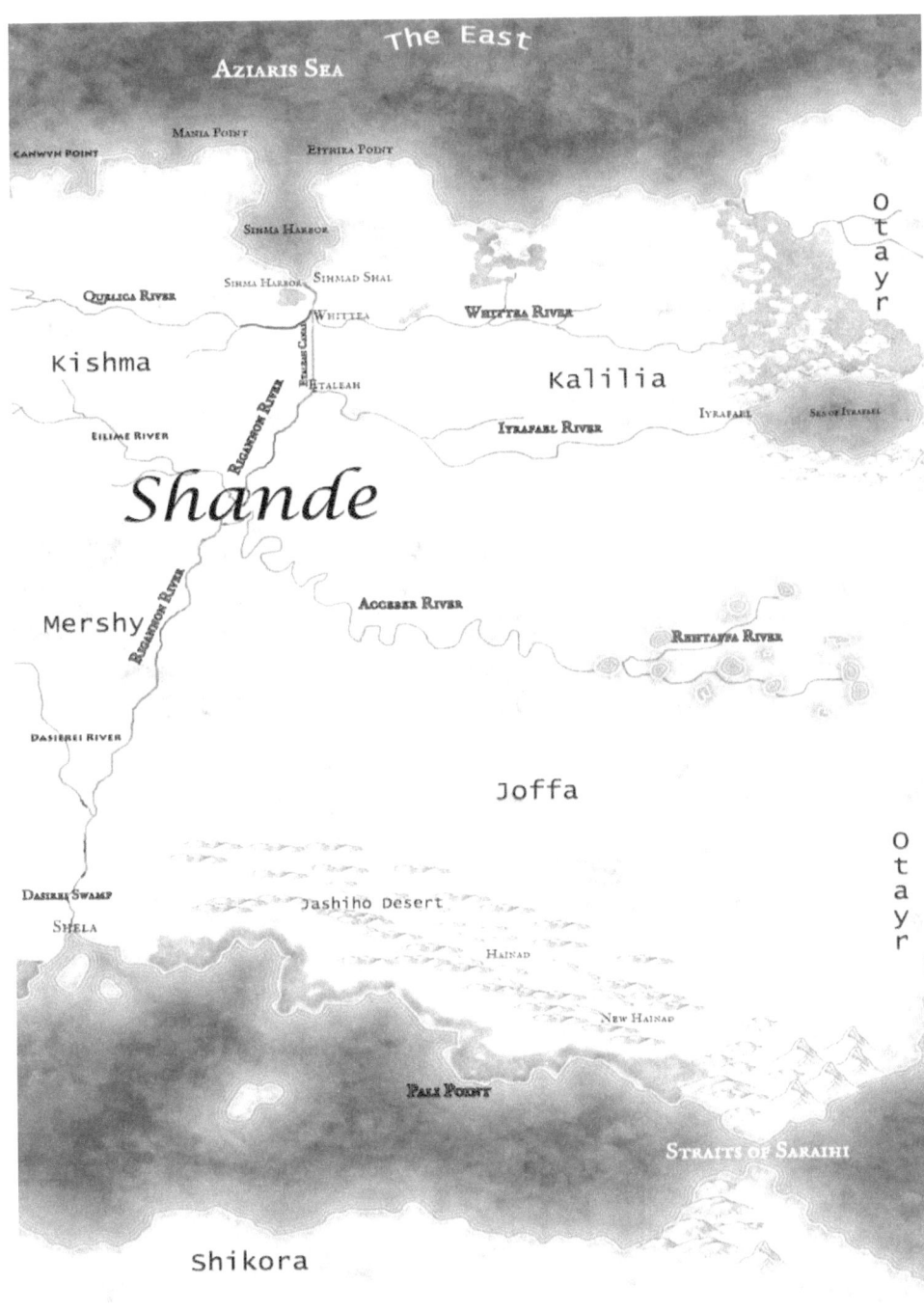

# PART 1. A PLAN

# 1: Honor

Khoti paused his pacing to study the pass from the mouth of the little cave where he'd sheltered Asteria but two moons ago. What took Chati so long? This second day of a cold-moon thaw crept into his blood, teasing him with the rushing sound of snowmelt. A south wind wafted into the snug cave, hinting that mountain winter might end early, taunting him with a false hope of sweet fruits and fresh greens.

He poked at the small fire he'd set and smoothed the painted hide holding a picnic feast. He had no time to idle, and since becoming the duke's aide barely the time to prepare for his next scouting duty.

At last, he heard Chati's cheery greeting over the sounds of snowmelt as the new Guard apprentice led Asteria's mount to a picket beside Khoti's own Fidra.

"I'll be out here," Chati said with that same lecherous grin Geleg always sported as Asteria peeked in, giving Khoti a quizzical smile.

"My Lady." Khoti executed a theatrical bow and gestured for her to enter the cave.

"What are you up to, Khoti?"

She settled on a cushion beside the fire as Khoti pulled a small bundle from his gear and knelt in front of her.

"What is this all about?" She laughed as she examined the picnic of wine, cheese, dried fruits, bread and meats spread out on the hide.

1

"You really don't understand our ways, do you?" He chewed his lip a moment. "Among my folk, when you pursue a lifemate you don't post it and put out a call for all comers like your people do, as if your fa were taking bids."

She watched him, breathless and smiling. The scent of the thaw clung to her.

"A Taschian man's first supposed to prove he can provide his share in a household, and the rest is just mutual likes." How could he explain traditions no one bothered to question? They just were. Heat rose in his face.

She covered her mouth with one hand. Her cheeks flushed as she waited for his explanation, expectant, as if she barely kept herself from speaking or breaking into giddy laughter.

"This feast is a tradition," Khoti continued. "And a nice one, I think. I had to wait so long because with that crowd in the Val there's no place for privacy, and your people don't like us even meeting alone, as is usual. And, well, it takes time to do these things right. See, I shot and cured the meats myself. The fruits came from stores, but the cheese I helped prepare. I ground the wheat for bread from Shiadin grain, and used my mother's method to bake it. I think there's something symbolic in that, but I don't remember the tale now. It's supposed to show I can bear some responsibility." He gestured at the cave. "This is all I have. But I should treat you in the home I'd offer as bridegift and we'd have a hearthstone from one of our parents, if there were hearths to pry them from." He held out the bundle in his hands. "And with shelter and sustenance proven there's the other needs of life. Clothing for warmth, I already gave you the dagger for protection, and what small things of pleasure I can give."

With trembling hands, he unwrapped the bundle. Certainly, this all seemed silly and crude to her, as if anything he made compared to a noble's gems or fine gowns.

First, he held up a necklace of stellan discs strung on fine metal threads wrapped along the length of a hide cord. Pounded leaf thin, he had impressed patterns on each disc: the image of a tawnkat on one, a fair likeness to Sefresal on another, the silhouette of the four mountains surrounding the Val, a pair of hands holding tera sticks, and an imprint of a star set in a stone the shape of the pendant Khoti still kept in his breast pocket. The necklace chimed as he held it up and tied it around her neck.

Her eyes had grown moist. "It is beautiful."

He held up the remaining bulk of the bundle. "I chose the best hides," he said as he displayed a hide tunic similar to the outfits worn by many mountain women. The accompanying trousers had room in the knee for riding and tied just above the calf to cover boot tops. He'd woven a fringe along the neckline of the tunic and decorated it with buff-and-pewter-colored beads. The hemline fringe sported green and beige, the colors long associated with Tasch-el.

She examined the seams, the sewing, the beading, the thickness of the hide. "You made this? It is so finely sewn. A little loose in front perhaps."

He tried to stop a sputter of laughter from escaping. "There must be room in front. I've never known a woman to wonder why." He chuckled as the color deepened in her cheeks.

"Then mountain men make their lifemates' wardrobes?"

"Only this bridegift," Khoti admitted. "The aim is to show you cared enough to try to make a gift more beautiful than others'."

Asteria stroked the soft hide. "I wish I knew such customs better. I steal its magic to expect an explanation."

Khoti shrugged. "It's only a tradition, a promise. Like your custom for waiting so long."

Again, he caught the scent of freshness, of thaw, of mountain wildness carried on the wind, clinging to Asteria's hair and cloak. Around him spread the comforts of the idle. He yearned to escape into the wild again, for the thrill and challenge of the hunt.

"It is a good tradition to wait," Asteria said. "Others can name reasons why the suit is inappropriate. There might be a better match, or the suitor's character or debts are in question. Perhaps the man is unaware of some dishonor to the woman. If no one contests the suits, the woman is then at leisure to decide."

Khoti shrugged. "We're in my world now, not Sefresal. It should be about love, not rumor. After all, you're selecting a lifemate, not a brood mare."

She studied him as if she could read his impatience, sense his desire to again take up the chase and challenge his mettle against their enemies. The headiness of the thaw, the freshness like dawn on the south wind, quickened his breath, awoke the sleeping warrior heart within him.

She touched the scrub of beard he now sported. "I will try to show my father his traditions are impractical, and that your way is the better," she murmured. "But this," she tugged at the sandy beard curling about his chin, "This must go."

He chuckled and pushed a chunk of dry apple into her open mouth. "Already you're trying to change me!" He tugged the hide table closer to reach for bread and cheese as she stroked the tunic in her lap.

"I would love to see how it fits," she mused.

He gave her Geleg's favorite grin. "Let me help you." He yelped when her hand came up. Scrambling beyond reach, he scampered from the cave to drink in the thaw, gulping deep breaths of the south wind, the wind that stirred in him the call, again, to battle.

When Khoti and Asteria rode into the Val side-by-side, Chati trailing behind them, Eithurdon faltered in his discussion with Tait, the new Mayor of Eilime, the young successor to the mayor who fell in the battle for the pass. He noted Tait's sudden scowl when he spied them. His daughter wore a coy smile, her head cocked to one side as Khoti spoke animatedly, one hand gesturing into the air as if he spoke of something rising up into the afternoon sun of the Val. She had dressed in the outfit of a mountain woman with some trinket at her neck glittering in the sunlight. He felt relief to see his aide nearby again, a tremor of something deep inside – his blood yearning for the spirits in Khoti's blood – something he hated to admit.

"Eithur, you have your daughter dressed up like a goatherdess," Tait sputtered.

"I do not decide what fashion she chooses." Indeed, she appeared more Taschian than shawnsi.

"It's unseemly, the way you allow her to gallivant around with him, a Guardsman!"

"Second in command of the Guard, an officer," Eithurdon said easily, not at all in the mood for suitor's games today.

"You want your daughter joined with a career warrior? Hardly the type to fit into court life. And her now even closer kin to the king! How can you imagine her with an uncouth miner's son, a fighting man? He'll have her toothless and old before she's thirty. You can do better by her, Eithur. She would do well by me."

Eithurdon sighed loudly. Asteria spent more time with Khoti than he liked, but always an appropriate chaperone accompanied them. Time remained in which to select the best suitor. Certainly, the two would soon tire of their infatuation with the other's differences and seek companions within their own culture. At least Tait knew the proper way of approaching a suit, with deference and the spirit of a match. Asteria barely acknowledged the man. Tait's, too, seemed an unlikely suit.

"Konner returned," Eithurdon called to Khoti. "We will meet in the common to hear Aibak's response."

Khoti nodded, touching Asteria's hand as they parted. His aide appeared ignorant of the baleful look Tait threw at him as he preceded Eithurdon and Tait into the caverns. Indeed, Khoti didn't stand a chance in such a match.

Those Arshal called the King's Council gathered at a long, rough-hewn table in the common, seated on rickety stools hacked from stumps. The tiny cavern that served as both community area and Arshal's receiving hall collected the echoes of crying babies and the stench of cookfires, a mockery of Sihmad Shal's sumptuous halls that he had so disdained.

"Aibak says they've no proof we got a king as can do anything," Konner said, his words echoing. "They're still too afraid Minaria will pressure them if they aid us."

The council shifted awkwardly at Konner's statement, a few mumbling aloud their rebuttals as the small room suddenly grew stuffy.

"That's ridiculous. We know Minaria won't settle for just Shande," Arshal returned sourly. Six weeks a king and he had no progress to show for it.

Konner shrugged. "Says he begged King Keyen to help us."

"Maybe he can help in another way," Khoti mused.

Eithurdon leaned forward. "Such as?"

"Well –" Khoti began.

"Such as more food stuffs?" Tait interrupted. "Well, that's no use to us. We need –"

"I was about to say, maybe they would work with the Pladde. If they arm the Pladde and keep them supplied, their resistance will continue to draw the –"

"Help the Pladde? Don't be stupid, boy. This foolish talk just wastes our time. We need the arms. Our country's the one occupied. The Pladde have had their little uprising for four months now. There's been nothing –"

"Because they need arms, Tait."

Arshal studied the Guard Lieutenant, whose patient tone barely hid irritation. Tait always seemed to have an argument against anything Khoti suggested, and too often these council debates ended in a shouted stalemate. If Arshal didn't need the link to Eilimean cooperation he'd never allow him in the room. Arshal hated to admit regret that he'd spent so little time in his father's court learning politics and how to shut up the worst offenders.

"They can't have an effect without weapons," Khoti continued. "They've got to regroup and resupply all the time so when they do get an advantage they lose it because they're ill-equipped. If they had weapons, some help from the Shiadins, they could strike a pretty nasty blow, tie up the Minarians on their own turf and leave us more room to maneuver."

"That's a good point, Khoti," Arshal said as Tait glared at the Lharan officer.

"I think it's a bad idea," Tait returned.

Arshal sighed. His war would never leave this valley at this rate.

"We should be concentrating on our own needs, not counting on some miracle out of Minaria," Tait stated. "You let some reckless rustic with no background in strategy cloud the issue with crazy ideas meant only to bring him glory and to support a rebellion with his father's name on it. That little Tawnkat foray brought us more harm than good. Look at how many good folk have died in the retaliations! He's just worried the blame will fall on his father's house. Well, it's foolish counting on the Pladde. They're deserving of the station they've got –"

"You're being a fool, Tait," Khoti said with a growl. "Think twice before you question my family's honor –"

"Begging your pardon, Your Grace, but look! See how his head is all grown big with all the laurels these fools have heaped on him? He doesn't even know his station. He can't even recognize the truth of the Tawnkat's failure. He doesn't belong at this table, Lord, but on the hillsides guarding a flock. And now this council gives this reckless boy too much leeway because of the inflated tales of his glory. You'd think he fought back the Minarians single-handedly the way he tells it –"

"Tait, that is enough," Arshal interrupted.

In one swift glance the king could see how Konner had straightened and gone red at the insult to his heroes and his people, how the Guardsmen in the room stiffened as the mayor publicly denigrated a favored leader, how Peshal and Zopher had dropped their hands to rest on the daggers at their belts, how Khoti himself barely held himself steady, his face a brilliant crimson beneath his tawny beard. Arshal knew he should throw Tait off his council this moment. Yet he couldn't risk further tribal division. How could a land beset with destruction remain so stuck in its ways?

"Forgive me, Your Grace, but mark me, he'll talk us tight into trouble. Already he proves his worth. These people think he can do no wrong. Well, he can. Hasn't he already shamed the duke's daughter? Of all men, he shames the one who gave him a boost up from his mean stock, a chance to better himself among decent folk–"

"What are you blathering about Tait!" Eithurdon demanded.

"Eithur, I've hesitated to speak up out of respect for her honor. But this goes too far. I saw him sneaking about with your daughter myself. Coming out of his rooms, or hers. And there's talk that when the king's people were in the pass your favored aide spent the night with your daughter when he could have been tracking the enemy who killed King Ebon. And you let him have his leave? This willful youth is the one whose counsel you think is prophecy?"

"You make grave accusations, Tait." Kefta's tone rang perilous. "We're discussing Shiad's place in our defense, not your slanted method of pushing your suit for a woman."

"I merely call attention to the fact you are all so swayed by his past prowess – no doubt exaggerated – that you are unwilling to hear reason. He's impetuous enough that he'd dally with the duke's daughter, yet you'd think his very words prophetic. It sickens me the way you cater to his vanity."

Khoti stood, his stool tilting back to slam onto the stone floor. His eyes reddened with a rage that made those gathered lean back. Khoti's hands twitched at his side.

"Excuse me, Lord." He nodded to Arshal. "I must leave before I bloody my knife on the Mayor of Eilime."

"That's right, boy. Leave this table in shame. You should be red from the things you did to a man that trusted you, gave you position. I don't hear you denying it. And you used that position for your own selfish aims. You should leave." As Khoti strode from the common, Tait smiled. "Shows you can't trust these hill people. Should we get down to business?"

When Konner, Zopher and Peshal, and a handful of observers bearing the marks of Tawnkats all rose to follow Khoti, Tait turned to Arshal. "Lord, may I make my case?" he demanded.

"I think you made it sufficiently," Arshal returned. "This is not a forum for suitor's games, Tait. We're talking about the welfare of a nation."

Tait held out his hands, palm up. "I've done nothing, Lord, but bring up a matter that needed addressing. This is a matter of strategy and security –"

"I believe the Mayor of Eilime has forgotten who at this table is king. I will hear no more from you." Arshal rose and departed, leaving Eithurdon alone with his daughter's suitor.

Too much needed to be done to be wasting time on such silly antics, the games of a land at peace, perilously foolish in a war. Arshal scowled as he made his way back to his alcove. Not just a suitor's game, it picked open unhealed scabs. Clearly, the undercurrent of distrust and tribal rivalry, supposedly set aside in Dynfearn's time, remained. He could accomplish nothing unless they saw themselves as Shandeans first. It made him long for the boring councils his father called among people who couldn't imagine something close to a tribal rivalry but would fight for hours over a point of protocol. Gods, they had only one true enemy, yet no one could agree on how to deal with it.

He slowed his pace. If he returned to his room, Cree would badger him about his 'powers.' Since their arrival Cree had beset him like a miner attacking a lode, always digging and delving to learn more about the power that called the fog into the Harbor. Even knowing such power existed made Arshal break into a nervous sweat.

Peshal waited by the alcove entry. "I suggest we follow Khoti's plan," Peshal said. "And Zopher agrees with me. I hope you didn't hear any of that filth Tait spouted about Khoti –"

Arshal cut his brother off with an impatient wave of his hand. Zopher and Khoti worked together to build a network of spies and scouts that daily brought trickles of valuable information back to the Val, information they needed for success. Zopher had easily turned to Khoti to learn the craft of one born to these elements. And Peshal seemed drawn to the odd young Guardsman, who seemed to have the same dark side Peshal had discovered in himself. Arshal didn't doubt both easterners would remain loyal to Khoti under any circumstances. The Taschian seemed to inspire devotion in all who worked with him, like Esthen, the kind of leader Shande needed.

Arshal had to admit even he felt something around the mountain man, something he couldn't name. Perhaps he only saw the oddity of a true Shandean warrior. Such sense led him to name the young man to his council. Khoti had his people's respect and appeared more conciliatory than dour Tsevon. Arshal had no regrets, until now.

"I don't need this, Pesh," Arshal said with a sigh when Peshal seemed about to give up on him. "I'm sick of Tait using every opportunity to turn discussions from the matters at hand. I'm tired of him stalling decisions and arguing each point. And his talk of negotiating with the enemy to stop the retaliations just makes me ill. And I'm tired of this in-fighting among my council! We have a country to retake and here we have people squabbling over a woman. That Eithur puts up with this –"

"He'll kill Khoti if he believes anything Tait said."

"If it's founded, Khoti deserves it."

Peshal shook his head as they entered the narrow alcove. Cree looked up from his books; the brothers ignored him.

"Our forces are nothing without Khoti," Peshal protested. "He's the energy, the heart of our resistance –"

"They once said that of Esthen, and now he's dead." Arshal didn't mean the comment to have such a bite that it stung even him.

"He has this uncanny map in his head: of where every spy or scout is, of enemy locations and strategic strongholds. He looks at a battle plan and instantly reads its weaknesses. We need a man like Khoti more than Tait –"

"Pesh, I'm sick of it. I don't want to hear –"

"Arshal, he is your army. Your best. Why else does even that stubborn stick of a duke indulge his every whim? Please, intercede if you can. You need him. You need these people united."

Arshal sighed. How could one man win such a following?

"He is good," Arshal conceded. "We also need to avoid tribal war. I promise nothing."

# 2: Premonition

Asteria cleared her throat on the other side of the curtain into Khoti's alcove, tentative, regretting already her decision to come. The curtain flung back to reveal Amhese. The woman's smile as she appraised Asteria's garb raised a warm lump in her throat.

"I didn't know Khoti had such patience in him!" Amhese exclaimed with a laugh, motioning Asteria to a seat at the alcove's plain table beside a scowling Tsevon. "You'll be the envy of every mountain lass in the Val. Even Tsevon didn't present me with one so fine! You must've won his heart indeed."

Rising from the table, Tsevon nodded at Asteria, and disappeared behind the curtain into the niche where he and Amhese slept. She could hear him working a knife on a whetstone with a rhythm that grew like a presence, a beat that matched the throb in Asteria's chest.

Amhese sat, hands folded on the table before her, exuding an aura of infinite patience as she waited for Asteria to begin.

"I have no mother, no one to speak to of these things." Asteria touched one of the discs on the necklace that chimed with her every movement. "Your kinswoman Latra sent me to you. She has helped me adjust here, to learn things so I am a help and not a burden, talked to me of," she sprouted a shy smile, "Men."

Amhese giggled. "My poor boy if Latra's your teacher!"

Amhese motioned Asteria closer so they could speak, out of Tsevon's hearing.

"Khoti should seek a woman of his own kind!" Tsevon grumbled from behind the curtain. "There's plenty of 'em, gawkin' at his every move."

Asteria rose. She'd been a fool to come among those who hated her. Amhese shook her head and put a hand on Asteria's arm.

10

"Don't listen to him. He can't accept any mixing of mountain people with other folk. It's a strange thing I could lure him from Tasch-el to take a Staphian lifemate. You've been good for Khoti. You make him think. He's always been rash. Now he's got reason to be careful." Amhese cocked an eyebrow. "You're frustrated."

"By many things: not knowing if Khoti will be patient and wait a proper time or if he will come back to me when he is away." She plucked at the beads on her hem, biting her lip. How could she tell Khoti's mother what had brought her here?

"The customs are different," Amhese conceded in her patient tone. "That's because lives here are short and intense compared to the lives of the shawnsi. What harm comes from waiting a few moons, learning more of each other? Here we know each other a lifetime. I lived in another village, yet Tsevon and I knew each other from our first memories, gathering at festfires and playing children's games. Time gave us an invaluable knowledge of who we are. Maybe you're afraid time will change your minds. We're at war. Maybe it's better not to encourage distractions. If Khoti's thinking about the trivial worries of courtship, he won't be thinking about his sword. If you're worried he'll lose interest, maybe the interest isn't genuine."

"Amhese." Asteria hesitated. How would this sound, like the fears of a reckless girl? She tugged at the beads at her hem. "It is not merely interest so much that concerns me. Latra sent me because you also read dreams and she thought you should hear mine. Have you ever known in advance misfortune was about to fall?"

Amhese sat back, nodded.

"Khoti is in danger. I know it. I keep seeing him coming home dead, bloody, broken. In another dream I see him leaving, not returning, a tragic parting. We cannot be separated because.... It is all so confusing. I dream that somehow his life depends upon me; if not for me he will die." She shook her head. "I know they are just dreams. But the feeling that something terrible is about to happen is like a presence I can almost touch. My father insists tradition be followed to maintain honor, yet if Khoti leaves without me –"

"Yet you've already risked your honor," Amhese said in a tone that made Asteria falter. Amhese laid a reassuring hand on Asteria's. "How else could Khoti present traditional gifts? You take many risks. A mix of culture is hard, especially now. Like Khoti, you're reckless."

11

Asteria tried to rise. She should never have come. Amhese grabbed her hand and forced her to sit again.

"We can't afford to have hard feelings between our people and yours."

"But these premonitions –"

"You can't stop what's meant to be, Asteria. You see him dead then see him dying again, later, because you aren't there. Maybe you don't understand what you see. Premonitions are common here, honored. You may be making more than's meant. Your father won't yield. You have no choice. Perhaps separation's a good idea for you. As a noble, Asteria, you've an awful lot to risk by your behavior."

Tsevon yanked open the curtain into the niche. "My son dishonors the Duke of Lharan's daughter?" His voice coiled with menace. She wanted to flee, but could only stare down at her hands in shame. Where could she go?

"They're innocent," Amhese stated. "Rumor's the enemy."

"Among Eithurdon's folk? Innocence to them's a man learning his lifemate's name the day they take hands. The duke grants suit, he says, but it's others of better line that'll claim the prize. It's a game, and Khoti's the toy kicked among the players. The duke'll learn of this and the rumors get an ear. I refuse to face a shamed father seeking to kill my son!"

"If they stop seeing each other now, there'll be no problem."

"This foolishness will bring shame on both our houses! The boy should learn his station and end it now!"

Asteria wanted to fade into the cavern walls, to melt into one of the hard puddles of wax spilled on the floor of the niche. Among Khoti's people their meeting had been innocent, but it wouldn't be in her father's eyes. What possessed them when they knew the consequences, and the suspicion between their peoples? Tsevon spoke true. Her father would never accept the shame if he learned of it. No matter their innocence. A mountain boy might steal a kiss from the neighbor girl. But an heir to a duke? Would he learn of their unchaperoned night together? What if she must face her shame alone because her premonitions came true and no one would listen? She could only sit silent between Khoti's parents as their argument waged on, her hands wringing the green and beige beads at her hem. What had they done?

12

Eithurdon flung back the curtain to Tsevon's alcove and pushed his way in.

"Where is he?" Eithurdon's voice rang out as he filled the alcove with his anger. He found his daughter, as he'd feared. Asteria took a step back, shielding herself with Amhese, who took on the posture of a hen herding chicks beneath her wing.

"Is there a problem?" Tsevon demanded, stepping forward to block the duke's way. Had all the world come to meddle in his role as parent? "What brings you barging into my home like this, as if this were your hall, not mine?"

"Your son shames my house." Eithurdon peered around Tsevon at Asteria. "You will promise Tait."

"I will not."

Where had she learned such insolence? Khoti? "I cannot accept as son a man who would dishonor me, defy me, use me." Eithurdon choked on his words. An image came, unbidden, of Khoti surrounded by spirits, absorbing his duke's pain. He forced the memory aside. "That I trusted him!" he said. "I gave him rank in my Guard, set him above men who have given me years of loyal service."

Asteria grasped Amhese's hand. "Tell him, tell him! I did no wrong! You cannot make me accept someone I hate merely to get even! It is my life you are selling! Tait is a pond worm. Worse! He lies to press a suit. It is unjust that you believe him without hearing Khoti's defense."

Amhese stared at Eithurdon, defiant, still shielding Asteria. "You call Khoti who's risked his life only to help you, who gave you his blood, a man without honor?"

"Asteria is my –"

"Aren't there enough problems in war without such nonsense?" Amhese demanded. "What's the harm of young people talking of hopes and dreams, dispensing with tradition, when they can't even know if they'll live through the next day?"

Eithurdon's mouth opened, but no words came. What was tradition, but the foundation of everything he was?

"How could you –" he stammered.

"In a time of war there's worse things than impetuous young people and rumors to fear. Would you prefer a death? That's already augured. Khoti's no different now than before this Tait spilled poison in your ears –"

"I refuse him," Eithurdon stated. "It was never meant to be and I never would have allowed the match. I did not think he would risk my honor, my daughter. I thought only to keep the peace until he went away to battle." Eithurdon spoke in a dry whisper. What had he just said? Khoti's parents, Asteria, stared at him as if upon a ghoul. Certainly, they saw the gods had designs on Khoti that exceeded mere mortal hopes for the youth!

"A game then, a lie," Tsevon stated in a tone like Khoti's, righteous and wronged. "Is this how you repay loyalty and trust? It proves you still think the mountain people who bleed and die for you are worth nothing. Shame'll come, Duke, if you drive your daughter from you and bring a feud into this valley to destroy alliances. Khoti's got many friends who won't stand to see him treated this way. All this because of Tait, jealousy, and a custom with no place in the Val."

Eithurdon had never heard Tsevon so bitter, nor restrained. The Tawnkat's veins stood out on his temples, ridges on arms reaching from clenched fists. A brief memory came to him of the man Khoti had trailed deep into the mountains in search of his captive people.

"What's more," Tsevon went on. "I've never known women's foresight to be wrong. The lady sees my son returned to us dead. If that's so, then indeed you'll have shame on you. Though the greater loss might be to your Guard, the scouts, his people."

Khoti dead? Eithurdon faltered. "You believe such visions and that it is right to try to cheat a fate the gods devised?"

"It's foresight that sent me to Minaria," Amhese said. "I never questioned the woman who told me to go. No one there could perform my task. The Tawnkats might have failed." Tsevon nodded as she spoke. "Was it fate?" She shrugged. "I heard your daughter's tale and fear what she sees. The spirits are strong here, Duke. You find our medicine alien, but to us, it's natural. The spirits are in us. We live closer to them. If you didn't reject Khoti's blood you'd know that." Amhese took Asteria's arm and guided her behind the curtain into Khoti's niche, already laying claim to his daughter.

Eithurdon stared after them a moment, his words stuck in his throat. He turned his back on Tsevon, the Tawnkat fuming and hateful. Was it his fault or Khoti's that a rift deepened?

He barely noticed people's stares as he went to his own niche. The rumor had raced through the Val like wildfire, so quickly it had beaten him to even Tsevon's rooms. Custom entitled Eithurdon to challenge Khoti to a contest to the death or wounding. Or, more commonly, as Lord of the Province of Kishma, he could judge and banish the Taschian. Would he challenge Khoti to a contest, the youth win only to heal him of

14

the wound? The Duke of Lharan couldn't die frivolously. Banishing Tsevon's son would gain nothing but the enmity of Khoti's people. How could he even think such thoughts of the loyal aide who proved the old suspicions should have been quenched long ago? Yet if even a small portion of what Tait claimed proved true.... He could only blame himself. He should never have permitted such a hopeless suit. The welfare of his people must come before his daughter's suitors. As wronged as he felt, Eithurdon had to care what happened to this warrior he had made. The mountain folk practiced strange arts. Perhaps Asteria's premonitions did come through Khoti's medicine, the youth's blood crying out a warning the giver couldn't hear.

"Geleg!" He shouted at the curtained doorway to the outside hall. Geleg stuck his head in. "Where is Khoti?"

Geleg's gaze narrowed. "Why?"

"Do not be insolent with me," Eithurdon warned. "I know where your loyalty lies. I will not harm him. I am told he is in danger. I want to ensure he stays in the Val for now."

Geleg shook his head. "He's already left for Sefresal, Lord, as if Ghyldus himself chased him."

"Get him back here, now!"

As Geleg spun away, Eithurdon let his head fall on his arms. Had Tait exaggerated? Khoti never answered the charge. Eithurdon had too many concerns to let affairs of the heart, affairs of honor, distract him. The king, if a more seasoned sovereign, wouldn't have put up with Tait interrupting the council so often, or so successfully. He himself should not have given Tait so much leeway to denigrate his officer. Yet, Eithurdon felt helpless to stop listening, stop thinking about it. Ground into him from birth, he guarded revered traditions like a family treasure, like a title, a castle or a crown. Khoti once told him that Sefresal was just a pile of rock and that his concerns should be with people. He'd seen that wisdom then. But how much more of his identity must he yield? Regaining Shande should be his one priority; must they destroy it to save it?

Eithurdon realized he had few options. Indeed, as Tait claimed, they had given Khoti too much power, let his glory exceed him. Now they had loosed something too powerful to contain. Eithurdon felt it in his blood, in Khoti's blood in him, in some niggling warning from the 'spirits.' He sensed winds of change coming, the carrion-fell winds of war. And Khoti would be at the center of the maelstrom.

# 3: Messenger

The call came so loud it forced Nali awake. Kicking aside his sweaty blanket, he sat up and stared into the dark. His stomach grumbled for the short rations of life in occupied Sefresal, loud against the quiet of the pre-dawn city outside his tiny window. The dark silence gave him an eerie sense of isolation, though Bertal's breaths came soft from a pallet beside him, undisturbed by his fa's restless sleep.

Every night for the two weeks since they arrived in Sefresal these blasted visions made him toss in his sleep. They grew only louder, warning him, urging him to act swiftly. He must find Arshal. In his dreams he felt naked, as if revealed to a pursuer he couldn't escape. Yet the pursuit – likely some agent of Ghyldus or Fyraer – didn't seek Nali in particular, but some unidentified threat it needed to dispatch before it could come into its strength. Arshal? Cree claimed Fyraer and Ghyldus lost their visionary powers when One exiled them, as had Cree when he remained behind. They no longer saw all that occurred in the present. Yet, more powerful than Cree, certainly Ghyldus and Fyraer recalled visions of the future shown to them then, and knew the portents for Arshal. Doubtless, as greater gods they retained some godly power that might allow them to sense the danger of someone guided by the true gods of Ea.

Rising from his sweat-soaked pallet, Nali felt that moment of ache he knew each morning without Olna beside him, her scent absent from his pillow, no sounds of Kia and Rena giggling over breakfast cakes. He wallowed in the silence a moment, staring at the deeper shadow of sleeping Bertal and let the memory sting him alert.

He needed to act now. The nightmares came as urgent as those preceding Nali's meeting with Arshal. Then, they had barely roused him in time.

As he pulled on the black tabard of his occupation, he grimaced at the odors no washing could remove. The Minarians had assigned 'Jani Hostler' to serve in Sefresal's dungeons, the one-time cellars of Eithurdon's Hall. As Jani, Nali fed the occupation's prisoners, emptied their waste buckets, and when brutal interrogators went too far, finally removed their bodies. The stench of death and fear clung to the cloth. After a few days of such work, he no longer complained about the meager rations allotted the Hostler household. It made him fear even more for Olna. Did she and Nalel languish in the Eilime lockup in such a place as these dungeons? Did his daughters comfort her? Or did they now labor for his enemy? The familiar tight fear for Bertal's safety wormed its way up his gut. How long could he keep such a boy cooped up in a shuttered house, pent in a dank cellar when he might be seen? He slipped from the room, pulling shut a creaking door to the main room.

"Up early," Rathil Hostler mumbled when Nali shuffled to the table and sat, plumping his elbows on the table with a weary thump.

Nali leaned forward to peer at Rathil, still feeling the urgency of his dream's call and the hopeless fear he'd felt as his enemy pursued him. It was dangerous to ask just what Rathil knew. Thus far, Nali had spurned the veiled offers to help the old farmer's friends. He feared losing his son, or dying on some foolish raid just for organized hoarding, costing Arshal a trusted counselor.

"Rath, remember my concerns about Sefresal?"

Rathil's eyes narrowed. He nodded.

"The folk I'm looking for aren't here and I've heard no hint that they ever were. I've got to find out what happened to them, get a message through if they're still around."

"It's important?" Rathil shrugged at Nali's nod. "I'll see what I can do. It's hard prying. What's the message? It's dangerous to know anything."

"Just one word: Kedtair. They'll know what it means."

"The Demonstar?" Rathil's eyebrows rose into bushy gray question marks. When Nali didn't elaborate, the old man studied his hands. "There's any number of folk holed up hereabouts. I can't wander about randomly hoping to strike on your people. How would I know them?"

How to say it without revealing too much? "An easterner. Young man. He traveled with many," Nali muttered, hoping he hadn't said more than he needed.

Rathil leaned back, not hiding his shock. Nali knew instantly the old farmer drew connections, conclusions. Certainly, Rathil remembered all the lists on which Nali Drulson had appeared. That he knew exactly who Nali meant, also told him Rathil belonged to something bigger than hoarding. Nali thought he would choke on the lump in his throat.

In the hour before Nali must report to work, he watched Rathil approach a burly, scar-faced man lounging in the square. The two spoke a moment, beyond Nali's hearing. Then the man gestured toward a fair-haired young peddlar offering various wooden wares and bone items, the man fawning when Minarians neared, only to stare after them with an icicle gaze. He didn't try to sell any of the needles, hinges or other odds and ends displayed on his little hand cart. Most of the time, the man scanned the square, studying all that passed with a covert gaze.

Rathil approached, casually examining the wares, digging in his pocket for one of the flimsy tin coins struck with the face of the governor of the Minarian Protectorate of Shande on it. Nali didn't even see Rathil's lips move, but suddenly the wood-crafter's gaze pierced Nali, jerking Nali's breath from him. Something ... had he seen this in a dream? Why couldn't he remember if he'd dreamt of friend or foe? The man nodded, handing Rathil a pack of needles, then returned to his quiet scrutiny of the square.

"Who was that?" Nali asked when Rathil joined him on a sunny bench sheltered from the wind.

"Best you don't know," Rathil warned. "Forget you ever saw him. He's usually not so bold as to show here. Too risky, as he's well-known here-abouts. The Minarians strung up one of his best friends with that last reprisal. I imagine he came to pay his respects. Be sure, your message is as sure as delivered."

Nali shivered as that gaze briefly touched him again, a shiver like when Arshal first looked on him. Nali sensed – not sure how – that with this one query he had recast the future. The thought chilled him. What power did he have when he tossed that pebble in the pond Cree warned them about? What fate had he altered when he fled his home?

Khoti logged the look of the man in his memory alongside Rathil's cryptic message, knowing all too well to whom it referred. He wouldn't have trusted this eastern stranger if his spy network hadn't long ago found Rathil Hostler a wealth of information, and trustworthy. Hadn't he heard talk a while back about Rathil taking on some refugee from the east, someone prominent on the Minarian lists? Anyone on that list was a friend of Khoti's. Something about the stranger gave Khoti a shiver of second sight. The Taschian had no time to consider any of it. Geleg conveyed orders to return to the Val and Khoti couldn't refuse. He imagined Eithurdon evicting him from the Guard, banishing him. Surely the duke could not believe Tait's charges! The duke would recognize the differences between the two peoples and the close quarters of the Val that made contact unavoidable. Khoti didn't want to face the man who had given him so much, made him, and admit to breaking a trust.

By the time Khoti left his cart to another man and slipped from the city, he had gathered news that made his blood boil up within him, the warrior heart. Another traitor, another act of treason had been detected. How many now since word of Mol Azezial's death came to Sefresal with the order for reprisals? The Minarians exploded, rounding up forty former defenders and burning them alive as tribute to Ghyldus, who now openly sat upon the Minarian throne. While the Pladde insurrection drew forces from the ranks of Minarians in Shande, reprisals continued and Shandeans suffered for their neighbors' deeds as well. The destruction of Lagdche had done good, but at a great cost. As Khoti had predicted, fear now led once faithful Shandeans to sell their knowledge for safety, extra rations, life. He couldn't tolerate treason. It would destroy everything. Ordering Geleg to kill a Shandean was hard. They just couldn't allow the man who betrayed Toban to go unpunished. Seeing Toban's good-natured face twisted with agony in his death throes, his body left on display in the square where scavenger birds gathered.... Khoti hoped Geleg left the traitor suffering for hours in a lonely death.

Khoti found Fidra waiting, rested and content, in a hidden cleft near the bottom of the pass. Though Geleg stressed urgency, Khoti rode slowly, ever alert for Minarian patrols and natural hazards. He felt no need to rush to trouble.

Kedtair, what did it mean?

As he picked his way back up the pass the anger in him abated. Eithurdon might expel him from the Guard, but he remained a Tawnkat. He touched the Tawnkat tattoo at the base of his neck. What need did he have for all the royals and rulers crowding his simple world? Pretense, protocol and etiquette had no place in the mountains. He had no time for suitors' games.

He should have listened to his fa and kept to his own kind, stayed out of these outlanders' lives. If Asteria's interest in him went beyond more than flirting to stave off boredom or trifling with the forbidden, wouldn't she have ended this all by now and told her father she would consider no other?

Khoti wanted action. Idleness brought them all this trouble. They awaited something from the young king: powers the king hesitated to use, but apparently needed.

Kedtair. The easterner had looked at him so oddly, as if he knew him.

Shande needed time, information, an army, and organization. At least Khoti had a role in the most necessary aspect. The plans, the decisions they made, every action would hinge on the information Khoti and Zopher's spies and scouts gathered. They had no time to trouble with dishonored fathers and the games of lovers.

Kedtair. What could the demonstar mean?

Khoti looked up at the sky and scowled. Another storm grew in the northwest. It brewed in the damp wind, blustered in the roll of the clouds. Hoping to reach the shelter of a cave before the weather turned, he sped Fidra's pace. He didn't think of his spy network or Eithurdon or even Asteria. Rathil's message, the word Kedtair, echoed in his mind, like an urgent cry, a plea, a warning.

# 4: The Stone

As winter grew old in the mountains and the easterners settled into life in the Val, Cree forced Arshal to face that thing he had hesitated to examine since the night so long ago when ships entered Sihma Harbor. Arshal knew he needed to master that power, some gift from the gods that they clearly intended him to use. And if he must face Ghyldus, as Cree claimed, he would need to project a lot more of himself than a fog that just about killed him.

Arshal had hoped to name some champion as the kings of old had. Though a scrapper, Arshal certainly didn't have the makings of a warrior. And no mortal champion could face a god with a sword and hope to come away victorious. Cree insisted he must learn to use the powers the gods granted him. It seemed Cree would have him die trying.

Though a bitter cold day, the wind coiling in strong drafts deep into the caverns, Arshal sat drenched in sweat at a table in his alcove, so weary he couldn't move. Shards of powdered pottery surrounded him on the table and floor. He couldn't control the power in him. It had him drained, and terrified. Even the minor efforts Cree called for resulted in massive amounts of energy and strength. Cree asked him to concentrate on lifting a mug of ale from the table. As Arshal imagined moving the mug a little, it smashed into the wall. Just that little effort made him dizzy. How could he ever harness this power as Cree said he must? He grew certain Cree knew less than he proclaimed.

"Arshal, I have it!" Cree announced from the doorway of the alcove. The old seer's excitement made his eyes even more piercing, more powerful, more like that awful visage in Arshal's dreams.

Arshal rubbed his blood-shot eyes and felt the hazy edge of hopelessness that always accompanied any use of the power.

Cree claimed that weakness came because the power took its strength from the spirit. To use it destroyed the will. With such encouraging words, Arshal must prepare himself to meet a sorcerer that would steal his will away. Arshal thought them both fools for imagining he had any weapon with which to challenge a god.

"Your power is too strong for you. When you unleash it you cannot control it."

Arshal rolled his eyes and let his head fall on his arms.

"We need a vessel to hold it. It was done before, long ago. If we lock the power inside something, then only a minor effort would wield it efficiently."

"Put it into something?" Arshal lifted his head, trying to imagine what Cree described. "You mean it's something we can actually pour or place somewhere?"

Cree shook his head. "You must see. If you can project your thoughts into space to move an object," he gestured at the powdered fragments of the mug. "Then you can project them into something sealed. Leave them there. With a slight effort you call on them to act through the vessel. Then they will not be drawn from within you, using your spirit as their home."

"How can you put thoughts into anything, as if they were a physical thing?"

"A fragment at a time. Like you thought the fog. Think of the power entering the vessel then lock it inside. Imagine how you would call it. It should be there at need."

"How can I think a fragment at a time? You forget how these small tasks have backfired."

"Think of the fog as a large task, the mug as a small. Put the energy of a mug into your thoughts."

"Cree, I don't think in terms of energy," Arshal sputtered. "I say to myself move the mug, and the mug flies into the wall. I thought, conceal the harbor, and a fog came. I can't control it!"

Cree pulled a small box from a shelf above his cot. He dug among the objects in it, at last holding up an opal the size of his eye. Its depths glowed a deep blue among many colors.

"Here. We will use this." He laid it on the table.

"How?"

Cree remained silent a long time as if he flipped back through pages of his life in search of a memory. "It must be close to your skin, blood, part of you, so you can fuel it with your intent, but not have to risk sharpness of thought and concentration. See, the power is in your mind." He plunked Arshal on the forehead with a finger that felt hot with the Visionary's excitement. "That is where the energy, the drive comes from, from your spirit. If the power is already concentrated, then a mere thought can wield it."

"I doubt this will work, Cree. What can I expect? How do I go about it? Will I be hurt? What if the power's irretrievable? If we pierce the stone to mount it –"

"I was thinking of inserting it."

"Inserting!"

Cree held up his palm. "King Dynfearn had a sapphire placed in his palm. He could blind his enemies with his powers without weakening himself in battle, able to remain sharp, astute."

"Dynfearn also had powers fresh, not lost over time."

"He made it work. I was not with him when he empowered the stone. It was another Visionary from my line, too distant to call upon if he remains undiscovered. You must try. It is my only hope for you to manage the gift. Your energy is indeed strong. That is what hinders us. Yet, King, I believe you will need it if you will help Shande."

For hours Cree dredged all he knew of how Dynfearn had used his stone: how he had placed it, tidbits of lore about the powers Dynfearn once wielded and how he managed them, how he had to think in detail – not broadly – to avoid unleashing a tempest. Finally, as the day grew old and a storm raged outside, Arshal decided he could be no more ready.

The stone lay on the table in front of him, the flicker of the candle firing its multi-colored depths. Wanting to know each flaw, the nature of each fleck of color, the shape, Arshal had studied the gem these long hours while Cree unearthed his memories. He hoped he would not merely bust the beautiful gem to fragments, but tried to ignore his reservations. Cree repeated his warning: doubt threatened control.

Staring intently into the stone the sweat dripped from his face as his eyes swam with flickers of royal blue, emerald green, fiery red, amethyst and gold. He imagined power flowing from him to the gem, a path, a slow filling of the opal's minute recesses. A rivulet, a stream, a river of energy ran from his mind into it. His head ached, his eyes, every part of him. What kind of energy did this river suck from him, from his spirit, his will? What if he again lost himself in the room inside his mind? The glimmer of fear broke his concentration, disrupted the pattern, the image, the flow. The river became a torrent as he struggled to control the power now raging from him into the stone, at last firing its colored depths.

The opal flared, a spectrum of light, blazing, brighter, brighter.

With a sudden blinding flash like lightning striking the table before them Arshal shouted and flew back in his chair, and crashed to the floor, the darkness complete, his eyes unseeing.

Cree froze.

The stone on the table glowed on its own for a moment, then faded back to the blue-green surface of an ordinary opal. The King in Exile lay in a sprawl on the floor, his eyes and mouth open wide, but still. True terror filled the Visionary, an emotion he had never felt among men. What had he done!

He bent and felt for Arshal's lifebeat. Nothing. He peered into unseeing eyes, shaking the king and calling his name. He pressed his hand to the man's forehead. No spark, no sense that anything remained of the king. He had called him back from near death before, leading him from that inner room, but that door stood locked fast against him. Cree sagged.

He heard a hiss of breath and turned to discover Eithurdon staring down at Arshal's lifeless face.

"We are lost," Cree said. "He is gone. We must prepare him for the rites. Call for Peshal. We must prepare him to be king –"

"No," Eithurdon returned, bending to hold his hand before Arshal's lips. "He lives yet."

"But I cannot help him! No spark remains. He has gone too far! I have no power to bring him back from this. I have failed us all," Cree wailed. "Peshal will –"

"You old fool! How can you bury a man before his time!" Eithurdon shouted.

"You would leave him lost in nothingness for eternity, lost in a world of empty rooms he cannot fill! We cannot bring him back! We must try to prepare Peshal to stand in his place. The gods were in Arshal's blood! If we draw his blood for the rites, offer it, we might empower Peshal in his place." Cree bent to slash Arshal's neck as Eithurdon struggled to shove aside the stronger Visionary.

Cree cut deeply, but no blood flowed.

Cree leaned heavily on a chair, trembling, terrified by his terror, his ineffectiveness. He had been a god! "The gods must know he failed –"

"Ytri!" Eithurdon shouted. The Guardsman dashed in, took in the scene, drew his sword and straddled Arshal's body. "Keep this seer away from him, even if you have to kill him."

"You do not understand," Cree protested. Eithurdon pushed by him, his face a pale mask of lost hope.

# 5: Kedtair

Khoti brought with him the scent of fresh air and cold as he brushed a few flakes of snow from his hair.

Ytri stood guard over the king, who lay in his bed. The one they claimed a fallen god sat, dejected, at the alcove's little table, fumbling with a large opal Khoti learned caused the king's malady. Princess Resala tended her brother, the woman as pale as the king's white streaked hair. To pin a kingdom's hope on a single man cursed with the frailty of mortality seemed to Khoti a bit rash in a war.

"It will do no good," Cree mumbled. "Leave the man his peace."

Khoti's glance silenced the words the old seer's lips continued to form.

Khoti took in the bloodless gash on the King's neck and the vacant stare in the man's eyes. After searching in vain for a lifebeat, he at last brushed his fingers across his forehead. He sensed a faint spark of life. "What was his injury? The wound hasn't bled –"

"Cree meant to bleed him," Resala whispered.

Khoti scowled. "He's still alive."

"Cree claims Arshal's locked in a room and no one can release him. He thought bleeding him for the rites they might somehow transfer Arshal's powers to Peshal. He only thought to help."

Khoti considered his own 'room,' that place the spirits took him when he'd over-extended his medicine. So perhaps this king did have powers and, like Khoti, must learn his limits. What did Kedtair mean, this word that had dogged his days in the pass?

When Kefta built up the fire the king's room grew smoky as poor ventilation forced most of the smoke back at them instead of finding its way along the ceilings and out into the Val. Khoti's eyes already burned and itched. Kefta set Khoti's knife in the fire as Khoti dug his tera sticks from the bottom of his pack. He hesitated as he pulled them out, felt the touch of the wood against his fingertips, the strong wood of spirits. Resala brought a candle closer as he again examined the king. This was not like tending a visible wound. He considered what he remembered of Konner rescuing him from the spirits. He touched the small scar Konner had placed on his forehead. A rustling told him Cree had moved closer: he ignored the Visionary.

"The neck first, or he'll bleed to death," Khoti muttered.

As Khoti applied his medicine to the king's neck – the room filling with the spirit music of his sticks, the symphony of mountain stone and forest – he wished he'd availed Konner of the teaching he'd offered. He hadn't wanted to be a part of this brotherhood of healers, to be called upon like some festival jester to perform for the spirits. Perhaps he should send for his fa, who might know more of such injuries. The cold in the king's skin told him he had little time to spare. They'd delayed long enough searching for Khoti rather than seeking Tsevon or Konner. He closed the wound on the king's neck, the spirits light in his hands.

Khoti then took a deep breath and cut a small mark in Arshal's forehead, tracing it with his stick, and placing his bloody hand on it. He called the king's name, the shawnsi so far gone, so distant, so near lost forever that he seemed unable to hear Khoti across the vast distance. What had been the significance of Kedtair? Khoti said the name aloud, Kedtair, the word so prominent in his thoughts, insistent.

The king's eyes closed; his chest lifted with a deep breath. Khoti continued his plea, pouring all his hopes for Shande into that odd message he carried. The spirits flooded him, more intently, rushed him. Something passed through Khoti, cool like a breath of breeze in mountain spring, yet more. Khoti gasped. It felt stronger than any touch the spirits had ever given him, a burst of something that made him want to weep, made him want to cry out with a passion deeper than any he'd ever felt. He ached. Everything within him ached for the breath of a moment, longing, passionate, like Ea itself gasping for breath above the blood soaking her soils.

The king's gray eyes opened to gaze on his healer, a haunting depth in them like wet-laden clouds on a hot spring day.

"I trust you," Arshal whispered.

Resala cried out in relief as Cree gripped the princess's hand, staring at Khoti as if looking upon a vision.

"Strange first words, Lord," Khoti said.

"Terremar's in you," Arshal breathed. "I know him. He's in you."

"Terremar is strong in this man," Cree agreed, leaning around to peer into Khoti's disbelieving face. "The lost powers in a mountain tribesman. How is it so?"

"It's my fa's medicine. He passed it to me. No strange thing here. We've always had healers. The spirits bring the medicine."

"It was different this time, Khoti," Kefta said. "Your music's a comfort. This time, there was something more. Like you weren't here and someone else –" Kefta stammered to silence.

Khoti shivered to recall the breath that passed through him. What had happened here?

"Why did you name Kedtair?" Arshal asked, his words thick on the edge of sleep.

"It's the message of a man in Sefresal seeking you. An easterner. Dark-haired, bearded, a raptor's gaze. Looks a bit of a ruffian, with a limp –"

"Nali!" Arshal tried to sit up.

"He goes by Jani. I wouldn't trust him from his looks, but he's vouchsafed by a good man. He had a one-word message for one he said was an easterner, young, who had traveled with many. He said merely to tell that man 'Kedtair.'"

"That could only be Nali. How did he know to be here now? How did he know I'd be –"

Khoti pressed on the king's shoulders. Arshal lay back without resisting. "He seeks you. Rest, King, you've a land to reconquer and we need a strong king."

With a nod, Khoti took his leave and hurried to Asteria's rooms. He needed to know how the duke had responded to Tait's allegations. For some reason Khoti didn't feel as exhausted as he expected. He should need rest, a deep and dreamless sleep. Perhaps, as the Visionary suggested, more worked in him, and the king, than either knew, some purpose guiding them. He didn't like the sensation. So, if he had these arts for a purpose had he fulfilled them now by sparing the king? Would Eithurdon now say he'd fulfilled his role and thus should be banished? He hadn't seen the duke yet and didn't want to. He only knew he wanted to control his future, his actions, who he healed and fought, and why. Perhaps now his strength would wane, no longer be needed. He sensed in it a vain hope.

While not exhausted, he did feel a weariness growing in him, a slow overtaking as his limbs grew heavy and his pace slowed.

For all his desire to put aside Asteria, he needed to see her now. She'd be alone, as she shared her alcove with Resala. Just a moment to see what the duke had said, then find his rooms and sleep. Tomorrow he could face Eithurdon.

Though he woke her, Asteria looked at him clear-eyed when he touched her hand. He stroked her forehead, feeling a light fever there, sensing illness beneath his fingers.

"It is nothing, just a cough," Asteria said. She took his hand, touching the sticky palm where blood still congealed in the wound. Her touch should have stung, but it didn't. What magic of the spirits had filled him? She sat up, peering at him in the darkness as if she could read his tale. "I sensed something would happen. Are you hurt?"

"The king. He'll be fine." Tension charged her hand. He smelled it on her breath. "What is it Asteria? You may be more ill than you think."

Her head shook in the darkness, her hair falling across his arm to raise gooseflesh. "I have this terrible feeling something is about to happen to you, Khoti. Something horrible. And I ... I am afraid."

Khoti chuckled. "With all the trouble I get into? I don't think you need to worry. I'll take no more unnecessary risks. I promise. I have enough battle scars and nothing more to prove."

"My father," she began.

"Tomorrow. Tomorrow I'll deal with that." He sighed. "That's a deep wound. I can't forget my role."

He brushed his hand against a hot, wet cheek, wishing instead he could crawl in beside her and comfort her fears, hold her, soothe her, feel her breath against his neck. As he left, her gaze bored into his back. Something had her worried. A premonition. Khoti couldn't think about it now. As he drifted to sleep in his bed, his mind went from Asteria to the strangeness of healing the King of Shande, and the name Kedtair he found himself calling with a voice, not his own.

He woke to the old Visionary poking him in the ribs with a bony finger. He hadn't slept enough. He now felt the weariness of a healing aching in him, a lethargy that took his edge. He knew outside the day remained dark with pre-dawn as Cree led him to Arshal's rooms. There, Cree demanded Khoti insert the gem in the flesh of Arshal's hand, then mend the wound so the king would suffer no pain or fever. In spite of his protestations, even this one who claimed kinship to the gods didn't seem to understand that the medicine took his edge. Or didn't care.

Not enough that he healed the king a second time, already medicine-weary, the Visionary then ordered him, on behalf of the king, to Sefresal to retrieve this fellow Nali. The king knew this man who appeared no more than a scraggly beggar. Yet, something about the man wormed into Khoti's thoughts, his dreams. At least it would delay an encounter with Eithurdon. Still, so much medicine in so short a time dulled Khoti's attention. He'd have to enter Sefresal, a place infested with Minarians after a long dangerous ride down the pass. He tried to explain, but Cree dismissed him with an imperious wave, leaving this mere Lharan soldier sputtering protests, tired, his bloody hands and exhaustion of no concern to a former god.

On his way out of the caves, he stopped outside the alcove Asteria shared with Resala. He slipped around the curtain. Asteria still slept. It would be best for both if he never saw her again. He couldn't just end it, but he knew it would come to that. He'd heard the rumors: the duke denied him, claimed him unworthy. That wound, too, remained raw and unhealed. He reached out to touch her, but she stirred in her sleep and he yanked his hand back. She mumbled something and fell still again. He turned to again race down the pass.

# 6: Treason

As dawn spread over the Val, Eithurdon looked up from the figures he'd studied through the night. Kefta stood before him, ill at ease. "Where is Khoti? I sent you to fetch him."

"He's gone, Lord."

"I sent Geleg for his return! I gave orders he remain here!" Eithurdon rose.

"The king sent him to Sefresal. He believes his counselor Nali –"

"Khoti is in danger, Kefta! You must stop him!"

"It's too late, Lord. He's long gone, hours ago. There's few dangers to slow Khoti –"

"Do not doubt me, Kefta." Eithurdon ran a hand through his hair, pulling it, needing the sting to help him think. Asteria had seen.... Maybe the blood he shared with the healer belatedly called to him: he felt it, sensed it like an entity that hung, life-like, in the air of the Val. Khoti was too important to be wasted on errands that could be taken on by some other. Look how he had saved the king! Khoti knew every plan the Shandeans had, the names and locations of each spy and informant and scout, every battle plan. They could not lose him.

"I am at fault," he mumbled, falling back into his chair. "I chose wrong."

Standing at his post by the woodcrafter's hand cart for only an hour or so, Khoti searched the Sefresal square for any sign of Nali, whose image stuck in his mind the way the name Kedtair had. He stifled a yawn. Medicine-weary with only a few hours of rest snagged on Fidra's back during the long hours again racing down the pass, he knew he should be more alert. If he could at least find Rathil, he could deliver his message, find a place to rest then return to his duties.

As he waited, Khoti tried to imagine a fisher-scholar who had commanded a group of merchants, fishers and farmers with enough presence to stymie the Minarian attack on Sihmad Shal, a rare feat among easterners. Khoti wanted to draw the picture of a powerful warrior with wisdom on his brow and sword muscles honed and corded. That certainly didn't fit the man with Rathil.

He yawned again. The square seemed too busy. A few more-than-disinterested glances thrown his way by passing soldiers unsettled him. The certainty grew in him slowly at first, then all in a rush. He needed to leave. He couldn't just leave the cart in the middle of the busiest part of the morning without drawing attention. He pulled out a stone rasp and worked the points of a few partially completed needles.

Instinct screamed at him. He looked up just as a sword pressed against his chest. Before he could finish his breath, soldiers closed off any route of escape. A spot of blood darkened his shirt where the blade touched his skin.

"You are arrested, charged as a fugitive from the justice of the Minarian Empire," the swordsman stated.

Khoti threw his rasp and needles at the man with the sword, flung his stool at another and tried to leap over the cart to escape. As he went over the counter, someone pushed him aside to slam him hard against the rickety cart. The air gasped from him. Before he could react, two men grabbed his arms and propelled him toward the doors of Eithurdon's Hall.

Khoti tried to wriggle free. He sent a soldier sprawling. Another grabbed his arm as he tried to squirm from their grasp. He whipped a foot out to strike a face. More hands closed to pin him. Could no one help him? They couldn't risk arrest. Alone. He continued to wrench from the soldiers' grasp, never quite free. Strong, wily, he anticipated their moves, but they outnumbered him. A kick sent his legs from beneath him. Another came and another, smashing his legs so hard he no longer felt the individual blows but only a constant fire. His legs wouldn't hold him up any longer. He fell. The soldiers continued to kick him. He tried to roll away in the slushy courtyard. Desperate, he knew it ended. At last, a foot smashed into his chest and took the last of his breath. Two soldiers dragged him gasping and gagging up the steps into Eithurdon's Hall and finally to the cellars that had become its dungeons.

Chains dangling brass-colored cuffs had been driven into the walls where once Khoti found shelves of wines or roots called for by the duke's board. Now, a thin layer of straw scattered the cold sandy floor, which seeped dampness into the cellar. A few small windows set high in the walls, barred and uncovered, allowed cold gusts of wind and snow to fall on the men and women chained there. Torches flickered and smoked with each near-extinguishing gust. Despite the draft the space stunk of cesspots and pus.

The rhythm of workmen constructing sturdy wooden walls to isolate future prisoners or felling others to open up unconverted storerooms beat in time with Khoti's pulse. Chained prisoners occupied almost all the space along the walls. Faces turned. They recognized him. He must do something.

Propelled against the wall, Khoti's head smacked the rough stone. A welt rose, sending a stream of blood into his eyes. He couldn't stand. Groggy from his beating, he couldn't force his arms to strike, his legs to kick. His limbs hung limp in the soldiers' grip as cuffs clamped onto his wrists and ankles, each strike of the mallet pinching his skin within the harsh metal. As soon as they released him, he threw his body at his captors, then fell, restricted by the short length of chains, and his inability to bring his legs up beneath him. Fury pumped through him in lieu of blood, the warrior heart raging. He hissed, the sound trailing into a low growl. A nervous laugh escaped one soldier, but they all retreated, leaving the prisoners alone in the dim dungeons.

His head hurt. His body hurt. He sprawled in the dingy straw, unable at first to move. His eyes accustomed quickly as he searched faces the length of the wall. A few appeared familiar, though he couldn't place them. Next to him lay a man sleeping, or dead, tall and lithe, with a familiar profile. As if sensing Khoti's gaze, the man rolled with a clatter of chain and rustle of straw to face Khoti.

"Welcome to Minarian rule," Steadon said.

Khoti's head dropped onto his chest as his breath escaped. Eithurdon had agonized over his brother for months, none knowing his fate. Khoti tried to pull himself up to sit and ease the pain throbbing in his legs and chest. The short length of chain wouldn't allow him to stretch out his legs, and sitting, his arms didn't quite reach the floor. They hung suspended at chest level. He tasted blood in his mouth as he pulled his knees up to his chin and rested his hands on them. Naked without sword, dagger, bow, Asteria's words echoed in his head, her warning. Was this what she'd seen? He heard his empty promise and pressed his eyes shut, never feeling more helpless, more out of control.

"They know," Steadon whispered from several feet away. "They know about the Val."

"You betrayed us!" Khoti returned, his eyes flying open.

"No, Khoti." Steadon's voice cracked. "They know what we should have known all along. How could they not notice the trails, the people –"

"We're careful."

Steadon shrugged. "Perhaps someone spoke, or followed. So many people must attract notice."

"We've had no attacks. They haven't even come close. The Val's guarded."

"Because they do not want to. They are saving us." Steadon's tone held such a deep bitterness it formed a knot in Khoti's stomach. "You must see. Guardsmen, they will be killed because they are a threat. People such as you are only important for the information they might pump from you and the damage you might do, in your case, perhaps the morale they might destroy among your followers. Me, my family, the nobles, we are bountied. The power in Minaria seeks us urgently. If we are turned in slowly, the price on our heads increases as Lagdche grows impatient. The Minarian officers of Sefresal can stuff their purses, gain their rank, knowing where a mine of bountied shawnsi are growing, bearing children. As long as there are many missing derna and nobles, including a royal family, as long as there is that, the reward will remain high."

"But they haven't come near –"

"Why should they? When spring comes and their dungeons are completed, when local resistance is crushed, they can turn their attention to earning a profit. They appear to have only just learned of the Val's existence."

"Are you so certain?" Khoti didn't look at Steadon. He tested the cuffs gripping his limbs, the adanan links of chain binding him to the wall, the rings through which the chain threaded.

"I am still alive enough to live through the journey to Lagdche when the weather warms, to be presented before their god. I am alive enough to sate their needs for revenge. That is proof. I have seen many men pass through these dungeons. I was not one of the forty burned. Toban came through here, many do. In a week maybe less, you too will be gone. I will remain until they can take me triumphantly to receive their reward."

"We must warn the Val."

"How? How do you intend to break from your chains, pass the guards, get up the stairs and through barred doors?" Steadon sneered.

"The window?"

"And break your chains?"

"To get a message out."

"Who is going to stand by the window to hear it? When you were outside, did you see many lingering around the windows?"

He'd won the debate, his triumph tempered by the cynical scowl that possessed his face.

A fire burned in Khoti's throat. So helpless. He tugged the chains again. No give. He pulled, wrenching his wrists in the hope they might slip from the cuffs. The metal gripped tight, and he only raised a chafe and blood.

"I am sorry, Khoti," Steadon said. "So young, and with such fire, you will be a great boon to them. They will beat you until you speak or die. And then you, too, will be gone."

Khoti stared at Steadon, seeing the rancor in the man's eyes, hearing the defeat in his voice.

"I'm not yet ready to give up. I'm sorry you already have." He spat blood from his mouth. "There's much in Ea we don't know about, things unseen, spirits, gods. It's in your blood. Yet you abandon it! Thank you anyway but I'll keep my hope."

Khoti turned from Steadon. He couldn't afford to entertain Steadon's cynicism. He needed his warrior heart to survive. He tried to recall how he'd called the word Kedtair, the way a breath of passion had poured into him. Instead, he saw Asteria's curious smile, smelled the scent of the thaw in her hair as minutes and hours passed with nothing but the dismal sounds of the dungeon for comfort. He was so lost in thought he never heard movement until he sensed someone before him.

Looking up, he saw a mug of water and chunk of bread held out to him. About to brush it away, he recognized the man holding it. His eyes widened.

"Nali?" Khoti breathed.

The man stepped back, beyond reach of the chains.

"Name's Jani," he muttered, his voice a tremor.

Steadon sat up beside him. "Do not trust him, Khoti," Steadon whispered. "They have traitors listening for secrets and this one is too quick and eager to the guards' summons. It is a good bet he is versed in treason."

"No," Khoti stated. "Not this man. He knows things that – I don't know how he knew." Khoti looked up at Nali, his voice a bare whisper. "How did you know?" Khoti didn't wait for Nali's answer. "I was sent for you, told to bring you to ... 'Kedtair.' I was betrayed."

Nali scanned the dungeon, hunching lower as if he could avoid being seen. No guards or workmen stood nearby. Their voices were so low Steadon appeared to strain to hear them.

"I've heard your legend, though I didn't know that was you. Only one man dared betray you, knowing what might come of it."

"Who!" Khoti's voice was a hiss.

"I'm told, Mayor of Eilime."

"Oh gods, we're lost!" Khoti's fists rose and fell in their chains. He gazed at the ceiling wanting to shout, to tear the walls down stone by stone. "Tait knows everything! Gods, he's on his council! How much did he tell?" He peered at Nali. "Do they know about the king?"

"All I've heard is that anyone working that hand cart's a spy," Nali mumbled. "They can round up the lot of you. I've heard no talk of King Ebon –"

"Arshal –"

"That I'd dreamt it any other way," Nali muttered as Khoti drank the tepid water and stuffed coarse, stale bread in his bloody mouth.

"You have to warn them," Khoti said around the bread. "My men'll be killed. You must get word out that they know where we're hiding. Thousands are at risk, including the king and what's left of his family!"

"I know few people here," Nali kneaded his forehead as if to absorb the news Khoti gave him. "Sir, I'm in danger! My name's on their lists, and I was betrayed in Eilime, as was Rath. Someone may ask questions, recognize a description. I've a son with me, a family taken prisoner. They've a lot to destroy me with."

"Then there's no hope for any of us. Whatever your plans were, whatever Kedtair means, it'll all be lost."

Nali wavered. "Why should they believe me?"

"Tell them a Tawnkat sent you. They'll believe you if I'm not there. They probably already know I've been –"

A door wrenching open sent Nali scurrying down the line to serve the other prisoners.

Three guards approached. One kicked Khoti in the chest, slamming Khoti's head back into the stone so hard he almost gagged.

"We will talk," the man said with a snarl. "And you will tell me all you know of this resistance."

The man rapped the handle of a lash in his hand as two others pulled Khoti to his feet and spun him to face the wall so he became tangled in the chains, his face shoved against the damp stone. Khoti glimpsed Steadon turning away, shoulders bent. As the lash fell on Khoti's back, insistent, the words of their demands lost in a haze of noise prying at his memory, Khoti could only clench his teeth, his fists, his body, trying to force into his mind only thoughts of Asteria and the promise he'd made to return. He embraced the words he wanted to spill to the guard, if only to halt the rhythm that pounded in his head. His skin anticipated each blow, gathering up into prickles of welted flesh that begged him to tell all and end the torment. His enemy's demands beat at him like the insistent wings of scavengers.

# 7: Verdaen

The stocky man with burn scars on his face stood at the woodcrafter's hand cart. Furrowed like a squall he appeared even less convincing as a merchant than Khoti. Nali scanned the square, seeing no sign of sentries. They had caught the big fish for now and gloated at its dimensions. They knew Khoti master-minded the hand cart as a focal point of resistance. And Khoti's name appeared as prominently on the Minarian's list as Nali's. His interrogator probably imagined he would have all the information he wanted by the end of the day.

Nali approached the hand cart, thinking only of the risk to Bertal and Rathil. The man scowled at him, wary. With trembling hands, Nali picked up a few of the crude dowels and nails and examined them.

"A Tawnkat sent me," Nali whispered through tight lips.

The man's eyes narrowed. "Why?"

"He's in the lock-up."

"Everyone knows that."

"Anyone working this cart is resistance. He also said they know where your people hide."

The man cast a covert glance around the square. "Who sold him?"

"Tait of Eilime."

"That's a dead man."

The man handed Nali a wooden spoon, then closed down his cart and walked away, leaving Nali standing alone in the center of the square.

Hours later when Nali returned to work, he waited until the guards left for an anteroom away from the stench of the dungeons before hurrying to Khoti. The Taschian lay in a sprawl, hide shirt shredded and bloody, his features swollen and bruised.

38

The man's gaze shot up at Nali with such flaring intensity the derna's heart faltered. Rather than pain, Nali recognized only rage in the man, as if a flame had burned away all but the pure fuel of his spirit. The fury in that expression filled the derna with shame. Nali had cowered for fear of losing one child when his whole family had been taken, tears the only weapon he'd raised. This man raged yet when nothing remained of him but torn sinew and broken bone.

"Who are you?" Khoti asked through cracked lips as Nali bent with water. The Taschian could barely shape his lips to drink from the ladle Nali held in shaking hands. "Why?" Khoti took a breath that made him wince. "Why do you have to meet with him? Do you bring hope, or more trouble?"

Nali shook his head.

"If I'm to die fetching you, I need to know it's worth it!" Khoti coughed, holding a bloody hand to his ribs.

"Don't give up," Nali mumbled, empty words, wondering himself if it was worth a man's life to deliver him. The man shivered. Nali tried to pull Khoti's shirt more closely about his shoulders against the drafts sinking down from the windows.

"The word, your message, gave him life. He was dead. How did you know?"

Nali shook his head again. He took a deep breath, held it then exhaled before he answered. "I was called in a vision. The gods send them." Nali expected doubt, a question. Instead, Khoti appeared relieved, as if a burden had been lifted.

The door opened into the dungeon, fluttering the torches as the air shifted. Nali hurried away to spread fresh straw over the dirty floor, wondering at the way his heart could flutter so with fear, he a man who had fought in Sihma Harbor, fought in Sihmad Shal. Yet it had never seemed so real before. The enemy had always been at the end of a sword, not in control, not in the position to destroy his family.

The man stopped in front of Khoti. He squatted on his haunches, just out of Khoti's reach, shaking his head.

"Back so soon?" Khoti snarled.

He couldn't let them think themselves victorious. He tried to sit up, pull himself together. It took every scrap of will he had left in him not to cry out when he moved, not to groan, not to sob, not to beg they stop if he just told them all he knew.

"You are not observant, Khoti of Tasch-el, Lieutenant of the Lharan Guard. That was not me." The man's voice came easy, relaxed. "So, you are the one our warriors named Verdaen, the Demon Warrior." He tapped a line of brocade on his cloak. "Hothur, captain of these hallowed halls, here to serve your pleasure, honored guest." Hothur spread an arm wide to encompass the dungeons, his tone sour.

Khoti's eyes narrowed. "Then it's you I have to thank."

"For the beating? The accommodations? Not really. I am not a brutal man. That is why such tasks are left to others. You I would not have treated thus. There are possibilities for you, things perhaps you have not considered. A great warrior and so young."

Khoti glanced at Steadon, who merely shrugged.

Hothur studied the closed door to the dungeon then pulled a small flask from inside his cloak. He took a sip then offered the flask to Khoti. Khoti gave him a wary stare and refused.

"It is no crime to accept a drink from your enemy if it can bring you comfort. My interrogator treated you hard, Verdaen, not my intent when I sent him. I have punished him. You are too valuable to destroy. See? You are a legend among your enemy! Verdaen, they call you, a name of respect, said with fear, as if they refer to Verdred, the Dread Warrior who is Minaria's Champion. I was at the Battle of Eilime. I saw you! Impressive. I have never seen such passion in any man. Minaria has a long history of great warriors. Perhaps you carry some Minarian blood? You make children of our heroes! I watched you ride alone in the midst of our army and slay our commander with your furious humor. That is the feat of a legend, not the image we have of Shandeans. You intrigue me, Khoti of Tasch-el." Hothur offered the flask again.

Khoti accepted it this time, feeling the chill of night feeding the ache in him. It was Kishman brandy, a fine lot. He took the flask's contents. Hothur screwed his face up into a grimace when he examined the empty flask.

"You were thirsty," he stated.

"Kishman brandy belongs in a Kishman," Khoti said, staring at Hothur with an unblinking gaze.

Hothur shook his head again, a bemused smile transforming his face. "Still your spirit is strong. What fires Verdaen? Give up this lost cause of Shande! You could achieve greatness among us. Do not pull such a long face. I am serious. Think of it! You are already honored among men who have most felt your edge.

You slew our best at Eilime. I hear it was your folk who deviled us all the way. I know you are the center of the resistance in these mountains. A true warrior needs only battle to sate him, has little need for the politics of allegiance. Naturally, we would not have you harm Shandeans. Our interests go beyond there. There are uprisings in Minaria that must be put down. There is Shiad, Arenh, Otayr, Shikora yet to conquer. You would never have to whet your knife on Shandean flesh. Why die, here, a wasted talent when your life could be glorious!"

Khoti gazed at the man. Was this some trick? How could they think he would consider it? Had their beating been so severe out of reverence? He saw few others with such wounds. He tried to shake his head, unsure if he did. The thickness brought by the brandy and the pain and poison of his injuries clouded his mind.

"I don't seek glory, only my land, whole and sound, ruled by my own people." Khoti's voice came soft, a bare whisper. He felt weak, confused, lost.

"Do not be rash!" Hothur cried, genuine concern in his tone. "They will kill you. I have no authority to protect you if you refuse. Do not be a fool! You will be made the worst example to the people of what resistance will get them, a retaliation made large to avenge Mol Azezial. You will have a horrid, violent death. Flogged to death perhaps." He gestured at Khoti's wounds. "Perhaps hacked to death, one by one the extremities cut away, to die in the open tied out for the scavengers to finish. I know among the mountain tribes that would be an end most abhorrent."

Khoti's mind drew pictures of vultures rending his flesh, not waiting for him to die as he lay in the gorge near Redside. He heard again the wolvers slinking about him, eyeing him from the shadows, their howls echoing among the rocks. Steadon's gaze locked on him. Did the shawnsi recall Khoti's weakness, the one he said might make a man yield?

How strong could he be? If the birds wheeled overhead, would he betray Eithurdon? The king? Asteria? Asteria. His gaze narrowed on the Minarian Captain.

Hothur straightened, took a step back.

"I won't betray my people. Do your worst. Instead of becoming an example of reprisal, I'd become a martyr, a symbol the resistance will rally to."

Hothur stared at him for long minutes. It was all Khoti could do to not look away, to not shiver with the cold. He wanted to wail his pain, gag with the sickness he felt.

"You are loyal, as a great warrior should be. That you were not Shandean! I think I would count you less of a man if you betrayed your people for yourself. I would not trust you. I hold no respect for the Shandean traitors, weak men, driven by selfish fears. It is a necessity of conquest that traitors must be made. Such a loss to destroy you! You have years yet to grow into the legend already built around you. It is a paradox. Shande's loss of you would be our gain. But killed in display? You are right. It would only fuel resistance. When they are done interrogating you, done with the destruction, I will insist you are given the rites due a man of your prowess and honor. You do not deserve ignoble death, but that which is quick and painless."

Hothur appeared to truly grieve over the death he would pronounce. Was it possible? He did not want to recognize humanity in his enemy. What if he must kill him? He thought of his mam, who still carried sorrow for all the innocent Minarians lost in Halieri's Flood. Then, she knew and it did not stop her: The cause too great, the need, the injustice of people you thought your friends turning on you. As far back as he could remember his fa and other miners had brought home Minarian apprentices, often inviting them to festfires. They had not seemed like bad men, a bit loud and boasting perhaps. They brought gifts, told fine tales, and leant a hand with chores. Khoti peered at Hothur, holding his enemy's gaze.

"Thank you for that consideration. I hope we can accommodate you in the same way."

Hothur chuckled. He pulled out a second flask and handed it to Khoti.

"You will need this to get through the night, I expect. I fear our interrogator will never break your spirit. And, believe it or not, I do hope he fails." With a nod, Hothur was gone.

Khoti looked from the flask to Steadon. Steadon shook his head. Khoti took the contents at once. The heat struck his stomach, the warm fuzziness working its way out from there. Hothur was right. Khoti needed to be numb to survive this night, and the nights to come. He only wished Hothur's flask had been larger.

A horse's hoof striking stone brought Geleg's head around. Who traveled up the pass under veil of night? He drew his sword and crept from beneath the ledge where he'd taken a short rest from the long hours' ride up the pass. In the center of an open stretch of the pass, a man rode as if unafraid of being sighted by friend or foe.

Geleg darted among the shadows of snow-covered boulders and slabs of stone, unheard. When the rider drew level with him, Geleg rushed out, yanking the man from his horse before the rider knew his danger. As the hood of the man's cloak fell away, Geleg grinned and chuckled to himself.

"Well, Tait, just the snake I was looking for," he said as he twisted his hand in the cloak at Tait's throat and brought the point of his sword to Tait's chest.

Tait held his arms up. "What are you talking about, Geleg! I came to see if watchers on the pass were alert."

"That's rich. You're the worst sort of traitor. One that returns from the enemy to gloat."

"It wasn't me, Geleg!" he insisted. His eyes flickered in the spare light thrown from the snow.

"And I hear it was. What kind of scum betrays their country to advance a suit?"

"It's not like that Geleg! I can make you a happy man. Share my bounty! We don't need upstarts and royals. Respected citizens can do well by this occupation if only we silence this rabble early. You don't know this enemy. There's merit to the things they say. Believe me. I met them while hunting. They weren't ogres. They treated me well, honored me as I deserved, for almost no other reason but my wisdom. Don't you see? Those loyal to Khoti, their days are numbered. I swear, as much as I would wish to silence him, it wasn't me. When I returned to the Val, I was going to report I saw Rathil Hostler speaking with a sentry today –"

"Liar! I've more witnesses that saw you. As if I'm to believe you had a purpose in Sefresal. How much did you tell them! Speak now. Who did you report? Your life grows short."

"One man!" Tait gasped as Geleg twisted the cloak tighter at his throat. "Only Khoti! He's dangerous! He'll get us all killed with his reckless ideas. He's so cocksure, putting us all at risk with crazed schemes. I have an idea, a plan. It'll work. I just needed to prove they could trust me."

"You sicken me."

"One man, Geleg! We can use this to our advantage! You'd harm the Mayor of Eilime, an influential person, over one man, one of many lesser men who can serve that role? He's only a mountain brat, worth nothing. Nothing! I deserve better than the treatment I've gotten because of him. The duke denied me because of some unwashed miner's issue who practices false superstitions and sleight of hand. He corrupted the duke's daughter; she needed to be saved from him. She needed to be saved."

"You betrayed us all! You told them about the Val."

"Not much, really. They knew we were around."

"What did you tell them!" Geleg pressed the sword harder against Tait's chest. The man's eyes bulged in the dark.

"That it exists. That's all! I'd be stupid to tell them everything. They'd have no need for me. Now I can play them into our hands. You could be a rich and comfortable man, Geleg! I'll be a person people will honor with a role in the province. I can help you –"

Tait's eyes widened, his mouth falling open as Geleg easily slammed his weapon home. "Khoti, you deserved better," Geleg muttered. The Mayor of Eilime slid from his sword. What spell did this enemy god employ that he could win over even a member of the King's Council? Had others been drawn to the lure of the medallion he found hidden beneath Tait's cloak?

Geleg sped up the pass, feeling vulnerable without Khoti and Toban beside him. The enemy might this moment be ferreting out paths to the Val. And Khoti! That he hadn't made Tait suffer first –

When Geleg at last burst into Eithurdon's rooms in the Val the next day, he could barely gasp out his news.

"Khoti's been arrested."

Asteria stood, paling.

"He was betrayed," Geleg went on. "And the Minarians know about the Val." Geleg took a deep breath. "It was Tait."

"Tait! When his people are sheltered here?" Eithurdon twisted a hand in his hair. "Are you certain?"

"He wore a medallion."

"How much did he tell them? We must know!"

"He's dead, Lord."

Eithurdon gave him a wary glance then nodded. "Asteria, leave us."

"No. I want to know –"

"Leave!"

She rose, stiffly, and slipped into the hall.

Eithurdon took a deep breath. "There is nothing we can do. We cannot take on all of Sefresal to rescue one man, even though that man has special gifts and is dear to us. Khoti is lost, Geleg, like Toban. There are no options." He smashed his fist on the table. "And they know where we are! There is nowhere else to go. We will be forced to face them here."

Geleg waited, impatient, as Eithurdon sank onto a stool. Geleg had never seen the duke so beaten, so distraught. "We can't just leave Khoti to them, Lord! They'll destroy him, execute him! And the things he knows –"

"What am I supposed to do? Stroll into the square and demand his return? You think this is a small matter to me? To lose a respected officer and aide? I do not believe Khoti can be forced to betray me." Eithurdon's eyes closed. "I tried to keep him here, ordered it. They said something would happen to him."

"Lord?"

"A premonition that Khoti would return to the Val, dead." Eithurdon waved his hand, dismissing Geleg. "His rashness got him killed. If he had just faced his punishment he could have been warned when I denied his suit."

"It was at the king's order." Geleg waited for some resolution from the duke. He hadn't risked all to tear up the pass and have nothing done. He owed Khoti his life. Eithurdon owed him. Everyone had some measure of duty to the man who put such fire into their cause. Finally, he had to leave. Eithurdon was no help.

# 8: Headman

In the dark, almost fading into the shadows of the stone walls, Nali held vigil. No longer glinting with defiance, Khoti's eyes remained closed, dark shadows against the pallor of his skin. Returning often, the interrogator repaid Khoti for the punishment the Tawnkats meted out to Minaria, and the dressing down Hothur must have given the man. Nali didn't know what possessed him to hold this vigil. At any moment some guard might challenge him for sitting in the dungeon staring at the prisoners, ask why he traded duties with another to be here. Nali didn't want Khoti to die alone. Khoti came to lead him to Arshal and for that he now died.

Nali dared approach the Taschian to discern the severity of his injuries. It could be anything killing him. Poisons crept into deep lash wounds and broken bones. A fever raged. There might even be internal damage, the kind no one could repair. Steadon claimed Khoti had special healing skills. What good could they be if he couldn't mend himself?

So, Nali waited, hearing the cold damp of the dungeon settling into Khoti's chest and his breath rattling. Tonight, maybe tomorrow, Nali knew, the man would die. Khoti must survive. Nali felt it, a sense that Khoti belonged to the same purpose that moved Nali and Arshal. The Guardsman had a role yet to play.

Sitting in the dark, knowing his enemy surrounded and outnumbered him, Nali dared to entertain a plan.

Punctuated by a wink, Nali told the sentry he needed some air. He slipped into the shadows of the square, scurrying home to find Rathil awake and restless, every few moments peering out the window.

"Rath, we have to do something," Nali insisted.

"What can we do, son? We're just as cowed and powerless as anyone else."

"Don't give me that, Rath, you've got connections here. And that man was one of them. I know the dungeons, the guards, the shifts, the routines. I can get us in there. But I need help."

"You'd do so much for one man? Now you're willing to risk orphaning your boy and messing up whatever purpose you got sending messages –"

"A man's dying because of me! How many more will? If I help his friends, maybe they'll take me to my friend, find refuge for Bertal. And there's other fine folk locked up in there."

Rathil turned and lifted the curtain, looking out a moment before dropping it. "He's been in there for days," he said without looking at the derna. "From what you've said he's so bad we can't save him. These things take time to plan."

"There's no time. It has to be tonight. I think he'll be dead soon."

A light tap struck their window. Nali shot a glance at the room where Bertal slept as Atnil opened the door. Nali recognized the burn-scarred cart tender.

The man pointed at Nali while looking at Rathil. "I saw this man sneaking across the square from Eithurdon's Hall."

Rathil nodded. "I told you, Geleg, he works in the lockup. He can help."

Nali turned to stare at Rathil who ignored him as if he were just some tool in his plans, not a friend sharing a roof.

"Then you've seen him?" Geleg's eyes focused on Nali, who inclined his head. "His own commander won't do a blasted thing. I owe my life. He knows too much. I refuse to give up."

"I was telling Rath, if we don't get him out of there soon, he's gone. And there's others, Steadon –"

"Steadon! Steadon's there!" Geleg glared at Rathil.

"I didn't want you wasting the entire defense of the Val on one fool royal with a stubborn streak and an equally pig-headed officer," Rathil admitted.

"I was trying to convince Rath that if we just had enough men, I know the dungeons well enough to get us in, and where and how many guards we'd face."

Geleg stroked his beard, sizing up Nali who barely reached the top of Geleg's muscled shoulder. Then he nodded. "My men are already gathered. Rath already guaranteed your help."

Nali gave Rathil a wary glance. The old man still ignored him. "Then he promised too soon. I won't help you without something in return." Nali thought Geleg would strike him dead. The scars on the man's face went crimson.

"Such as?"

"Your man was sent to fetch me, and I've a child with me. I'll help you if I'm promised that me and my boy are taken where Khoti intended to bring us."

"We don't know you to trust you."

"You trust me well enough to get you in the dungeons," Nali retorted. "And Rath's 'parently vouched for me."

"We won't have time for your boy. It may be a battle."

"He can wait by your horses. He's strong, a survivor."

Geleg studied Nali a long moment then nodded. He signalled out the window and soon ten of Shande's scruffiest-looking men crowded Rathil's kitchen. Each wore battle scars, their features weathered, but Nali felt comforted in their presence as he had when he'd stood among the fighting men of Sihmad Shal. They made their plans in whispers as if the enemy had an ear pressed to the windows.

Only an hour later, Nali stepped into the dark, wintry square. He tried to calm his breathing. This was no time to panic. After all, he'd fought in Sihma Harbor, on the walls of Sihmad Shal and braved the elements to cross the country. Risk and fear were old friends.

He gripped the knife beneath his cloak and limped across the square. He found it easy to stagger, to appear somewhat sodden as he returned to the guardroom leading to the dungeon, his nervous feet unsteady beneath him. What if he failed and lost Bertal? He knew what to fear: this dungeon. Ignoring the furtive shadows creeping along the wall and waiting just out of the circle of light thrown by a torch at the door, he smiled a greeting at the guard, his eyes bare slits. As the man opened the door to admit him, he gripped his knife more tightly, stumbled on the sill and fell into the man, knocking him to the floor.

The other four guards started to laugh, the guffaws loud in Nali's ears. They didn't yet realize the first guard's startled expression came from the knife wedged between his ribs. As Nali made as if to stand, his hand sticky and warm, in that brief second before they grew alarmed and their attention remained turned from the door, Geleg's men swept into the room.

Nali kicked the door shut behind him and slid the bolt. The guards were so taken unawares no one had time to cry an alarm.

Geleg slapped Nali on the back as the derna found his feet and tucked the bloody knife inside his cloak.

"Just two more you said?"

Nali nodded as he wiped the blood from his hands on his victim's cloak.

"This is easier than I thought!" Geleg grinned, an oddly lecherous expression on that scarred face. Nali led the way down the dim stairwell to the dungeons, leaving behind the bodies of five guards slicking the stone floor and one of Geleg's dour companions guarding their escape.

The two guards posted at the dungeon door stood alert. They'd heard laughter, what sounded like a scuffle. Nali again staggered as he approached. One guard grinned and nudged the other as Nali missed a step and grabbed the railing, his knees coming from beneath him before he pulled himself back up. One man grabbed Nali as he made to stumble into them. They spun him around so his face pressed against the rough door.

"Looks good enough to hang," one muttered from behind him as they argued over how best to make an example of him.

Nali tried to grin with his best drunkard's look, but only managed a sickened smile. A knife pressed against his collarbone, raising a thread of blood, but at that moment the grip on his arm loosened, and the man fell to the floor.

"C'mon," Geleg whispered. "How long before they notice?"

Nali didn't respond. He touched his neck to be sure he wasn't hurt then dug through the guard's cloak until he found what he sought: a pair of metal shears for cutting the shackle pins. He held them up in the torch light as one of Geleg's men unbolted the dungeon door.

Nali went first to Khoti. The Taschian hadn't moved, but he still breathed. Swiftly shearing the shackle pins, he then moved along the wall, freeing all the prisoners. When he returned, he found Geleg, the man's rough features gentled as he knelt beside Khoti and held the Tawnkat's head to dribble water on cracked lips.

Khoti's eyes opened a slit, a hand lifting, but not quite reaching to touch Geleg's face. The bloody mouth whispered 'Asteria'. Geleg glanced at Nali.

"He's truly ill if he thinks I'm a woman," he muttered as he lifted Khoti to his shoulder.

Nali hurried to support Steadon, whose long confinement left him weak and unstable on his feet. In only a few minutes the dungeons emptied, the prisoners scattered, as Nali and Steadon followed Geleg and his burden to the mouth of the pass.

A flash of metal caught Nali's eye as they approached. "Bertal!" Nali whispered.

"Fa?" A small voice came back. The metal disappeared as the boy sheathed the knife and unhobbled the horses. Geleg laid Khoti over his horse's back and tied him to the saddle. He pointed to one of his men.

"Keep an eye on Rath. They'll come to him to find Jani Hostler." The man nodded and was gone as Nali at last followed Arshal's path up the pass.

That the Taschian survived the grueling journey up the pass seemed a miracle, a testament to that something extra about the man that Nali sensed, and the special care his friends took of him. Nali felt it himself: an unexplainable bond with this young warrior from a tribe Nali hadn't even known existed. More than wonder at his strength and the tales of valor that followed him, it simply amazed him that anyone could contemplate betraying him.

When they reached the valley so deep in the mountains that Nali thought they might never reach the other side, the strange looks thrown his way by the hardy lot of people pressed into the caverns made Nali clutch Bertal to him as he followed Geleg. He, a derna, felt nothing but awkward beneath their stares. He stood in the corner of a tiny alcove as they lay Khoti's body on a bed in his parents' rooms. Steadon caught Nali's eye, nodded, a warm gesture, as a shawnsi woman trailed by several children pushed through the crowd, to throw her arms around Steadon. Nali could only stand numb as more and more people crowded in to verify the rumor of Khoti's return, the rumor of his presence a hum through the caverns, in the whispers of people who craned to see over the crowd.

A white-haired figure with one bandaged hand entered, the crowd parting for him. When the man turned, Nali sucked a sharp breath. Arshal stared back at him, his features brightening as he shoved past Steadon and his family to reach him.

"Nali! It's true! You sent the message that saved my life."

"You've changed," Nali said. "Like the man I dreamt." He reached for Arshal's unbandaged hand, where the gleam of the signet ring caught his eye, then stared up at the king to find the sapphire at his brow, set in the circlet crown.

"He died as I dreamed it."

Nali stared down at the top of Bertal's head, clutching the boy's shoulders. Bertal squirmed only a little as he tried to see around the press of people. "As I feared," Nali said softly. "They don't come to pass exactly as I see them, but close enough to be concerned about."

"Your family?"

"Bertal and I escaped."

Arshal turned away. "We'll talk later," he mumbled. "I'll have someone make room near me for you and your boy." Arshal absently stroked the palm of his injured hand. "We'll have much to talk about. Now, I must learn what I can of Khoti's condition."

Nali noted a tall man who strongly resembled Steadon ducking through the doorway. When the man's gaze fell on Steadon, Nali knew instantly it must be the Duke of Lharan. The shock of seeing his brother so thin and ragged seemed to suck the heart from him. The duke looked away a moment only to find Khoti's tenders cleansing and clucking like old midwives as they worked. A man Nali knew must be Tsevon sat on a chair beside the bed, his hands caressing his son as he sought broken bones.

As the duke reached his brother, he stared at the shackle cuffs still attached to Steadon's wrists and ankles.

"I feared the worst," the duke said.

"I knew the worst." Steadon gestured toward Khoti. "He is disgusted with me because I gave up hope. Says there are powers in the world I do not know, and they even run in my own blood. He said that he would not die there, that it was not his time. I did not believe him. But here I stand, beyond hopes, and there he is, and still I do not believe."

"He is not dead," Eithurdon offered.

Steadon's sharp glance cut like a cold knife. "Not yet." Steadon would say no more.

Tsevon hadn't been himself since his journey to Minaria, likely not since he tended Khoti in that cleft near Redside, an effort that seemed to drain the spirit from him, maybe as far back as that night he'd rescued Amhese and learned of Von's death. The memory conjured an image of the medallions he touched, warm yet with their wearers' furor.

He could no longer ignore the changes in himself. He grew old though others his age did not. His lifetime of healing gnawed at his spirit. His sandy hair and beard had grayed. His limbs felt so weighted he wondered if he could even stand the rigors of a hunt, or even still hold a ram for shearing. A lifetime had passed in less than a year. And now, again, he spent his blood to save his son.

51

He felt used up as he stared down at Khoti's face, which had swelled and purpled so that he could barely recognize him. Tsevon and Konner worked together, with midwives and wise women, all of them tending him because no one could undo all the horrors the Minarians had done. They worked furiously, no time to hesitate or they would lose to the poisons that had settled in Khoti's blood and threatened to take him beyond their reach, a place Tsevon had already gone once for his son. Healing even one wound took a toll. Khoti had many. As he set his bloody hands on each poisoned wound, Tsevon knew he and Konner broke from their guild, from all they knew to be wisdom. With a war of wounds and ills around them, they had decided Khoti should live. Khoti may have great gifts, but was Tsevon's son more important than any other son in this war?

Konner tapped a tribute to the spirits that guided the healers' hands as they took a rest from their labor. Tsevon stumbled to his niche and fell on the bed. He had never felt so exhausted. So much must be done yet. They found no internal wound, yet the interrogator had been thorough. Tsevon didn't have Khoti's skill, and even together he and Konner could not mend it all. Tsevon never felt so helpless in his life. He could do nothing. He ached so much he couldn't move to pull the blanket over himself.

After a few minutes, when the verge of sleep pressed in on him, he gasped at a horrible weight on his chest. His eyes flew open and he clutched himself, struggled to pull the weight away and find the breath so bound up within him. Amhese rushed to his strangled call, Konner behind her. Too late. He knew it as his gaze looked last upon Amhese and the spirits called from far away.

The mountain man that had been the heart and spirit of Tasch-el, the one constancy in upheaval, closed his eyes and lay still. The wail that tore from Amhese echoed through the caverns as the Tawnkat's spirit left him, the last of his energies given his son.

Konner sank down beside Khoti, bereft, the heart in him soured and so medicine-weary he could barely move. He held the healing-scarred hand of the young warrior who but a year ago, less, never imagined himself a headman. Konner made no move as the well-wishers and curious emptied the alcove, a few taking a moment to tidy up before they led Amhese away to where the wise women would prepare Tsevon for the rites. It should be in his own cabin, in his own bed that they washed him and prepared him for his journey. Konner sent them away, Konner Tsevon's Second, but who was he now?

Soon, Konner would need to free his long-time headman, a man he had grown up beside, had thought would always be the unbreakable stone to the world's pick. And here Konner, a mere Second, remained the only Taschian left who knew all the rites.

Only Konner and Asteria remained in the alcove, though Geleg, Kefta and Ytri spoke softly in the corridor beyond. Still, Konner sat, unable to think, speak, Khoti's leg resting in his lap as he pried at one of the cuffs embedded in swollen flesh. He knew he had a duty to free Tsevon of this place, but perhaps, too, the fa might want to look upon the son he had thought he'd lost, for just a few moments more.

Konner glanced out at Asteria, who sat at the table staring into her hands. It made no sense for her to be here. On hearing of Tait's betrayal Eithurdon declared an end to the entire mess by proclaiming only one suit could be tendered the Lady: Anlon of Mershy, if he still lived in the far reaches of Tormor Wood. Even if Khoti lived, and that seemed a frail hope to those expecting him to succeed his fa, Eithurdon would refuse him. As he had always intended.

These shawnsi and their customs sickened Konner. Not even a shawnsi, Anlon's father, Habdelion, brother of Queen Sala, adopted Anlon from a Dasirean tribe. The boy merely stood heir to the title; Habdelion's younger daughter by blood would hold the ancestral seat, leaving Anlon free to join Asteria in Sefresal where she would succeed her father. How ridiculous to think of ancestral seats occupied by an enemy, their title-holders bountied, the kingdom in a war that had no time for suits and traditions and peerage. The duke claimed to have solved their problems as rumors about Asteria likely hadn't reached Mershy. Of course, the duke ignored Khoti in this plan. His loyal aide, harmed in service to the king, the duke deemed as nothing but a mountain man, of no account in the end. And there Asteria waited. To bid him goodbye? To beg him talk sense into the duke? Or did her premonitions overwhelm her, or Tsevon's death? Did that matter to her at all now that she would join some southern lordling? For Khoti's sake, Konner wanted it to matter to her. He held out no long hope.

Konner had no words for her. The tragedies befalling his people had him too shaken to think beyond the moment. To lose two such fine men in one day? If Khoti lived, certainly he'd be broken for life. Little could Konner mend each day without following Tsevon to an early death. He alone remained the keeper of Tasch-el's rites. Even Khoti would need to learn much to stand in this place for Tasch-el.

Konner leaned against the rough, mat-covered cavern wall, absently wiping away the fresh blood he'd raised on Khoti's ankle as he worked at the cuff. He'd felt rage at first, for the treason that led to Khoti's capture. He grieved now, to see the brutal way the Minarians had treated Tsevon's son. Here ended the fine line from which Tsevon came. The people wove legends around their simplest feats. No doubt, some day they would say Khoti fought his way out of Sefresal's dungeons and felled his enemy with just his glance.

It seemed when Khoti took care, trouble found him; yet, when he flew recklessly into battle, he came away almost unscathed. Why did the spirits bestow gifts in such measure, if Khoti would die now, goal unachieved? Had it all been for that one moment when he called back the king, or even the duke?

Looking up from his bloody hands, Konner found Khoti's feverish eyes gazing back at him through puffy lids.

"Asteria?" The word came thick through swollen lips.

Asteria came into the tiny niche to stare wide-eyed at Khoti. She grabbed up the hand that wore the battered shackle Konner had worked on earlier. Konner had pried it loose enough to return circulation but not yet enough to get his snipper beneath the metal.

"You knew," Khoti gasped. Asteria nodded. "If I live –" Khoti gasped as some pain wrung through him and the sweat rose on his face. "I can't dishonor him." His eyes lost their focus, and slowly his lids drifted over them.

"Be strong!" Asteria insisted, squeezing his hand. If he heard, he made no response. Asteria glanced at Konner, but he only shrugged. Breathing hard, she pried at the shackle still clenching Khoti's left wrist, digging her nails into his skin for the grip to tear off the cuff. Konner tried to push her away, but the shackle pulled free, slipping over a thinned and bloody wrist, and she fell into Konner almost spilling him onto the floor. Red faced, Asteria found her balance and stiffly walked from the niche, clutching the cuff to her as she went.

# 9: Timing

Nali sat at the hewn table in the center of the alcove Arshal called home, watching the king unwind the bandage Khoti had wrapped around his left hand. King. It felt right, natural, as if it had always been. As the last strip of cloth pulled away, an opal glimmered out from the midst of a wrinkled scar in the palm. Nali took a deep breath and held it. He remembered obscure lore from his days as a scholar striving for derna certification. Dynfearn the Lost, legend said, bore magic in the palm of his hand, with which he struck his enemies from his path. Had Cree hoped to make of Arshal a warrior king like Dynfearn? Dynfearn's mother was one of Terremar's children. Arshal's blood barely remembered its ancestry.

"I'll need your help with this," Arshal said, staring into his palm. "Cree's been worthless. He barely speaks. I think he's lost his mind, if that can happen to Visionaries."

Nali stroked the soft royal blue of the derna robe that had remained tucked away in the bottom of his pack. Feeling the satiny material against his skin brought back some of the certainty he'd once felt as they planned the defense of the Harbor and Sihmad Shal. A derna of the First Degree, he earned his role as the king's advisor. The king needed confident counsel to guide him on a sure path, not the hesitant musings of a Visionary who no longer remembered the future. In the few days since Nali's arrival, they had managed to avoid discussing their most pressing issues. They talked long hours about the paths they traveled and their fears for friends and family left behind. All those times when Rath had come to him wanting him to be more than a crafter, and left rebuffed, Nali regretted now. He'd set aside his mission for his own personal concerns. What had it gotten them? He again shouldered his cause as if he could slip it back on like his long-packed derna robe. Might things have been different? He vowed to never again forget his goals, his mission: to see Shande whole and sound again, the Minarians defeated, and then, finally, his family could return home.

"I don't know where to begin with this," Arshal said at last as they both studied the opal in his hand. "Here it is, in my body, almost the tool of my death, already the cause of another's death: Tsevon's, perhaps Khoti's. I can't let their sacrifice be wasted. And Cree won't help me discover this gem's strengths now that I'm stuck with it. He's afraid I'll go where he can't retrieve me. I'm afraid, Nali. If I can't control it who would save me this time? Khoti brought me back with your message. Will I need him again? I felt Terremar in him. Terremar! Can you imagine that? In a mountain man a world distant from all our musings in Sihmad Shal. A brutal warrior like Khoti, and Terremar's in him. There has to be a reason we're thrown together with this warrior-healer, and your message coming to him, the only man who could help me."

Nali straightened, pulling his robe about his shoulders. "I was called," he said, peering at the king. "Nights on end the same vision. After each vision I awoke, as if someone roused me. We're supposed to be doing something that we aren't. The enemy searches for what he knows stands between him and his goal: you. We must do something."

"And what is that?" Arshal whispered.

"Get ready for an event. Kedtair." He knew it as certainly as the thought came to him. "That's the sign. When Kedtair rises next we have to be ready."

"Why Kedtair?"

"Why not? The star influences us and binds us. Wouldn't it be when we're strongest? With all that Kedtair does to Ea, there'll be conflict and turmoil, supplies scarce, a goad to those who might otherwise be afraid to act. It's a universal timeline that everyone can follow. And leading up to the rising, they'd be fools to send reinforcements by sea."

"Why would your visions be urgent, only to wait more than two years before we act? Not that I'm a knowledgeable strategist, but wouldn't the enemy merely become entrenched? That's one of the concerns Khoti and Eithurdon always raise."

"Don't you see, Arshal? That's when we should strike, not for the first time, but for the last time." Nali shrugged to himself, stunned by his own sense of conviction. "That's when we should be facing Ghyldus, when our gods are strongest, when our spirits are most in their element. To harness enough of all the strength of Ea, we have to act now. If the enemy does sense some power threatening him, he'll bend his energies this way. It's like when everyone retreated into Yckeb. We're all waiting in this valley. One blow could wipe us out. Think of Steadon's warning. We have to move now!"

"And do what? For more than three months I've been here, struggling with all the possibilities, haggling with my council. I've gone over every one of our visions for hidden signs, but found nothing. I haven't dreamed for ages. I thought, perhaps mistakenly, it meant things are going well. What can we do? We have thousands to feed, protect and conceal. There are no farms and stockyards to provision these people. Launching an attack from the Val will be just as impossible as defending Sihmad Shal, Nali. We're just too few, and they're just too many and better organized."

"Think about what you just said," Nali snapped. "You described exactly what we must be doing now: building the army we didn't have when Sihmad Shal fell, a real army with real soldiers that know what they're doing, people like the Lharan Guard and the Tawnkats. Look at the problems we had! What Sihmad Shal knew, Sefresal learned a month later. What Sefresal knew, Sihmad Shal learned too late. We need organization and communication to strike from all parts of the kingdom at once, a cue, a symbol, a goal, a way of letting all the defenders of Shande know exactly what we expect. I'm told Eithurdon could've done more to hamper the enemy, but let Tsevon's Tawnkats – a handful of Taschian refugees – fight a war because he couldn't act without authority from the king. When that approval came, he'd already turned away an army! We can't have that kind of uncertainty. When you say how few we are, are you thinking of just this valley? There's all of Shande! Think of all the farmers around Sihmad Shal that weren't called up. Think of all the farmers and ranchers in the Kishman countryside. They could be trained, prepared to fight on cue. Mershy, Joffa, the other countries of Ea."

"Shiad knows we're here, but won't help us. They don't believe there's a King of Shande or any way of stopping the –"

"Then prove it." Anger crept into Nali's words. He had risked his family, and Rathil's, to reach the king. Always he had hesitated to counsel, uncertain of himself. Now he knew what had to be done and saw it more clearly than the king. He had no intention of letting Arshal urge the way of moderation. "Use that stone of yours!" he demanded. "We can't just sit on our hands like this!" He jumped to his feet, pacing around the little alcove. "What other great men like Khoti and Tsevon might be awaiting merely the direction? What possessed the gods to grant Khoti healing powers and battle prowess? How many other would-be legends are working on the wharves of Shela, or tending horses in Kalilia, or blowing glass in the Jashiho Desert, or felling timber in Mershy, or mining in the southern mountains? We won't know unless we act! Zopher and Khoti have spies returning daily with more and more information. Arshal, we're finally thinking! We aren't ready yet. You can't put it off any longer. But as long as you're here, we've thrown our entire measure in the pot. We have to keep you moving, untraced, but helping us build a coalition of support."

Nali was thinking aloud now, Arshal merely staring at him in wonderment.

"If we don't move soon, we'll miss that one opportunity when perhaps those powers of yours will shine, when perhaps the other Khotis of Shande will be at their finest, when, as a kingdom, we can pull together and regain Shande."

Arshal stared at the dark surface of the stone in his palm. "For an instant before it blinded me, I saw my power, a physical thing: the alien entity that could conceal a harbor or smash a mug against the wall. I'm bound to it now, irreversibly. It's part of me. But something of me in it is able to strike back at me." As if responding to his memory, the colors in the stone shifted. It flared red in his palm. He glanced up at Nali. When he looked back, it glowed royal blue.

"What can I do with this?" he asked of himself.

Nali shook his head. "That, we have to learn, too."

Arshal reached into a pouch hanging from his side and pulled out a small etched vial filled with blue liquid. He inclined his head to acknowledge Nali's recognition.

"Tend me, Nali?" he asked. "I must seek answers through the osfothye, and the journey's a long one."

Nali nodded, thinking he should, instead, protest. He didn't know the properties of the liquid. He remembered only Cree's long sleep and Arshal's obvious discomfort with his one attempt to find guidance through osfothye dreams, as if the visions that came to them without their consent weren't enough. Before Nali could protest, Arshal had taken a bare drop in a glass of cider, the room growing oppressive with the heavy minty scent. Too late to protest now, time, instead, to witness.

# 10: Madness

That the man still lived after all this time gave Konner hope. Each day he paced the long corridor to Khoti's alcove and took a morsel of Khoti's torment into himself. Yet Khoti, doubtless, would remain bent and broken like the gnarled pines clinging to the peaks above the treeline, Konner like the crumbling rock feeding his roots. It seemed with each touch, Khoti took the older man's strength, as if burning a fuel that couldn't be replenished. Is this what used up Tsevon? Would Konner's fate be to follow his old friend into the spirit world? Who would remain to keep the Taschians a people? Khoti could name no Second but Konner.

This day, when Konner strode by Asteria to pull back the curtain to the niche, he found Khoti staring at the ceiling, seeming to boil from within as he pondered some rage.

"Khoti?" Konner asked, finding the man the most alert he'd been since his rescue. Khoti turned to him, the expression on his face making Konner's heart catch. He could see the fever had fled.

"I betrayed us all," Khoti whispered.

"You did nothing of the sort."

"I told them everything. I had to. Konner, I'm a traitor! Nali tried to stop me. But I told them who he was." Konner jumped back as Khoti grabbed for the dagger at Konner's hip.

"What're you trying to do, son?" Konner stared at the younger man, seeing the demon of madness. "That's cowardice, Khoti. It's not our way to end our lives. It's the decision of the spirits when to call a life home."

Asteria stirred from her vigil at the table then rushed away. Konner ached, just ached down deep.

"We kill traitors. I told them where to find us, destroy us. I can't live with that. I deserve to die. Let me –"

"What did you do?" Konner stalled, trying to stay out of Khoti's reach.

"I told them everything!" Khoti threw an arm over his face as Steadon and Nali pressed into the niche, Asteria behind them biting a bloody lip. "The scavengers. When they came, I just couldn't stop myself Konner. I kept picturing them tearing me apart, scattered so far the spirits would lose me. Nali was there. He told me I wasn't alone. But they came anyway."

Konner turned to Steadon and Nali. "What's he babbling about?"

"They learned nothing from you! You betrayed no one." Steadon, said grasping Khoti's shoulders.

"I felt their beaks and talons ripping at me."

"There weren't no birds, Khoti. It's the lash you're thinking of –" Konner began.

"No," Nali said quietly. "It's rats he's remembering."

Konner paled and a small sound escaped Asteria as she turned to escape, only to find her father behind her, his face like stone. He pulled her against his chest.

"I shooed them off, Khoti. You said nothing," Nali soothed. "Maybe inside you did. Nothing came from your mouth but curses and prattle."

"I remember. Numb on Hothur's brandy. Questioning me, asking me what rights I had to be here."

"It's your mind, Khoti, that questioned you," Nali said, his eyes taking on a shrewd, hawkish stare.

Khoti turned away, gasping. "I would've told if I could."

"You warned me that every man has a breaking point," Eithurdon said. "You are not a god, whatever their gifts to you. You are capable of every weakness of any other mortal being. It is not treason to be tortured into delirium."

"So much trouble I've brought," Khoti mumbled. "I'm in my fa's bed. I killed him, didn't I? I felt his touch. I took his spirit. Because of me, he's gone. Tait betrays us because of me. If I had just led Asteria to Sefresal that day instead of chasing my own bloodlust, no harm would have come to her, no question of honor –"

"And King Arshal would be dead because we would know only Tsevon as a healer, and he could not have brought the king back to us," Eithurdon said firmly. "And I would be dead on the battlefield, and thus perhaps the pass would not have been open for the king's retreat. Consequences transpire from choices. We have discussed this. Without you, many Tawnkats would have died trying to rescue their families taken captive. Sefresal would have been set out for the enemy like a feast, and Steadon en route to Lagdche. Is not being made a legend, even among your enemy, enough? You learned there are limits to what you can do. Tait might have betrayed us anyway, Tsevon died anyway. Are you only just discovering weakness in yourself? Self-pity is unbecoming in the man who would succeed Tsevon."

Khoti's breath came as a gasp. He wouldn't turn to face them, his right arm thrown over his eyes with its brassy cuff gleaming dully in the flickering candlelight.

"Is that what frightens you?" Eithurdon demanded. "Actually facing the consequences?" Eithurdon's face had gone red, veins standing out on his neck and forehead. "So, they broke you. So, you will never be the soldier you were. Is that all it takes to turn you from your obligations to your people, to turn a legendary warrior into a coward?"

Khoti's body had knotted. "I remember Nali waiting for me to die but I couldn't see him. Their faces were pressed so close I couldn't see past them. I kept trying to see Nali, but they kept coming closer, demanding to know what right I had."

Nali moved around the bed, and crouched down on his haunches where Khoti would be forced to look at him or have to turn to face Eithurdon. "You said that before. Who asked you that? Whose faces? Was it your own doubts?" Nali's voice was gentle, but his gaze remained blade sharp.

Khoti shook his head. He removed his arm and looked at the derna who had dressed in his blue robes. "From somewhere else. They asked me what right I had, what my purpose was."

"And what purpose did you say you had?"

"I said I didn't know. To stop Minaria."

"But that wasn't the answer?" Nali demanded.

Khoti shook his head.

"The answer was larger than Minaria. It had to do with your gifts of prowess and healing. It had to do with all you knew of Arshal and his stone. It had to do with your purpose for being who you are."

Khoti pulled himself up a little, grunting with the effort it took to lean on an elbow to peer at Nali, the sharp attention in the derna's expression that of a scholar unearthing the answer to some great mystery.

"It was the spirits, Khoti, challenging you to live," Nali declared. "You were wasting yourself, not meant to give up. You took the voice as a claim you'd failed. Instead, I believe it's an appeal for you to be strong, so you won't fail. You're called, Khoti, like me and Arshal. There's a force in you that makes you more powerful than you know to deal with. It's all part of something more than regaining Shande, but dealing with the power behind the threat. It's the ambition of Fyraer, of Ghyldus, we've been called to battle."

Khoti lay back. "Then no matter what I do, I've got some fate I have to fulfill? I didn't die in battle because it wasn't willed?" Khoti's words had turned sour.

Nali shrugged. "I think you could die anytime, even now. But you're given gifts and a will strong enough to sustain and protect you, perhaps more than others. As much as it seems like fate, I think we can abandon it, or even alter it through our actions. Even the visions I have only guide us to make the right choices, or maybe are meant to guide us away from the wrong decisions. The gods can't will anything for us. They can only give us the tools and maybe lead us a little. Maybe the challenge you heard was their appeal to that part of you still fighting for life. I know you're guided by the gods. I have no doubt. They didn't will you to name Kedtair to bring Arshal home. But they made it so strong an image you used it. They gave you your gifts, prowess, healing, spirit, to be used, for whatever purpose only they know, not wasted lost in a dungeon somewhere, and not by your own hand."

Nali straightened. The madness Konner had seen in Khoti's eyes had faded. The tension in his muscles relaxed as he again covered his face with his arm, his cheeks crimson. "Ah, gods. What good am I now, Nali? All my posturing to Hothur, all the promises I made for revenge. I have the body of an old man."

"Only because you think you do," Nali said in the cryptic tone of the advisor, brushing by a startled Eithurdon as he left.

"And you, duke, what punishment do you bring? Have you already tried me without my accounting? Would you let the maimed man who you think dishonored you remain in your Guard, a man who would now be headman to his people? A fool that doesn't know delusion from reality?" Khoti's face remained hidden beneath his arm.

"Your concerns should be with your health and your people. Other matters can be discussed later," Eithurdon stated coldly.

A silence fell on the alcove.

When Khoti lifted his arm from his eyes, he was alone.

Even Konner had gone. Stretching his arm out, Khoti stared at the cuff still clinging to his right wrist. Scabbed gouges marred his left wrist where Asteria had torn the other cuff away. He flexed his arm. The muscles screamed at him, but responded. So, everything his people had suffered was because of the intervention of arbitrary gods seeking to end a menace they unleashed on Ea. The sweet spirits that filled his sticks with song couldn't be the same as would concoct so cruel a fate as a healer-warrior. Who would bring him back from death if he acted the fool again? He had consumed his fa. Konner already appeared a decade older. To save one warrior, healer, reckless man.

Sitting up, he tested his limbs. It would be a long while yet before the bones in his legs completely mended, perhaps never. Konner had already taken on so much. He didn't dare let the man touch him again. His ribs, too, felt tender, aching with each breath. But the muscles remained intact, mended by Konner and Tsevon's blood. Muscles could be made strong again.

He grinned to himself, the grin that scared enemies from his path. He felt a touch; a breath seemed to pass through him from somewhere else, cleansing, comforting, exhilarating, like the south wind before the thaw. They said Terremar. Instead, he sensed Tsevon.

# 11: Visionary

Cree sat on a log at the edge of the small lake at the base of the Val. One of those warm days in the first moon, the Evenday promised spring to come, though the wind falling from the slopes still crackled with winter. Water slowly spread over the ice on the lake as snow warmed to the sun. A large section kept ice-free, serving as the Val's water supply, teemed with ducks and geese fattening on the small leavings the dwellers of the Val gave them. The sun felt comfortable, the hubbub a welcome buzz in the normally silent valley. Children chased in the trees behind him, thrilling in a day warm enough to escape the crowded caverns. A group of girls hauled buckets of water to the just-built cistern perched on a ledge by the South Slope caverns, their giggles and chatter like the waterfalls rushing from the snowpack. The clamor of fowl, the wind in the pines, and the thunk of an axe on wood all melded into a symphony with none of the notes of discord expected in a song of occupation.

Cree pondered his centuries of service to kings that came and went in a lifebeat, though a lifetime to them. That service ended with the death of King Ebon. Always he had retreated for a generation or two to wander the world or take up with some family of promise, a brother spirit filling his role as some king's advisor.

Now, Nali filled that role: a time, Nali had said, to undo the effects of the gods on Ea. Was this part of Terremar's plan, the future Cree should remember? But then, the future changed with each moment of the present and past, different threads woven into the pattern of life with each unforecasted change. Wisely, Nali recognized the legacy of Fyraer, saw the purpose of the gods. How, Cree didn't know. He only knew that the time had come for a shal advisor to the king. He felt content that Nali could serve that role. Once, he remembered something about Nali, something ancient, when Cree knew the future. Now, he couldn't remember it.

He turned and looked up toward the pass to the east. He'd heard something. Or foreseen it? He shook off the sensation of being watched. Scouts and Tawnkats lurked throughout the Val and the pass. Nothing entered the place without them knowing.

He turned and looked again. Something stalked him.

How had his powers passed so far from him that he could no longer read events of even the present? He couldn't even read Arshal anymore, could not face him. He, Cree, had not even known such a thing as Khoti's gift existed in the world yet. That he didn't know almost killed the king. Now what feeling did he have that he could not define?

A loud bellow of anger, surprise or pain, and a horn blast that echoed to the peaks and startled the fowl into flight, brought Cree to his feet. Children and water bearers stared east, riveted by their shock.

"Move!" he screamed. "Into the caves!"

He tried to shoo them before him, his arms sweeping wide to drive them, his ancient legs powerful. A Minarian patrol rode hard at them. People scrambled everywhere as arrows flew in both directions. A Minarian leaned down and scooped up a fleeing shawnsi woman. They approached fast. Cree, filled with the youth of the gods, still couldn't outrun horsemen. A Minarian caught up to him, leaning forward to strike him with his sword. Cree stopped, the man brushing by. Cree pulled a dagger from the folds of his robes. The horseman reined in and circled back, eyes gleaming. Though Cree bore a weapon, the Minarian grinned as if looking upon an old man, or perhaps his foe saw a Visionary and only counted his bounty.

The horseman struck with the flat of his sword to knock Cree from his feet. Cree stood fast, ducking to the side in a swift move like a tensed branch slapping into place. The sword missed. Cree slashed with his dagger, striking the man's leg. The look on the horseman's face registered his shock at the strength behind the blow. Enraged, he swung back. He brought his sword around in a sweeping arc. At the same instant, Cree flung his dagger so it lodged in the man's neck. The sword struck Cree in his unprotected side.

He remained standing, unnoted by the other enemy horsemen riding through the valley. Cree pulled aside his robe and looked. It might kill a man. But him? He smiled, one he knew had a truly ethereal glow. At last he would go home, be shed of all the trials of Ea. Yet he stood. Had he erred?

A horseman rode at him, sword drawn. Cree lifted his arms to face the man, unarmed. The sword tip pierced his chest.

The weapon flew up in a burst of light like lightning, splintering into shrapnel as sparks arced. The man's arm shattered like the sword and metal shards shredded his face.

Cree fell. A crackling thunder echoed around them, driving the enemy's horses before it as a puff of snow smoke on the mountain peaks signed a distant avalanche. The fowl squawked and rose in a beat of wings from the lake.

When the patrol retreated back into the pass Cree remained behind, lying in the churned and bloody snow with his god-like smile, the rain of sword fragments lying over him as a dusting of snow.

When silence returned to the Val, reports filtered in that the patrol took four captives and left two Guardsmen dead in the pass. Signs indicated the patrol arrived singly, averting detection. Then, searchers found the dead Visionary near one of the three Minarians killed in the brief battle.

Nali alone knew what to do. Those who understood what it meant to have a god living among them, a god killed by an enemy they as mortals must face, mourned in stunned silence. As they tallied the losses that came from Tait's betrayal, Nali ordered a massive pyre built. He called on the gods to prepare for their lost spirit's return to One. Flames touched the ancient skin Idenai took to live among his children.

At last Cree went home, one less prey among the hunted.

# 12: King's Council

Khoti sat in his bed, sword across his lap, distracted from honing his weapon to study the brass-colored cuff on his wrist. Not for the first time he wondered why it hadn't been removed like the ones at his ankles. The soft metal could be pounded tight on the wrist and easily removed, yet resisted his efforts to pry it off. The more he considered it, the more he felt it should remain.

Looking up, he startled to discover Asteria standing in the doorway watching him. He almost cut himself on the sword's sharp edge. Her glance touched the weapon. She hesitated, looking over her shoulder before pulling up a stool.

He smiled, gesturing, to demonstrate how he practiced to strengthen his arms.

"I considered prying this off," he held up the hand with the cuff. "But I don't know now." He extended his hand to her.

Again, she hesitated before she took it. Her palm felt damp in his.

"You're afraid of me," he stated, suddenly seeing it in her. He yanked his hand away and tossed the sword. It clanged against the wall. His own reaction stunned him.

"My father promised me to another," she said softly. "I hoped you could speak for me."

"What can I do?" His words stuck in his throat. He ached inside. He hadn't thought it would feel like this. He'd had battle wounds that didn't knock the breath out of him the way Asteria could by just looking at him that way, her eyes soft, moist, frightened. She feared him! "Perhaps, as they said, we were wrong," he muttered. "We can't cause a war in the Val. I'm a headman now, like it or not, ready or not. For the Staphians too, since they came to Fa's call. Von said Fa would never live to see a cub take his place, foolish words then. I have duties to my people, duke and king. There's no time for – and since he refuses me –"

He swung his legs to the floor. A wince choked off his words. The bones hadn't completely knit. The muscles remained bruised and weak. He reached for the wall for support.

"No, Khoti, you are being a fool," Asteria cried when he tried to stand. She pushed him back. He lost his balance and fell hard on the bed, a cry of pain escaping him before he recovered and grasped her arm, yanking her close.

"Why come to me now?" he demanded, frightened by his own emotions. "You'll bring even more trouble to me if your fa finds you here. I see your fear."

"There was an attack on the Val," she said, not responding to his assessment. She tried to pull free but he gripped her arm tighter. "There were captives, a death, mourning and rites to be performed. Everyone is meeting, to try to find answers, to –"

"An attack? They came then? That dog Tait!" Khoti released her, flinging an arm over his face. "And I'm helpless."

"You will be strong again. You live. No one expected that."

"I warned you this couldn't work from the start. Look what came of it! Tait might never have done this if he hadn't been so obsessed with showing me up."

"He wore a Minarian medallion."

"It's over. I should have known. Your fa never planned to agree. Yet you come here to torment me, risking his wrath."

"I would not."

"Then what're you doing!"

She shook her head, shrugged. "I do not want to lose you," she said in a small voice, crimson. "You were dead, just like my dreams. Then seeing you mad –"

"I was feverish. I remembered an illusion and thought it real," he said softly. He took her hand again, afraid if he drove her away, as he must, he would never see her again, never feel this strange sense of wholeness she gave him.

"Who's meeting, what're they planning?" Khoti asked when the silence grew awkward.

"King's Council, I think, to devise some plan of attack. The derna's message was urgency." Khoti tried to rise. She held his shoulders, gripping so hard it hurt. "Someone will tell you what they decide. You are weak yet. Regain your strength."

Khoti took a deep breath and held it a moment as he stared at her, caught that scent of thaw in her hair again. Had she been out giving a treat to Fidra as she'd once admitted? Had spring

68

come out there, the rocks singing the season? Why did her eyes have to take on that sparkle so like the dark gem on the pendant in his pocket, no, around his neck where someone had hung it while he lay in his fever?

"What's his name?"

"Anlon of Mershy."

"You know him well?" he asked through clenched teeth.

She shook her head. "We met once when we were children. He is Dasirean, not shawnsi, heir to Habdelion's name only."

"Congratulations," he said sourly, releasing her hand. "Will it be a large joining ceremony? A gathering of royals? In the halls of Sefresal perhaps, or will the king honor you in Sihmad Shal as you're so close in his line."

"Bitterness does not suit you."

He knew the wound struck deep. He stared at the brass cuff on his wrist. She waited, as if unsure what to do now.

"Do me a last honor. Will you?" he asked softly.

She nodded without hesitation.

"Help me walk. I've laid a-bed too long already."

Elbows propped on the rough trestle table in the common, Arshal sat staring into the dark knots in the wood's surface. The few assembled pressed elbow to elbow. Tawnkat squad leaders perched on stools against the walls, the King's Council and Resala crowding the little table with Arshal while Chati and Tre fumbled to serve wine and bread and refresh the ink with which Nali intended to pen their decisions.

Arshal leaned back to look up at Kefta, who stood in the doorway. "Then Steadon's fear holds true."

Kefta inclined his head. "Lord, scouts followed the patrol to the Staph-el bridge, where it appears they transferred the captives to a wagon, likely making for Lagdche. The wagon had been waiting. They've planned this for a time. From what we know, the Minarians will be well-rewarded for any shawnsi, Visionary or derna delivered alive to Ghyldus."

"Then why did they kill Cree?"

Kefta shrugged. "He may have just looked like an old man in their way. We'll never know. I merely report what we know, Lord."

"How much did Tait reveal?" Arshal muttered. "Do they know I'm here as well? Or do they think a Shandean king's no threat."

"They assume the King is Ebon," Eithurdon said from beside Nali. "They never wrested even that truth from Khoti."

"To our advantage," Arshal declared, thumping his fist on the table and almost overturning Nali's ink. "Nali's come to urge action, now. That was over a month ago so already we're behind. I think his counsel's wise. We must build an army, the right way, and prepare for one great signal for all the land to heed. We need the help of every person still loyal to Shande."

"Well, Lord, in a way, we'll have Aibak's help," Konner said from the other end of the table, leaning forward to peer around Zopher. "He's agreed to arm the Pladde. They may not believe we've got a boat's odds in a waterfall, but they know if the Pladde make life miserable for Ghyldus, Minaria'll be slow to attack Shiad. That'll pull a few troops home from Shande."

"It's something," Arshal conceded. "But what of the rest of Ea? How can we convince them to help us?"

"They must be told the Minarians are coming for them next," Steadon said from beside Eithurdon, his fingers rapping the table in a staccato rhythm that made Nali turn to study the man's too-thin face. "Hothur gloated about how they would conquer all of Ea soon. They believe they have a divine right, as a people, to control the world. If we can convince other countries —"

"How?" Zopher's gaze challenged Arshal. Beside him, Peshal leaned back with a small smile. Resala straightened, her expression of boredom giving way to attentiveness. "Our own people refuse us," Zopher stated. "We told them we have a king and an intention to fight. Prince Euzzeldir in Joffa sent our man back with jeers, saying our failure to halt the occupation is proof we have nothing to support our claims."

"Ah, such distinction to be the first King of Shande challenged by his own provinces," Arshal said. "Then we must prove ourselves." He held up his palm with the stone burning a fierce blue in it. "We need word of our plans to reach the right people, remind them of the prophecies, set a date for action, and form a strong plan. All will serve to build our case. Bring Aibak here; we can take him into our confidence. He's remained a true ally. With the right information, maybe he can convince King Keyen to support us. They must see! The scouts report Minarian troops called home to put down the uprising. While they may have soldiers in every corner of the land, they're spread thin. Our people quail before them out of fear because they don't know they're not alone in resistance. They don't know we intend to fight back. And neither does our enemy. They assume we're complacent. As long as the osfothye, the produce and livestock keep coming they assume success. They don't dare mention to superiors the little knot of resistance here, not when that would wreck their tyranny and the potential for profit in captives. They think they can sit back and grow fat on Shande. We must prove them wrong. We can retake –"

"How can we hold any conquest?" Zopher protested. "They'd soon learn of it and reinforce their position. It would be a waste." Zopher ignored Arshal's impatient sputter and glare at being interrupted.

"A waste to position Shandeans openly," Nali said. "Some must be covert, like those working in Sefresal now. If you take some fellow, say Geleg, whose features could be Minarian, and dress him up like a Minarian, and have him imitate a Minarian accent, then they'd be slow to learn it was Shandeans giving the orders. Peshal himself, a shawnsi, passed among them in the guise of an Eidhalt, and none were the wiser."

"Well, some were," Peshal conceded with a grim smile. He ran his finger across his throat. "They didn't challenge me again."

A round of chuckles eased a little of the tension and a few of the men gave red-faced Geleg mock thrusts as if their swords had skewered his Hogde-like features.

Arshal laid his hands on the table, palms up, looking from face to face until they fell silent. When the common returned to silence, he launched into a description of the plan he and Nali had crafted these last weeks since he'd sought guidance in the osfothye dreams, taking in as he spoke the wide eyes of his listeners, their shock at his declarations of intent, the brashness of his plans, the scowls of the doubters.

Segan cleared his throat as Arshal finished, emerging from his place at the wall. "It's a vast kingdom, Lord," he said. "If Minaria diverts more men here, if they get suspicious, what's to stop another army from crossing the river, or setting sail? We don't have enough of us to hold a city alone."

"Look at what just a handful of you did!" Arshal expounded. "I hope to have all of Shande working on the same schedule."

"What stops communication from being hopelessly muddled from one province to the next? If I send scouts to warn the provinces and other rulers, what do they say?" Zopher asked. He'd supported the idea as Arshal spoke, nodding at key points; now his tone reflected doubt.

"Kedtairday is the date we take back Shande. That's a bit more than two years to reach everyone, build an army, weed out the enemy and eliminate traitors. Then, on Kedtairday, we strike the major blow on the largest bodies of the enemy. Kedtair is when we'll be our strongest, an easy date to set." Arshal leaned back in his chair, scanning the skeptical faces turned to him.

"What stops them from sending even more troops, as Segan suggested?" Eithurdon asked with a sigh.

"They must send more. It must be a decisive blow. We must draw Ghyldus to us in that month when Kedtair stands overhead. Then, I must face Ghyldus, likely my last act."

"We hope on a great number of possibilities, Arshal," Eithurdon said after a lengthy silence. "You count on Ghyldus leaving his comfort to face you, an upstart king who poses no apparent threat. You count on nations who now turn, smirking, from us, and province leaders who laugh in our faces. You count on the response of cowed people facing a brutal occupation and who knows what condition they will be in two years hence. You count on the Pladde, who had no identity until the Hogde provided it for them, on just too many things."

"We must make Ghyldus afraid." Arshal stared at his hands. "That's the hard part. There's reason to believe Ghyldus already has doubts, or perhaps fears some retaliation from the gods. He seeks us, the royal family, sends Eidhalt, out of fear of an overlooked threat. Perhaps some captive will relate tales to enhance those doubts. If we capture a few Minarians and they report to him ... I don't know. It's for such details a king calls a council.

"But as for the rest," Arshal glanced up at Eithurdon. "I also must convince the leaders of Ea it's worth the risk. They know me only for tipping an ale in the Harbor or winning wrestling matches. They don't know me for my determination to regain my birthright and avenge my family. No messenger's word will convince them of the changes this war has wrought in me. Even you, Eithur, doubted orders from Sihmad Shal. Now we must be a united land. The people must see a king in whom they can believe. When Zel of Joffa laughs in my face, I'll have an answer for him the scouts cannot provide."

Voices rose in protest as those gathered understood the risk the king suggested he undertake.

"We can't place all our hopes on you, Lord, then let you wander off to places where we can't protect you," Konner's voice rose above the din.

Arshal held up his hands for silence, the stone bright in his left palm, casting a blue glow on his features.

"Clearly the Val is no longer safe. As long as I remain here, we're in danger. When Ghyldus learns from where his captives came, we'll have even more trouble. As I said, we think Ghyldus is unsettled. If he identifies this fear and links it to rumors of a king – if he hasn't already – he'll spend all of his energies trying to find and extinguish the threat. This is no longer a safe place to hide, no matter how secure the Guard and Tawnkats make it."

"Lord, an armed escort will attract attention in an occupied land," Kefta warned.

"I will go alone, save for a guide and defender."

Sputtered denials grew toward a crescendo in the tiny room. The stone in his hand blazed out, silencing them.

"The kings of Shande have often relied on osfothye to guide them. Such guidance is god-born and has never been wrong. I must go, in person, without retinue or escort." Heads shook, frustrated features twisted in grimaces of denial. "Which king would you believe could face Ghyldus? The king protected by thirty men-at-arms? Or the one who came alone because he has no fear? The fewer with me, the fewer who can be forced to betray me. I count on gathering help as I travel. I have a gift of the gods to protect me, a stone as Dynfearn the Lost used to drive his enemies from his path." He held up his hand again, the stone blazing so white they had to shield their eyes.

A palpable silence reigned.

"I need a guide from the mountains, perhaps some Tawnkat."

"The Tawnkats know this area like their lifemates' smiles, Lord, but anything beyond Lhata or Sefresal you're looking at about as much help as you'd get from Ghyldus himself," Konner grumbled.

"Eithurdon had scouts –"

"Of those still alive, all are crisscrossing Shande gathering news, can't be reached or are more necessary in other places," Zopher said.

"There isn't one man?" Arshal challenged. "I need a guide, just through the mountains! And protection. I admit I'm not the class of swordsman a Lharan Guardsman is."

"Khoti's the best," Kefta mused. "Been up and down the range and has a natural canniness for such things. He can't even walk."

"Agreed, Khoti would fit both bills. He is unlikely to see battle again," Steadon said. "His body is broken, perhaps even his spirit."

"Might I be consulted!" Khoti demanded. All heads turned to find the Taschian headman leaning on Asteria as he shuffled past Kefta into the crowded common. Tre reached him swiftly, helping Khoti to a stool, which he fell onto with a grimace. The duke glared at his daughter as she stood behind Khoti. The woman's chin thrust out defiantly.

"Khoti you're too weak to –" Konner began.

"Do not underestimate him," Asteria warned.

"By the gods, Asteria," Eithurdon retorted. "Look at him. He cannot even walk."

"He walked here! You can do nothing yet, and you know it," she returned.

"The scouts won't be back for months," Zopher admitted.

"You still could not leave until the snows melt," Asteria said. "By the light moon, what then? Look at him! Konner said he would die. Two weeks later his fever broke. People said he would never walk again. Three weeks later he walked here. So, in three weeks, he will need no support. And three weeks after that, he will be fencing with Kefta. And three weeks after that he will be ready to ride into death if that is what you demand. By then, the snows will be gone."

They all stared at Asteria. Khoti sat silent, his stony gaze warming at her words. Clearly, she knew, as all knew, Khoti's warrior heart could never be left behind to languish in idleness.

Arshal looked from Asteria to Khoti. "I must have a guide," he stated. "Better yet if he's a swordsman. I wouldn't again dare these mountains in winter. There's much to be done here, yet. We need to refine our plans. It isn't time wasted. By the light moon, if another scout's returned who can guide me and Khoti's not ready, then there's no loss for the wait. If I need a defender on this road through the mountains, from what I'm told, I doubt I'd find better than Khoti. I saw many things in my osfothye dreams, such visions as the gods would grant me. I sense a greater danger than just patrols closing on me. I will need someone with great skill to help me remain ahead of the pursuit. Besides, Khoti's gifts weren't meant to be idled any more than my own. Time will allow us to figure out how to bait Ghyldus into our trap, and permit me to explore this stone."

Arshal stood, signalling the end of the conference. He smiled at Khoti who stood pale and sweat-slicked, his gaze calculating.

"I find it hard to believe you're the same man brought back for dead but weeks ago. If this is a sign of mountain strength, I can't wait to see what the Tawnkats can do together."

With a nod, Arshal departed, leaving the leaders of the Val to grapple with their doubts about the soundness of the king's plans, so brash, assumptive. And each must find a way to make them work.

# 13: Diplomacy

"I'm called to it, Resala," Peshal whispered as he leaned on the table in the alcove Resala shared with Asteria.

Resala shook her head as if refusing to hear him. "Why are you telling me this? So, I can prepare to mourn another brother? Do you really think Arshal wanted his seeds of fear planted this way? It's too much to risk. If something happens to Arshal, who'll take his place?"

"You," Peshal said. "Look, I sat in on all the discussions Cree and Arshal had, and some with Nali and Arshal. I know what they need. I know what to do. I know what I face."

"And if you fail, it's a wasted effort."

"And if anyone else fails –"

"No one said yet how to do it. He merely postulated that captives might plant doubts." Resala's breath came fast. It wasn't fear. Peshal knew Resala's reaction to fear, a grim silence, a patience to see what would come of it, a flash of anger. Not this odd, breathless excitement.

"And if you don't see him," she continued. "Then what? If they kill you, your efforts are worth nothing. What if you're sacrificed and never even reach him? You don't have to be alive for them to collect their bounty. What if you came too soon and he strikes early, when Arshal's not ready for him. Or if you're killed before you can make him doubt enough? We can't count on one man, Peshal."

Peshal's eyes narrowed. He stared at her, waiting as footsteps faded outside her alcove before he responded. "Then what do you suggest? For whatever crazed reason I can't fathom, I believe Arshal's plan can work. But Ghyldus must feel threatened, and at the right time, to fall into the scheme. There's always the possibility it'll fail."

"I think your idea is sound, but not alone. Together, you and I, between us we can make it work."

"You?" Peshal recoiled. She had changed as they crossed the plains, always stronger than anyone thought her, always a pillar of faith for the people. So strong she could suggest this? To let herself be captured to gain access to their enemy? "Resala, your gift is in comforting our people. They need you! If I fail, and if Arshal fails, someone must remain –"

"Remain for what? What weapon do I have to face Ghyldus?" Peshal sat back from her rancor, which struck him like a blow. "Do you think if Arshal fails, I'm likely to ride up to some ruler and convince him I'm worthy of his support? They'd truly have something to laugh at then. My strengths may be compassion. That I concede. But other strengths, purposes, exist in the world. Do you think Arshal and Esthen were alone in the dire prophecies? All of Ebon's children were blessed with their doom. Seek my name in the Lierye, brother. You'll find my purpose has nothing to do with comforting troubled souls."

"You sought your name in the Lierye?" Scholars might consult the tome, but not the children of kings, not people who might change their fate by knowing.

She nodded, smiling grimly. "I know there's more expected of me. I discard prophecy, or at least I used to. Then, Arshal fit his, Esthen his, Father his. I would ignore this prophecy, choose against fulfilling it. But Pesh, I feel it. I must do this. It struck Arshal when Father called the kingdom to arms, Esthen when he commanded an army, now me when you suggest the logical means to meet our needs. Arshal knows it must be done. He'd never ask for such a sacrifice from any individual. But we bear the same blood. He merely has the curse of birth order. The gods work in us, too. And this is what I'm called to." She had grasped his hand, gripped it, as she stared into his eyes with her appeal. The sunburst mark of the shawnsi on her right temple had grown dark, bold, as her face reddened.

"Zopher will never allow it," Peshal warned.

"It's not Zopher's decision to make, but mine. It's my contribution to Shande. We can't tell anyone, Pesh, not Arshal, not Zopher. They'd stop us. The two closest to the king running off into the arms of the enemy? By the time they find out, it'll be too late."

"My heart goes against this."

"And my heart goes against you doing this," she retorted. "For myself, I know what must be done. If it's what you truly intend, we can work together. Together there'd be double pressure on Ghyldus and a surety if one of us fails."

Peshal studied her a long time, at last nodding. He felt a deep dread. He had an unexpected image of Esthen in a far-away room extolling the glory war might be. "Then it's settled. I hope we aren't just the world's greatest fools."

"We aren't."

He gazed at her a moment. "What was that forbidden name in the Lierye that drives you?"

"Artras. A name Cree would not allow uttered."

Peshal stared at her in horror as his childhood lessons brought the ancient word to his tongue in an instant. "Martyr? Oh Resala, this is no decision to make lightly. You can –"

"I can do no more than I was meant to, as you." The

expression on her face, so full of pride and purpose, froze the words in Peshal's throat. He could only close his eyes and nod.

Khoti sat with Kefta beside the communal kitchen on the South Slope of the Val. Joking with the women and young girls working there, they'd begun to feel a bit of the wine Kefta brought to cheer Khoti on his way to health and to welcome spring. It wasn't long before the women had Khoti red-faced and grinning as they competed for his attention, many teasing him with offers of a joining. A few dared suggest other options short of permanence as their companions shrieked, giggles shrill in the warm sun raising a hazy mist from patches of snow. These were his people, with a history proud and deep that he learned more about each day as Konner tried to instill in him what a headman should know.

Khoti grinned up at Kefta, not feeling the chill as a gust of wind fell down the slope. It felt good to be here, with a Guardsman and friend. He idled with the two canes he used to support himself, feeling better with each day that gave him more freedom from his bed.

"So, when are you going to let me pry that thing off?" Kefta pointed at the brass-colored cuff on Khoti's right wrist; the metal glinted in the hazy sunlight. Khoti had pried it apart enough so that it no longer pinched and chafed his skin.

"Never," he said. "Whenever I've gone into battle, I've called on some memory to make me strong. I'll be in battle again. When I am, I'll have this reminder on my sword arm of why I'm fighting.

It has more power than that. It keeps Tait's memory fresh: the power of treason, as if I could forget."

Kefta motioned at the canes. "Battle, you say? I doubt you're even strong enough to handle your wine, or this gaggle of giggling women."

Khoti gave him Geleg's best lecherous grin. "Oh, I can handle a lot of things you don't think I can. Don't be so foolish as to underestimate me, Kefta."

"Ah, and you keep telling me that, and I haven't yet. But one day, boy, you're going to come up against something bigger than yourself, bigger than that vanity of yours."

Khoti's gaze dropped to the cuff. "I already have."

Kefta was about to retort when someone called out and pointed at the west end of the Val. He reached for his sword. "What –"

Khoti silenced him, head cocked to catch the distant taps carried away on the wind.

"Aibak," Khoti said, lurching to his feet. "But he's with dozens of people."

"Maybe he brings fighting men."

Khoti let out a whoop as the stones passed along what the tapper saw. "He brings Staphians!"

As others heard the message a buzz of voices grew. Konner hurried from the cavern, speeding down the path to the lake. Soon he returned, walking beside Aibak and followed by a bedraggled file of women and youths who marched along the lakeshore in stoic silence as if they refused to hope on their future.

As Amhese hurried from the caves to greet her kinspeople and find them homes in the caverns, Aibak came to Khoti, embracing the Tawnkat he had met only briefly before.

"I grieve for your father," he said. The Shiadin stood back, his gaze going from the canes with which Khoti supported himself to the cuff at his wrist, then the small Tawnkat tattoo at the base of his neck. "I see you are your father's son. I know you will fill his place in the hearts of these people, and in the spirit of the Tawnkats."

Khoti inclined his head at the tribute.

"I am here first to meet with the man who calls himself your king. He claims he must prove something. Do you believe his tale, Khoti? I remember Tsevon as wary of Shandean kings. Should I treat with this man? Will he convince me King Keyen is wrong?"

Khoti studied the Shiadin's round face, his open expression. "He convinced me, Fa and Konner of his worth. That's no small feat. I think you'll find this king, if any, will see Ghyldus's demise."

With a nod Aibak followed Konner to the common, matching his pace to Khoti's.

Only Arshal, Nali and Eithurdon sat at the trestle table, as Tre set out wine. When Khoti hobbled in with Aibak, Arshal smiled, his expression a reward for Khoti efforts. Eithurdon found something of interest in his hands.

"Aibak brings a gift to fill our hearts, Lord," Konner said. "The Pladde found dozens of Staphian captives in a labor camp in Minaria and delivered them to Aibak's care."

Arshal jumped up, motioning for Aibak to sit beside Khoti. "Then the Pladde remain successful. Wonderful! Any Lhatans?"

"These people knew of no others, Lord," Aibak said. "The tribe of Lhata remains dead."

"I hope I haven't inconvenienced you," Arshal said after a long moment. "I must convince you we're worthy of Shiad's aid, that King Arshaldon of Shande will not be denied." Without further preamble, Arshal launched into an explanation of all the Shandeans planned to achieve in the coming months, ignoring the incredulous expression growing on Aibak's face.

"You expect a lot, Lord," Aibak said when Arshal finished. "And if you succeed, what can you do to Ghyldus? Will he not merely destroy you?"

"Perhaps," Arshal said. "As I explained, there are other powers working in Shande. Nali here is touched by them, Khoti, myself."

Aibak peered first at Nali, then at Khoti as if expecting Khoti to display some miracle. Khoti shrugged and looked away.

Arshal held up his hand. The stone blazed a royal blue, so bright Aibak's eyes watered. "In this stone is the strength the gods expect me to use against Ghyldus."

Aibak gave the stone an appreciative appraisal. "We have seers that make crystals glow. What distinguishes this stone? What power does it grant that will not be outmatched by Ghyldus?"

"It can produce many things. It nearly killed me to empower it."

Aibak's gaze remained skeptical as Arshal ran a hand through hair grown in completely white.

The king nodded to Tre. The apprentice placed his sword on a stool just beyond the edge of the table. "Stand back," Arshal called. The youth moved away. "If threatened, I might use the stone thus," Arshal said with the tone of a teacher. When Aibak looked from the sword to Arshal, the king raised his hand. A burst of white erupted from the stone, followed by an explosion of metal. Sword fragments scattered throughout the room.

Nali wiped a bead of blood from beneath his eye as Aibak stared open-mouthed at the sword.

"You need a bit of practice," Nali warned as he pointed to the scratch on his cheek. "You go before some foreign king and cut him up with your demonstrations you'll have more than just war with the Minarians."

Khoti dug a shard of metal from his wine before he took a drink. Sensing Aibak's gaze on him, he looked up and smiled.

"Is this what convinced you?" Aibak asked him.

Khoti shook his head. "When I healed him."

"What about that convinced you?"

Khoti shrugged. "It's hard to explain. When you call a person, you come in contact with their thoughts. When I went to find this king, I found a mind filled with something other than pain, something that passed through me. I felt the spirits in him. I knew there was power in that stone because I saw what it did to him."

"What passed through you, Khoti?" Nali asked.

"Terremar," Arshal stated.

"Maybe," Khoti said with a shrug. "Maybe it's just the gathering of all the spirits in you." He tapped his head. "You can see a man's life if you look hard enough. When you don't find pain, you look for another source of the problem."

"What are you talking about?" Eithurdon demanded, appearing pale. Khoti gave him a quizzical look.

"A healer has to assess his risk," Konner offered. "Khoti says he sees things. It's really feeling things in such a way that you know them as if you can see them. I touch a body I know the injury by its feel. Once you find the injury, you usually don't look no further, so there's no call to explore deeper. When the injury don't seem enough to have felled the man, then you might look further and find he still mourns a lost child or has lost a love and this keeps him from fighting his illness."

Eithurdon took a deep breath and stared into his hands.

Nali nodded. "So, Khoti, what did you see in Arshal? His future? His past?"

"Well, it's not so much like a vision, Nali," Khoti mumbled, feeling Aibak's gaze on him. He squirmed to discuss something so private as healing. It felt as if by scrutinizing it, it would lose its mystery. "It's knowing what's going on in a man's head. Here was a soul driven by special needs, knowledge. I discovered what you did in Sihma Harbor that night," Khoti held the king's gaze a moment. Should he speak of something so personal? "How you felt about that gave it reality. I didn't understand all this right away. It all comes upon you in an instant. It's the same instant I felt something exhilarating pass through me. Then, I just knew. There's no time to think on it. You're worn from the healing. It takes time to sort out. But I knew from then."

Aibak studied the shards of sword Tre swept together. He glanced back at Arshal. "It wears on you." Aibak gestured at the king's trembling hand. Arshal nodded. "You think you have the stamina to fight a battle against such a force as Ghyldus?"

"I must," Arshal stated.

"I would hate to tell King Keyen to supply you with armament merely to have you destroy it all."

"Then you will encourage your king to support us?"

Aibak nodded.

"The demonstration convinced you?"

"It is convincing that you have a special power, yes. Khoti's testimony holds the most weight because I know of him and respect him. Perhaps you could control your demonstration better." He smiled as he pulled a shard of metal from his braids and dropped it on the table. "I will do my best. What would you ask of King Keyen? Arms? Supplies?"

Arshal nodded to Nali. "He can tell you best. The help we need from Shiad is to aid Nali in his task."

Arshal motioned for Khoti, Tre and Eithurdon to follow him from the room.

As Nali settled into an explanation of his plans in a low voice punctuated by his hawkish gaze, Arshal paused outside the doorway to wait for Khoti.

"I gain an advocate in my demonstrations," Arshal said with a smile.

Eithurdon lay a hand on Khoti's shoulder. "Perhaps Khoti should accompany you on your entire journey, if it was his words that convinced Aibak."

"That's because Aibak knows me," Khoti said, leaning heavily on his canes. Khoti caught an undertone in Eithurdon's words that he couldn't place. He couldn't dwell on it. He felt light-headed with the prolonged spell away from his bed. "I doubt I could convince those who don't know me." The buzzing in his ears returned. He needed to lie down.

"I'd like to discuss with you those things you said you saw, Khoti." Arshal's words made the humming in Khoti's ears louder.

Khoti gazed up at Arshal. He could feel the sweat spreading from his forehead and down his back. His eyes clouded. "Not now, Lord. I think I should rest a while."

He pitched forward into Arshal. Eithurdon caught him before he fell.

"Must he guide you?" Eithurdon asked, but dismissed it as swiftly. "He will kill himself to prove himself. You will have a shell of a man for a guide, and I will lose a fine officer."

Eithurdon didn't wait for Arshal to respond, but looped an arm around his lieutenant's waist for support and led Khoti back to his alcove.

Khoti eased himself into bed, wanting to just close his eyes and sink into the mattress. He waited, awkward, as the never-silent caverns seemed to grow quiet around them.

They faced one another alone for the first time since Tait made his charges, the duke refusing to speak to him until his health could be assured.

Eithurdon's features jutted red and angry like the face of Redside. "Your cavern in the pass, is it a pleasant place?" the duke asked in an easy voice, belying his expression.

Khoti nodded, leery, uncertain where this discussion headed.

"If this were not a time of war, and you not indispensable, I would have ordered you banished, at least cast from the Guard for defying orders." Eithurdon held up a hand to silence Khoti's protest. "But you are too important. Your scouts, your people, would not accept it and ... I would not forgive myself if harm came to you. I am fond of you and would never want your enmity. Honor runs deep in my people, Khoti. I am told you have broken with Asteria. It is a wise move that tempers my decision. But she is willful enough, like you, that she will not back down from whatever she wants. It is best if you do not see her, do not even speak to her. She is promised to another."

"You're ordering this banishment?" Khoti gasped.

"It is no banishment."

"I honor the duke to whom I swore, but I'd again break your orders. In the confines of these caverns, not seeing one another's impossible."

"You have your cave. You will be closer to your scouts in the pass and easily called to council –"

"Exiled."

"Reassigned."

"Thus, the people I serve as headman and my family can't see me as long as your people are our guests –" His sarcasm seemed to escape the duke.

"They can visit you." Eithurdon raised his brows when Khoti gave him a disbelieving glance. Both knew the pass too dangerous for anyone but scouts to venture into. "They will be here when you return from service with the king –"

"And if I don't?"

"They will continue on without you. This is war." Eithurdon took a step back from Khoti's expression. "You have duties that will bring you to the Val," he added with haste.

Khoti's head throbbed. His ears hummed. He sank back on the bed, feeling as if the duke had yanked the floor from beneath him. The duke ducked from the alcove, his words the fuel for Khoti's dark dreams of carrion birds circling above.

# 14: A Warning

When Khoti, trailed by Chati and Tre, hobbled into his little cave the next day, his face broke into a wry smile to see what his friends had done for him. Plush mats covered the stony floor, thick comforters stacked in one corner. Firewood and tinder stood by as did baskets of food and skins of wine. A hide over the entry kept out the wind, provided privacy and would shelter Fidra and her feed. They had left soaps, towels and water. Even a bathing tub awaited only the hot water to help ease his healing muscles; a flute, Khoti's only talent among the finer arts, awaited a soft breath. Only the crude sword rack beside the entry marred the picture of a peaceful castle.

Chati and Tre built up the fire, urging their mentor to relax. The two would stay nearby to supply and guard him until he proved himself fit for the tasks. While they chattered and teased, the cave grew comfortable and warm. Khoti leaned back against a pile of pillows to enjoy the homeyness of the place. But when they went to their watch on the pass, leaving Khoti alone with the cheerful fire, he felt the press of silence. An ill man, forced from his bed, from the comfort of friends and family and the people for whom he'd become headman before Konner could teach him all of his responsibilities – exiled – his thoughts soon soured. The duke seemed blind to the injustice.

On his third day idling in the cave Khoti heard a commotion outside that sent him limping to grab his sword.

Geleg held a challenging stance before Tre and Chati. Beside him stood a man dressed in the garb of a Minarian officer. Had Geleg caught some spy they would now fill with the story they wanted carried to Ghyldus? By the way Geleg gestured toward the cave, Chati shaking his head, adamant, Khoti knew the dispute involved him.

Khoti pulled aside the curtain. "What is it?" Khoti demanded.

Geleg left the Minarian with Tre, Chati letting the Guardsman approach, but with his sword held up as if he didn't trust Khoti's long-time friend.

"I found this Minarian coming up the pass like he didn't care who saw him," Geleg stated, his scarred face set in its most serious expression. "About to just kill him straight away, he pleaded peace and asked to see you. Imagine that. I told him anything he had to say could come through me, but he insisted. He claims you know him. I'd have killed him on the spot, but he just didn't seem to be lying. He says it's urgent."

Khoti peered out at the Minarian, trying to imagine how any of them would think he would know or trust them. He felt the cold working into the metal cuff on his wrist and on the verge of telling Geleg to just kill the man and be done with it, the Minarian turned, the sun revealing his features. Khoti's breath hissed between his teeth.

"Hothur. Captain of Sefresal's dungeons."

"Then he's dead," Geleg said with a growl, turning as he drew his sword. Khoti grabbed Geleg's arm, almost losing his balance on shaky legs.

"No," Khoti insisted. "I think if any of them have a shred of honor it's Hothur. Gave me two flasks of Kishman brandy that saved my life, left me so numb I laughed at the interrogator. He also gave a promise that when I died, I'd be treated with honor. In my mind, that's a step beyond the instructions given by his superiors."

Geleg clearly remained skeptical as Chati shook his head.

"Bring him, Geleg. You can stand by to kill him if he makes any threatening move. Chati, just let them pass. But be watchful."

Bowing on arrival, Hothur's face brightened when he saw Khoti sitting easily on a splitting log as if no harm had ever befallen him. He'd slipped the canes out of sight. Hothur's gaze went to the cuff.

"Why do you wear that?" Hothur pointed at the brass-colored band, incredulous.

"So the memory of your hospitality fuels my sword," Khoti said easily. "Wine, Chati, and for our guest. Unless we still have Kishman brandy in our stores." Geleg grumbled something under his breath, but Khoti ignored him.

"I came because I must," Hothur said. "Indeed, and truly Verdaen, you are the kind of warrior our people revere. You escape our dungeons. You have men with cunning and skill willing to risk their lives to rescue you, who you train, like this Geleg here, to act in the best intents of his leaders and not kill any enemy he sees on sight, as I'm sure he wished to. And you survive the interrogator's worst abuses to sit before me as if unscathed." He took a deep draw on the wine, watching Khoti over the rim of his mug. "I asked you to join and fight for us." Hothur acknowledged Geleg's gasp and the stunned expressions on Chati and Tre's faces with an embarrassed smile, the corner of his mouth twitching up, then down.

"And I refused."

"Of course you did. The best choice," Hothur agreed. "I told you I feel nothing but contempt for any man who betrays his people. But," Hothur looked up at Khoti with an expression that bared the torment of his decisions. "But when the ruler is wrong, then traitors act, not losing dignity or honor but affirming it. Perhaps your Tait of Eilime thought the same. We come by our deceit from different places. To me, Ghyldism is a trifling thing that will pass when its novelty wears off. My goal is the glory of Minaria, a land with the strongest people, but the most wasted property on Ea. I do not, however, believe in bountying women and children to fuel brutal rituals. I do not believe in haranguing a people to death for profit. Officers in Sefresal will grow fat supplying chattel to Ghyldus from your valley, because of your traitors. Some person avenged you with the blood of Tait of Eilime, but his damage is done. Your people will continue to be captured, and herded to Lagdche to sate Ghyldus whose sick desires – unbelievable – we are told are to breed a race of warriors able to challenge the gods, warriors with shawnsi blood that remembers ancient powers. I know of a creature he has made, and the result in a mere man is horrifying – and him not a shawnsi – so fell they name him Dread Warrior, Verdred. To then apply these magics to those who could use them? I believe in my people, but not when they fall under such a spell, tricked into revering lies. That is why I come to you, against everything I believe, but in recognition of the honor earned by Verdaen. Another patrol will be here in three days, and like the last they will be swift. More of your people will be captured. In a few weeks' time another will arrive. That is all I came to say. Move your people somewhere the patrols will not find you. We occupy Shande. What more do they want?"

He stared now into trembling hands. "We should not destroy lives. It is wrong. We conquered. We should now be benefactors, not tormentors. I appeal to you, a man of honor, to save your people. Let no more shame be heaped on Minaria. Naturally, I would like to live. But, as you can see, I am not armed."

Khoti was silent a long minute, a flood of ideas churning as he studied his one-time jailor. "We won't hurt you," Khoti said, still staring at Hothur's down-turned face. "But we're not done here. Tre," he turned to the youth standing poised to kill. "Fetch Arshal. I think there might be some worth to Hothur's confession." Khoti smiled and splashed more wine in Hothur's cup as he sat back to wait.

When Arshal arrived at Khoti's tidy cave he stopped and stared as he ducked through the doorway. He stood on the threshold, stunned by the strange rapport between Khoti and the Minarian. Glancing over his shoulder at Nali, who entered to stand a step behind him, it struck him how the derna's blue robes and dark beard, coupled with his severe expression, gave him a sense of sage wisdom in a way the king hadn't seen before. Nor did he expect to find Khoti at his ease on a splitting log, sipping wine as he chatted amicably with a stocky Minarian warrior. If any man had reason to hate the Minarians, and if any man had an impulsive temper, it was Khoti. Yet Khoti played the perfect host. Then Arshal caught the calculating glint in Khoti's emerald eyes.

"What's this about, Khoti?" Arshal demanded when he found his voice. Khoti rose slowly, as if rising from a feast, not because he needed the support of canes that appeared conspicuously absent. Arshal would have told him not to bother with the deference, but clearly Khoti built upon some illusion. "You drag me out here to show me a Minarian? Believe me, I've seen them before."

"Jani," Hothur whispered. "A derna. I never would have guessed. And right in our own dungeons, plotting Verdaen's escape." Hothur chuckled softly, shaking his head. "Indeed, Verdaen you are a powerful man to have gathered such a retinue."

Nali merely gazed back at the Minarian in silence. Arshal waved at Khoti to sit again and accepted the wine Chati offered.

Khoti's gaze had that intensity that so unnerved a person.

"You had a message you wanted sent, Your Grace?" Khoti said, emphasizing an honorific the two had long ago dispensed with. "This man came to warn us of more attacks on the Val. He doesn't want Minaria's victories stained by traffic in captive shawnsi. Captain Hothur won't betray his people, but wants to protect his conscience and honor. Maybe he'd carry this news to his superiors: that you exist. He can say he learned it as a captive. He is my prisoner until I free him. They think we're inept. It shouldn't take much for a Minarian officer to escape us."

Arshal smiled. He'd never seen Khoti like this, gracious, patient, his words schooled and formal. He'd had a glimpse of it in his council. Those meetings always ended in a battle of wills with Tait in attendance. Arshal glanced at Hothur. "Do we want them to know where to look for me this soon? The visions –"

"You must move your people somewhere else. The patrols will continue to come –"

Khoti silenced Hothur with a slashing motion.

"His plan is sound," Nali said softly.

"What do you think of Ghyldus, Hothur?" Khoti asked.

"Think of?" Hothur shrugged, confused. "I do not believe in all this talk of gods. I am a warrior for Minaria, not for some creature more concerned about personal revenge than accomplishing our aims."

"Do you think any man can defeat Ghyldus?" Khoti queried.

"No, but then, you have proven me wrong." He gave Khoti a private smile. "Perhaps I over-estimate Ghyldus."

Arshal could tell Khoti weighed his next words. They reached the point where Khoti prepared the ground for the seeds he wanted to plant, and by the small smile tugging Nali's mouth awry, Arshal guessed Khoti did well. "Why do you think you so easily overtook us?" Khoti asked.

"Because we are stronger," Hothur declared. Khoti shook his head. Hothur chuckled. "Because we were swift, and you were unprepared. We caught you without an army, no unifying strength, no expertise. That was the plan and it worked. Be proud though. This region has been the most difficult to suppress. Likely because there was a standing military unit with the discipline and chain of command to enable it to act. Many men alone may be angry. Without unity they could not stop us."

"And if there was unity? If a great leader arose would that threaten your occupation?"

"Ah, the great Verdaen. I see your ambitions were higher than mere warrior for Minaria. You seek Shande for yourself. I believe you could take it." Hothur stopped when Khoti chuckled, holding his ribs.

"No, if we had a king with a mission from the gods to stop Ghyldus, a king with a birthright and the ancient powers of the gods to make him strong," Khoti said, wiping at his eyes and taking a deep breath.

"You had a king before. What use was it? I am sure the old man still lives among your people."

"He's been replaced," Khoti stated, "with a man that can destroy Ghyldus. Don't doubt me, Hothur. You know I wouldn't embrace false hopes."

Hothur stared at the cuff on Khoti's wrist. "What game are you playing with me? I know I am meant to serve some purpose. Be straight. Why do you trifle with me when I have been honorable?"

Arshal cleared his throat as Khoti followed Hothur's gaze to the cuff. "He's not trifling with you. He introduces you to me," Arshal said. "We want Ghyldus to see his threat."

Hothur studied Arshal. "It is not a personal affront, sir, but you look hardly the man to be a threat."

Khoti laughed again, an easy chuckle. "You are addressing King Arshaldon Dyndevas. Don't underestimate him either."

Hothur studied Khoti's smiling face as if encountering a new creature. The smile erased the marks of a warrior to reveal a young man who might be chatting about his flocks. Hothur turned to Arshal as the king raised his hand to display the dark opal. As Hothur watched, the opal blazed a royal blue then whitened to an almost blinding fire like sunlight on a mirror.

"This stone heralds the end of Ghyldus's claims," Arshal said as the stone flared so brightly that Arshal's hand could no longer be seen and Hothur shielded his eyes.

"What can it do?" Hothur asked as Arshal closed his fist and extinguished the light.

"What I ask it to."

"And you expect of me?"

"To let it be known a king exists with ancient powers, comparable to Dynfearn the Lost and the gods of old," Nali stated.

"My word will not serve your purposes, Verdaen," Hothur warned as he drained his wine.

"It's another drop of evidence. That's all I ask of you," Khoti said.

"And you will be ready when the patrols come in three days, and two weeks from then?"

Khoti smiled. "This is a strange enemy we hate."

"There can be honor in a justified war, Verdaen," Hothur replied. "Not one fought against innocents. I do not believe in sacrifice, nor in killing children, nor in child labor meant to destroy the minds and spirit of an entire generation. Look how many generations it took for the Pladde to find the spirit to rise against their masters. I am not a traitor. If you come into my city, you will again be in my dungeons. Bet on it." Hothur smiled and stood.

Geleg's hand went to his sword, but a motion from Khoti stayed Geleg mid-motion. Hothur glanced from Geleg to Khoti, then at the bright cuff on Khoti's wrist. "My interrogator made a grave mistake when he failed to listen to me, Verdaen. If you were a formidable enemy before, you will be a terror now." Hothur swung back the curtain and was gone.

"Will he say anything?" Arshal asked as Hothur's crunching steps receded, Chati hurrying to follow him.

"He has to. He's an honorable enemy. You're a threat to the occupation." Khoti sagged a little, letting Tre help him to pillows nearer the fire, his legs wobbly beneath him.

"But will it be too soon?"

"It's only the beginning," Nali said. "They won't believe just him. When others tell the same tale, the plan will work."

"In the meantime," Geleg said, "an attack will come in three days. This place will not be safe. He knows you're here."

"Move back to the Val, Khoti. I don't want to worry about you hobbling around out here when I need you regaining your strength to guide me," Arshal said.

Khoti shook his head. "This is my punishment, spurned by the man that made me. I'll await here for your call."

Arshal hesitated at the cave entrance. He should order Khoti to return. Then he'd have an angry duke. He didn't need such conflicts when they already fought just to exist in this occupied land. As he let the curtain drop he wondered which of the proud men, Eithurdon or Khoti, was the bigger fool.

# 15: Bait

Hothur's warning heeded, in those short three days dozens of defenders hid throughout the pass and along the valley rim. On the afternoon of the second day the Val hummed with a flurry of activity as each family prepared for the day they could not go to the kitchens or lake or light a fire. The valley and pass echoed with the taps of Shandean scouts. That night, as if the weather heard some silent plea, an early greening moon storm deposited a span of snow, concealing the scouts' passage and giving the Val the illusion of desertion.

As the first streaks of dawn filtered up the pass, Peshal and Resala stepped from beneath the ledge where they had hidden through the night. An eerie silence clung to the Val below as they climbed up the slope to the spot from where the last attack had come. Holding to the shadows of the pines to avoid being sighted by the valley's defenders, they at last sat together at the base of a tree in the natural funnel leading from the pass down to the Val. Even with the light blanket of snow, the passage of a year's traffic formed an unmistakable rut in the slope, a clear trail and almost the only path a horse could follow.

They leaned against the wide bole of the tree as they tried to warm the chill of night from them and silence chattering teeth.

"We are fools, Pesh," Resala whispered as a cold wind followed dawn, filling the trees above with a mournful song.

"Uh-huh," Peshal grasped her hand.

"I don't want to die."

"It's a little late to decide that now, Sal."

"If it must be done, if I must die –"

"Dying will be the least of your worries."

Resala stared at him. A shiver took her.

Only an hour into morning they heard hooves drumming the rutted trail, an occasional staccato in the beat as horseshoes struck the litter of stones beneath the snowcover. The two royals stood slowly in the path, holding hands. As Resala moved, frozen by her fear into an unthinking state, Peshal's mind instead churned over the terrors he'd seen the Minarians visit upon Shande, wondering how he could allow his sister to make this sacrifice with him.

A small patrol raced down the path, a few sporting bloody wounds, riderless horses trailing behind. The pair fought down the last temptation to flee as three Minarians cut toward them while the rest rushed on down to the Val.

Before they could gasp at the speed of their capture, the siblings had already been knocked from their feet, and thrown over a spare horse, their last image of the Val one of flying snow and the crack of something hard against their heads.

While Minarians sped Peshal and Resala away, the remaining members of the patrol rode into the deserted valley. Hidden archers decimated the Minarian ranks to a few badly wounded men who at last turned and fled.

In the common, the King's Council gathered, badgering each incoming messenger for reports of the near total destruction of the patrol. While a dozen made it through to the Val, at least another dozen fell in the pass. Those who escaped the assault in the Val most certainly had fatal wounds.

Zopher strode into the common, his features scrunched up in a scowl. "I can't find Pesh anywhere. He knows we were to meet. Resala's not to be found –"

"They were captured." Asteria's whisper from the doorway brought all heads around. She held up a slate, her face pale.

Zopher ripped the chalked note from Asteria's hand, swiftly scanning it. His features froze. The slate fell with a crack to the floor. He looked up at Arshal in disbelief, then whirled and rushed from the room.

"They intend to bait the enemy. They are certain they will be taken to Ghyldus," Asteria said as she retrieved the chipped slate. "Resala said it's the meaning of her birthname, Artras."

Nali buried his head in his hands. No one said a word as Arshal rose, and with the gait of an old man, retreated to his alcove.

As the greening moon dragged on, mountains reluctant to admit spring, the Val erupted with activity that beat winter's idleness from limbs. While the sun tempted by day, warming the stone and melting the snows from peak and valley – only to freeze into an icy crust with sunset – Kefta trained his new Guard. The remaining men of Eithurdon's hardy unit mostly served as scouts or spies in far posts under Khoti and Zopher's direction. Now the men of Sihmad Shal, Sihma Harbor, Eilime and Sefresal underwent the harsh training Khoti remembered with a mixture of distaste and fondness. Tawnkats joined in, despite their already proven talents, to learn the arts of sword fighting. Besides, Khoti would not allow his Tawnkats to hold the Guard in disdain. Shande needed a unified army made up of independent corps.

As young men such as Chati and Tre at last gained full rank in the Guard, they instructed a new group of apprentices capable of fighting if their Guardsmen fell. While young for promotion to regular service, Kefta gave the the two exceptions based on their experience.

The Val's women had no intention of remaining defenseless when the Guard rode to war. They saw in Amhese a model of the strong defenders they could become. It gladdened hearts to see Amhese shaking the malaise of Tsevon's death, standing beside her son, her Tawnkat tattoo proudly displayed and sword in hand. She assured the king she would build a force that could serve as the vital supply link to the army when at last it marched out of the Val. Long hours into late evening Amhese instructed the lowlanders in archery, daggers and even light swordplay she learned from her son. The mountains had never heard such a din since their making, as Shande's refugees fenced and sparred and wrestled and barked orders in the early spring sunshine.

Though still not hale, Khoti returned to his duties. Zopher had left, alone, without provision or even word of his intent. Scouts found no trace of Resala and Peshal, but they detected Zopher's pursuit of the remnants of the patrol: he spared no Minarian in his path. With Zopher gone, Khoti again oversaw the scouts and the spy network alone. Though he still limped and his breaths occasionally caught in his ribs, he shed his canes and again wore his sword at his side. Soon, he took to riding Fidra into the pass to check positions and meet with his men, the spring breath of the mountains and the spirit of his warrior heart like a tonic. Yet, each time he dismounted his body reminded him of his interrogator. The jarring gait made his back ache and his legs felt stiff and sore after each ride. Always he kept Chati, Tre or Geleg beside him, uncertain he could save himself if he encountered his enemy in the pass.

By the time the third patrol dared ride up the pass, new Guard members had augmented the scouts. The Shandeans picked off most of the enemy. Those Minarians who reached the rim of the valley met a volley of arrows fired under Amhese's direction. No rumor ever returned to Sefresal, but that of a shawnsi warrior, on a mission of vengeance, ranging the mountains in search of a stolen love. None, it seemed, saw him. In his wake remained the bodies of his victims, supposedly including the entire patrol sent to the Val.

As spring wore on, one evening, sitting alone in his alcove – as he often did since Resala and Peshal's capture – Arshal stared into folded hands, hating the blue glow that winked between his fingers. Once, he thought the caverns crowded and noisy, an impossible place to think. With Cree and Peshal gone from the small room they'd shared it seemed a place large and silent. He peered into the smoky corridor now and then, as if expecting to see one of his brothers blustering to greet him, or his sister with demands for the morale of the people, perhaps even his parents coming to call. His decision brought his parents here. Esthen heeded his call to battle. And now Resala and Peshal had taken his appeal more literally than intended. If he failed who would lead them? The Duke of Lharan disdained all that passed east of his realm and possessed no such mingling of blood and birth as burdened Arshal. If Arshal failed, what could any leader who might fill the void do? Without the gods' gifts, what tools would they use to take on Ghyldus?

The curtain lifted. Arshal looked up to find Khoti scowling in the doorway.

"Yes, I'm brooding, moping and pouting," Arshal said with a growl.

Khoti didn't smile. "I have news for Nali. I thought you'd give it better," Khoti's words fell softer than his expression. "Word came from Eilime. They hung his wife, an infant boy killed, two young girls shipped off to labor camps."

What heart remained, everything fell out of Arshal. He thought he might never take another breath. "It'll destroy him."

"It'll make him harder, like the rest of us," Khoti retorted. "It's warriors we need, King, not philosophers. Besides, since that day he's known what was possible."

Arshal could tell Khoti wanted to say more as the Guard Lieutenant took a few more steps into the room. His glance went to Peshal's few belongings arranged as he'd left them. Cree's effects had been packed and stowed away.

"We've all lost someone, Arshal," Khoti said, laying a familiar hand on Arshal's shoulder. "You've got to let that make you stronger."

"Is that what makes you such a campaigner, Khoti, so ruthless?"

Khoti snorted a little at the description. "I suppose some might say ruthless," he admitted. "I'll never forget how Von died, or Tasch-el burning around the dead, or what Mam had to do. It's also every injustice that's happened since. Not just me and my family or friends, but all of it: exiles, traitors, martyrs, and what drives a man like Hothur. He could be my friend! Yet he's my enemy. He gives my enemy a face I wouldn't choose to see. So proud and honorable a man as Hothur is repulsed by the deeds of his own people. Perhaps that's reason to grow 'ruthless.'"

"So, I should shed my self-pity and think like you?" Arshal asked with a sad smile.

"Yes." Khoti eased himself onto a stool his legs slow to bend. "You expect me to lead you on a hard road through the mountains. You should be preparing for that journey. I'll refuse to guide you unless I think you're strong enough to take on the job. And, Arshal," Khoti tweaked the muscle of Arshal's arm. "You aren't ready."

"Are you, Khoti? I've seen you walk at the end of the day."

"By Longday, make that by the rising of the light moon, when the danger of snow is past, I'll be ready." Khoti pointed at Arshal's hand where the stone lay dull in the palm. "Will you know how to use that?"

Arshal studied the opal embedded in his palm. As he did, it flared blue. He closed his palm to a fist. "It doesn't do what I thought it would. I tried to build a fog, like I did that night in Sihma Harbor. Apparently, I'm limited to the vessel and the vessel's limited to me. What power I wield must flow from my palm. In that, perhaps, I'm weaker now."

"You had the power to blast a sword to shards –"

"With a burst of light from the stone. Maybe it's heat. What the stone does is throw pure energy, fire, light, me. It won't create illusion. It won't make something of nothing."

"It's still a power. It'll serve you."

They turned as Nali entered, Bertal in tow. Khoti jumped up, his expression trapped. In two strides he'd gone halfway through the entry and into the corridor.

"Khoti, just the man I wanted to see. Please explain to this trouble of mine he's too young to apprentice your Guard!" Nali said in his gruffest tone; the derna's eyes smiled.

Bertal's jaw had a stubborn set.

"You look like you'd do fine, strong man that you are," Khoti said. "We have rules and they can't be broken. Rules say: no one under twelve." He gave the boy a measuring look. "While you can't apprentice, I think if you reported to Chati, we could probably get in a little training for you to have you ready when the time comes." Khoti glanced at Nali. "It wouldn't hurt the child to know how to defend himself."

"The boy's just come on eight," Nali protested.

"War spares none for age," Khoti mumbled as he guided Bertal toward the door, ignoring Nali's protest and leaving Arshal alone to break Nali's heart.

Only a few days later Arshal, having spread out maps of Ea and Shande on the table in the common, looked up to find Khoti studying them. Arshal gave him a grim smile.

"They show the Quelica as if it were a straight river flowing easily into the Rigannon. I know it's as easily a river as the Dodfrenyen marshes are a sea."

"Then you'll have to rely on your instincts," Khoti said. "We heard from Otayr."

If it would be the same as word from Arenh and Shikora, Arshal didn't want to hear it. "So soon? That's a long trek to make in only six months."

"He caught passage on a sympathetic ship to Ymmenay Bay. The King of Otayr claims his hands are tied. There's been no threatening overtures from Minaria, and there's no way they want to get involved in our little mess. They still have diplomatic ties with Minaria and really don't believe we've got a spark's chance in a rainstorm for uprooting the Minarians. He did, however, claim pity for our plight and concedes we may not be treated in a humane way."

"A lot of good his pity does," Arshal returned.

"Can you convince him we can and will throw out the Minarians?"

"You must!" a voice boomed in the small room.

Zopher, weather-worn and bearded, stood in the doorway. Long parallel gashes marked his forehead; his eyes held a feverish glint. Khoti quickly reached for the marks on his face with the scarred palms and instincts of a healer.

"I met Khoti's patron cat," Zopher said without humor. "If they are anything alike in a fight –"

"And you escaped with just that?" Khoti asked. "No wonder they make a legend of you."

"A few more, chest, shoulder, back." Zopher gave him a weak smile, leaning on the table. His features sagged with defeat. "I startled it. I doubt I could have fought it off if it hadn't been injured."

"Peshal? Resala?" Arshal demanded.

"They took them northeast, toward Saran." Zopher shook his head. "I bolted for the Staph-el falls. By the time I backtracked and found the trail, it was too old to be good for long. Muddled by others' passage, rain, I lost them." Zopher stared down at his hands gripping the edge of the table.

"We'll find them," Arshal said without conviction. "We'll put our best scouts on the last trail –"

"No," Zopher interrupted. "Just make your plan work, Arshal. Rid us of these animals."

"It's my fault, I –" Arshal began.

"When did Resala or Peshal not have their own minds? Put away the guilt Arshal, it's unbecoming in a king." Zopher's tone tasted like sour wine on the tongue. "At first I was outraged, that Resala would just abandon me, that she never told me her intent. How is it any different than me flying off after them? To do what? They acted as they thought they must. I only hope it wasn't wasted." Zopher shrugged, appearing to visibly shed the burdens he wore. He tested a slight smile as Khoti yanked open his shirt to examine for himself the injuries.

"I don't need a healer, Khoti." The open shirt revealed more parallel gashes.

Khoti nodded, inspecting the wounds. "They aren't deep. Konner's got a salve that'll speed the healing, fight the fever." He looked up at Zopher and grinned. "You mastered a tawnkat, did you. Well, he still got a pretty good chunk of you, injured or not." Khoti stabbed a thumb at himself, the brass-colored cuff on his wrist glinting. "Takes a lot to bring down a tawnkat."

"Thing is, the cat won. Ran off. Pray its next victim is Minarian." Zopher shook his head. "Convince them, Arshal. Don't let Resala and Peshal's efforts be for nothing." Zopher slipped into the corridor, his steps slow.

Arshal glanced at Khoti then returned to the study of his maps. Khoti taking it as a dismissal, followed Zopher.

"Khoti," Arshal called softly, waiting as the Taschian turned. "We must not fail."

Khoti inclined his head then let the curtain drop, leaving Arshal to his maps, the king knowing that they placed too much on one sovereign's shoulders, one hope. What if he failed? The king stared at the stone in his hand. The gem glittered a bloody red.

# PART 2. WAKING

# 16: A Little Pilfering and Sabotage

Jan stood beneath the dark overhang of pines edging Tel's farm. The shuttered shack where Nali's family had hidden from the siege of Sihmad Shal stood a darker shadow in the moonless night, empty. He heard movement among the trees, footfalls muffled by the thick carpet of needles and the mushrooms popping up in the warmth of spring. He heard the unmistakable brush of pine branches against clothing, and the swish of a branch swinging back into place. A twig snapped. He crouched, hand groping for the knife hidden beneath his shirt.

"Jan?" Tel whispered.

Jan straightened as the timid farmer approached.

"She told me you was out here. What on Ea for? It's a risk you oughtn't be taking with Aron's mouth running the way it's been since that Minarian king was laid under the soil."

"I heard there's been a change in the fugitive list," Jan breathed. "Is it true? Nali?" He couldn't see Tel in the darkness, but sensed him shaking his head.

"I don't think so." Tel's tone conveyed a deeper sorrow. "The list was changed from Family Drulson, Nali, wife, two girls and one boy, to Nali Bertalson. No family listed. They must've been caught and he escaped. It's got to be the same Nali. Bertal's a family name. It makes me fear for Olna and their minnows."

"Any other changes?"

"Not the ones you're interested in. Though it looks like they must be having problems out west."

Jan perked up, leaning closer to Tel. "Why's that?"

"The list must've been modified a couple of times. They cross out names then add them back to the bottom. Folk from Sefresal. And they got a whole list of people under the Duke of Lharan's Guard, others named as spies, and it just seems to get longer and longer every time they post it, instead of shorter. And all the ones they add are from Sefresal."

Jan grinned. They had made it. That must be the result of having the king out west. "I wanted something else, Tel. I'm ready to start up. Have you let the word out?"

Tel shifted in the dark, his knuckles crackling. "We could be caught. Even if they didn't know what we're up to they'd get us on that rule about unrelated folk gathering without permission."

"We need a militia. Did you get any responses?"

"Well sure, there's folk that're angry and all. Jan, they're all just plain scared. They can't think what good they'll do but get themselves killed and leave their families in a bind. They're worried someone like Aron –"

"Tel, all those people out west that are getting the Minarians riled, they're probably being goaded on by someone. You know that. I figure to be getting' a visitor one of these days, someone asking me if we're ready. I don't want to say I was too busy arguing with a bunch of cowards to get anything done. We got to be prepared. There's no reason we can't have a system set to call the folk up on a moment's notice. Who's to say some pilfering and a little sabotage wouldn't do all our hearts good."

"Pilfering?"

"Well, a militia's gotta train, don't they? So, we steal a little here and break a little there. All in good fun."

He could hear the smile in Tel's words. "That might make more sense, Jan, whatever the motive is. Meet here, at the cottage, tomorrow night. Have some ideas if you want to hold their interest."

Tel disappeared back into the pines, leaving Jan to fade into the darkness, thinking that maybe he'd promised too much to Arshal, never expecting the people would bend to the enemy with such a supple waist.

Less than a week later, Jan and a handful of men puffed their exertion lugging burdens to the side of a loosely constructed warehouse built over the ashes of Sihma Harbor. Their breaths roared in his ears. He studied the poor workmanship of crooked window frames that left a gap in which his crowbar easily slipped. With the bare groan of a single nail, the frame pulled away from the wall. He half expected the entire side of the building to fall in.

He glanced at the figures waiting for him. He nodded and two younger accomplices heaved themselves onto the sill and slipped into the darkness beyond. The rest crouched low when they heard the sentry pacing toward them along the charred timbers of the boardwalk. In the east the sky grew light with moonrise. They had to hurry.

A door opened and Jan slipped inside the warehouse, pointing to what he wanted. His men quickly emptied the building of crates of dried fish, packets of osfothye and sacks of winter wheat. In their place they left dried grass and seaweed dyed the blue and gold of osfothye; uncured fish locally known as floaters that had been plucked, dead, from the Harbor surface and ripened for several days, and the moldy, bug-infested sacks of wheat left behind after the Minarians selected the choicest crops for their own tables or shipment to Minaria.

As his men disappeared into the darkness, bearing fish that would feed families grown thin under the Minarian rule, wheat that would make fine bread, and osfothye ready to smoke or season the traditional dishes, Jan smiled. He slapped the former Reve, Pedr the Drayman on the back.

"Eh, Pedr," Jan said as they pulled the window frame back into place. "We're Gnats again."

"Aye, and it feels good." Pedr grinned back. "Soon we'll be bolder. People will start talking and our ranks will swell."

"And then we'll get back what's ours," Jan agreed.

"And make the Commander sorry he weren't here to see it."

The two men slipped back into the shadows as the sentry once again passed the shoddy warehouse standing over the remains of Jan's burned inn on Sihma Harbor's boardwalk, unaware that even the governor's pet Jashiho lizard had again changed color. In the days since Tel put out the word that the Gnats gathered again, Aron had come on his knees to Pedr, begging forgiveness, claiming fear had first loosened his tongue. Now that his eldest daughter Laria clearly served as no mere handmaid, bruised with Adesia's jealousy and the governor's desires, now that he knew what fate his other nine children had met, Aron Keeper again abetted the Gnats, prepared to repeat to his governor the lies seasoned with truths Pedr provided.

As Jan took the dark road home, he felt like skipping. He wished only that Nali could share their victory.

Nali and Bertal waited among the pines overlooking the place on the Ymmenay River where Aibak had gathered weapons for the Tawnkats. He shifted the heavy pack on his back then adjusted the smaller one Bertal disappeared beneath as Aibak paddled to them in a tiny boat like a twig against the churning snowmelt-swollen river.

When Nali climbed in, at home even though not his tidy fishing boat but instead a rickety craft that would carry him over the rapids ahead, he finally felt as if he embarked on the journey to which the visions had prodded him. With his every move he wondered how a low-born fisher could have so much to do with the world. The memory of the life his family once had, that ache, fed a desire to again take up the sword in a role he had once disdained. He had only a few moments' fears for Arshal. He left his king in good hands. He would see him in Sihmad Shal soon and this nightmare would end. He would gather his girls and Bertal and they would rebuild their world in the little cottage overlooking Sihma Harbor. Olna and Nalel he'd lost forever. Kia and Rena, somewhere, he knew, waited for their fa to bring them home.

The river sped them by the towering peaks of the northern-most Lharan Mountains, at last spilling them two days later into Ymmenay Bay where the silts and sands of the mountains built a myriad of islands dotted with twisted pine and birch.

Aibak paddled them to an island where they set camp to wait. Two days passed before a Shiadin ship dropped anchor in the bay. Aibak paddled them out to climb up its sides. The Shiadin waved as the ship hauled anchor and he beached his boat to trudge back up river toward his home.

After settling Bertal in their cramped quarters, Nali wandered out on deck to draw a nostalgic breath of sea air. Staring north, he noted a Minarian ship beating against the wind to reach the cape of Shiad. He shuddered as he gazed upon the distant vessel, not knowing what it was about the sight that so disturbed him, but it gave him a pervasive and sinking feeling like seeing something that marched unaware to its doom. He sensed it suggested something from a dream. He only knew the very sight of the ship left him feeling stained, his thoughts gone dark. Had Peshal and Resala disappeared in a vessel such as this? The thought turned his blood cold.

# 17: Guardian

Resala fell against Peshal as she stumbled onto the deck. She whirled to face her captors. They merely laughed as they collected their coin and departed in the tender that would take them back to shore.

The Pladde rebellion had made the more direct overland routes to Lagdche via the Staph-el Falls dangerous. Instead, their captors took them many days north and east to the Saran River where a ship loading Kishman osfothye agreed to transport them.

She glanced at Peshal as the ship's captain approached. Her brother's eyes had glazed, the prince oblivious to his surroundings. They had barely touched her, treating her with a care that proved her value. Clearly, only Peshal's body need arrive in Lagdche for the captain to collect his reward. Their captors had nearly starved and beaten Peshal to death. Resala slipped bits of food to him to keep him alive. What fools they'd been. Their grand schemes meant nothing. Peshal would never survive to journey's end, would never survive long enough to even plant a seed of doubt.

As if to prove it, the captain struck Peshal so hard the prince flopped to the deck at Resala's feet. She stared at the captain in stony silence as he thrust his face into hers.

"Thought you could evade justice, did you?"

She spat in his face. He lifted his hand, about to strike her, but instead, aimed a kick at Peshal's stomach.

"Does it make you bigger to strike a defenseless man?" Resala demanded.

"This is no man, but demon spawn, as you," the captain shot back. "We rid Ea of vermin like you to make the world again pure and safe from your wizardry and evil charms."

"There's a strong King of Shande now, and he'll see the end of your persecution."

"King of what? A governor oversees Shande. A shal ruler, as the God of Ea intended. Your kind can no longer oppress us. You will not think yourself so clever when the God of Ea finishes with you." He sneered, but his eyes held a hint of doubt.

"My brother, the king, has the power of the true gods guiding him. He'll blast your false god into nothingness. It's you that'll not think yourself so clever."

The captain kicked Peshal hard in the side. "Where do your people hide!"

"Ask your friends who brought us!"

He kicked Peshal's face, eliciting a low moan from the battered prince crumpled on the deck. "You tell me!"

She clenched her jaw and turned away. He grabbed her arm and whipped her around, shoving her down close to where the blood trickled from the corner of Peshal's swollen mouth.

"Is this your lover? Is it with this creature you hope to produce more demons?"

"My brother," she gasped around his grip on her neck.

"This is your king?" He laughed.

"I have two brothers."

"And this great king could not even save his siblings. I feel no threat. It is posturing." He dismissed her with a shove so that she fell to the deck beside Peshal. With an airy wave of his hand, the captain strolled away. Soon several sailors dragged Peshal, and pushed her, into a dark corner of the hold for the long voyage to Lagdche. Such fools to think they could defeat an enemy at his own game.

As the days passed into weeks on this dark voyage a rumor spread throughout the ship: the cargo caused the ship's misfortunes. Not the osfothye cramming the hold, taken from the green hills enveloping the Saran River, but the shawnsi pair brought aboard there. Anyone coming in contact with the two suffered some calamity, it seemed. Frightened sailors declared the pair sorcerers: the ship's captain slipped in rigging he had traversed for decades, and fell to the deck with a broken neck; rough seas near the cape of Shiad swept overboard the man charged to bring the captives food; the wind drove against them for weeks, seeming to shift with their every tack, eventually forcing them so far north they lost sight of the coast they hoped to hug, then ceased completely, becalming them; and now many fell ill with some malady that made their joints swell and a fever rage within them, several more succumbing and dying on this ill-fated voyage.

With growing discord among the remaining crew, Ghyldus's priest went to the acting captain.

"We must sacrifice them now to sate Ghyldus's anger," he said.

"Take the male. The orders about females are clear."

"You will have a mutiny."

"If it comes to a choice between mutiny and facing an angry god, I will risk the mutiny," the captain returned.

"Perhaps just one of them will bring favorable winds and end the illness," the priest conceded.

The threat of rebellion charging the air greeted Peshal when they hauled him up from the hold into the bright glare of day.

"Be sure not to spoil his head, or deface the mark of the demon on his face, or we lose the bounty," the black-and-orange-robed priest told the captain.

"Aye. It better be a great reward to repay us for this voyage."

The priest sang incantations over Peshal, who hung limp between two sailors whose faces reflected their fear of him. The priest's words sounded like gibberish, a humming like an infant's play. The captain kicked a crate into position near the rail. They awaited sunset, that hazy line marking day and night when the deity supposedly preferred tribute.

Peshal's eyes glazed as the captain pushed him to his knees. His treatment had not improved, his fever likely the same as felled many of the sailors. The pain, the hate, all of it would end now.

His eyes cleared enough for him to recognize his danger. A sharpened knife poised to slit his throat. The sailors propelled his neck down onto the crate. How odd that he felt no self-pity this moment when he might be entitled to it. Instead, his heart pounded with fear for Resala, for Arshal, for the way their plans had gone awry. Deep inside the anger built. How his people suffered, the injustices they faced, all of it came together in him in a moment of boiling rage. In a startling clear image, he saw Esthen falling near the gate, though Peshal had been days distant at the time. The image stood out in his mind, a point on which to focus.

He struggled to his feet, arching back from the crate as the sun fell into the waves. A sailor swiftly bound his legs with brass-colored chains that pressed close to his skin the dark shroud bearing Ghyldus's symbols and the herbs that would send a pleasant aroma to the receiving god.

Peshal struggled. They tried to again bend him over the crate.

"I'll be no tool of Ghyldus!" He spat through cracked lips. "I'm a prince of the House of Dyndevas, second-in-line to Shande's rule. I'll give you no rest! It's the true gods who torment you!"

They laughed, nervous, pushing him closer to the crate and rail.

"Resala you must succeed," he breathed, knowing she couldn't hear him and that he'd foolishly wasted himself. Like Esthen, he, too, would die before seeing Shande restored, Ghyldus vanquished.

Hands gripped him. The priest raised his knife. The emaciated prince yanked free and flung himself toward the rail. They grabbed for him, tugging the free end of his bonds. His momentum, and the surprise of his move, left them too late to stop his plummet from the ship's side into the cold, still waters of the sea.

Cold water didn't cool Peshal's rage. While the chains dragged him into the depths, Peshal bellowed at the gods for the injustices they let stand. As water filled his lungs, as he tried to kick free of the weight binding him, the shroud clinging to him, he cried out for Terremar, with an aching anger, a hatred so consuming, so overpowering, Terremar could not fail to hear. The gods could not abandon him. His blood ran as pure as their chosen. He, too, had a name, a destiny, inscribed in the Lierye.

He thought he would burst with the ache, the fear, the rage he felt. If only this last moment of life could be one of peace. He suddenly remembered Arshal's locked room from which Khoti had retrieved the king. Peshal had listened for hours as Cree taught Arshal to find that room, to seek that place where pain and fear could not touch him. Peshal feared death, feared the pain of the water filling his lungs, feared the waste of his life, cringed to wonder what fish might strike him first, creatures he couldn't see in this blackness of water, scavengers like those the Taschians feared would scatter their spirits too far for the gods to retrieve.

Sinking ever deeper, he at last found the small niche in his mind. He embraced the peace it gave him, the comfort that would accompany him on the lonely walk to the lip of the chasm of which Khoti spoke.

Something soft and charged brushed against his legs as the water grew turbulent around him.

He tried to open his eyes to see what scavenger prowled about him. He didn't need to.

The mournful, deafening call of Maura coiled about him. She brushed against Peshal, encircling him, surrounding him with the powerful charge of her being. Again, he bellowed his rage, now at being called from his peace back into pain. She calmed him, called him to come with her, to meet his new world as sparks thrown by her power flashed through his closed eyelids.

As he drifted downward into the darkness of the sea, instead of fear, he embraced Maura's comforting presence spinning around him, giving him breath. With each touch life returned to his dead limbs. Though she spoke no words, her song surrounded him. He fell into the surreality of her command. He belonged to her now, to remain at her side now and forever. He would guide the faithful, destroy evil, guard her fisheries and the fishers living from Ea's seas.

Peshal discovered himself alive, felt the throb of blood in veins, the spark of spirit in his existence. No game of a mind at the verge of death, the gods had heard his plea and sent him Maura.

She continued to spin around him, weaving a protective spell and teaching him through her mournful song the ways of the deeps of Ea. When at last she took him to see the brightness of her sister Luna shining high above Ea, a night sentry lighting Shande's struggles, air filled his lungs and sensation greeted the protective shell she'd woven around him. He might never again greet his family. Yet he could watch, guard them. He knew his purpose at last, embraced this strange fate, this awful power. At last he understood the name Cree long ago ordered penned in the Lierye, though no one foresaw how he might come by his title. Fate bade him join Maura as Guardian of Shande, her consort. His fate hadn't been written unchangeable, he knew. Instead, his instincts brought him home to waiting Maura.

The captain smiled. Carrying only dispatches, letters and a few passengers, his ship caught a favorable wind that would speed him back to Shande. Survivor of that terrible voyage from the Saran River with the two shawnsi aboard, a load of osfothye cramming the hold, his troubles ended with the man who claimed to be a prince. The winds shifted; the seas calmed.

109

When the woman departed at Lagdche he took on replacements and vowed to never again transport such demons and their ill luck. He would merely earn his pay carrying the riches of Shande home to his people. His smile became a grin when he thought of the large reward, the official commission of this ship and the commendation he received for delivering the princess to her new master.

He stared into the bow wave as wind filled every span of sail; these demons had delayed him too long. He wasted almost a month fighting the wind and trying to man a ship with only half a crew. Froth curled outward. Spray reared up as the ship met each trough, the bow briefly lifting at each crest.

Excited calls reached him above the whip of wind. He followed the gazes of men in the rigging and those along the rail. There, off the port stern! Like a ship sailing beneath the waves, an immense creature suddenly broke the sea's surface, propelling its entire bulk into the air to splash back in a thunder of water and spray. Such majesty! He stood agape. Air and water it seemed to rule, spiraling and turning as it played. Certainly, he viewed a sign from the Great God of Ea that his fortunes had indeed turned, the beast a symbol of how his vessel sped through the foam to carry the boon of Minarian conquest.

He cried out with the exuberance of his men and cheered as the beast continued its play, pacing their ship. Suddenly, the beast veered toward their vessel. The joy died on men's lips. Diving beneath the ship, the creature arched its adamant back. Its massive tail smashed the vessel, sweeping sailors from the rail to be pulled down in its passage. It swung back again, its giant eyes like torches as it breached the water to strike them. The bulk of its weight slammed down on the decks, the droplets of water shed from its skin becoming sparks that burned the sails as more men disappeared beneath the surface. Terrified their speed would stress weakened timbers the captain ordered the sails lowered. How to stop this rampage?

His sailors flung loosened timbers and knives at the beast. Officers shouted that the ship took on water. The feeble efforts of the sailors only seemed to anger the beast more. It launched into a more furious attack. Its head moved above the water at tremendous speed with only a hint of the dark giant beneath as it bore down on the crippled vessel. While the captain stared upon the tragedy again befalling his crew, as the priest stood at the stern beseeching the Great Ghyldus to hear their pleas, as he took note of a second beast frolicking off the port bow, at last the beast's rampage broke the ship in half, sending it into a watery grave, the realm the beast ruled.

# 18: Martyr

Resala fell in a sprawl, blinking through watery eyes as the blindfold ripped from her face. They had bound, gagged, and blindfolded her before leading her from the ship; she caught only one telling glance of the destruction of Halieri's Flood. Though long weeks in the dark, airless hold of the ship made her eyes burn when the blistering Minarian sun struck them, she still recognized the wrath of waters long held captive in the remnants of crumbled buildings, uprooted trees, and flotsam washed ashore.

As the ship's captain led her through the streets, she couldn't see the crowds who jeered at her or threw stones. She tried to count the paces, the steps into buildings, the turns and twists of corridors as, once inside, they led her deeper and deeper into the damp and musty cellars of Ghyldus's Halls.

A guard pulled her up by her bound wrists, cut the cords and yanked the rag from her mouth and eyes. She had to cling to a sweating pillar that braced the ceiling to keep her feet.

Before her stood a man who on first glance could have been Cree. Now Arshal's dreams made sense: Ghyldus. Instead of coarse blue-black robes and the cowled hood concealing tousled white hair that had been Cree's hallmark, this man wore black satin threaded with orange and red and a profusion of gold brocade. His bald head remained bare but for a gold band bound across his brow. The band encased a giant ruby that perched in the center of his forehead like an additional eye, or a beacon, a compelling feature that drew her. While certainly his face carried that hint of age, yet agelessness, that Cree's had worn, she saw no hint of the knowledge and patience Cree emanated. This expression held ambition and lechery, a look that made his eyes seem to gleam with madness and menace. In anger Cree had appeared formidable, a paternal expression, that of a father disciplining a child with love. A smile, that on Cree appeared ethereal, on Ghyldus appeared so twisted, heinous and carnal it made Resala's heart quake. She froze as if bound by some physical thing from which she could not break free. Or, perhaps, rather than his smile, the odd stone at his brow made breathing difficult, her words gathering in her throat unable to escape, her limbs inoperative.

"So, this is a princess," he sneered, his words booming so that the very rock she stood upon trembled. "A Dyndevas."

He spat the name as if it summed up all that he hated. He walked around her, a vulgar inspection, wearing an obscene smile. A charged hand touched the base of her chin, then gathered up the top of the hide tunic she wore in one fist and tore right through the hide, ripping away the bodice and shift beneath to bare her chest. "High title for a servant," he declared with a chuckle like icicles breaking from eaves.

Summing up a strength she didn't know she possessed, she broke from his spell and spat in his face, trying to pull the ripped tunic up to cover her. His eyes blazed as he swung at her, a seemingly effortless swat that sent her sprawling on the rough stone floor. She tasted blood and felt it dribbling from the corner of her mouth down her chin.

"You will revere me," he stated as he ripped the remaining shreds of her shift from her back as she tried to crawl away from him.

"No," She found her wits through the ache running from her jaw to crash into the base of her skull. "There's a new king in Shande, empowered by Terremar – you remember him. He'll obliterate you."

"Liar!" he howled. His backhand slammed her head against stone.

She feebly tried to rise, to pull the shreds of herself together as the guards leered.

"Princess Resala." He sneered. "It will be a joy to teach you who it is that rules Ea. See how your false gods help you? Any rebellion will be crushed."

"Like the Pladde?" she challenged, unable to stop the words from escaping now.

"When I present you as courtesan, producer of my offspring, the hostess of Shande's deposed house serving my every whim as my devoted servant and toy, they will see that even you have given up such pointless resistance. Your false gods will cringe to see how wasted and unfounded their expectations. They will

113

abandon Ea at last, uncontested. My offspring will war for me, drive the last of your cringing 'gods' from my empire, the last of your tainted blood. You are in my world now, my halls, and you will serve me!"

"I'll cheer when the king blasts you to your death, to face One."

"No man can harm me." His words seemed to shake the walls.

"The king is empowered by Kedtair, Terremar –"

"Speak that name again and I will tear you in two!" He hissed, a sound like a thousand snakes. His face swam among the lights flickering before her eyes, the red stone seeming to shift into eyes, multi-faceted. The face took on the aspect of a snake, its black tongue licking out to smell its prey. She recoiled, too late to avert the blow of his fist in her face again.

"You will learn," he laughed, a sharp gesture dismissing his servants as he closed on the fallen woman.

Powerless, under some spell she felt too weak to escape, she could no longer crawl away as furies assaulted her senses: an evil stench rose around her like the odor of battlefield carrion; foul tastes burned her tongue and choked her throat; mewling, bleating, begging sounds assaulting her ears. The red eyes became fanged creatures that groped and sniffed her like hogs snuffling the ground for feed, their snouts exhaling hotly at her neck, their fangs tearing away the riding breeches she wore. She tried to pull herself into a protective ball, to swat away the lurid beasts. Her senses beating at her, she at last screamed, unable to close her throat, as fire burned over her flesh leaving her behind like the dark withered fragments of ash.

Resala's every muscle and bone cried out when she stirred. In the dim dungeon only the light of one torch glowed somewhere distant. Mice scuffled through stinking straw for crumbs. She wrapped around her a dirty blanket to cover her bare, bruised skin. Pulling her knees to her chest, she buried her head. Had Peshal known she risked this when he tried to stop her? Thinking of Peshal brought the ache into the back of her throat. She tried to swallow it away. She had no time, no room for self-pity and grief. She boldly walked into this. Now she must survive, salvage what she could of her plan, and pray it bore fruit.

She tested the chain running from one arm to the wall, and searched the bruises on her face for broken bones. She didn't want to dwell on any thought but survival. She wanted to wipe Ghyldus's grin from her mind and forget her debasement, the horrible things that had assaulted her senses. She examined the shackle on her wrist. An image of Khoti, emerald eyes defiant, stood so clear before her. A silent laugh that made her ribs hurt took her. Had she already lost her mind to find humor in any of this? When she studied the shackle again, she at last recognized how Khoti had harbored the rage, molded it, used his pain and anger as a weapon to make him unbeatable by his tormentors. The shackle was his talisman for his revenge.

She sat unmoving, assuring herself she lived, concentrating on each part of herself, a toe, a knee, feeling the bruises but knowing she remained whole. Did it matter? Likely she would never see friend or family again. How could Zopher even bear to look at her again? Would he be horrified? Resala had no future now that she could see.

She didn't despair more than a moment. Thinking about the healthful spirit music in Khoti's tera sticks, how he drank with his enemy, she knew that like Khoti she must survive and overcome, count on the unknowable in her world. She would mold her shame and disgust into a rage, a quieter rage than Khoti's, but a rage nonetheless. Foremost, she was a Dyndevas. An image of Esthen touched her, thousands rallying to his upraised banner, heeding a call that carried clarion over the din. Only Arshal remained of her entire family. Zopher would never accept her. Forcing into her thoughts the images she most wanted to erase, she built of them a cloak, a wall, a barrier she could hide behind to harbor her strength. She concentrated on Ghyldus's gruesome smile, his laughter when he presented her to the guards for their pleasure when he had done with her. If the last thing she did, she would see Ghyldus dead, she vowed.

She looked up to find someone watching her. An emaciated shawnsi woman with bland eyes, hair knotted and dirty, her belly appearing about to burst with child, held out a cup of water and a chunk of bread. Resala thought she might have once recognized this woman, but could not place her. Resala unclenched aching fists to find red half-moon marks in her palms. She accepted the proffered food in silence, finding the bread fresher by far, and more tasty, than the stuff tossed to her in the hold of the ship. How much longer could she maintain her strength with nothing more wholesome? Her lips curled as she tasted the acidic water. It made her thirstier. She stared at the woman who waited, silent.

"What am I to expect?" Resala whispered when she thought the quiet could grow no more oppressive.

"More of the same if you do not cooperate." The woman said, emotionless.

"Did you cooperate?"

"Too late," she muttered. "Once his seed grows in you it's better."

Resala closed her eyes with a shudder. When she opened them, the woman was gone, her shuffling footsteps echoing long after.

The woman's words, so blandly said, continued to echo in Resala's ears as she studied the far wall where the shadows wavered with the flickering of an unseen torch. Cooperate. Could she do that? She had to survive to draw Ghyldus into their trap. How long could she continue to fight them, before becoming that other spiritless woman? Would she instead achieve more by playing the game with them, leading them, willing, into her trap? She didn't know if she was cunning enough, strong enough, to play such a dangerous game.

She looked up to find a leering guard staring at her as if imagining some fantasy of his own.

"You are summoned."

Resala forced herself to smile. "Really?" She tried to sound breathless, expectant. She pulled a long face. "If only I could bathe first, it would be more pleasant."

Stunned by her smile, her tone, the man didn't appear to hear her choke on the word 'pleasant,' or note how only her lips smiled.

He grinned. "That is more like it."

"And some proper clothes, scent if you have it," she mused. "I shouldn't go before one of such stature appearing so ragged." She gave him a coquettish smile, leaning back against the wall to wait. The blanket slid down, half revealing one breast. The guard whirled and scurried away. Could she thus fool Ghyldus? A god, they claimed. If so powerful, could she even trick him? She had to force the bile down in her throat. Who would be the fool?

When brought before the self-proclaimed Great God of Ea, Resala did not resemble the exile who had sat in the dark hold of a Minarian ship for two long months. The guard had procured a garish, figure-hugging satin dress left behind by one of Mol Azezial's courtesans. He chose one of royal blue, perhaps an oversight, but the color flattered. After bathing, she had found

116

powder to lighten the bruises on her face, and scent, and unwound her long braids for the first time in months.

If one could stun a god, Ghyldus certainly gave that impression. His mouth fell open at the sight of her. The low-cut dress clung to her hips. White bows held the garment together, a peek of flesh exposed before each tie. She felt like a bridegift. The irony almost made her choke. Having practiced as she prepared to meet him, she now smiled at the object of her hatred as if looking on the most desirable creature on Ea. She had already lost Zopher. She ignored the sense of betrayal.

Ghyldus's smile felt no more appealing, but less menacing. He led her to the soft chair the guard had brought and ordered wine, cheese and salt meats, then dismissed his servants.

He gazed at the low-cut dress. A bow loosened and the dress parted a little. Then another bow untied itself. The red stone on his forehead blazed. She felt a flutter like a bird wing brushing against her. Looking down she found, indeed, a bird tugged one more bow. Then it dissolved into nothingness. She looked up.

"Does my power amaze you?"

She nodded. Indeed, it did.

He stepped behind her to take up his wine. "It is wise you have come to your senses." He reached around the chair to stroke a breast revealed by the loosened bows. He looked around at her to find a smile frozen on her lips. "You will only benefit from this change of heart. You would have fought and died for those false gods while they lifted no hand to aid you unless threatened themselves. Instead, now you will live well as long as your service pleases me. You will bear me children that I will train in the arts of enchantment and magic like the gods of old. They will serve me, loyal. They will honor me as their life giver and god. They will at last rout the last of those false demons your people have worshipped. And for your service you will have fine robes, soft beds, the choicest food and wine. You will always be guarded, but no more shackles. You will see. It is much better for you this way."

How his touch sickened her! Something fluttered in her lap, loosening bows. She couldn't look, turning instead to gaze up at him.

She froze at the flash of the ruby on his brow. It caught the flickering light thrown by candles, filling her vision. The blurred face beneath appeared more godly, powerful, than she remembered. Perhaps beautiful, ethereal. She tried to wrench her gaze away, sensing she fell under some enchantment. That his words, his presence, could command such power ... could Shande face such a god, barely weakened, living in a house unassailable? This was no Visionary, years from the fold, but a god of powers the equal of Terremar's. She had already learned that he secured these halls with sorcery to prevent such a breach as the Tawnkats had made. Who would dare even attempt to face such a great power? She shook her head, barely imperceptible. What was she thinking? Arshal hoped to face him!

"I should not have resisted ... I was afraid. You are truly as great as they say." Her voice came out a whisper as she struggled against a fog of confusion and doubt filling her. His vanity absorbed her flattery.

"It is a pity our first meeting could not have been more pleasant for you."

His words sounded kind in her ears, undulating, rhythmic, alluring. Her mouth fell open as she fought for breath against a tightness in her chest, his hand on her breast.

"No doubt the lies of your elders deceived you. They led you to believe a false tale of evil as if I had a desire to destroy my beloved Shande. I only wish to save it, for the people." His voice had a note of incredulity in the compelling resonance that called her.

She felt invigorated, motivated by his words. His touch kindled something deep inside her. Yes, she had heard such things, an innocent child believing what her elders told her. No lie twisted his tone. She pulled her gaze from the strange stone on his brow. Now his eyes held her captive. Deep and dark, black, they held a gleam that danced like sparks, bright stars of the heavens, in front of her eyes. The face below reflected the sufferings of the wronged, appearing soft and vulnerable as a child frightened by thunder. She wanted to wipe away the tears she thought she saw there, comfort one so wronged by malicious gossip.

"You must understand," he said as her chest continued to constrict, her heart labor under his spell, her breast strain to more fully fill his hand. "I am the one wronged. They stripped my honor from me, my creations and titles erased, only because I thought to question a superior. So much punishment for a mere question? When the gods divided Ea, those called Visionaries took the best for themselves and left nothing to the other tribes of Ea, tribes who sought me to right this wrong, use my special talents to help them. I wish only the return of my birthright, to rule as intended, to ease the centuries of injustice the people of Minaria suffered. They deserve somewhat of Ea's bounty."

As he spoke, a picture formed in her mind of a land ravaged by greedy gods. Her heart pounded so loud now she heard each lifebeat, felt it in her skin pulsing beneath his touch. Mouth still open, eyes riveted by his, her breath came in small gasps as the warmth of his hand became a blaze inside of her. She imagined herself a small and delicate child gone astray, that had now come under his wing to be led back onto the right path where he would mold her, make her into something beautiful and desirable, powerful, a woman, no longer an erring child. What he said sounded so right as his words continued to fall into her ears like a soft breath, making her want to serve him like no other desire she held, to suffer if he wished, to sacrifice everything within her to be used for his good. Perhaps Arshal had been wrong. Arshal.

As she thought of her brother, the blue glow in his palm lighting his face, another image again returned: Esthen's rakish grin, his eyes encompassing his troops, his banner fluttering above his head beside an upraised sword. She at last pulled her gaze from Ghyldus's. Her head nodded, affirming what he said. She sensed him smiling, triumphant, beyond her vision, as the hands he touched her with grew charged and hot with his power.

Despite the warmth inside her, her nod meant something else. She saw her danger, a spell she'd fallen under. She had a mission to fulfill. Again, her rage and anger and revulsion rose up in her as she struggled to hide it. She must remain wary of his eyes, his voice, and the red gem in his crown.

His hand took hers, and he pulled her to her feet. He reacted briefly to something in her expression, as if he could tell he didn't fully have her. Her willingness must have confused him as she couldn't imagine him not seeing right through her. He led her to a bed of soft pillows. This time he did not need to beat her unconscious to gain submission nor assail her with enchantments. While he might have thought he had at last found a beautiful and willing partner who would only strengthen his hold on Ea, she fought the desire to vomit, closing her eyes to keep him from seeing the hatred she felt.

When he'd finished with her and servants led her to sumptuous rooms adjoining his – where a guard licked his lips to watch her wash and scrub as if she would never be clean –

she stared out at the bay below thinking she couldn't wait to see him burn in the flame of Arshal's stone.

As each messenger gingerly approached, he invariably stopped to stare in amazement at the shawnsi woman decorating their omnipotent ruler. Ghyldus leaned back and gloated over his good fortune. Both knew the rumor of his conquest would race across Ea. Daily, Resala stood behind the ornate throne Ghyldus sat upon, flanked by a gallery of attendants twittering with speculation at his every movement. She rested one hand on the god's shoulder with her gaze riveted on Verdred, his black-garbed champion, the Dread Warrior who guarded the door to the broad stone chamber where Ghyldus held forth.

Verdred clung to the shadows, a creature that could darken a bright day. His face hid beneath helm and hood, his hands sheathed in black leather. In Verdred Ghyldus had created the most fell of the Eidhalt. Ghyldus made his corruption mute so he couldn't reveal the private counsels he heard though his spare hand signs could be understood by all.

Resala found a morbid fascination with Ghyldus's creation. The man's spirit and will had been purged, leaving behind a deadly tool. He repulsed her. In Ghyldus's design, Resala would give life to more such tools. Her revulsion became her greatest defense against the enchantment that daily beat against her, leaving her weary and weakened. The abomination of Minaria's Dread Warrior fed her hatred, strengthened the mortar in the wall she had built inside her, kept her certain of her purpose, and her gaze from drifting to the stone on Ghyldus's brow.

At first, Ghyldus gloated that he controlled her. Soon that claim of conquest proved false. To outsiders, certainly she appeared the willing courtesan. He dressed her in flowing gowns, cut teasingly low and clinging sensually at the waist. Gems flashed at her neck, in her hair, in the rings on her hands. And her acid smile hinted of the chase.

Though petitioners saw a willing courtesan, a certain sign the House of Dyndevas accepted the conquest, sleeping with the enemy proved dangerous even for a god.

The first messenger to present Ghyldus with a glowing report of progress in the Lharan Mountains spoke of mines and tithes and the amount of produce shipped. As he departed, his footsteps fading from the hall, Resala leaned forward, letting her barely covered breast brush the god's shoulder, one jewel-bedecked hand played down his arm.

He looked up at her; her gaze always just missed him, aimed somewhere toward the hall's entry and Verdred.

"Perhaps my master's messenger forgets some news of that region," she said with a coy smile. "Some bit of resistance, perhaps." She laughed then as his hands tightened on the arms of his throne.

"Of what do you speak?" he demanded, but not too loud, lest his gallery overhear.

"Why, I lived in the Lharans for many months, Great Ghyldus. Perhaps your messenger has forgotten to speak of those who escaped the dungeons of Sefresal? Or perhaps he hesitated to mention all the dead Minarians littering the mountainsides. I'm sure he wouldn't want to present such bad news to the Great God of Ea. Or perhaps he merely forgot." She laughed again, the sound both cold and musical like water beneath ice. His face puckered with anger but he said nothing more.

When the next messenger arrived with news from the Lharans, Ghyldus interrogated him with purpose, each question wound about with the threads of enchantment. Slowly Ghyldus drew from his messengers talk of a missing patrol here, a body found there or goods sabotaged. With each truth revealed, in a voice sharp as a shard of ice, Resala would remind Ghyldus that her brother still lived, building resistance.

As the months passed Resala boldened. She seemed to gain her own power over her captor as she alternately played to his vanity, then dashed his confidence. Though she resisted the full depth of his enchantment, he didn't seem capable of destroying this symbol of his control over Shande. He might demand his services in ways that repulsed her, but he could leave no mark to hint of unbroken spirit or willingness feigned.

For all his power, he confessed he couldn't quite see into her as he could his other conquests. He need only demonstrate the depth of his power to make her quiver. Yet she would not bow to him.

He claimed her like the goddesses he had once known, twisting his passions with an ethereal power. Some power in her tweaked his desire until he could not ignore her, yet in the same tone with which she praised his virility, she laughed at his inability to defeat the new King of Shande. He told her he wanted to destroy her; but he couldn't.

As tainted fish and grain arrived, damaged goods slipped in among the fine crafts of ships' cargos, and the Pladde revolt continued, Ghyldus fumed. Advisors schemed to eliminate him. Though they unmasked the traitors and in public display Verdred's captive and hungry wolvers and desert cats tore them to pieces, it nonetheless pointed to discord in his world. A Dyndevas was the architect of this trouble and he knew it.

Then came a dispatch signed by Hothur, Captain of the Sefresal dungeons, advising that some man in Shande who held strange powers Hothur himself had witnessed, now proclaimed himself king, supported by an army of warriors akin to the legendary Verdaen.

Resala laughed coldly when she returned to her own bed at night, telling herself that she sowed the seeds of Shande's revenge even as Ghyldus sowed his own in her. As they cast spells about one another, both played and dealt a dangerous hand.

She knew he wanted to stop Arshal before he gained more strength, and at last win this battle of wills with her. He would demonstrate his power, surrounding her with a dark dream of horrors befalling all those she loved, ringing her bed with evil conjurations to keep her there. He laughed in her face as he sent his spies out to range the world in search of this king.

Even Verdred, a champion foul and corrupt, the sheer malice of his maker, went in search of the king.

Resala needed Verdred. She never realized how much until he left. He had anchored her hatred and kept her resolve firm. As the weeks of his absence passed, Resala felt Ghyldus's battle for her spirit gain. At last, when she thought she couldn't last another day under Ghyldus's relentless gaze, Verdred returned and threw a captive bound and bloody at his feet.

Verdred pulled the head up to display the face. Resala gasped, a poignant memory from the Val lurching from the dark threads of enchantment – Khoti's kinswoman giggling and sewing beside Resala and Asteria, a woman rich in the lore of her people who clung to that spirit that ran so deep in her people. Latra.

Latra's gaze found Resala. Her swollen eyes widened to disbelief before they became hateful slits that did not hide a certainty Resala had betrayed them. Latra's hatred stung like pickling brine in a deep wound.

"Yes, this is your princess." Ghyldus laughed, that wicked booming laugh that could shake the ground and make Resala's heart quail with fear. "A Dyndevas. A wasted line of kings, I hear, but their women are most pleasing."

Verdred prodded Latra to her knees.

"And you must know something I wish to hear if Verdred brings you to me. It is an honor, woman! Do not cringe so! Look at your great princess. See how she reveres me?"

Resala's heart pounded as Latra's gaze found Ghyldus. Though she came from a strong race, the privation of her captivity already weakened her. A glaze spread over the woman's eyes as Ghyldus leaned forward, peering at her with a triumphant grin.

"So Verdred found you, a person who knows of this so-called king. And he brought you here to tell me your tale. You are of a mountain race, are you not? Was I not told that even this princess was captured among such people?" Ghyldus leaned back, crossing his arms on his chest as Latra's eyes widened again.

With effort, the woman glanced at Resala, her will still strong enough to pull away. While enchantment already worked in her, while the spell of Ghyldus took control, Latra appeared to remain lucid enough to see: Minaria did not know where the king dwelt.

"It is these mountain people of yours who resist. For shame! You will tell us where they are. Perhaps, instead, you wish to watch your people die, one by one, until you speak?"

Gasping, Latra tried to turn away from Ghyldus's mighty presence; her gaze again fell on Resala and that moment Latra took a deep breath of strength. In silent entreaty, Resala's gaze bore into the beaten woman, willing Latra to remember her mountain roots, her strong race, her lifemate Ahrwesz whose smile could make her giggle, her children who the Minarians would enslave. Resala could see a rush of emotion flooding Latra as Ghyldus bent his power on her. He clenched his fist; Latra grasped her throat. She continued to stare at Resala. Jaw twitching as Ghyldus demanded information. Latra clenched her mouth shut, biting her lips until blood ran down her chin.

"Where is your king!" Ghyldus yelled with such command in his voice that Latra's mouth flew open and the words fell out.

"Left mountains," she gasped as the words tore from her. She tried to put her hands to her mouth to muffle them. "To Mershy."

Ghyldus leaned forward again, glancing briefly back at Resala as if she had something to do with the woman's resistance to his spell. He had won the toss.

"You will speak now," he commanded, a gesture of his hand forcing out the words.

Resala wanted to weep for the great will of such mountain folk as Latra. While unable to stop the words, Latra's loyalty remained strong. Ghyldus could draw news from her that she sought to conceal, learning of Shiad's aid, but he couldn't make her reveal the location of the Val. Neither could he draw from her much news of the king, beyond mention of Mershy, because Latra did not know.

Resala had learned from this fallen god, though he didn't appear to realize she could draw such conclusions, that the gods of Terremar kept Ghyldus from seeing what passed beyond his land, just as they had barred his knowledge of the future. For all he tried, he didn't learn all from Resala that he thought he could. He needed such captives as Latra, and even they seemed capable of shrugging off his enchantments.

At last, when his anger had built so that he gave off a great heat beneath Resala's touch and the information he took gave him nothing new, he gestured and Verdred moved from the shadows, placed a hand on Latra, and with no apparent effort, broke her neck.

Long seconds passed before the breath left the woman. Spell broken, Latra stared at Resala with a gaze that begged the princess's forgiveness. Resala glanced at Verdred, needing to see that menace for the strength to turn her grief into more mortar for the internal walls she built.

Ghyldus leaned back in his mighty throne and laughed, a sound that shook the rafters. He gripped Resala's hand on his shoulder in a talon-like grasp.

"Who wins now? Your sorcery is no match for mine," he declared.

"I claim no craft," Resala protested in an icy voice that barely hid her hatred.

Ghyldus turned his gaze on her. Rage rushed her blood; his spell found nothing to which it could cling.

"You have your spells. I sense them. They cannot match mine. I saw how that woman rallied for you. As you see, where your brother might have a power, as his sister clearly has, it measures to me as nothing. You may control the witless. But I am larger than both of you."

He laughed again, but his words had no hold on her. Latra filled her gaze.

"Verdred, gather the Eidhalt," he called. "We will find this upstart king if we must tear Mershy apart. We will end this stubborn resistance. If Shiad thinks to resist me, it is sorely mistaken." He cast a glance at Resala's stony face. "We will find this mountain haunt and end that as well." He rose and strode from his hall.

Resala stared at Verdred where he waited at attention for his master to depart. She sensed nothing in the creature but a blind obedience, a malice, a terrifying desire to destroy all things, as he was destroyed. She could only shiver and wonder how long before she, too, succumbed to such emptiness.

# 19: Return to Peshal's Tunnel

Light rain and fog concealed the far bank of the Rigannon River. Jan glanced at the dark line of haze, his goal, then at Pedr standing by with a rope to keep Jan from being swept away by the current. With a nod, Jan plunged into the chill of spring in the water. The coil of current and the slick and rocky bottom threatened to pull him under.

Straggling from the water on the eastern bank, he shook off a shiver as he made for Peshal's Tunnel. Aron Keeper claimed the Minarians never discovered how the royals escaped. From the Gnats' veiled interrogations of the humbled man, clearly he'd heard of no tunnel. Jan didn't trust Aron's reversed loyalties, and doubted Loch Asmodiel told Keeper all that passed in the world. What little Aron would share the Gnats treasured and sifted carefully for deceit. Aron returned to the governor with Pedr's seeds of rumor planted with the care of a gardener.

Now the Gnats needed the cache of arms and food stored beneath the city. Jan couldn't expect men to work all day filling the Minarian wagons and then labor all night to steal it away, leaving them no means of defense if caught. The rumor of the Gnats had indeed spread. A dozen folk found their way into the circle of Gnats, itching to do more than just pilfer from warehouses and sabotage goods. They had a blood thirst.

Vines and grasses overgrew the tunnel so completely Jan at first thought the spring floods had closed it. It remained dry and open as it had for centuries, above the highest flood possible with the management of the Etaleah Canal's locks far to the south, and concealed by the brushy banks and the curve of the river.

He groped in the dark until he found a torch in its bracket. A flint spark sent into a nest of puffweed fluff flared. He touched the tinder to the torch and watched as the tunnel suddenly appeared before him, wandering into uncertain darkness ahead. He padded through the curving corridor until he came to the great cavern beneath the market square of the city above. A forgotten blanket, an empty wineskin, a child's straw doll brought memories of the exiles back to him, poignant and fresh. He sat in the cavern for at least an hour, studying the patterns of stone, the swirl of color left by centuries of dripping water. He needed courage to make the last leg of his journey. What if the hidden storerooms had been discovered, and with them, perhaps even the entrance to the tunnel? For all he knew, Minarians had long ago explored the tunnel, assumed the royal family made their escape this way, but found no purpose for it.

With a sigh he continued, climbing the stairs into the last long passage. When he came to the door shut tight behind the last exile, he stood long, listening for any sound beyond. From the inside they had seen no visible handle, bar or bolt. On this side, a bar secured the door, a distinct line demarking its edges, and a handle turned the bolts and locks to open it. It appeared Minarians had never found the tunnel entrance. But did they know of the storerooms beyond? From a few who had learned the hard way, he knew at least some storerooms had been converted to dungeons for recalcitrant Shandeans.

At last, Jan lifted the bar and turned the handle. First the door resisted his pressure. Surely the storerooms had been discovered and something moved to block the doorway. The door suddenly pushed inward, soundlessly swinging open into the expansive darkness of the hidden rooms.

They appeared undiscovered and by far better stocked than he'd noted in his hasty retreat. He shook his head and grinned, allowing himself a low whistle when he raised his torch to examine crates of weapons wrapped in oil cloth, barrels of pickled vegetables, crocks of canned meats and produce, kegs of wine and sacks of seed. Candied and dried fruits filled the rooms with a smell of sweetness reminding him of the harvests of the past, wiping away memory of the most recent harvest when famine ruled.

He wandered through the cellars, amazed that a country that barely remembered war, and starving through a siege, had such foresight. He found bins of nails, and bolts of cloth. Boxes held items from needles and shears to cutlery and cookware. Bundles contained royal blue cloaks. Chests held leather armor, and the various papers and records of the realm. The Lierye remained encased in its trunk, and beside it the small casket containing the ceremonial crown. Gems and coins gleamed in caskets, and osfothye seeds packed with care remained unspoiled. All the necessities for rebuilding Shande could be found: tools for working timber and stone, gear for farriers, leathercrafters and blacksmiths and armorers' plans. In the jumble of stores he found trunks of medicinal herbs and dernas' books of medicine, lore and history.

Jan sat on the floor in the middle of the largest room, ringed by the torches he'd lit, his throat tight and his eyes burning. This was Shande: these hand-written parchment tomes, the crates and caskets and barrels and bags, a culture in its material remains. For hours he wandered in a reverie of the past, and in a litany of events that began almost a year ago to this day.

At last, Jan stood, stiff, face red as the turn of his thoughts brought him to his son's capture. He moved on to find the door to the known parts of the palace. He listened, now hearing the sounds of the dungeons echoing down the hidden passage. Again, he forced himself to swallow fear and open the door, then trudge up the stairs. The steps coiled upward to a doorway on a landing. Beyond it he heard the suffering of prisoners. The way he'd entered long ago had closed. He continued up the coiling stairs, his steps slower. By now he had to be almost level to the living area of the palace.

When at last he came to the end of the passage, he tried to recall how long he'd been in the tunnel. Was it daylight or dark? He pushed against a door likely unopened since the day it was built. Jan tossed aside the torch. As the door slid open, eyes accustoming to the total darkness of night in the palace, he realized he looked upon the back of the curtain behind the dais in the reception hall. He knew, too, that behind the dais a stairway led to what had been the king's private chambers. Already the seeds of a plan took shape.

After pushing the door shut, he barred it and grabbed his torch. He hurried down to the cellars, sealing off the passage behind him. When he reached the little room closest to the entrance to the tunnel, he pried open a few of the crates. Taking the empty pack from his back, he stuffed it with daggers, then atop those, for a special treat, he stowed candied fruit. He tied together a bundle of swords and fastened them to the base of his pack, and with a grin to himself, emptied his waterskin and tapped a keg of wine to refill it. He hadn't had the taste of a good wine for months and this had aged a year from a good harvest.

He allowed himself one savory swallow, but spared the rest to share among the Gnats, and again slipped through the door, bolted it, and trotted down the tunnel toward occupied Shande.

A soft splash rose from below when the boat dropped into the water. Beside Nali, the Shiadin captain's hands rested on Bertal's shoulders a moment as his men loaded the boat. He glanced at Nali, shaking his head.

"You take a mighty risk. Yourself, especially the boy," he said.

Nali searched for the line of coast. The moonless night gave no sign of shore but the distant boil of surf.

"It's a risk that's got to be taken," Nali said as sailors stowed the last bundle in the rowboat.

"It was just luck no one caught you at Saran. In a land so oppressed you might have more sympathy. But here? More know you to report you." The captain peered at him in the darkness as if he looked upon a doomed man. "Think of your boy!"

Scowling, Nali didn't answer, merely climbed down to the little boat and waited for a sailor to help Bertal into the craft. He seldom let the boy out of his reach, much less sight. He couldn't help but think of him. He wrapped the oarlocks in rags to muffle the sound as he rowed for shore. He didn't make his first foray to a hostile shore. He went alone to Saran, with only a name Zopher provided of a man loyal to don Saran.

If Nali had known the state of the occupation along the Saran River, he wouldn't have feared his reception. Osfothye commanded Minarian attention like no other export. Something about the plant's properties and Minarian bloodlines resulted in a more euphoric response that gave osfothye a worth to them equal to all the gems in Shande.

Minaria's intense demand for osfothye already showed in the land. Even Nali, a fisher, could smell the diseased fields on the wind. So, when Nali's little rowboat floated past the sleeping sentries at the mouth of the river, and proceeded beyond the eyes and hearing of the Minarian watchers on the river wharves, he found an eager welcome when he at last pulled his weapon-laden rowboat ashore.

Yet this shore was not Saran.

The small boat came to rest on a patch of sand. Nali touched his foot to shore. That moment, a shadow loomed out of the black night and in the same instant he found himself on his stomach on the ground. A hand grasped his hair. Pressure forced his head into the sand as the point of a knife nicked his throat.

From the corner of his eye, Nali saw a circle of figures surround the little boat. Bertal cringed in the bow, the spare starlight not enough to light faces. Someone yanked the boat clear of the water, nearly throwing Bertal backward onto the deck. The circle tightened.

"Fa?" Bertal's voice trembled.

Nali shushed him, turning his head enough to make out a silhouette looming over him. The lead figure studied Bertal as if doubting a child sat in the bow of the little rowboat. One figure gestured at the name printed on the boat's stern.

"What do you want here," the leader challenged. "What brings Shiadins sneakin' to shore?"

The knife pressed harder against Nali's throat. A trickle of blood oozed away from the point with each painful swallow. He brought his hands up, trying to pull away the knife so he could speak.

"Pedr?" Nali gasped as he struggled against the pressure.

Nali's assailant leaned back, letting the knife fall at his side and pulled Nali over onto his back where he could peer into the derna's face.

"I don't believe it," Pedr muttered under his breath. "You've come back, like he said you would." The man held out his hand to help Nali to his feet.

Nali rubbed the cut on his throat, glaring at Pedr in the darkness. "Gods, Pedr, I come to help and you folk treat me like some spy. They don't need to sneak ashore they can dock in broad daylight."

"A Shiadin rowboat?" Pedr jerked his head toward the silhouette of the ship at anchor.

"Friends."

"We can't be too careful. I'm sorry, Commander." Pedr signaled for his men to move back as Bertal again whimpered his fear. "The child, it's dangerous to have him here."

"He's all I've got. Who do you serve, Pedr?"

"My name's as prominent on that list as yours," Pedr said. "Though, 'pears you been busy out west, Bertalson." He stressed the name with an admiring note. "A bit of resistance there."

"More than a bit," Nali admitted. He grasped Pedr's arm in greeting, then whirled to lift Bertal free of the boat. The boy clung to Nali's shadow. "Jan's safe then? You're organized? Are you in control that you prey on helpless sailors?"

"Helpless I doubt," Pedr snorted. "When a ship does something odd like anchor out there instead of coming into port, well we just had to check it out. You never know what kind of windfall you might come upon. We aren't organized, yet. Just got started. There's a lot to do. By the gods, Jan'll be happy."

"You got weapons?"

"Some. Jan brings back a load from the tunnel now and then. But we're growing, and you can only carry so much at a time."

"Then you might have a need for my cargo?"

For the first time Pedr peered at the canvas covering the bottom of the little boat. He lifted one corner and gave a low whistle. "Won't go far," Pedr said. "But it's much appreciated."

"Won't go far? Pedr, what do you s'pose is on that ship?"

Pedr's mouth fell open as he gazed out at the shadowy vessel. "A ship full of swords?"

"And bows, arrows, daggers, axes, spears, armor, and there's more. Out west there's a dearth of metal stuffs. So, we threw in knives, shears, needles. And there's medicines, tack, raw metals and everything you need to set up a forge. We even got a Shiadin invention that I've learned to use. It shoots a dart with such force it'll pierce the sturdiest armor. There's a bit of everything we could think of. And then there's me, and the word I bring, the plans I've brought."

"What word, what plan?" Pedr urged.

"That can wait. I've a whole ship to unload, a child to shelter. And there's things I just don't want to say aloud right yet. I've been betrayed before." Ice crept into Nali's tone.

"We've got a few of that kind here," Pedr admitted.

"Out west, you speak, you're dead."

"We haven't gone that far."

"It's time you do. It's the one thing that could wreck everything. The time's come to fight back. Are your folk ready, Pedr? Can you have me back?"

"The Gnats are nothing without you. Jan was alone a long time, but we're growing. You got yourself a command again, Nali."

"I'm more expecting to be an advisor."

Pedr ignored the comment, already signaling for men to unload the cargo, and lead Bertal to safety. As soon as they emptied the little boat, Pedr and several of his men climbed in to row back out to the ship where half a dozen more rowboats waited with arms for Shande.

It took several days to disperse the ship's cargo to dozens of hiding places, making numerous trips back and forth from Mania Point where they buried weapons beneath the sand. Nali and Pedr kept to the dark nights, in constant fear of being seen. Nali had waited so long to once again look upon his home, but he stood mute with faltering heart when at last he saw the Harbor from a ridge above town. Crammed with warehouses, the once colorful Harbor, rebuilt from charred timbers, looked like a dark smudge against the bluffs. The boardwalk served only as a loading dock for Minarian ships, no markets or idle gossips. The statue of Maura lay on the ground, defiled. Instead of The Old Scow's windows looking out on the bay, crude halls swallowed sailors into dark and smoky confines that emitted the clamor of drunken discord. Nali scowled to find Otayran, Arenhian, Shikoran and even Shiadin ships at anchor, their wares stacked on the docks as their mariners, too, joined in the pilgrimage to the pubs. Here and there, once prominent Shandean merchants or artisans worked as waterfront labor. A few Pladde labored beside them, their eyes averted, the Shandeans beginning to take on the same subservient postures.

Before Nali could absorb the changes, Pedr urged him on, warning that the price had grown so high on Nali's head it would tempt those who had yet to cooperate with the occupation.

Pedr led Nali past Tel's farm to the little house where Jan had grown up. Pedr left the derna hiding among the trees until dark, where Nali drank in the scents of his home province, trying to stir Bertal's young memory of a time before war. As night fell, Nali couldn't mistake signs of a gathering, nor miss the light leaking from the barn.

"So, Pedr, why are we here?" a man asked as Nali followed the Reve into the barn.

"Nali's come," someone said.

"Ah, 'tis in your head. He's gone. You've seen the lists."

"True he's –" the speaker faltered.

The Gnats stared open-mouthed as Nali entered the lantern light. Nali realized here, too, legends had grown.

"Commander, it is you," one young man whispered before surprising Nali with an impulsive hug.

Nali reddened, looking around him in consternation when he realized that all the Gnats gathered numbered barely a Tawnkat squad, and certainly less experienced. Only thirty men sweltered in Jan's barn.

"You can see the paths here, and the light from the barn could be seen an hour distant," Nali told Pedr, who nodded apologetically, motioning for a man to throw a blanket over a chink in the barn wall.

The door creaked open, then slammed shut. Jan almost bowled Nali over with his exuberance as the man grabbed him and swung him from his feet then did a little jig after he had set his friend down.

"I knew it, Nali! I knew you'd be back; you wouldn't forget us!"

"This is home, how could I forget?"

"It's just the trials we've been through –"

"Everyone's suffered," Nali returned. "In the mountains the Minarians hunt shawnsi to sell west to Lagdche. The people's resistance has brought them suffering that'd make your life here seem pleasant." The bitterness in his tone made them look away.

Jan's smile soured. "Maybe we're ignorant of the rest of Shande," Jan admitted. "But it hasn't been easy here either. My Jali was taken for the camps –"

"And Olna was hung for treason, my infant son murdered, my girls shipped off to labor, betrayed by a man I broke my back to help when he lost everything to the Minarians. We've all got troubles, Jan."

Nali settled on a crate, Bertal obediently sitting at his feet. Nali wanted to find a way to explain to these men the real meaning of this occupation. Certainly, they had troubles. He could see change, but nothing like in the west. Certainly, they had the dead and the children taken away. He gripped Bertal's shoulder, not looking at the boy, but knowing the child stared at him with wide eyes, accustomed to his father's strange moods.

When the silence seemed like it could bear itself no longer, Nali began the tale of the western cities and villages, of the farms on the Saran River, of captives tortured. The words came in fragments as the weight of so much suffering made his chest grow tight, his throat constrict. He feared as he described Khoti's interment he would give in to his emotions, the helplessness he'd felt and the blame he assigned himself. When he finished the men sat in silence, a few even wept. Nali had to prove to them the importance of the little victories, that such suffering built a platform for rebellion, worth the risks.

"Arshal, the king, a magic. He'll use this magic to regain Shande?" Pedr asked.

"He can't do it alone. He needs all of Shande, and the Gnats," Nali said.

"We've so few men," Pedr protested.

"Then we need to grow," Nali said. "And root out the traitors. I know it's hard to hurt a man you might've grown up with. But look at what harm's done. If people know they'll be killed if they talk, they're less likely to risk it. After they found Tait's body, in the months before I left we had no more betrayals."

"Where do we even start?" Jan asked.

"First, we need a place from which to operate. It's too risky meeting in a barn like this. It's only a matter of time before you're discovered. How about Peshal's Tunnel? The stores would be close. It's a safe hiding place for fugitives and the cavern would be a perfect staging area." Nali stood to pace.

"And after that?" Jan asked.

"Eliminate the known traitors –" Nali began.

"Even Aron?" Pedr asked.

Nali thought a moment. "For now he's useful. If he steps out of line, if only to tap a toe over, take him. Next, we recruit more. Do a lot of training. I picked up a few things from the Guard. We could gain a lot by scouting out their strengths and weaknesses." Nali ticked off his fingers, surprised how easily he slipped into the role of commander. It seemed so natural he found it a bit frightening. He had a memory of Rathil praising him for 'thinking organized.'

"And in the end?" Jan asked.

"In the end, we retake Sihmad Shal, the Harbor."

The men looked at each other as Jan whistled. "That's a mighty big ship for thirty men to man."

"That's why we recruit. There's folks never called up before, thousands. We find out how many Minarians are here, their rotations and supply schedules. It may not take that many to get control, but then we got to hold the place once we get it."

"Hold it?" Jan echoed. "But what do we know of –"

"We've got a lot of training to do."

Nali paced to the barn door, peering out into the steamy night, the first week of the heat moon baking the fields. The moon sank in the west where Nali knew, in mountains so far distant they couldn't be seen, Eithurdon's men fought the same fears as he.

"We'll start by moving into the tunnel," he said, looking at Jan, his hands again resting on Bertal's shoulders. "Anyone whose name is on that list should come for certain."

They nodded, mechanical. He had taken charge, more so than long ago when he tried to stop the army in the Harbor. As the men drifted away, he felt a hand on his shoulder and turned to find Jan. The man's eyes had a misty, nostalgic cast to them.

"We finally made a commander out of you, Nali."

Nali sighed looking down at the top of Bertal's head. "It took a lot, but yes, I guess I am." He glanced up at Jan from the corner of his eye. "But gods, Jan, I don't know if we'll ever make you a soldier."

Jan grinned, thumping him on the back. "You'd be surprised."

They slipped from the barn to pack Jan's few belongings and warn Cookie she was moving and to bring her big pots. As Nali stared out the little window at dawn tingeing the rolling countryside, a place that smelled green, with a far horizon, no snow and little stone, he found it hard to believe he stood in a troubled land, hard to believe he had spent his winter holed up like a burrowrat. He paced, wanting to act, to begin working toward the goal for which he lived, his vengeance.

It seemed, at first, Nali might never achieve it. The Gnats grew only slowly, and though they trained diligently, the security they employed to prevent too much leaking out about their resistance made recruitment difficult. Weeks passed in which his militia grew to only a hundred, each recruit forced to endure a ritual similar to the Whittean come before them one summer afternoon.

Standing before Nali, blindfolded, the man's head cocked as if by listening he could decipher his surroundings. Echoes chased throughout the caverns and tunnels.

Almost all of the Gnats had gathered in the cavern, which served as a meeting hall. Many still perspired from fencing. Others cleaned the precious cross-bows from Shiad with which they practiced. Some sharpened broadheads, or honed swords, knives or axes as they took seats on the floor of the cavern, their faces turned toward where Nali, Jan and Pedr sat on stools built from emptied crates. The man before Nali, like many before him, had passed word through the intricate message network to make his petition to join the Gnats known. Days after sending the message Gnats abducted the recruits from home or work and brought them blindfolded before the Gnat tribunal of leaders. In each step of this secretive process, Gnats judged, evaluated, and vouchsafed the candidates. The Gnats could risk no lesser caution.

"What do you want?" Nali demanded, leaning back against the stony wall.

The Whittean's face turned toward Nali's voice. His hands, tied behind his back, moved with an instinctive gesture that would have been placating. "I want to serve with the Gnats," the man declared.

"Why?" Jan demanded.

"'Cause I want to help. I would'a fighted before, but we weren't called." The man twisted his head, as if seeking faces to speak to. "But we listened to the criers. We hid things. I got me some butcherin' knives of my fa's that'd likely do in a pinch." The man would have blushed if he'd seen the room of soldiers smiling at this admission as they cleaned their weaponry.

"Have you heard what happens to traitors?" Nali asked with a hint of menace in his tone.

"I heard some."

"So, what would you do if a friend, maybe even a family member, sold secrets?" Jan challenged.

The man sighed. "I'd tell someone else, a Gnat, that so-and-so was talkin' out of turn. I gotta be honest. If it were a friend, I couldn't harm 'em meself. I guess I just couldn't have a friend pleadin' at me." The man's brow creased. "Does that mean I can't join?"

Nali scanned the hall. "You heard this petition. Comments?"

A few noted they had heard praise of the man's family and loyalty. One mentioned a child taken from the man's home. The man's shoulders sagged, his head tilting toward the floor. Nali scanned the back of the cavern to find Bertal in Cookie's care. He felt naked without the boy beside him.

"A show of hands?" Nali called. "Ayes?" He counted the number of hands raised. "Nays?" None. Even one objection would have been thoroughly investigated before approval. Nali nodded to the Gnats guarding the man. They freed the recruit's hands then removed the blindfold. He stood blinking, looking around and gasping at the caverns and the arms stored there. He blushed.

"You're a Gnat, now," Pedr said. "You'll train with us, likely live with us since your home's so far, kill and maybe die for us. In your head are some mighty dangerous secrets. Be advised. If you're ever captured, the torture the Minarians use will be nothing compared to what we'll give if you talk."

With a nod from Nali, the hearing ended. The Gnats returned to their tasks, one recruit more numerous.

Not all the decisions for command came so easily and too often Nali had to carry out the threats he made, to prove by example.

One moonlit night, he stopped Jan as he prepared to depart with a squad of their best.

"I heard it's Rollynd," Nali whispered.

"Aye," Jan said. "I wanted to see myself. No need for you to trouble, Nali. The boys do fine on their own. I shouldn't even be there."

"But I should," Nali said softly, following them into the dark.

Night had grown old when at last they spied their target hugging the shadows as he slipped toward home. The man whimpered at the sight of the squad of dark-cloaked men, hoods pulled down to conceal their faces. His eyes widened when moonlight glinted on drawn swords.

"What did I do?" The man wailed. "I've done no wrong to you. I've cooperated."

"How have you cooperated?" A Gnat demanded in Minarian dialect.

"I gave you names. It's not my fault they left. It was a farmhouse west of the river, an hour's walk south of the Harbor. They were there, honest!"

"Who?" Another demanded.

"I told you! Jan the Innkeeper. It's his farm. And Reve Pedr. They're the ones responsible for the trouble—"

"Ah, so 'twas you that finked," Jan crowed. "And what else did you say?"

The man peered up at the cloaked men with wide eyes as if finally seeing the capes of royal blue, not black. A small cry came from his throat.

"I had to!" he cried. "I had to find food for my family. I'm innocent compared to Aron Keeper. Look how high he lives! Why don't you go after him?"

"Perhaps we will," Jan replied.

"He grows fat on my labor! They're starving us."

"They're starving everyone, Rollynd," Nali said at last. "What makes you better than the next man?"

Rollynd trembled violently. "Nali?" he whispered. "You understand my troubles! We grew up together! We've always been friends! You can't –"

"I can," Nali stated. "It's traitors that destroyed my family. It's cravens like you that bring Shande to her knees." Nali grasped the man's collar and twisted. "What else did you say? Vindicate yourself now! It's your last chance."

Rollynd's eyes appeared to bulge in his head. "Just rumors, nothin' important," he whispered.

"Let me decide," Nali ordered.

"I ... I just mentioned there was a resistance organizing. They knew that! That you claim the king is coming. That rumor's flown high as well." His words came faster as one of the men pressed a sword against his throat. "And I mentioned ... I heard it at market, it's just a rumor ... that there's maybe a hundred of you and that you're planning to raid the warehouses on the new moon –"

"You make me sick." Nali spat as Rollynd's voice trailed away.

"I won't say no more if you just let me go. I promise! I lost my wits from hunger, the young ones naggin', my wife lookin' like a wraith."

"You're right you won't be speakin' again," a Gnat said savagely. Drawing a dagger, he grabbed Rollynd by the jaw, forcing him to his knees.

"You know so much I'm sure you know there's no second chance," Jan warned.

Nali stared down at Rollynd who clasped his hands as he begged Nali for a life Nali couldn't give. He couldn't yield. The sight sickened him, a physical ill. Rollynd displayed a cowardice and weakness that seemed too prevalent in Nali's home region. It took more to make a traitor in Sefresal. This man had been his childhood playmate, a neighbor, a fellow fisher who kept his little boat tied beside Nali's. Could Nali give the order he must and yet claim himself better than a Minarian?

Before he could reconsider, Nali ran his own dagger across Rollynd's throat. He turned his back on Rollynd to find Jan, who grasped Nali's arms, but thankfully said nothing about the man whose breaths still gurgled.

"Cut out his tongue. It shows we mean business," Nali said, then strode away into the night. He drove away a little of his remorse forcing himself to think of Nalel's body being flung aside, his daughters' tear-stained faces, Olna struggling in the grip of her captors, Khoti's beaten body sprawled in his shackles.

The next dawn found a dead man propped against a burned-out shack along the busy stretch of road outside Sihmad Shal, 'traitor' scrawled across his face in charcoal, his tongue nailed with a forbidden metal spike to the shack wall. Hundreds saw the grisly message before the Minarians hauled it away.

The battle to retake Sihmad Shal had begun in earnest.

# 20: Champion

In the king's alcove, a smoky taper left a haze in the air, the flame barely enough to light the shallowest shadow. Yet Khoti quickly marked the removal of Peshal's belongings. Rumor claimed the king dreamed his brother consumed by a giant fish and thus surely dead. Khoti only cared that he dealt with a king who possessed all his faculties.

Swiftly, Khoti searched Arshal's packs, adjusting an item now and then to redistribute weight or prevent a rattle. He examined each article to assure himself the king had gear suitable for the journey, discarding the redundant. Arshal watched him, bemused, but said nothing.

After so many hours together planning this journey Khoti had a hard time looking on Arshal as a king or even a shawnsi. Just another man whose mission meant much to Shande, he found the king a likeable sort but mountain-ignorant, one more lowlander for whom Khoti must take responsibility.

At last, Khoti picked up the king's sword, which gleamed in the candlelight. He studied the intricate engraving, the sharp stellan edge and the curve of the hilts. He gave Arshal an appreciative nod.

"It's a fine weapon," he said. "Though not of Lharan craft, it'll do." He raised the blade, absorbing the feel of its weight and balance.

"I think the armorer did a fine job selecting the devices," Arshal said, pointing out the tracery. "See how the eagle clings to the wildcat's back? The craftsman figured the eagle represented foresight. I've always thought it to be Nali. And the way the wildcat tramples the flames, I think the flames are Ghyldus, and the wildcat symbolic of royalty."

"But I'm the cat!" Khoti teased tapping the tattoo on his neck. "You can't be a cat unless I say so. So, you must be the eagle. I'll be the wildcat trampling the enemy."

"I'm certainly not going to challenge you!" Arshal said with a laugh, motioning at Khoti's confident stance, hand resting on the haft of his dagger. "The important part is they work together to overcome the enemy."

"And you know how to use this weapon?" Khoti asked, handing it to the king.

As Arshal swished at the air, Khoti drew his own sword, always at his side. He parried each of Arshal's thrusts. Without effort, Khoti pressed his king into the corner. In moments the shawnsi gasped for breath, bathed in sweat, each parry more desperate and clumsy than the last. Finally, Khoti forced the sword from Arshal's grip. The Taschian jumped back, scowling, barely breathing hard.

"This isn't good." Khoti picked up the weapon and returned it to his sovereign. "I wasn't even trying to hurt you, especially with an edged weapon and not a practice piece. All this time you've had to prepare and you never thought to train? You might've improved. Now we're out of time. You're woefully ill-prepared for battle, King."

Arshal shook his head. "Don't let anyone try to say your injuries dulled your edge –"

"But they have! Kefta would've had me weaponless in moments the way I fought. I'm not ready! And here you are, relying on me. We should improve our skills before we take this on."

"Do we even need them?" Arshal held up his hand to display the opal set in his palm.

"Why use it if you don't have to? You said it wears on you. You could leave yourself vulnerable. I know my medicine does that to me."

The king hefted his sword as if measuring it against the gem.

"You should use it only to learn its properties. The rest of the time you should rely on your own sword skills."

"Of course, you're right," Arshal admitted, falling silent for a long moment in which he scrutinized Khoti a bit longer than felt comfortable. "Have I told you yet how valuable I've found your participation on my council? You always amaze me, Khoti. It proves how ignorant we were in our defense of Sihmad Shal."

Khoti shrugged as heat rose in his face. "I only do what's natural. I don't know why folk make such a to-do of it."

Arshal turned away, staring down at the sword in his hand. "I don't like to admit it, but I have this problem with battle. It angered Peshal. We were retreating through Thaila; the wall had fallen." Arshal's words seemed to carry him back to some far memory; his hands gripped the sword, white-knuckled, the tendons in his arms taut. "Pesh was hurt. We were trapped by Eidhalt. Killed them. Pesh thought I mourned my enemy. It disgusted him. I wasn't mourning. I felt like I wasn't in control, as if someone else's hand struck that fatal blow. I just can't seem to kill with –"

"Then you'd better learn, King," Khoti said, not bothering to soften the brutal edge to his tone. "If you intend to face Ghyldus, you can't look on your enemy as anything but an enemy. You can't fear them. You can't doubt your powers, your skills, or any motivation that moves you in that conflict. You can't feel remorse if you hope to survive. They don't. While you mourn them, or wonder at what you've done, they'll be defilin' your dead. You'd best learn to use that 'someone else' you fear to your advantage. I admit, at Eilime I felt possessed. I don't know that it wasn't just something I didn't know I could do, or maybe the spirits did it. If I'd stopped to wonder and marvel, I'd be dead. Don't let it trouble you! Learn the skill. The feeling doesn't have to be there. But when you're faced with a choice between life and death, I'd rather you save yourself, and save me the trouble of healing you. Besides, I can't rouse the dead. So, if you really bungle, you're done for." Khoti struck a battle pose, but Arshal shook his head, still trying to catch his breath.

"There isn't enough time, Khoti. You can't make a warrior of me by tomorrow." Arshal threw his sword on the table and sank onto a stool, studying the Taschian. "You could easily kill me," he admitted. "Please, if you're ever angry with me, ask first and make sure it's not a misunderstanding?"

Khoti grinned. "I'll whip you in shape before I'm done with you," he warned. "I've got too much riding on you to leave you helpless in the wilderness. No wonder Sihmad Shal fell. If you were commander, I can just imagine what your troops were like."

"Granted," Arshal admitted. "After seeing the Lharan Guard and the Tawnkats, I realize we were lucky to last as long as we did. Steadon still insists we could just retake Sefresal, as if it's so simple, and work from there. He doesn't understand that the rest of Shande is not like this place or that this journey is something I have to do. If only I'd had men like you in Sihmad

Shal, we might never have fallen, nor needed to send a king on a dream chase."

"Remember, we failed before we succeeded."

"But it's something else. There's more to it. It's the warrior in you Khoti." The king fell silent a moment, then straightened and stood. "Kneel before me, Khoti."

"Pardon me, Lord?" Khoti returned. What was this game?

"I'm your king, Khoti. You owe fealty. I recognize you as the representative of the Independent Lharan Tribes, but that doesn't free you of fealty." The stone in Arshal's palm swam from royal blue to a blaze of white.

"I've knelt before no man," Khoti said softly. "Not even my duke, not my captors. Is this a time I'm to ask if there's a misunderstanding before I become angry? Is my friendship not enough that you demand I debase myself to make you seem greater?"

Arshal held out his hands, the stone brilliant. "Friendship and fealty are not the same. It's no debasement to be named King's Champion."

"Champion?"

"No one's used the title in generations. Kneel, Khoti."

The king's voice held such authority as if some order of the spirits had come from Arshal's lips. Slowly, Khoti sank to his knees, hating himself for succumbing. He kept his gaze down-turned. What did his capitulation mean? Arshal stuck his head out in the corridor and called Chati and Tre, who waited to accompany their headman back to his cave. Would the king now debase him before his own? He could sense his aides' tension, their dismay at this dishonor.

Arshal held the sword by the blade before Khoti's down-turned eyes. "Place your hand on the hilt." Khoti obeyed. "Look at me. By the gods, you'd think I'd ordered your death."

Khoti glared up at him defiantly.

"Khoti of Tasch-el, son of Tsevon, Headman of the Independent Lharan Tribes, Tawnkat leader, Lieutenant of the Lharan Guard, member of the King's Council, I name you King's Champion that you will serve as my sword, the Sword of Shande."

For the first time Arshal seemed truly regal, his voice rich with that odd and compelling tone. "Chati the Cooper's Son of Tasch-el and Tre the Imager of Tasch-el serve as witness to what I have done this hour. Get up now."

Khoti slowly stood, still gripping the king's sword. "As champion, you're the leader of all my armies, the Sword of Shande. You will be my protector. Khoti, I trust you."

One side of Khoti's mouth rose as he recalled the king's words when Khoti roused him from his death walk. "And I you, my lord," Khoti whispered. He caught a glimpse of Chati and Tre, their eyes bright with pride in their mentor. He could tell. They heard it, too, something in Arshal's voice.

"Think of this not as debasement, Khoti, but the greatest honor I know to bestow on a warrior," Arshal said. "Odd to find this fragment of history usable. How I hated those lessons. But it's exactly what we need. You're my champion. No higher post can there be for a warrior. I'll have the papers drawn and witnessed before we depart. Now, wine to seal our pact."

Khoti found himself trembling, the king's sword still gripped in his hand as Arshal poured wine, the shadows turning the wine the color of blood. He hoped this omen meant he drank to his enemy's shed blood, not his own. He drank, sensing that nothing would ever be normal again. His fate spun him ahead of himself, beyond his control. Perhaps the pride he'd witnessed on the faces of Chati and Tre instead represented awe, horror.

But an hour later, Khoti dared enter Asteria's alcove, Chati and Tre prepared to warn him if the duke approached. Khoti stared into his hands in his lap as he sat with Asteria's warmth leaning against him.

She rapped her knuckles on his head. "Hello in there." He turned to look at her.

He grinned but the smile faded after a moment. "I don't know how long I'll be gone."

"I know. You must do what you must," Asteria replied.

"I'd better leave now. Before your fa –"

She turned to him with a guarded expression. "You will be gone by the time he learns of it and when you return he will no longer be angry. But do not dally. Come home right away. Eventually he will see the wrongness of this banishment."

"You aren't thinking straight, Asteria. You're promised to another. There's no hope for us. It's foolish of me to come here. I don't know why I came, except that your friendship has meant so much to me."

"I do not want anyone else."

"Then I'm equally sad that your father sends with me the message of your acceptance to your promised."

He stared into her dark eyes, drawn to them, wishing he could forget her as the duke demanded. The harder he tried the more persistent he found her in his thoughts.

She didn't respond. Her expression didn't have that caged look that mention of Anlon of Mershy generally brought. Khoti's gaze narrowed on her. Something in her demeanor felt less than sincere. Was she now suddenly intrigued with this man of Tormor?

"Have you special greetings for your suitor?" Khoti asked. "I'd be obliged to carry them since your father so thoughtfully assigned me the task of bearing his welcome." He blanched at the baleful look she threw him before she wiped the expression away.

"There comes soon a time when you leave and you will not return," she stated, gesturing with her head at the cuff on his wrist to remind him of the truth in her premonitions. "You will not leave me behind."

Hating himself for the weakness, he pulled her to him and held her a moment, drawing deep of her scent, feeling her hair soft on his cheek, her breath on his neck. Then he pushed her away and grasped her hand. He shook his head at her. "No, Asteria, you will remain," he murmured. "We've got to let go. You'll learn to love this Anlon, and our … friendship will be just another memory, a lesson on the cultures of the world. I serve my king now. I can make no promises or hold any hope of surviving him. I can be nothing but his champion, because that's what I am now."

Before she could protest, he left. Among his many errands, he would carry to her suitor Eithurdon's guarantee.

The Lharan mountains rose forbidding around them, Arshal wholly in Khoti's hands as he lost all sense of direction in the deep valleys and gorges, each slope seeming much like the one before it and the directions hopelessly lost in the small square of sky above. He found Khoti possessed an uncanny knowledge of this world of loose slopes, where each cleft, gorge or cave would offer a safe rest, where they dared light a cook fire, where to lay flat and silent to wait for the passage of a Minarian patrol. Khoti knew in which mountain streams he'd find fish, or where sweet berries grew with abandon on avalanche-scarred slopes. Arshal knew they moved slowly for his sake. Khoti aimed to teach him what survival skills he could in their time together, and prepare the king for the harsh roads ahead when his champion would no longer be with him. On their second day out of the Val, Khoti brought down a mountbuck. They took a few days to smoke and cure it into a delicacy like nothing Arshal had tasted before. While Khoti always cautioned that his wisdom ended in the foothills at the edge of the mountains, Arshal had to wonder if he was a fool to think he could travel alone when Khoti left him in the relative safety of Arenh. Perhaps a king should keep at least his champion beside him.

A few days later, Khoti stopped then made a slight hand signal. Arshal leaped from his mount's back to follow Khoti to the cover of dense scrub overlooking a steep gorge. Arshal knew better than to second-guess his protector.

It seemed they crouched in the scrub for hours, holding their breath as the horses shifted behind them. Finally, a Minarian sentry emerged from the concealment of the scrub on the slope below and surveyed what Arshal realized was a crudely cut road snaking along the bottom of the gorge.

Arshal watched Khoti. A cord worked in his champion's neck and jaw as the sentry stood in the road with an assured posture. After a few moments Khoti pushed himself back from the rim of the gorge and returned to Fidra.

"Staph-el Road," Khoti said when Arshal joined him. "We have to cross. They must still expect trouble from Tawnkats if they've set a sentry." Khoti chewed on a twig as he pondered their next move. "Ahrwesz's Avalanche closed the road just beyond the canyon, right near the waymeet with the Lhata Road, though they've carved a re-route, it's above the treeline and too open." Khoti's gaze had narrowed to cat-like slits. "We can probably cross on the Tasch-el side of the canyon. Then, if we keep to the east of the Lhata Road we'll likely have easy riding for a way."

"Well, that sounds like the best plan anyway," Arshal said. "To take the easier path."

"Think that through, King. The easiest way will be our enemy's route of choice. Besides, that trail takes us along the edge of the marshes. It may be budding spring up here, but down there blood-sucking pests have been waiting for that sweet shawnsi blood."

Arshal grimaced. "It sounds as if we have no choice."

"We can pick up a trail a day or two south of Lhata that'll take us back into forest and upland. It'll be easier going then. The mountains are lower, forested with fewer loose slopes."

Already Arshal liked the sound of this route. He didn't share Khoti's fondness for the northern range. While breathtaking in the short mountain spring when a crush of wildflowers carpeted everything, including the sheer faces of rock, Arshal wouldn't miss the jolts of missteps while crossing loose slopes, or passing beneath crumbling ledges. Swift, treacherous waters ran in the valleys, boulders strewing their path. Trees, twisted and stunted by wind, blocked their way. At night, animals growled and hissed. By day, only a few rodents sunned themselves on rocks, lazily watching the riders until they neared then scurrying under cover with their noses twitching. Each step they took seemed to announce their passage with a clatter of rock and eerie echoes. Arshal would happily bid farewell to Khoti's haunts, the quickest path out most appreciated.

From his pocket, Khoti pulled a pair of palm-sized stones, smoothed by decades in a mountain brook and hollowed and chipped with use. He made a few short, widely-spaced raps on the rock.

"Are these the talking stones Eithur lauds?" Arshal asked when it seemed Khoti had finished.

Khoti motioned him to silence, cupping a hand to his ears. Arshal heard nothing, but Khoti smiled and rapped out a slow pattern different from the first. After listening again to sounds Arshal couldn't distinguish from the snap of rock in the sun, Khoti dropped the stones in his pocket and mounted Fidra.

"Well?" Arshal asked.

"Nothing moving on our route. If we hurry, we'll be able to cross before dark and maybe make a safe camp."

"You got all that? I didn't hear a thing."

"You weren't meant to. If you recognize the stones without knowing the language, so can the Minarians. One of my scouts is about a half-day's travel east of here, near Tasch-el. He passed this way safely but two days ago."

Arshal couldn't hide his amazement at the distance Khoti's message traveled in but minutes. "These stones seem a stealthy art for Shande," Arshal mused as Khoti led the way.

"It's an old skill, as far back in our lore as the art of the healers."

"Terremar has always been in your people then."

"Ah, King, your gods may be in your veins, our spirits are in our hearts." Khoti gave him a winning smile that made Arshal want to laugh as his champion nudged Fidra ahead.

A few hours before nightfall they made the canyon where Konner and Eithurdon and less than three-hundred and fifty men and boys had turned an army of thousands back but a year ago. Arshal had heard variations on the tale, which gave much credit to his champion. Khoti blushed and muttered something about exaggeration, but offered no revision to the tale.

After a cursory search for signs of recent use, Khoti sped them across the road and into what seemed a mere continuation of loose slopes and jagged stone. Arshal had almost expected the terrain to change suddenly, not gradually as it did. By the time they made their camp in darkness, he noticed a stronger scent of pine on the wind, the heavy aroma of wildflowers muted. The mournful whistle of wind in stone softened to a swish through a few pines looming in the darkness. The soils felt heavier and more stable underfoot, and the damp thickness of moisture flowed up at them from where Khoti told him marshes stretched below.

After a cheerless night, one of the few when Khoti refused to set a fire, Khoti pushed them on well before dawn. Arshal felt Khoti's tension building as the day lengthened. The Taschian's head turned constantly as he sought something in the undergrowth or in the way needles lay in their trail, his muscles knotted as he occasionally reached for his sword.

When it seemed to Arshal the charge in the air around Khoti could grow no more intense, Khoti suddenly stopped. He yanked Fidra's head to one side and goaded her up the slope with Arshal's mount laboring close behind.

Khoti stopped just beneath a sharp outcrop of rock blocking their path. He drew his sword as he dismounted, then peered down at the trail below.

"What is it?" Arshal whispered beside him.

Khoti put a finger to his lips and pointed. Three horsemen passed through open spaces among the trees on the path below. They stopped where Khoti had left the trail. Two wore the markers of the Eidhalt on their helms, the third obviously a tracker from the way he led his two superiors. Khoti dropped flat, Arshal following more slowly. The tracker studied the ground a moment then stared up toward them. The noon sun flickered off rubies in the medallions they wore on their chests. Arshal glanced back to see the horses well-concealed behind the lichen-coated branches of a fallen tree. His breath came out a hiss as the Minarians dismounted and climbed the slope.

Arshal eased his sword from the scabbard at his side, hearing in his ears Khoti's warning that he could not fight all his battles with the stone in his palm.

Khoti rolled to the cover of a log so decomposed it had almost returned to soil. With an intricate hand signal, one of the many Khoti had taught him, Khoti sent Arshal rolling to the other side of the path they made climbing to the ridge. The king hid behind the base of a tree that had been split in half by lightning. Still alive, the trunk had peeled back to form a wide base behind which Arshal could stand, yet peer out through the split. Arshal's hands had grown sweaty and he tried to dry his palms on his breeches to keep a strong grip on his sword. His thoughts raced with the warnings of his council: how ill-advised to travel without a full escort, what risk they entailed placing so much hope on one man alone against thousands of conquerors.

When the Minarians reached a spot almost level with Khoti, they again stopped, studying the signs where Khoti had rolled to one side and Arshal to the other. A horse stomped, drawing the Minarians' attention to the fallen tree. They went on, cautious.

Khoti eased his bow from his back and nocked an arrow. He drew, aiming at the last of the three, and shot. At the last moment, the Minarian turned. The arrow struck the man in the shoulder, a flesh wound. The injured man bellowed an alarm as Khoti stood to face them.

They smiled, triumphant to face a single man. As the enemy neared, Khoti freed his dagger, holding it in one hand as he brought up his sword in the other. They blanched at the expression on Khoti's face, one filled seemingly with a bloodlust. Arshal sucked in his own breath to see his champion, the way he appeared fluid, like his patron tawnkat as he sidled. Khoti crouched as if about to pounce, poised and confident, a man given up for dead but months ago.

The wounded man hung back as the leader rushed Khoti. Khoti spun away as the man flew at him, parrying and stabbing as he turned to wedge his dagger in the Minarian's side. The man's momentum carried him on down the slope. The Eidhalt slowed and turned, ready to face Khoti again. But the tracker stepped forward now that both Eidhalt were injured.

The tracker approached more warily, sidling and forcing Khoti to keep turning to match him.

The tracker's eyes widened. "I know you. You were at Eilime! You are –"

"Your executioner," Khoti said.

149

Arshal went cold. This was not the man he'd come to know, but 'someone else.'

"The reward will be great when Verdaen is returned to the dungeons where he belongs."

Khoti lunged. The Minarian fell back, almost stumbling over the crumbling log behind which Khoti had hidden. The man with the arrow wound pulled a throwing dagger from his belt. They took no chances. Khoti dropped and rolled, the knife the Eidhalt threw sticking into the ground, useless. In that instant the tracker lunged for Khoti while the Eidhalt leader crawled up the slope toward them, reaching for the sword lost in his fall.

Arshal still hid behind the tree. About to rush out and dare to face the Eidhalt with the arrow wound, he saw Khoti's danger. Khoti struggled to gain his feet as the tracker's sword blows fell. But with each parry, Khoti again lost his balance. The Taschian could only scoot away as he fended the tracker off. Gaining his knees, Khoti tried to pull a leg up to stand as the Minarian continued to hammer at him only to meet Khoti's sword.

"You are not so tough," the tracker declared.

"That's why I'm not dead yet." Khoti sneered.

The Minarian lunged again, this time throwing his balance behind it.

Arshal darted from tree to tree, always moving closer to the Minarian with the arrow wound who, so engrossed in the battle, failed to see his danger. Arshal sucked in a deep breath, then leaped forward and swung his sword at the Minarian's neck, feeling the sickening scrape of metal against bone. The man fell, Arshal straddling him to ensure he didn't rise again. Just then, the other spied him and cried out an alarm. The Eidhalt threw his knife at Arshal. The king ducked it, his concern now for his champion.

The tracker had the advantage on Khoti now. He had thrown his weight behind him and had again toppled Khoti to the ground. The tracker stabbed with his dagger, the blow glancing off the cuff on Khoti's wrist raised in defense. In a breath of an instant, Khoti erupted from the edge of defeat. Regaining his feet, he took the offensive, driving the man down the slope toward the Eidhalt who held the bloody gash in his side.

Arshal tried to follow, determined to prevent the Eidhalt from aiding the tracker. Khoti's fury forced a downward charge, wielding his sword two-handed. Their battle carried them by the wounded Eidhalt and on down the slope as Arshal chased after them, helpless without bow and with no knife to fling.

As Arshal came abreast of the Eidhalt, the Minarian raised the medallion in his hand, pointing it at the king. He bellowed some incantation and light flickered from the gem. The breath caught in Arshal's throat as, suddenly, giant hounds as large as a mountbuck – larger, agile and sleek – leaped from the net of trees behind Arshal. Howls shrieked from them with unearthly menace as they raced at the king. Great spikes of teeth gnashed, white, like swords in moonlight. Snarling, gurgling sounds of hunger erupted in their throats as red eyes blazed with the fire in the medallion. Arshal couldn't move, too stunned, as the apparitions jumped for his throat. He smelled their scavenging-foul breath. Before he could react, he felt teeth puncturing the leather armor he wore. He swiped his sword before him in defense. When he struck dark and wiry flesh, a jolt made his fingers tingle, the creatures exploding in a fury of sparks. They vanished, leaving behind only the hot odor of lightning.

Arshal gasped, leaning on his knees. The medallion remained raised in the man's hands as the Eidhalt's mouth shaped some incantation.

The Eidhalt sidled down the slope, keeping one eye on Arshal as he closed on Khoti, who still battled, near oblivious to the king's dilemma. At last, Khoti thrust his sword into the tracker's chest, shearing the man's light mail and driving on through. But Khoti hadn't escaped danger. His back to the Eidhalt officer, he couldn't see the Eidhalt letting the medallion fall at his chest. He raised his sword high over Khoti's head. Arshal's champion yanked his weapon from the dead tracker's chest and turned, last moment, as if sensing his danger. A flash of light blazed, followed by the snapping explosion of the sword held in the man's hand. Khoti shielded his eyes as shards of metal scattered, most of them rending the Eidhalt.

When the rain of metal settled, the Minarian lay dying from wounds from his own sword.

Khoti glared at Arshal as he wiped blood from his face and arms, picking at bits of shrapnel. "I told you not to."

"Oh, and you'd rather he cleaved your skull?" Arshal still gasped for breath, shaking from the encounter.

Khoti continued to scowl as he inspected the minor scratches he'd received from the sword shards.

"Next time use your sword." Khoti trudged up to Arshal to check him over as if he examined booty won in a battle.

"I did," Arshal retorted, pointing up the slope. Khoti grabbed the king's shoulder, pushing his fingers through holes the hound's teeth had ripped in the leather. The skin had bruised beneath, but not broken.

"This is a puzzle," Khoti mumbled. Khoti's face screwed up into a speculative frown. "Did they know who they called this magic upon?"

Arshal couldn't answer, he'd tucked away his circlet crown for this part of his journey, but the signet ring still gleamed on his finger. Would they have noticed it in battle? Khoti gathered their horses. Some unspoken anger had him scowling. Arshal concentrated on fighting down the revulsion for the feel of his sword striking bone, the way his mere thought had shredded his enemy. He needed to force himself to use his anger in battle. He couldn't afford to mourn his enemy, nor let his fear of the enemy's magic paralyze him.

# 21: Mershy

Khoti scorned the trail now, taking a slower route through tangles of brush and undergrowth, or beneath the low sweeping branches of pine. He forced even more care, their camps quiet and cold, and their talk in low whispers. Yet, Arshal had never felt as safe as traveling with this Taschian weapon.

Three weeks brought the king and Khoti to the edges of Tormor Wood. As they passed beneath the forest canopy it closed around them, warm, like a blanket.

Khoti scowled at the thick forest canopy with suspicion, stopping just under the cover of the eaves.

"This is a watchful place. I've never been here. I don't know what to think of this." He scanned the giant trunks of trees marching into murky darkness where only the barest green light reached down from the thick canopy to be lost in the mush of leaf litter. "There's no air here, no wind. I feel watched."

"It's a far piece from your world of stone," Arshal agreed.

"Things grow in our valleys and forests, King. We tread on another's ground here. Our scouts report this to be a dangerous place peopled by a violent tribe."

"The Tachi. They're protective, not violent. My Uncle Habdelion lives here and it's here we must go. His stronghold isn't on the forest edge."

"No," Khoti agreed. "But I don't like this place."

They rode east for hours, picking along the small trails of some wildlife for which Khoti never found a print. The forest all tracked the same, even with a rise or a dip, a little hill or open glade now and then. When at last they made camp, lost without starlight penetrating the canopy, Arshal dug in his pack for tinder.

Khoti shook his head. "The dark is safety."

"Maybe we could use a little publicity if we ever want to find my uncle. I doubt many Minarians lurk so far from any road."

Khoti gave him a skeptical glance. "There's plenty of people moving on the forest's edge. For all we know a road could be just ahead. We know there's Minarians on the Akora River overseeing the timber operations, wherever that lies from here."

"We're just too far from anything. There's no one to fear here."

"No one?" Khoti scoffed. "My scouts are brought to your uncle as prisoners of someone."

"No different than if his scouts went in search of the Val. I said, the Tachi guard my uncle, as the Guard protects the Val. I've been here before – when I was a child – to visit my uncle. He made peace with the Tachi, earned their respect and honor. They're a people not unlike the Taschians I've known. Independent."

"And they may have made the independent decision to side with the Minarians."

"Light the fire, Khoti."

Khoti glared, but lit a small fire, refusing to let Arshal build it up beyond a small flicker of coals to warm their tea and stew dried fruits. Arshal could see his champion tensing again. What did he feel that wound him so tight? Did his instincts read forest as they did stone?

Arshal had just settled himself into his bedroll when even he sensed something, a pause, an absolute silence in the wood. He opened one eye as Khoti jumped to his feet, kicking out the fire and drawing his sword.

Arshal couldn't see anything in the pitch blackness of the forest, but heard a scuffle in the deeper shadows beyond their camp. He quickly tossed a handful of dry leaves on the coals, sending up a flare of light. Khoti wrestled with a dark-haired man dressed in the browns and greens favored by the Tachi. He'd dropped his sword and now pulled his dagger.

"Hold!" Arshal demanded. "Khoti, no! It's the Tachi. Give him your weapon!"

"You're crazed!"

"They're my uncle's friends."

Khoti scowled and dropped the dagger. The man swiftly kicked Khoti's legs from beneath him. Khoti fell, struggling to roll free, but at another word from Arshal he went limp. Khoti's gaze even in this dim light felt perilous.

More Tachi dissolved out of the darkness. A man he vaguely recognized shoved his face in front of Arshal.

"Tedwa," Arshal said, the man's name welling up out of his memory. "I seek my uncle. Is he well?"

The leader of the Tachi nodded. "We take you to him." One of his men bound Khoti's hands behind him, attaching a length of rope like a leash.

"This is my champion. He won't harm you," Arshal assured Tedwa.

The man gestured at a swelling bruise beneath his eye and a small cut on his shoulder where Khoti's dagger had made contact.

"In self-defense –" Arshal began.

Tedwa cut him off with a gesture. "I know who you are," Tedwa said. "Him, I do not know."

"He's Headman of the Independent Lharan Tribes," Arshal objected, considering that the title Tedwa would respect most.

Tedwa shrugged. "I know no mountain people."

Tedwa yanked on the rope, pulling Khoti to his feet. The Tachi leader gestured for Arshal to follow the shadowy Tachi in front of him. Other Tachi stowed Khoti and Arshal's gear and unhobbled their horses. When they kicked out the fire, the world of Tormor Wood became darkest night. Ahead of him, Arshal heard Khoti stumble and fall in the dark, the hiss of Khoti's breath full of rage for the humiliation his king made him suffer. Arshal only prayed his champion would hold his infamous temper.

Arshal swallowed a pang of guilt when Khoti stumbled again in the black night beneath the canopy, no hands to give him balance, hauled along at his captor's pace. Tedwa lit a sputtering torch that made the forest shadows seem even darker and the stifling heat of the forest only more oppressive.

The ground grew soft beneath their feet as they neared the marshy headwaters of the Akora River. The Tachi steered away from the river, guiding them east of where Habdelion's family had managed the southern timber industry. Shela might be the largest city and only port of call in southern Shande, but Habdelion's family had chosen to live here, in the heart of Mershy's forests rather than in that balmy seaport.

Khoti tripped. Arshal saw him pitch forward, falling face first into the damp earth before the guide could right Khoti's balance. Tedwa called a halt, stooping to peer into Khoti's blistering glare.

"You rest?" Tedwa asked in the musical dialect that had always mesmerized Arshal.

Khoti hissed as he struggled to his knees.

Tedwa shook his head. "Hard to walk in dark places unknown." Tedwa's men fanned out around them at a signal Arshal couldn't detect. Tedwa held a skin to Khoti's lips. Khoti turned his head away. Tedwa smiled, his face appearing less severe even in the dimness of the forest.

"Is good, trust me." He chuckled, a sound like the gurgle of the brook they sat beside. "Is hard work to walk with hands bound. Be proud. You do better than other men. Your scouts."

Khoti glanced up at Tedwa with a wary gaze, accepting the syrupy liquor from the skin. "My scouts?" he said when Tedwa took away the skin to offer it to Arshal.

"They come. They say they work for you, and if you ever come you make us suffer for their treatment."

Khoti snorted, trying to bury his face in his lap to muffle the sound. "And I would've, if I'd been allowed," he warned when he looked up again. "I've only been bound once, by Minarians. Those men are dead now." Khoti's tone carried the serrated edge of his indignation.

Tedwa stiffened then pointed at the cuff on Khoti's wrist. "Your trophy?"

Khoti nodded. Tedwa said nothing more. But when he called for his men to again move along a trail only they could see, Tedwa grabbed Khoti's arms and yanked them up behind his back, slashing the cords binding him.

While Khoti rubbed the stiffness from his wrists Tedwa peered up at him. "We are Tachi, not Minarian." Tedwa gave Khoti a shove that would have sent him sprawling without his hands to balance him. They moved on through the darkness of Tormor Wood, warrior and king. What vain hope had driven them to such foolish roads?

They'd been walking for hours before Khoti noticed a dim light growing around them. Khoti couldn't tell if dawn neared, or if the sun had been up for a long time and its rays just pierced the canopy. Already the stifling heat of day settled among them. At last Tedwa called a halt, motioning for Arshal and Khoti to follow him to a sprawling shack built among the trees. A small stream flowed in front of the ramshackle building, eventually finding its way into larger tributaries to the Akora. It looked as if the shack had started out as a one-room hut, and slowly grown with additions linked by roughly thrown-together passages, some of which circled the massive trunks of the ancient trees.

Khoti doubted this could be the home of the Duke of Mershy. A family born to the timber industry certainly had a better sense of carpentry and construction. Yet, he could barely distinguish the structure built so loosely among the shadows of the trees from the jumble of windfall, the mosses trailing from the branches above and the mulch of leaves carpeting its roof. One must seek this structure to find it.

A Tachi led away their horses. Khoti watched the man as he took Fidra's lead with a soft hand. Absolute silence closed as they stood among the shadows, Tedwa refusing to allow them to step over the little rivulet running just a stone's throw from the rough door, nor offering any explanation for their reception. After a few moments a man carried their packs into the structure. Some time later the door opened and Tedwa motioned for them to cross the rivulet and enter the shack. Khoti had to remind himself that his own scouts would be just as wary.

The entryway belied the hodgepodge of the exterior: a sumptuous carpet underfoot, a servant at attention by the door dressed in the duke's rich brown and hunter green colors. The polished wood of the interior walls hid behind thick tapestries delineating generations of the duke's household. Everywhere Khoti saw the trappings of a world to which Eithurdon and Asteria belonged. He entered no mean hovel in the woods.

A servant led Arshal and Khoti through a maze of rooms and passages, some centered around the base of a tree, others passing dozens of closed doors. At last they came to a room that would be a solarium if the sun could find its way to the forest floor. Only two men awaited them, Arshal and Khoti's gear strewn upon the floor before them. Khoti knew the elder must be Habdelion, the shawnsi birthmark on his temple muted by the darker complexion of southern bloodlines. With his jet hair he appeared a shawnsi version of the Tachi. Khoti remembered that despite grayed hair, Habdelion's sister, Queen Sala, had favored the southern tribes, unlike her children. The younger man clearly had to be Anlon. He bore no marks of the shawnsi, his lighter Dasireian features and auburn hair a contrast to his father's.

Habdelion and Anlon rose and bowed. The duke reached for Arshal's hand bearing the signet ring and kissed it.

"King Arshaldon," Habdelion whispered, testing the name as he remained bent over Arshal's hand.

Khoti almost laughed, but Arshal took the gesture seriously.

"I bear sad news," Arshal stated, hand dropping to his side as Habdelion straightened. "As you have surmised, my father is gone, the rest of my family with him. Esthen fell before the gates of Sihmad Shal. Minarians captured Resala and Peshal. Your sister died of grief and the hardship of our long road into exile."

"And we thought our lot hard," Habdelion muttered, gesturing at their home.

He paused as a servant brought chairs for Khoti and Arshal.

"This is not why you came." Habdelion said as they took their seats. "You would not risk your life to tell me of the queen's death when your scouts brought the news months ago."

"The king comes to ask you to fight for him," Khoti declared.

Habdelion's gaze measured Khoti. "Is this your spokesman, Arshal?"

Khoti stiffened at the duke's tone.

"Such a young man, dressed in hides, Eithur's colors, and wearing such an undiplomatic face?"

"I'd give everything for a thousand like him," Arshal stated. "I named Khoti King's Champion. He deserves more than your respect. As young as he is, he's headman of the mountain tribes, member of my council and an officer in the Lharan Guard. I expect him to marshal my armies as the Sword of Shande."

Habdelion sat back in his chair, regarding Khoti like a buyer sizing up a horse. "I have spoken with your men, heard of you, Khoti of Tasch-el. One Toban –"

"He's dead," Khoti said, sour with his embarrassment that his king had to defend his honor. And he didn't like the judgmental cast of Anlon's gaze on him. The duke's son wore a surly expression, his lips curling with distaste at Arshal's account. And this was Asteria's promised. Khoti felt his warrior's rage twisting in his gut just thinking about Asteria with the duke's heir, imagining him touching her –

"It seems many of your best are dead, Arshal," Habdelion said. "Why have you risked the Dyndevas line to come here?"

"As Khoti said, to enlist you in our cause," Arshal stated. "You turned away Toban with rebuke." He barely suppressed the indignation in his tone. "You turned away Mitte Salman and Ytri. You, brother of the queen, uncle to the King in Exile, told them you saw no reason to risk your men."

Arshal rose to stride to the window overlooking the leafy wood. Anlon puffed out at the rebuke his father received, glaring at Arshal's back. Khoti fought down the urge to snarl.

"You denied me, Han! I'm your king, no matter what you think of my abilities!" Arshal spun around to face the duke. His tone carried a dignity, and again Khoti heard that power in it, that something that compelled and admonished in the same instant. Arshal stood so regal before them, truly a king, gray eyes hinting of a power not entirely locked in his palm. "Perhaps you don't think I'm capable of filling my father's place. I'm not my father. Trade, merchants, entertaining heads of state and ruling on petty grievances, those were his concerns. My role is to destroy Ghyldus. I'm charged by the gods to rule Shande. The country will be mine!"

"What makes you think you can succeed?" Habdelion asked, the bluster and arrogance gone from his tone.

"This," Arshal declared. He held up his hand, the stone blazing a blinding and brilliant royal blue. "Dynfearn the Lost had such a stone with which he smote his enemies. I'm not Dynfearn with power fresh from his godly ancestors. But I empowered this stone with gifts from the gods."

Khoti sensed a slow anger kindling in the king. As he spoke, the stone grew to a blazing white light that Arshal had to shield with his fist to avoid blinding them all.

"What do you expect will happen, Han, if you continue to sit here so cozy in your shack in the forest?" The bitter words made Habdelion sit back as if from a blow. "You've made your home pleasant, no doubt. What of your charge to your people? How will you protect them when the Minarians subdue the resistance and have time to harass the Tachi, and find your people and root them out? How can you sit here, with any semblance of self-respect when our people are dying? How can you sit idle when Minarian patrols hunt members of your own family, selling them to sate Ghyldus's bloodthirst? How, when children are marched away to labor, when families starve to death, how can you sit here in your comfort and refuse my call? How can you turn away my men when they beg of you only the fealty you owe me? Have you become a traitor, Han? Are your loyalties elsewhere?"

Habdelion rose at the challenge. "King or not, how dare you enter my house and charge me with treason! I am sought as other shawnsi. How could you suggest –"

"How could you deny me?"

Habdelion plopped down into his chair with a scowl. He glanced at his son, who studied Khoti with open skepticism, the Taschian intently ignoring the scrutiny as he watched the king.

"Anlon, your assessment?" Habdelion asked.

159

"Helping him could destroy us." Anlon declared. Khoti couldn't stop an indignant snort from escaping. "We have power here yet, enough to protect our people. In time they may grant us stature again when they move on –"

"They're killing shawnsi!" Arshal exclaimed.

"Some will always survive –" Anlon began.

"Your father, mother, sister?" Khoti asked.

"I will protect them," Anlon stated.

"What of others?" Khoti demanded. "I bear the Duke of Lharan's agreement to your request to be joined to the Lady Asteria. Will you consign her to the Minarians?"

Anlon shrugged. "If it is for the greater good. She is not here. If she were? I barely know the woman. She holds nothing now but a title. Perhaps her father is too eager to be shed of her. Is she perhaps damaged? Perhaps the Minarians –"

Khoti jumped to his feet, his hand going for the dagger no longer in his belt. Arshal's blazing hand restrained him.

"Your role, Champion," Arshal warned as Khoti sat hard on his stool. Anlon squirmed under Khoti's glare.

Habdelion sighed, making a slashing motion with his arm toward Anlon. "Tell me, King, what you plan, the place you see for your uncle Han," he said at last.

Arshal launched into a description of all that had been set in motion from the Val. Khoti sat in stony silence, watching Anlon. At least Habdelion listened. As did his son.

Night fell and deepened. At last servants led them to soft beds while the duke remained pondering all that Arshal had told him.

Despite the reprieve from bedrolls and stony ground, Arshal tossed, keeping Khoti awake.

He claimed a plague of dreams assaulted him, seeming to warn him of danger, imparting an urgency that made his heart pound so loud Khoti could see the king's pulse. Other dreams Arshal claimed provided glimpses into the mind of Ghyldus, visions that told him that powerful being sought him. Khoti couldn't imagine such a torment, but to imagine his own nightmares of scavengers nibbling at his flesh.

Each time the king awoke, he found Khoti watching him, the Tawnkat alert to every sound around him even within the safety of guarded walls. Arshal would whisper to Khoti of his doubts, questioning assumptions. Had he been wrong to flee the Val like this? Each time the king drifted back to sleep, he again dreamed warnings that told him to keep moving, be wary and stay out of Ghyldus's grasp. The king must grow yet into his power.

Khoti held vigil.

Champion now, leader of the collective Shandean army, if it ever materialized.

From careless mountain youth he had somehow bypassed all those men of rank and blood to marshal Shande's forces: what an awesome challenge for a man of only eighteen years, the second son of the headman to an obscure tribe the king had never even heard of. His role both beckoned and terrified him. How could he leave this king in the wilderness with the survival skills of a child? The Sword of Shande must oversee the duties he and Arshal had mapped out over late campfires. But the King's Champion should ensure his king's safety. What worth in any of these plans if the enemy captured and killed his king? The night dragged toward dawn with no resolution, and no rest.

When Khoti and Arshal at last rose, they found Habdelion dressed for travel and waiting to accompany them to the edge of his shrunken realm.

The heat of the last days of the light moon wrung the sweat from them as Tachi led them to the western edge of Tormor Wood. The forest felt peaceful, a world away from the privation of occupation. Habdelion walked beside Khoti and Arshal in a daze, often staring at Arshal's hand, or studying Khoti, not asking whatever questions made his lips open, only to clamp shut.

They paused by a small stream sending tepid water in search of the Akora River, the Tachi fanning out around them.

"I do not know what I can accomplish, Arshal," Habdelion said as they soaked their feet in the stream. "I have perhaps five hundred loyals throughout Tormor Wood, and of course the Tachi. The army you expect from me must fight a war, pitched battle on an open plain with horsed swordsmen, not skirmishes among the trees. I have no knowledge of such things, no experience to impart. If I can only put some few –"

"What of Shela?" Khoti asked, disgusted by Habdelion's vacillation.

"I cannot come near the place. The Minarians caught and executed the city leaders and elders by example. They are a strong presence there. I know the people of Shela chafe under the occupation. But what can they do? They are even more closely watched, more oppressed than your folk in the mountains."

Tedwa stared from one to the other, at last pointing at Khoti, his finger plunking Khoti in the chest.

"You want Tachi to fight. That we do. Here and there, one or two. But you want a different battle. If you want that, you show us how. You are a warrior. It is your job."

Khoti glanced at Arshal. "You're still determined to go this alone?"

"I need you to get me through the mountains into Arenh, from there I'm on my own. I'm safer there than here. I can't ask you to accompany me. You have other tasks. Though I'd feel safer if you could join me, this I must do alone."

"Then if I were to go home, gather a few men and some weapons, I'd be free to help Habdelion train his army?"

"I named you champion and sword, Khoti. You must assess our needs and marshal those resources. I know you grip a grudge like that sword of yours. You arrived here a prisoner –"

"I have no reason to doubt his ability," Habdelion stated.

"I'm more concerned about Khoti," Arshal hedged.

"Don't be." Khoti stood. "They'd have had no better greeting had they sought the Val. The Duke of Mershy needs us, we need him. Aren't most alliances formed by mutual need?"

"They are. Let us start afresh, as allies at our next meeting," Habdelion said.

Tedwa gestured at the long scar on Khoti's neck.

Habdelion nodded. "I look forward to your return, Khoti. We want to see if the man made the legend, or the legend made the man."

Arshal grinned as they clasped arms in parting. "I think, Han, you will find it the former."

When Khoti took up Fidra's reins at the eaves of the forest where already they felt the cooler air falling from the mountains, a grip on his arm stopped him from mounting. Tedwa held out a pear-shaped pin of polished dark wood carved in the image of an Akoran leaf.

"It vouches for you and those with you," Tedwa said as Khoti pulled his cloak from his bags and fastened the pin at the collar.

"I have nothing of value to offer," Khoti said. Tedwa smiled, a musical chuckle escaping him. The Tachi raised his hand and moments later had disappeared back into the forest.

Khoti gazed ahead at the brightness of dry hills leading into the mountains. They'd traveled south from where they entered the great forest into a world strange to Khoti's eyes. They surveyed the brown line of distant road for signs of traffic before goading their mounts to a gallop in search of the cover of another forest, the kind Khoti knew, one of pine and cedar competing with mountain peaks for the best vantage. In such a world, Khoti mused, it would be good to have a good-faith token.

# 22: Azren

The King of Shande rode out of the unbearable heat of the ripening moon in the midday of southern lands. The soil beneath his mount's hooves had baked to brick. A salty film coated the king's skin, his body unable even to sweat. With relief, he left behind him the choking desert to crest a ridge overlooking the inviting seaside city of Ar-Tebez. The sleepy Arenhian town, its bright whitewashed walls edging the aqua shallows of the Sea of Tebez, moved at the careless pace of a land at peace. Flowers spilled from planters perched beneath windows on mud-block dwellings, or crowded up to the dusty yellow-dirt paths as children played in the shade of broad trees that dominated the squares.

Despite the heat, Arshal pulled his cloak from his saddlebags and draped it over his shoulders, pulling up the hood to conceal the marks of a shawnsi in his features.

Keeping his face in shadow, Arshal made a few cursory requests, at last directed to an unimpressive building overlooking a harbor encircled by low brown mountains. The sweltering sun sent heat waves rising from the streets, the few people moving about keeping to the shade thrown from the village's buildings. Even the market stood shuttered and closed until late afternoon.

Like Habdelion's shack, outward appearances said nothing about the King of Arenh's home. The polished stone floors and walls of the reception hall, and windows open to the sea side, provided a cool respite from the streets. The bright building staggered across the hillside, its large open passages, courtyards and verandas opening out onto the vista of the town and harbor below.

A servant approached, dark eyes sleepy, hair tousled as if he'd just risen from his bed. His smile, bright in a sun-coppered face, appeared friendly as he asked Arshal's business. Even placid Shande screened the king's petitioners more closely. Arshal merely stated that he wished an audience.

"Name?" the man asked, bowing. When Arshal hesitated, the servant stood back, his gaze narrowing as he gripped a pull cord beside the entry.

"King of Shande," Arshal said, mustering all the sense of mission he could put into his words and fearing the pull cord might call armed guards.

The servant peered at Arshal's shrouded features. The Shandean offered no more. After a long moment in which Arshal feared all of Arenh could hear his heartbeat, the servant left, returning minutes later to lead the King of Shande to a shady courtyard. A jet-haired man with coppery skin still smooth and not yet care-worn lounged beside a spring-fed pond that spilled over a sluiceway to drain out through a small channel under the courtyard wall.

King Azren didn't hide his scrutiny of Arshal's weather-stained cloak and hide breeches, the hood pulled low, or the tip of a sword scabbard peaking from beneath the cloak. Arshal couldn't help but note the man's eyes. They held the haunted yet compassionate cast of one who thinks too deeply about his decisions.

"You look nothing like King Ebon," Azren stated. "I met him years ago before I became king, as a student of your dernailye. He was an older man. You have the hands and stature of one much younger, younger than me. Has my servant unwittingly admitted some ruffian?"

"King Ebon is dead, killed by a Minarian patrol," Arshal said, pulling back his hood. "I'm my father's eldest son, named King in Exile. I come to appeal for aid from a neighbor who has always been our friend. We need your assistance to resist the occupation."

"Would that I had seen wrong," Azren muttered. He gestured to a seat as a servant quietly left a tray of cider on a small service table. "I am honored you come yourself, King Arshaldon. But what can I do?" Azren asked in a southern dialect that placed an odd emphasis on Arshal's name, his tone soft and patient. "Arenh is not prepared for war with Minaria, much less to arm our neighbors. We cannot risk being drawn into confrontation. If it were not for the heat of afternoon, you might never have arrived at my halls alive. Many Minarians work here. Some of our people might take note of a man with shawnsi features, and sell that information." Azren shook his head. "Are you so desperate to risk your life so needlessly? I grant I do not believe wars of conquest should be the extension of failed negotiations –"

"There were no negotiations. What they do is the systematic extermination of a people. And yours are next," Arshal warned.

"That is a harsh assessment for conquest."

"But true. My sister and surviving brother were abducted only because they are shawnsi. The Minarians have declared a mission to eliminate us from Ea, as well as Visionaries and derna."

Azren stared at him, incredulous.

"You heard none of this? Such proclamations are posted on the walls of Shandean towns. It's not merely shawnsi. At least one Lharan tribe has been obliterated."

Azren shook his head. "The auguries, the visions, each time they sounded the challenge I would not listen, could not believe. What can I do? Arenh is a small country, Shande vast. What help can we give but our wishes and sympathy? I must think of my people first. For the king to choose sides in a foreign war is against their best interests."

"Do your people support Ghyldus?" Arshal's tone brought a chill into the warm courtyard.

Azren leaned back, gaze narrowing on Arshal. "Certainly not, at least not that I know. Ghyldus is blasphemy. I know the histories enough to be sure Ghyldus likely acts at another's direction. But Minaria's folly is not our concern."

"You know better, King. It is your concern," Arshal said, something in his tone seeming to strike Azren a blow. "Minaria's plans don't end with Shande. They brag of conquests to come. Ghyldus wants all of Ea. It's a vengeful quest, to repay his exile and defeat." Arshal peered into dark eyes soft with compassion. "You can't sit back and say 'it's not my concern.' It is your concern. The Pladde rebel. Shiad aids us. Resistance takes root in the far reaches of Shande. With a united effort, we could drive him out."

"Where? He will just continue to –"

"He must face me and be destroyed."

Azren took a sip of his cider, watching Arshal over the rim of the cup. "You do not appear capable of defeating a vengeful god," he said. "Though I do believe I sense in you something more than appearances –"

166

A blaze of white light, like lightning cast loose, shot from Arshal's hand. Azren gasped and dropped his cup just as the base of the pond beside them exploded, the stone smashed to powder. The water, no longer contained, rushed down the channel, dragging chunks of stone with it as it raced to pool against the drain in the vine-covered courtyard wall.

When the light faded from Arshal's palm, Azren caught his breath, again running nervous fingers through his hair.

"Why not just smite him in Lagdche and be done with it?"

Arshal leaned back in his chair, wiping his sweaty face with a handkerchief proffered by the King of Arenh. "The time isn't right. We've learned Ghyldus's halls are sealed by sorcery; and we're told he observes what passes in Minaria by merely directing his thoughts that way. It would still leave an occupied Shande and a strong Minaria into which Fyraer could send yet another of his acolytes."

"Yet you vow to destroy Ghyldus."

"The defeat must be total," Arshal said with a weary sigh. "We need to draw Ghyldus and his armies to us, under our terms. After suffering so great a loss under the guidance of a false god, his subjects will hesitate to hear any future comer."

"And you think you can make all these plans work?"

Azren stared at him as if he somehow read into his thoughts, an uncanny thing that reminded Arshal of Cree, even Nali. Azren had studied with derna, and clearly knew the histories to see Fyraer in Ghyldus.

"Why did you risk everything to come here?" Azren asked.

"You ignored my messengers. Would you believe if you hadn't seen me yourself?"

Azren smiled, inclining his head. "Point taken. The auguries hinted of challenge, undoing and destruction, without detail. Yet I saw clearly that this is the gods' war, not ours. Are you so certain it is your role to face Ghyldus?"

"What do you know of Fyraer, of Ghyldus? Have you heard that story?" Arshal asked.

Azren nodded. "I pondered it long when I learned who replaced Mol Azezial. I saw it as a matter of state, not a matter of heart. Perhaps I was wrong to assume it merely a political thing."

"The gods fight this war. I'm their weapon."

Azren stood, throwing a glance at his draining pond. "It would be the gods' way. In your ancestry is the power of the Making. Perhaps, too, the power of Unmaking," he said, his words cryptic, his dark gaze lost in the shadows lengthening in his courtyard. "I will consider this. You are safe in my house. No harm will come to you."

Arshal remained beside the shattered pond, so weary of his journey already that he couldn't force himself to move. In the quiet of the courtyard – water splattering from the spring onto the mossy base of pond bottom – Arshal wondered what Azren saw. Unmaking, he said. Unmaking of what?

Azren found him late that night on a high veranda that looked out over the star-lit bay where a few ships' lanterns glittered. King Azren's man guarding Arshal grinned companionably at Azren, who returned it with a smile tight and fleet.

"It is hard to take your ease a hunted man," Azren said by way of preamble.

"I haven't my champion's skill at recognizing danger. Am I now in danger?"

"No. You have another disciple. I knew it all along. It is difficult to commit when you know your decision will cost lives. But, as you said, a vendetta directed by Fyraer or Ghyldus cannot help but touch us all. I do fear your goals are loftier than attainable, but I cannot withhold aid so deserved. You may even succeed. What do you ask of us that I have the power to give?"

Arshal gave him a weary smile as he launched into details so conservative, Azren vowed to do more, arranging to speed Arshal to his next destination.

It seemed so easy: two leaders yielded what could have been given without risking the king's life, things that could have been granted through scouts who had come begging again and again. What was it they saw in him? Was it the stone? Was it the reality of a young king?

A few days later, a dozen of Azren's faithful Kingsmen ushered the King in Exile from Ar-Tebez in the dark of night. The journey to the southern tip of Arenh, following the eastern edge of mountains bordering the sea, took them just over a week. Though they traveled without incident, Arshal knew it to be a trek he would never have survived on his own. While rains fed by the Sea of Tebez fell on the western slopes of mountains that fell sharply to the sea, making that stretch of Arenh a verdant garden, east of the range the land lay parched. Most of Arenh's people huddled in the rain forests of the western slopes. The eastern deserts harnessed dew to support the clumps of scrub, the few dwellers husbanding a hardy breed of horses on a range so vast ranchers lived a day's distance from their grazing herds.

Arshal's guides knew where to find water locked in some plant hoarding rare rainfall or in some deep well dug to supply the horses. They warned him from poisonous creatures, and averted the sun sickness that might have felled him. In this land, he realized, Khoti would have been only a companion to die beside.

When at last they arrived at the narrow Strait of Tebez where the cold waters of the Sea of Tebez mingled with the warm and shallow Sea of Simiriel, building afternoon storms that rained out over the rainforest of Detarian, Azren's men prepared to bid farewell to a King of Shande more confidant in his ability to win the people of Ea to his cause. The plan he'd presented to his council back in the Val no longer felt so impossible.

Azren's men led him to a tiny boat, little larger than Nali's, that would carry him among the myriad islands of the Sea of Simiriel. He struggled to absorb instruction in how to use the little square of sail with its removable mast, which stars to mark and warnings that the calm sea he looked upon hid a treacherous face. At last, he stowed the food, water and crude maps marking currents and shoals and bid farewell to Arenh.

While across Shande his agents carried out carefully timed orders that hinged all on one man, one hope for defeating Ghyldus and Minaria, the King of Shande, euphoric in his confidence, set sail, alone, journeying into a barely charted unknown.

The power of Unmaking, Azren had said. It niggled the back of his thoughts. It was too late to ask just what Azren had seen.

# 23: Jali

The groan woke him. His own, Jali Janson realized. He tried to roll, to move his face from the yielding thing that made him retch so that he choked. His hands remained bound behind him by the frayed rope that had hauled him over rock and bramble to this place, ripping the skin and clothing from his body, bruising and battering him, so that his tormentors left him for dead. Too old, too independent, too much a troublemaker. That streak came from his fa, Jan, a famous Gnat officer. A pang of memory for Sihma Harbor struck him. He was so far from home! But not alone.

He tried to rouse the girl still bound at his back by a cord at his waist, near torn through.

"Libria!" he whispered into the dark night. Only the soft sounds of death answered.

He began to tremble, his skin cold, his face hot, wishing he could go back to the long sleep that had kept him ignorant. He tried to squirm from beneath her slight weight. Her head lolled back and forth across his back. He knew where he lay: a pit dug beside a dry stream, the refuse pile of his camp. His captors had dragged other young people from Sihma Harbor here and tossed them aside with the bones of meals and mine tailings. They dumped others as well, youths from strange places he only heard of through covert stories told late at night when the guards thought them sleeping.

Troublemakers like Jali Janson became heroes at night when pupils like Libria Keeper roused themselves to anger at the whispered tales told of a freer time. This camp taught no great wisdom as Libria's father Aron had promised the parents of Sihmad Shal's children. Minarian labor camps taught only death and hatred and broke spirits of youths kept far from places where people might learn of their plight in terrain too inhospitable to support escape. If they cooperated, learned to yield, they might hope to work their way up to some less onerous labor. If they survived. And now dispatches would be sent to Aron Keeper and perhaps even Cookie, relating how their children died consumed by a rampant fever, or some lung ailment, or buried in an avalanche, or in a fall from a precipice.

Libria Keeper died because Jali convinced her to resist learning the new way. Jali died a troublemaker. They made a convincing demonstration when dragged behind a horse along the rocky trail into camp so that all would see the bloody punishment for those who made trouble, who resisted. Yet, he lived.

He tried to rouse Libria again though she felt cold against him. The stench of the pit dulled his senses, made him groggy. Again, he choked and retched, at last squirming upward, the loop of rope that held Libria to him biting into his chest. He crawled, hands still bound behind him, for the clean air he knew awaited above, his skin screaming its torment as knees gripped the stone. He must escape.

A whiff of fresh wind came down at him, carrying the scent of venison over a fire like a far memory of an inn in the Harbor. A distant light flickered between the boughs of pine. Did he imagine it? He lurched forward, his stomach churning at the scent, his mouth watering for the aroma. He slipped and skidded back down into the pit, falling on Libria's yielding body with a gasp. He bellowed pain and frustration into the night, his hunger, to where the small light flickered like a mirage in his vision. He hoped his shout brought Minarians who would at last end this misery.

Dawn remained only a few hours off when Khoti set camp in a dell that seemed secluded enough. He had shot a mountbuck and needed to cure the meat to last him the remainder of his journey. He'd just stretched out strips of jerky to dry beside the flames when he heard a loud cry only a short way off. In an instant, he'd smothered his fire, the scent of needles and dirt and bracken smoldering with an acrid smoke that might still give him away. He unhobbled Fidra and tossed his pack over her back in case a foe outnumbered him and he had to flee. He led her behind him as he cautiously ventured along the edge of a dry stream bed.

A stench grew in degree from the odor of perhaps some dead animal, to an entity that made him gag. His eyes watered as he descended farther into the gorge, sword drawn, blood racing, pumping through his warrior heart.

Fidra snorted and shied from a lump lying in the gloom thrown by scattered trees. Fidra continued to prance at the end of her lead as Khoti lowered his sword. He caught the glimmer of bare human flesh. Fidra refused to step around the body. Khoti didn't have time for this. He needed to assess his danger.

He bent to drag the bound, mostly nude body from his path; no, not one, but two bodies bound together, stretched out like a feast for the ravages of scavengers. He startled when his hands met warmth, a pliant arm beneath the cool burden on top, the sensation of illness and injury rushed his fingers and made his palms itch. His healer's blood raged through his warrior heart. He pushed the body onto its side. Beneath it the slight figure of a boy still breathed, moaning softly as eyes opened to stare at Khoti with fatalistic acceptance.

Khoti unsheathed his dagger. Eyes glittering in the darkness watched him, making no move as he cut the rope that had bound the boy to the dead girl. A few hours remained until dawn reached this valley and Khoti couldn't discern in the darkness the seriousness of the youth's injuries, his age, or tribe. He didn't dare light a fire here, nor did he consider expending his much-needed energies to call on the spirits to mend someone who could be his enemy. Morning would force him under cover to avoid the numerous enemy patrols in this part of the mountains. Khoti had to pick his way through unfamiliar terrain in darkness. He looked up at the peaks above, trying to trace where the boy had come from and the hours before dawn.

He couldn't just leave the youth, injured and helpless, and he desired nothing more than to escape the stench of this place. He dug his blanket from his pack and wrapped the trembling youth in it, then hefted him to his shoulder. The youth gasped, his eyes closing.

He wished he could just ignore this healer's instinct and just move on as he led Fidra back to the small hollow where his fire smoked.

A cool night for the middle days of the heat moon had settled in. He set his burden beside the shallow fire pit he had dug with his sword, and rekindled the flames. As the warming firelight fell on the boy's face, he recognized the build of an older youth of perhaps fifteen, but slight, as one who has suffered a lengthy illness. Clearly not from a southern tribe, the freckled youth sported a shock of red hair and bones pushed at skin as fair as any northerner. Khoti probed the scrapes, burns and bruises in search of broken bones, with no response. When he dripped cold water on the cuts and seeping scrapes, blue eyes flew open to stare at him.

"What do you want?" the boy challenged in a scratchy gasp.

Khoti peered at him. He had an eastern dialect, a familiar lilt. "Only to help you," Khoti said as he bathed wounds with water that made the youth's skin twitch and clench into gooseflesh.

"Why?"

Khoti gave him a quizzical look. "Because you're injured, fool. Why else?"

"You aren't one of them?"

"What, a Minarian?" A snort of disbelief escaped. "Do I look like one? Do you think I'd be tending you or killing you?" He studied the youth as he plucked a second blanket from his pack and wrapped it around the boy's shoulders to help stop his chattering teeth. "How'd this happen?"

The youth looked away, his gaze scanning the small camp. "Where's Libria?" he demanded.

"The girl?" The youth appeared to understand the finality of the question. "What's your name? What're you doing here?" Khoti asked as he examined each wound in the spare light and offered his own name. The youth had only a few cracked ribs, and many scrapes and bruises, not as serious as it could be. Khoti applied the salve he carried in his saddlebags as the youth mumbled his name and home city, just this minor ministration seeming to ease his pain and fear of Khoti, as if merely Khoti's company provided comfort.

Khoti paused in his application of the salve to sit back on his haunches. "So Jali, is Jan the Innkeeper your fa?" Jali tensed, turned away. "Is he?" Khoti insisted.

"Why should I tell you?" Jali's tone turned surly.

"Well, you offered your name," Khoti said with disinterest. "I know a friend of your fa's."

Jali's expression remained wary as he sucked on his cheek.

"It's a long way from Sihma Harbor," Khoti offered when the silence grew uncomfortable, the youth staring into the fire, trying not to flinch as Khoti's hands passed over purple bruises and bloody scrapes.

"I know it," Jali said. "Don't anyone know about us?" He stared back in dismay when Khoti shook his head. "They haul young folk off to labor camps and no one notices?"

"There's labor camps here? For what?"

"Adanan mines, stellan, a little gold and some gems. The older ones do the heavy stuff, diggin', bracin'. The younger haul it up, stoke the furnace, cook, serve the guards."

"Children mining adanan?" Khoti's mouth fell open. The strongest of his tribe didn't do such debilitating work for more than a few weeks at a stretch, leading to the rotation schedule at most of the mines. "How many? Where?" Khoti demanded, leaning close.

Jali sat up and circled his bloody knees with his arms, huddling under Khoti's blankets. Khoti leaned back when he realized how he'd intimidated the youth. He handed Jali a piece of dried venison and his wineskin.

"I do thank you," Jali said as he swallowed the venison. "I thought I was dead. And Libria, I kept hearin' her screamin'. I thought she was dead, but I kept hearin' her screamin'. Tried to rouse her. Didn't do no good."

He accepted more of the wine. The strong vintage from the Arenhian hillsides near where Khoti had left Arshal brought a pinpoint of color into freckled cheeks.

"I don't know how many mines there are. I don't even know where we are, just that it took forever to get here." Jali shrugged. "Daris knows everything. She's so smart. They don't even know she's a troublemaker. She's in my camp, but somehow she passes word to other camps where she has friends. She helps kids in trouble, like me. I always get in trouble. I'm old so they expect it so they catch me when I try to remind the little ones about the way things were, try to tell them not to learn the new way and snitch what we can. Daris is old, like me, but she can get away with stuff 'cause the guards ... like her."

Khoti stared into his hands as Jali spoke. "How many children do you think?"

"I guess maybe a hundred in my camp. Eight or ten camps. We lose a lot and new come in. The pit ... over there," he nodded to where Khoti had found him. "It's full of the dead. Troublemakers like me and Libria, and those killed by cave-ins, or who get crushed or burned real bad. They might live a while but they always get sick and die if they get hurt. They don't treat 'em, just send 'em out to the pit 'cause they know they won't live. They just die there. Sometimes they take away food for a while, or beat us when they think we're resistin'. The new way's we're supposed to just do what we're told. They fill the little ones' heads with all sorts of lies. I can't believe no one's done nothin'!"

Jali seemed to waiting for some outward reaction, but Khoti remained still, staring into the coals of the fire.

"Can't anything be done?" Jali wailed.

Khoti looked up. He felt for Asteria's pendant on the chain around his neck. "What happened to your clothing?" Khoti asked him suddenly.

"It's gone." Jali trembled again despite the wine and fire. "I didn't need it where I was goin'."

Khoti put an instinctive arm around the youth's shoulder to help still chattering teeth. "Can you go back there?"

"For what? I've spent the better part of four months tryin' to find a way out!"

Khoti held up his hand to silence him. Jali's eyes locked on the thatch of scars in Khoti's palm then moved to the brass-colored shackle locked on his wrist.

"Who are you?" Jali whispered. "You don't seem too troubled wanderin' here, armed."

"I told you, name's Khoti. The Minarians call me Verdaen. Doesn't mean much to you, does it?" Khoti said with a grin, leaning back to take a deep drink of wine. He had to project confidence and hide his revulsion at what Jali had told him, and what he hadn't told him. "It's not too wise for me to sit here in mountains crawling with Minarians and tell you my purposes. You'll just have to trust me."

Khoti dug out of his pack a heavy woolen sleeved tunic he'd brought against winter, too large on Jali's shoulders, and breeches too long. Khoti's soft sandals, worn last in the forest of Mershy, were a little large, and flimsy against sharp rocks on the mountains' stony trails. The clothing seemed to return a measure of the youth's confidence. He gazed up at Khoti as if he looked on a hero, the savior for which one might dream.

"But why send me back? Can't you take me with you?"

"Because I need your help." Khoti tried to define his hazy plans to himself so he could explain them to Jali. "Look, your fa's an important man in Sihmad Shal, right? Do you understand any of what he was doing?"

"He's a Gnat," Jali said with pride. "I stood watch for the Gnats, waitin' for the Minarian fleet, pulled a few capers after the occupation, mostly stealin'."

Khoti continued, impatient. "Did you know his derna friend?"

"Commander Nali?" Jali asked.

"I know Nali, and ... the other man he came east with, the King of Shande. What I want's your help. Can you handle that?"

Jali nodded and drew on the wineskin as Khoti explained a plan just emerging in the back of his mind. He packed up Fidra and the dried meat, then again studied Jali's wounds. Already as the color came back to the youth's skin the injuries appeared less severe.

"I've got to get out of here before I'm caught. If it's too risky for you to stay at the camp, at least go back long enough to tell the plan to your friend Daris and hightail it out."

"To go where?"

Khoti paused only a moment. "Tormor Wood. There's a Tachi headman there named Tedwa. Ask for him and tell him I sent you." Khoti removed the leaf clasp Tedwa had given him and clipped it to the collar of Jali's shirt, hoping Jali had the survival skills to get so far.

Jali watched in a silence Khoti knew as disappointment, perhaps even dismay, as Khoti kicked out the fire. He rolled a small bundle of jerky up in a bit of vine to offer the youth some sustenance.

"I hate to leave you like this, Jali, without even a cloak. But it's just too important. I have to hurry so I can get back here." Khoti mounted, pulling Jali up behind him to be dropped off near where Khoti had found him. "Just remember, the full moon of the waning moon, just after the Evenday, I'll be here."

As Khoti rode away in the growing light of morning, he knew Jali stared after him. What went through the youth's head? Had he just consigned the boy to more undeserved suffering? He smelled the spot where he'd discovered Jali, long before he reached it, having forgotten its evil odor. With dawn upon him, he now saw the first of the birds rousing to come to the pit. The wine he'd drunk went sour in his throat when he saw the enormity of something Jali barely mentioned. The pit held the decomposing bodies of more than a dozen children, tossed in with garbage like clothes in the laundry. Some were bones, others bloating. Khoti looked up at the dark birds looping silent against the dawn as he pushed Libria from the path to roll down into the pit.

And he'd sent Jali back.

# 24: Rift

Khoti had barely passed the line of the Staph-el road when he heard the taps heralding his homecoming. With each new valley he entered the stones rapped greetings, their news filling him with pride. Tawnkats, scouts, spies, virtually canvassed the entire mountain range from Staph-el to the Val, from the Ymmenay River to Sefresal. Zopher had expanded the network he and Khoti forged. He grinned to recognize the various traps from which they warned him. Though he felt them watching him, he saw no scouts among the rock and stone of his mountains.

Khoti pushed Fidra faster, wanting to sleep again in a soft bed, and see his mother, Konner, Chati and Tre and his Guard friends. And he wanted to see Asteria, though he knew he shouldn't. Maybe he'd just see her long enough to warn her away from Anlon. Wasn't that the way of shawnsi courtship that others could state why a match shouldn't occur?

When Khoti reached the Val late the next afternoon, he found the Val's folk already waiting to greet him in the summer green beside the lake, eager for news. Mountain folk pressed so close Fidra grew skittish as hands reached to pat his legs in greeting and offer him the sweet delicacies he'd missed from festfires and tell him of missed rites.

Their headman had come home.

Konner hurried out of the caverns, his face fighting with itself to show both happiness, and anxiety to hear Khoti's news.

Khoti grinned down at Konner as he chewed a sweet berry candy. When he looked up to see Eithurdon near the cavern's entry his smile faded.

"Habdelion's with us," Khoti said with a nod of greeting. A collective sigh preceded a buzz of speculation about the king's other likely successes.

"We'll meet in the common," Konner said, holding Fidra for Khoti to dismount.

"In time," Khoti said. "I want to change clothes, bathe—"

Konner's expression held such a serious cast Khoti hesitated only a moment before following his Second to the common.

As they took their seats, Khoti's impatience had him already detailing the things he'd learned of Mershy.

"I'm going to need a few Guardsmen to help me train Han's men. They're even more ignorant than Arshal's folk," Khoti said.

Eithurdon gave him a sharp glance then studied his hands. "You are still my aide, Khoti. You answer to me."

"I've an obligation, promises made by the king to send support. And I stumbled over camps of captive children. Children mining adanan! Children operating furnaces! There's hundreds awaiting me. What possible good can I do here to equal that?"

"We're getting ready to move on Sefresal," Kefta said. "Konner will stay rearguard in the Val. We need you, working either with the Tawnkats or the Guard. You have a responsibility for your people, Khoti. This is your home –"

"My home's Shande, the whole kingdom," Khoti returned. He felt the heat rising in his face. What kind of deception did they contemplate? This went against Arshal's goals. "I have a duty to carry out the king's plans. The Guard has more than a thousand men, young, but trained. Certainly that's enough."

"They brought in reinforcements from Eilime and the Saran River," Eithurdon said. "Someone has convinced the Minarian command the mountains pose a threat to the occupation. Eidhalt have begun asking about the Val and seeking the king. It is well he is gone. They will come for us soon. Word has it the woman Latra was captured."

Eithurdon ignored Khoti's soft hiss through clenched teeth. Khoti scanned the common for Ahrwesz, who returned Khoti's gaze with a fire like his own.

"They know where to find us and are unlikely to send merely a few men in a patrol. They have five hundred effectives in Sefresal alone. That does not include all the men in the mines and on the road and the various patrols and scouts."

"Five hundred?" Khoti allowed himself a low whistle. "Nothing can be done about it. Arshal needs Han and his people to be on schedule. They don't even know how to make weapons, much less use them. They rely for protection on the Tachi, a tribe that may be great archers from the cover of trees, but are no use in open-field battle. There's other Tawnkats who can serve my role in the Guard."

"Are you refusing the order of your duke?" Eithurdon demanded, straightening so that he towered over Khoti. "Do you forget who is your liege lord and commander?"

"Do you?" Khoti returned, a hint of menace creeping into his tone. "You respond to the king. He made promises. I'm not indispensable that you need to jeopardize our plans to have me at your side. For what? To mend you should you take injury?"

Eithurdon started to sputter a denial, but Khoti pushed on.

"What of children slaving in adanan mines? Dying. I'm expected by Evenday of the waning moon. They're counting on me. What difference will one soldier make in a battle? For that matter, three, I only planned to take two men with me."

"When it comes to you, Khoti, one makes a difference," Kefta said. "You've got a way with the men, morale. They like to eat your dust."

"We need tried leaders here or our plans could go awry as well," Eithurdon said.

"With Konner in the Val, you, Kefta and Ytri with the Guard, why can't someone like Segan or Ahrwesz, both able men, lead the Tawnkats? What do you need with more leaders?"

"You are too important to be running around risking yourself," Eithurdon said. "Remember as well, premonitions bode ill for you if you leave again."

"But it's all right for me to leave to do battle in Sefresal? The augury said I wouldn't return is all."

"I need you!"

Khoti shook his head. "I'm supposed to choose between my people, my duke and my king. My role has changed." He pulled a sealed parchment from his medicine pouch and let it drop on the table to roll to the duke's fingers. "The eve before I left, Arshal named me King's Champion and Sword of Shande," he said, watching as Eithurdon's eyebrows shot up as he read. "Signed, witnessed. I wanted to tell you at the right time. Not like this. As you can see, I can't think only of my own. I've got certain duties, such as marshal of the armies of Shande, not just the Guard."

Eithurdon's mouth opened but no words came out. Khoti could see the stunned expressions around the table, only Steadon appeared unsurprised. Chati and Tre stood a little taller at their posts beside the door and Khoti knew he had their trust first. They had not spoken.

"I have to look at where the most need lies, Lord," Khoti said, stressing a courtesy title he seldom used. "Would you defy the king?" Eithurdon's glance stabbed at him. "We have a good operation here. We're organized, trained, armed. Habdelion has a greater need. And if you heard the tale of these youths, you'd wonder how I could send poor Jali, beaten bloody, back to his tormentors to prepare his fellows for my return. You're forcing me to play favorites when we're supposed to unite Shande, all of Shande. You say 'help your people.' I'm Shandean. My people are the Hans and Jalis as much as the Konners and Eithurdons. When I pledged to the Guard, duke, I pledged to you. You're pledged to the king."

Eithurdon's face had reddened. "King's Champion. Sword of Shande. So, I have no authority over my officer anyway, as he can command me."

"I have no armies to lead," Khoti admitted. "I won't if we don't help Mershy. He names me Sword. That's a laugh. Champion, a title, no more. I'm still a Guardsman." He reached up to touch the mark on his neck. "And a Tawnkat. And a Headman of the Lharan Tribes. But why should Han listen to the Duke of Lharan's junior officer? King's Champion, Sword of Shande, he hears. I really wanted to tell you this under other circumstances. I'm needed there, Eithur. An obligation as great as King's Champion I can't ignore, but accepted ... with honor. Hearing his liege lords haggle over whose will has precedence –"

"You have a responsibility here, too –" Eithurdon began.

"Covered by his Second or any number of Tawnkats that can take charge, Duke," Konner interrupted. "Hear him. I don't want to be held as the folk that messed up the king's plans."

The duke nodded. "Perhaps I am selfish, wanting my best with me to take back my city."

The corner of Khoti's mouth rose. "We'll be doing better than that. You'll be with the nation's best, taking back Shande." Khoti stood, giving them a brief nod. "I'd like to see my mother, if you don't mind, and consult with the Lady Asteria after her premonitions and the words of her suitor, Anlon of Mershy."

Eithurdon stood a small scowl on his face. "The former of course. We agreed on the latter."

"That still holds?" Khoti asked, incredulous. "I delivered your words to Anlon. Not many in my position would've left him alive after hearing his response! You won't let me even greet her, give her Anlon's words? I've proven no worth to you? Am I untrustworthy? Or isn't King's Champion good enough to speak with her? What, must I become king to have a word with your daughter even as a friend? Do you put such restraints on Kefta or any others attached to your house?"

"You need not concern yourself with her any longer if Anlon is agreed. This is not open to discussion –"

"Agreed?" Khoti sneered. "Like a rancher judging breeding stock! Instead of someone giving her his heart, you promised her to a man uncertain he wants a woman who couldn't defend her ancestral seat."

"He refused? Then her honor was likely stained by rumor –"

"He agreed. Backhanded. He didn't care about her safety, though he suggested she'd been defiled by Minarians and perhaps that's why you'd sell her so cheap. You worry so about the House of Lharan's honor, yet you defy the king and sell your daughter for position. Admit it. I'm just not good enough for your house. It had nothing to do with Tait. You sought any excuse to keep me here to heal your wounds, plan your battles and bleed for you, but not to sully your bloodline with my low-born mountain roots!" Khoti strode to the doorway. "I'll be taking Chati and Tre with me, mountain-born like me, so no loss to you. I'll be out of your way soon enough, Eithur. I leave my Second to ensure the interests of the Independent Lharan Tribes and the Tawnkats. I have obligations. But don't you forget, I'm the Sword now."

As he stalked from the common, he felt as if he'd ripped his own heart out of himself.

# 25: Broken Promises

Geleg and Zopher stood, heads together, in a deep moon shadow in the pass, hands gesturing as they exchanged whispered news. Suddenly, Geleg gripped Zopher's arm. He jerked his head at an open stretch where the moon slanted down. A dozen mounted figures sat there, drawn swords glaring white.

They had nowhere to run. The patrol closed. One man called for their surrender.

"Certainly!" Geleg bellowed as he swung his sword, two-handed, at the lead rider.

When Geleg's blow shattered the bone of the man's knee, the leader bellowed the order for the others to attack. Zopher and Geleg leaped over rocks, ducked beneath horses and darted into the shadows to baffle their enemy as the horses churned up the sod that had grown in the short summer, mud flinging from hooves as the horses splashed through the narrow stream, their shoes ringing on stone more hollow than the clank of sword on sword.

"Demon!" a Minarian called as Zopher's hood fell back and the moonlight glanced from his face, revealing the birthmark on his temple.

The patrol closed on Zopher, encircling him. Zopher jabbed at any shape that moved, each moment bringing the noose tighter about him. They seemed to have forgotten Geleg, who darted in to strike, then shifted away, hugging the shadows as the patrol spent its efforts subduing Zopher.

Sefresal's dungeons might be survived, but Lagdche? More could be revealed to an interrogator now, and Zopher knew it all; he knew the names and locations of every spy and scout. He knew the king's plan.

Geleg fought with no thought of himself, dervish like a leaf caught in a swirling wind. He couldn't let them take Zopher. A soldier toppled from his horse, Zopher swinging his blade around into the man's face. Geleg drove two others from their mounts, his sword piercing mail to strike the belly of one. As he drove his sword into the neck of another, he barely felt the bite of a blade in his shoulder but to release that hand from its grip. At last, Zopher lost his sword. The remaining Minarians quickly knocked him unconscious and threw him on the horse of a fallen rider, speeding their booty away.

As the echo of hooves faded, Geleg fell to his knees, gasping as he leaned on his sword to avert falling face down in the churned mud. Five Minarians lay dead. A sixth crawled toward the shadow of a boulder. When Geleg caught his breath, he stumbled to the man and, with a merciful thrust, ended his enemy's pain. Then, sitting on the boulder beside the dead Minarian, Geleg let his head fall into his bloody hands. How could they have been so careless? Several minutes more passed before he forced himself to tap the message that the enemy held Zopher.

Khoti found Geleg in the shadow of a boulder hours later. He'd hurried from a campsite a short distance up the pass, racing down the treacherous trail in response to the stones' plea for help. Grim as he tended Geleg's shoulder, he barely spoke, scowling at the wound and responding to Geleg's muttered comments with only a grunt. Already everything unraveled. He should have left for Mershy to meet with Jali long ago. Daily, his mother delivered Asteria's dire premonitions about his fate, and through Kefta the duke assailed him to reconsider his stance on the battle for Sefresal. Khoti didn't need all these distractions. Even after hearing Anlon's remarks – the man not even sending his intended a token or personal message – Eithurdon still kept his daughter like a hostage held until the captor saw how the battle would turn. Khoti couldn't rid his thoughts of her and likely wouldn't until he could head south. Then he'd wasted precious time on Eithurdon's delaying demands, demands that had him halfway down the pass when he heard Geleg's call for aid and not gone to meet Jali. Soon winter would close the mountains. Even if he left today, Khoti doubted he could reach Jali on time. What repercussions would this missed appointment bring?

Now this. He couldn't leave his network to founder leaderless. Zopher mattered too much to leave rotting in some Minarian dungeon.

"What am I going to do, Geleg." He stared into the stream bubbling beside them, the waters wiping away the torn turf where the battle had taken place, washing at a horse's thrown shoe, a discarded knife, and the scuffs where he had dragged away the dead when he arrived. "I've got to get out of here. There's just not enough time. Everyone has all these demands, needs, like I'm the only one with answers."

"Well, y'are Champion."

"Not by choice!"

"Earned. Kefta always wondered what you'd be when you grew into your strength. If it weren't for that shackle, and having hauled you for dead myself, I'd never believe how broken you were just six months ago. You've got more the stuff of a champion than any I know. It's a title deserved." Geleg gazed at the sky. "It'll all work out."

Khoti took a deep breath. "Arshal owes me. As if I don't have enough responsibilities."

"Many taken on yourself."

"Granted," Khoti said with a derisive snort. "We aren't likely to break into the dungeons this time. How long do we have to wait before they move him? Can Zopher withstand the interrogator until then? I hate to even think it, but maybe we could slip him poison. Not as a coward's solution," he added at Geleg's scowl. "But if death's certain, to keep him from revealing what he wouldn't choose to, to do the work of Kishman brandy."

Khoti tied off the bandage on Geleg's shoulder.

"And you're worthless to me now. Go on, head up to the Val and send me Tre and Chati. I want to see if they're really ready for Mershy."

Khoti settled down to wait as another delay drew him closer to failure. What kind of capricious gods gave gifts that wore the spirit from the bearers? His concerns went beyond planning for battles, building armies, his disagreements with Eithurdon and his fear for Arshal. He wondered, too, about Latra. Had she told her interrogator that the House of Lharan dwelt in a vale near Sefresal, near Minaria, and that the House of Dyndevas dwelt here as well? Tait had revealed the location of the Val to Sefresal, but scouts reported Latra's fate had taken her to Minaria where they might be learning for the first time just who resisted in this obscure little valley. He tried to imagine Latra's twinkling eyes as she instructed Asteria in how to snare a man, or when she taught the Val's girls the lore of mountain women. Memory gave him only the look she'd worn that night Tsevon and Eithurdon rescued the Tasch-el captives. Terrified for her child, her eyes swollen and black, her tears for her brother Tegi had raised as a wail into the night. What more could his people take before, like the Lhatans, no Taschians remained?

He leaned against the cold stone of a narrow cleft as the night grew old and the shadows grayed and withered with dawn. He weighed the worn leather pouch Konner had given him, his Second walking him through the contents with the patience of a man who knew he imparted a dying lore. It bore Tsevon's mark and ties from which Khoti's tera sticks now hung. Inside, his fa had kept the herbs and potions of a tribal healer. Khoti fashioned a small cloth bag, no larger than his fingernail, from a bandage in his medicine pouch. When he'd secured a drawstring, he put into it a pinch of several herbs, keeping each separate until inside the bag and ensuring no residue remained on his fingers. When he finished, he carefully wiped off the outside of the bag and washed his hands in the little stream. He prayed this particular healer's potion would never be used.

Torches flapped in the draft when the door wrenched open. Zopher concentrated on the flame to ignore the interrogator's face pressed close to his demanding to know where the upstart leader of the resistance hid.

"You can tell me now, or talk for certain in Lagdche." The man struck Zopher so hard his head cracked against the wall. The interrogator grinned, the expression growing bleary before Zopher's eyes.

"Interrogator!"

The interrogator spun. "Captain Hothur! I –" the man began, but Hothur's fist had already sent him sprawling against Zopher, blood spurting from the interrogator's nose.

"You disobey orders?" Hothur's voice trembled. "It is treason to disobey, Interrogator. I ordered this prisoner left alone –"

"We are told he is tied to the resistance! He is shawnsi, sir!" The man stammered, wiping at his bloody nose as he disentangled himself from Zopher.

"I see his lineage, Interrogator. You take your commands from me. These are my prisoners. Leave, before I have you hung for treason!" Hothur gave the interrogator a parting kick. The man hurried away, still wiping the blood running down his face.

Hothur turned to Zopher, who tried to focus upon the man of whom he had only heard rumor. Zopher knew he could never survive the Minarian interrogator as Khoti had.

He finally managed to bring his eyes together on the Minarian officer. Hothur looked nothing like his voice sounded. Certainly, he dressed as a Minarian captain, his hair hung in long dark braids and a cloak in the colors of Minaria covered his mail coat. His face displayed prominently the strong features and burly height that gave the Minarians a menacing appearance. He didn't wear the medallion, and his hazel-brown eyes didn't carry that fanatical gleam.

Hothur sighed and tipped Zopher's head none-too-gently to the side so he could see the bloody welt where he'd struck the wall. "Can you hear me?" Hothur asked. "Are you alert?" Hothur snapped his fingers beside Zopher's ears, then in front of his eyes.

Zopher nodded, his face screwing itself up with confusion.

"You have a nasty lump. It will heal. The bruises on your face will mend. Others will still know your lineage." Hothur sat back on his haunches and lit a pipe filled with osfothye. He coughed as he puffed, grimacing. "Even Saran osfothye we corrupt. The soil is strained. The plants are worthless. You must know this strain well. Sipheron don Saran died defending it."

He tapped out the pipe on the floor, ignoring Zopher's reaction to first news of his father's death, barely even registering that Hothur knew of him. His fists and teeth clenched. He closed his eyes, wanting to cry his sorrow for his father, to say his apologies for not turning out the way his father had hoped he would, that he'd lost the woman Sipheron had wished to name Daughter. Zopher didn't have that luxury. For all Zopher knew, his father's only offspring would die now, obscure and unknown among the hundreds of shawnsi, thousands, already lost. Hothur waited, watching the curl of smoke as the osfothye burned away to ash. Several minutes passed before Zopher unclenched his fists.

"No informants came forward for a while after your people caught Tait of Eilime," Hothur said, still studying the pipe. "Then we brought in reinforcements. It frightened them just enough. Likely Verdaen told you I have no love for traitors."

As his mind cleared, the lump on his head a dull ache, Zopher noticed the rings of fatigue around Hothur's eyes. The man wore the haggard look of one who had not slept for days.

"I ask you to trust me, don Saran. I know you work with Verdaen. I think it admirable. Foolish, but admirable. I ask you to trust me in a way that will go against everything you know of us." Hothur leaned against the wall a few feet away to stare out the narrow grate above Zopher's head.

"I told Verdaen I hate what our people do here, and I mean it. It is a slur against Minaria, the things this so-called god does! I am an officer because I am a warrior, because I am fit for nothing else but battle." He swept an arm around his dungeons. "Look at that which I am given charge. It is still destroying men. Where is the contest when the challenger is shackled and defenseless?" He snorted, still staring out the small window. "Today, I ordered a man killed. He carried a gift from Verdaen to you." He held out a tiny cloth pouch, dropping it on Zopher's bent knee. "So you would not live to tell all in Lagdche, nor suffer. I know it was a bitter mix for a friend to package. You being a peaceful folk, you probably cannot understand. Verdaen does. The honor of the conquest is lost when the people are oppressed and innocents destroyed. While you may not be as innocent as many sent before Ghyldus, the principle holds. If we merely took the share I thought we sought then your folk might accept our leadership. So, you are a product of that failure, that breach of honor."

Hothur peered at Zopher, then looked around to see if any listened. "I want to help you, don Saran."

Zopher gave him a cynical smile. "Like you helped Khoti? Is this a gift so I can suicide before your interrogator returns, or are you to offer me a position in your army as well?"

Hothur gave him an obligatory smile. "I somehow doubt we would accept shawnsi in our army. Verdaen's treatment was unforgivable. I sent his message in good faith, and perhaps because of it, Ghyldus seeks your king most urgently. Unless, of course, he learned fear from your king's sister, the woman behind the throne of Lagdche, his courtesan."

A blast of ice chilled through Zopher's blood. His entire body knotted. He felt the blood in his palms as his fingernails gouged deep into his flesh.

"That is not what I offer. Nor do I expect you to suicide. I want you to escape."

Zopher sat up, his stomach churning, breaths uneven as he stared at Hothur, searching for deceit in his expression. Did Hothur work to destroy his will by mixing so much evil news with a tidbit of hope? The man's face remained open, clearly distressed by the decision he had made.

"You are going to risk death for me?" Zopher asked.

Hothur snorted his self-contempt. "I suppose that is what I propose. You must name a contact. That is where you must trust me. I promise you they will not be harmed if they leave immediately after I deliver my message. If they return, I will arrest them."

Zopher stared at Hothur. Did Khoti consider him worth such a risk to one of their contacts if he'd sent his gift of death? Or perhaps the poison proved Khoti thought him too important to risk living to be interrogated. What would he face if taken to Lagdche? The mountain people had a strength greater than any people he had known, yet Khoti almost succumbed, and Latra fell prey. He glanced at the pouch resting on his knee. How it must have pained Khoti to send it. Yet Khoti sent poison, not Tawnkats. What had they done to Resala that she hadn't scratched out the evil god's eyes?

"This I promise, Hothur," Zopher said. "If you don't honor your word you'll suffer the worst of deaths. If you're true to what you say you'll be spared when Shande's retaken."

"It is a noble gesture, whether I believe it will come to pass or not," Hothur conceded.

"Find Rathil Hostler," Zopher choked, praying he hadn't doomed the old man.

"Him? He is an informant, a traitor –" Hothur stopped when he saw Zopher's blank gaze.

"That is what you were meant to believe."

"But he gave us –"

"He fed you the lies we asked him to: the names of traitors, plans that would lead your patrols to ambush. He works for us."

Hothur wagged a finger. "Your people are learning, Zopher. Jani was a derna. You have Verdaen. Perhaps we have underestimated you." He stared down at Zopher a long minute, then scooped up the poison pouch and left Zopher to wonder whether he'd doomed another to this same fate.

The three Minarians assigned to escort Zopher to the Saran River for passage to Minaria were loutish oafs. If any of them had a brain beneath his helm, Zopher couldn't detect it. One had become so heavy he couldn't walk more than a few feet and likely would be winded in only a brief parry. If only Eithurdon knew the quality of the Saran reinforcements!

Their zeal and hatred for anything shawnsi gave them an odd power. They claimed to have heard Ghyldus speak and still hung on his prophetic words. Apparently, some spell echoed yet in their ears, something they fed upon like honey. Even their eyes held the enchanted cast of the fanatic. Once they'd left sight of Sefresal, where Hothur had given strict orders on the treatment of the prisoner, they had taken a giddy pleasure in tying Zopher in a manner most likely to break his back.

His guards tied him face up across the wide back of a draft horse, hands and feet bound beneath its large barrel. His head banged against the horse's side, blood rushing to his temples and hands, and his feet and legs had gone numb.

With each step, the horse's jarring gait sent stabs of pain up his spine, making him long for the poison Khoti prepared for him. Every so often the louts urged their mounts to trot, the jolts making Zopher gasp, or even faint to the sound of their giggles. Zopher wondered if he'd live long enough to get even with Hothur.

His captors claimed he possessed magical powers. If he looked at them a knife pressed to his throat. If any noise passed his lips, they tightened the cords binding his feet and hands and snapped the horse's bridle until it reared, jarring down to send fire shooting through him. They refused to give him water but threw it in his face. So, he baked beneath the hot sun of the plains, and shivered, cursing Hothur, as the cool waning moon nights crept into his bones.

On the fourth night of the journey, as a light frost settled into the marshy headwaters of the Quelica River, his escorts left him tied to the horse as punishment for requesting water. In the past camps they had cut him loose to lay in a stupor through the night. The chill night filled him, dizziness and nausea bringing a welcome unconsciousness.

Through a haze he discerned a message from a dream. To think he'd gone so far now to dream in the language of the stones. The dream taps ordered someone to the right, another to the middle. He tried to imagine what operation he supervised in the past that haunted him. None fit the exact instructions because the stones – here in the marshy lowlands sounding almost like the incessant chatter of crickets – seemed to refer to him.

He tried to force his eyes open and overcome the buzzing in his ears. The light of the Minarians' little campfire blinded him before he closed them again. A slight whoosh came from his right, followed by the startled cry as one guard looked down at an arrow protruding from a belly too wide to cover with mail. Zopher wanted to see what transpired, who came to his aid, but the horse beneath him grew nervous, jittery within the confines of her hobbles. The pain slammed against his skull, mingling with shouts as more arrows whooshed by him. He heard the clang of metal over the hum in his ears.

His bonds loosened. He heard a gasp and groan as marshy ground, cold with dew, supported his bruised back. Around him he recognized the voices of his friends giving instructions, cursing, giving him assurances. Everything gave way to the comforting darkness of some herb he tasted on his tongue. He smiled. His trust in Hothur, a Minarian, had been founded.

He let the darkness take him.

Khoti weighed in his palm the small pouch of poison Rathil had carried up the pass on the Hostlers' trudge to a new home in the Val. Hothur wouldn't even let Verdaen bear his full measure of guilt.

"Bring him closer to the fire," Khoti told Chati who dragged Zopher nearer as Tre labored to move the dead toward the marshy ground where the bodies would decompose in only a matter of days. With each body Tre ceremoniously lobbed the medallion far out into the deeper, darker waters of the swamp, then stripped the men of clothing and gear. He tied the Minarian garments into neat bundles to be taken back to the Val with their horses.

Khoti pressed water to Zopher's lips as Chati heated a tin of broth. Then the healer rubbed at the chafe of the shawnsi's raw wrists and ankles and massaged blood back into the limbs.

A harvest moon rose orange and pregnant to the east. As they revived Zopher so he could take more of the broth, only to become sick again and again as they tried to force the life back into the man, Khoti wondered what his delays had cost those awaiting him in the mountains far to the south. What had his broken promise meant to Jali? He should have known there'd be delays, should have returned first and then worried about the timing. He pictured what tragedy it might mean if they stumbled through his plan with no guide to lead them to the safety of

Tormor Wood. How many would die when the first snows came, likely before he could reach them? Though far south in a hotter land, the mountain peaks could still shed winter storms, and warm moist winds would pile snow deeper and more treacherously. What troubles had been wrought by that compassion that cursed him? Children had no place in Arshal's scheme. But Khoti knew Arshal could not have ignored their plight.

Khoti peered into Zopher's feverish eyes. They couldn't let Zopher fall into Ghyldus's hands to reveal plans so painstakingly wrought. They needed him to monitor the scouts, the spies, and trackers necessary to their operation. Besides, he had a feeling Zopher had a role in the pageant of Shande as well, though it gave him a crawling feeling to think of it. He glanced at the poison in his palm then tucked it in his pocket as Zopher's eyes flickered open. Zopher gazed at him – the man who had sent him poison, not a rescue squad – with gratitude. Zopher's features took on the stubborn set of stone.

"They have Resala," Zopher gasped. "I must go to her."

Khoti sighed, knowing that like Zopher's desperate search, he wouldn't be convinced otherwise. So, both would leave. It would be a while before Zopher would regain his health, but maybe Eithurdon could stumble along without them.

At last, Zopher kept the broth in his stomach and Khoti's gentle ministrations gave the shawnsi a little strength. As they packed their gear to bear him home to the Val, Khoti only wondered how he could be trusted to carry out Arshal's plans. What had his delay cost Jali?

# 26: Return to Staph-el

Astone skittered. A silhouette loomed before Ahrwesz, the bulk of the harvest moon behind it. The silhouette dissolved into a recognizable figure as Davin crouched, melting into the darkness outside the Staph-el mine.

"Parently, they don't buy what Sefresal has," Davin whispered as the Tawnkat squad closed in around him to hear his news. "There's only three at the entrance. They got a tiny redoubt up on the ledge above that, but it don't look over the mine, just the road. Segan's set up, so's Teckhan."

Ahrwesz nodded, glancing up the steep bank to study the fortification. From here they could only see one corner of the redoubt. The curve of the mountainside kept the new entrance to the Staph-el mine from view. Only a little to the east the moon lit the giant scar of Khoti's work. Only a few small shrubs and weeds had taken root on the loose slope. That cave-in still sent a slither of stone onto the road when wagons rumbled by.

"Any idea how many inside?" Ahrwesz whispered.

Davin shook his head. "Some Pladde. Couldn't tell for sure."

"So, we won't know what we'll face. We want to work this, not spend half a year digging it out again." He considered a moment, cursing and praising the moonlight. "No word from Velder?"

Davin shrugged.

"We'll have to work it as we see it, then," Ahrwesz muttered, swinging his hand in a wide arc to send his men fanning out to creep up the bank, his determination to avenge Latra a bitter taste in his mouth.

He took note of the bright harvest moon. Somewhere north and east this moon would be shining on Khoti's hoped-for rescue of Zopher. Here, it made the Staph-el road a bright dusty slash lined with the deeper shadows of tree and boulder. To avert raising alarm their timing had to be perfect. With only four

192

dozen men under four commands and whatever Pladde laborers they could find, they hoped to retake and control the mining region hundreds hadn't held. It was a bold, brash, plan so very like the Headman, Tawnkat commander and king's man who had devised it.

Ahrwesz knew Teckhan's squad crept along the lower edge of the redoubt. Segan lurked in the dell to the west where the forges threw an orange glow skyward. Far away, almost beyond reach of the calling stones in the stiff west wind, Velder crept upon the camp and bridge below the Staph-el Falls.

Davin and two others crouched at the edge of the shadows, their faces darkened with charred wood to absorb the moonlight glowing from the road. They set their bows, nocking arrows and holding for the perfect moment when all three sentries moved in range. If any missed his target, the redoubt might be alerted, dooming their entire effort.

Strings tensed, the bow limbs reaching back toward locked arms held ready, muscles straining as the men trained their sights on their targets. The strings hummed as one. A sentry stooped in that crucial second when the other two silently clutched arrows sunk deep in their bodies. Davin had already nocked another arrow, but the man's cry of alarm carried aloft. Minarian heads peeked over the edge of the redoubt.

Ahrwesz swung his arm forward, sending his dozen Tawnkats dashing across the road to the mine entrance, leaving the sentry who had raised the alarm dead in their wake. Showers of stone fell from above, and they heard an occasional clank as Teckhan's men fought the sentries in the redoubt.

Two men ran a short distance up the shaft to extinguish torches. In the darkness, Ahrwesz's squad held their breaths at the cave entrance as they listened for clues to what transpired above. Ahrwesz gripped his sword, wanting to rush to help his friends but knowing he couldn't. A heavy thud made them all jump as a Tawnkat fell from above to land at the mouth of the shaft. Davin sped out to drag the man, still alive, to cover. Already they had botched their mission. What of Segan and Velder? At least two more mines operated in the region. What if a wagon happened upon them right now, or if a Minarian escaped to warn that Tawnkats dared to again prowl the Staph-el Road?

It fell silent, an eerie sound. They tensed as a shower of gravel rained from above. Several bodies flopped to the ground. Ahrwesz smiled to recognize Minarian uniforms.

He tagged two of his men, who rushed out to strip the dead of their clothing and toss away medallions as if they handled soiled swaddling rags. A few moments later Teckhan scrambled down, already donning a Minarian uniform. The helm covered his fair hair, noseguard hiding his fine mountain features, and the cloak concealed the lazy-w tattoo at the base of his neck marking him a Tawnkat. He turned for Ahrwesz's inspection, broad grin cleaving his face.

"That was a little close," he said. "How do I look? Convincing?"

Ahrwesz nodded, reaching for his knife as Teckhan feigned a battle stance.

Teckhan jabbed a thumb toward Davin. "Would'a been nice if you'd sent Davin to warn us," he said. "We were expecting half a dozen. We were outnumbered."

Ahrwesz emitted a low whistle. "Then they are reinforcing."

Teckhan grinned again. "We threw you the spares. We got a full force of Minarian Tawnkats in the redoubt. Now if only Velder and Segan do their part we'll be set."

Ahrwesz singled out two Staphians who made the best Minarians, with their darker hair and larger build, to don the Minarian uniforms.

When dressed, the Staphians stood at the sentry posts as the rest of Ahrwesz's men rolled dead Minarians out of sight down the bank. Now they could turn their attention to the miners laboring deep inside the mountain.

Segan peered from between the sweeping branches of a stately pine as he overlooked the dell beside the Staph-el mine. A handful of sentries watched over two furnaces that roared and shot sparks into the night as men worked the bellows to smelt loads of ore into bars, which they stacked high between piles of slag, wood and charcoal. Others worked a forge and pounded out weapons in a smithy. As he watched, a heavy wagon rolled up and several men loaded it with a mix of metal bars and finished weaponry for the return over the Staph-el Bridge to Lagdche. He had just a dozen Tawnkats to take them all. Segan's men had only the advantage of surprise and he intended to use it.

He positioned his best archers in a semi-circle around the little compound, listening intently to the taps that told him Teckhan and Ahrwesz's squads secured the mine.

Needing a diversion, he pulled out the sling he carried with him to drive off a variety of predators. He wedged a fist-sized stone in the little cup, swung it over his head, then released it so that the rock grazed a horse harnessed to the wagon.

The horse lunged, dragging the team with it. The brake on the wagon held, but as the teamster struggled to control the animals, and as the wagon lurched – skidding on the dusty ground – the sentries and workmen rushed to help. With a slash of his hand, Segan's archers released a fusillade of arrows, finding targets in the torchlight. In those first few chaotic moments, the remaining half dozen Tawnkats rushed across the compound, bursting through the doors of the smithy where the din of the forge concealed their arrival.

Segan and his archers closed, continuing to shoot arrows among the enemy while trying to avoid shooting unarmed Pladde laborers who held out their hands and sat down to await their fate. The sentries wore mail. The shots had to be true and powerful to penetrate the mesh. Though bedeviled by flesh wounds, the Minarians' injuries didn't slow them as they dashed past the dead and injured in the compound and rushed up the slope toward the Tawnkats, who crept downhill with each release of the bowstring.

Segan dropped his bow as a sentry loomed before him. Drawing his sword with the same fluid motion as had flung the rock, Segan swung the sword over his head and let out the shriek of a tawnkat. The sentries hesitated, giving Segan's archers a moment to release their last arrows and draw swords. Only a pause in the sentries' momentum, the enemy again rushed to meet Shandean swordsmen trained by the Lharan Guard's best instructor.

Segan brought his sword down, aiming for the sentry's head. The man tried to dodge, Segan's blow falling on the sentry's shoulder instead. The strength behind the blow drove the man's mail deep into his flesh. Staggering, his foe used his loss of balance to lunge at Segan's unprotected middle. Segan jumped back an instant too late. The heat of blood spread from the slash across his chest. Segan maintained his feet, calling on his mountain-bred stamina to weaken his enemy. Blood seeped downward from the gash as Segan parried, trying to regain his breath. His foe continued on the offensive, each blow deflected, the assault slowing as the Minarian battled uphill on the loose slope, his breaths ripping at the night air. Finally, Segan shifted to the offensive, parrying each thrust with a stronger and faster blow. He drove the sentry downhill. When the Minarian stumbled over a protruding rock, Segan took his moment to end the battle.

He turned to see how his archers fared, fearing more battles when he'd already been injured. He grinned through the sweat running in his eyes. His Tawnkats lounged over the dead sentries, their swords in their scabbards, pantomiming a hearty applause as three surrendered Pladde looked on. He barked an order for them to get on with their business. Besides the sentries, the teamster and ten other laborers lay dead in the compound. Segan cautiously entered the smithy, finding the remainder of the Tawnkats sitting at a table laid ready for the workers' dinner break. Five laborers lay dead on the floor, with no signs of struggle. From his perch near the head of the table, Dagon raised a mug of ale in toast to the success of the Tawnkats, only to watch Segan collapse to the floor.

While Segan's men treated the bloody gash on their leader's chest, and Ahrwesz and his squad used stealth and a mining heritage to whittle away at the Hogde in the mountain's gut, Velder found his task just a bit more difficult. A few taps caught on the wind hinted of the others' successes, and that meant the security of the Staph-el mine now rested on him.

The crux of the Tawnkat's brazen plan lay in working the mines, with the Minarians none-the-wiser. With the help of cooperative Pladde, Segan's men would operate the furnace and forge, Ahrwesz's team work the mine, Teckhan's man the redoubt – all appearing as Minarian as possible. And while they sent inferior goods on to Minaria, as sturdy as wheat before the scythe, they would forge fine weapons for Shande and the Pladde uprising.

But Velder's task involved more than just one target. To build a stock of inferior weapons and other metal goods, give the Tawnkats time to settle into their roles and root out all of the Minarians, once again the bridge over the Ymmenay River must be destroyed, as well as the little redoubt guarding it. Minarian guards in the redoubt would recognize the regular teamsters. And since Velder's squad would now haul the goods to an exchange point just across the bridge, they needed a whole new group of sentries to staff the crossing that wouldn't recognize them. If they held the ruse, the Tawnkat teamsters would know of every Minarian patrol passing and likely even pick up news from the teamsters on the relay. They had a perfect plan, with one minor glitch. The Minarians had sent reinforcements and the entire plan required Velder's success.

Velder studied the bridge, now lit by a ring of torches, constantly replenished. The camp on the Minarian side, for a while only populated by relief sentries, now housed a large squad, the redoubt holding a contingent of a dozen men. Velder's people were dangerously outnumbered.

"It'll be a slaughter," Gelter muttered beside him.

Velder scowled, studying the scene from every angle he could twist his head. A wagon rumbled over the bridge and passed the redoubt, unchecked, taking the road to the mines.

"How long since the last wagon passed?" Velder asked.

"'Bout an hour," Gelter whispered.

Velder stared at Gelter, waiting for the other man to grasp his idea. After a few moments Gelter's face broke into a wide grin. He pointed to a man, and the two scrambled off into the darkness while Velder again peered into the enemy's camp. He tried to judge how many hours of darkness remained. If his end of the plan failed, everything would.

A short time later he heard Gelter's tap and rushed his men to the point around the bend where Gelter had a wagon stopped. The Tawnkats piled in, lying flat in the wagon's bed. One man threw the tarp over the wagon, then pulled the teamster's cloak over his shoulders and pulled a cap down low over his ears. A sharp wind blew in his face; he pulled the hood of the cloak up to hide his fair features and huddled low on the seat.

As the little wagon approached, a sentry peered out a moment then turned back to his business of examining the peaks and shadows.

The wagon crossed the bridge and made for the narrow gap that led to the team exchange, a new teamster prepared to guide the wagon to the river that would carry the goods west to Lagdche. But Velder signed for a stop in the gap, just out of sight and hearing of both the teamsters and the camp beside the Staph-el Falls. The men clambered from the wagon, hurrying from cover to cover as they crept on the camp.

They stalked the smattering of tents awaiting the construction of a sturdy blockhouse. Listening at each tent, the Tawnkats judged the number of sleeping occupants and their relative positions. When each Tawnkat stood over a Minarian, on one signal they lashed out with their knives, ripping through the thin tent. An occasional cry and struggle, muffled by a strong hand, was lost in the roar of the river and the whip of the wind through the gap.

Gathering behind the cover of the tents, they donned the gear of those they had killed. Then, one by one a half dozen drifted through the camp, approaching the bridge where the torches sputtered in the wind and the waterfall's spray rolled at them as a fine mist. Gelter and five men scurried up the road to the gap to dispatch waiting teamsters.

The bridge, built sturdier than ever before, held one flaw that they could see. Time hadn't allowed the proper securing of the logs to the piles with bands of metal and chains. Instead, heavy rope held the tree trunks to the piles and each other, looped through metal pegs driven into the hard rock of each shore. Velder's men kept to the shadows thrown by the torches as the harvest moon of the autumn Evenday at last dropped behind the peaks of lofty mountains to the west. When Gelter and his group returned, the Tawnkats slashed the ropes as they crossed the bridge, darting among the shadows to avoid being spied by the men in the redoubt. They stalked the redoubt, archers already pulling bows from their backs, swordsmen with weapons drawn.

"Hey, you are early to relieve us!" A voice challenged from the redoubt.

"Yes, important meeting," Gelter said in his best attempt at a Minarian accent. Skeptical faces peered over the redoubt.

"Why are your weapons drawn!" another sentry demanded. "Who are you?"

Velder's arrow struck the sentry in the face. Somewhere within the redoubt a sentry winded a horn. No reinforcements remained to answer the alarm.

The Tawnkats darted among the shadows to reach the high ground behind the redoubt as sentries fired through the little arrow loops built into the redoubt's walls. Velder had picked marksmen for his squad. Tawnkat archers shot through the loops, and shouts went up as arrows struck targets within. A handful of sentries burst from the opening at the back of the structure, rushing the Tawnkats.

Khoti and Kefta's patient instruction paid off as the men fought. The Tawnkats noted their positions carefully as they battled, keeping their foes between them and the enemy archers in the redoubt like shields. The enemy found only the rare target. When Tawnkats pivoted or turned suddenly, Minarian archers struck a few of their own. Now the Tawnkats, too, wore light Minarian mail beneath dark cloaks.

Before long, Velder entered the redoubt as his men finished off the remaining Minarians. Velder surveyed wounds, not a fatal injury among them. It seemed too easy.

At last, the tiny squad returned to the bridge. As the logs, requiring the strength of a dozen Tawnkats to push, rolled from the pilings to fall into the river with a splash, the Tawnkats again controlled the road to Staph-el.

# 27: Howl

Jali waited in the shelter of the little dell where Khoti had tended him as the harvest moon rose, heavy and orange, from the side of an eastern mountain, as if a giant lantern pointed them the way home. He barely contained his excitement, his hope, the dream that after so long it would soon be over. Peering into the dark shadows of the valleys leading away from the gorge, he sought the strong savior that had borne him from the pit, his heart leaping at each imaginary shadow his eyes revealed to him. He remembered the way the man's cloak flapped back to reveal sword and dagger, how his smile had assured, how scars and the brassy shackle had marked him a man to be reckoned with, the way a tattoo on his neck gave him the mystique of a warrior. Khoti rode through the mountains, boldly, as if no Minarian could touch him. If any could save them, this mystery would be the man.

After Khoti had left him, Jali returned to the edge of his camp breathless with Khoti's promise.

"What fool are you!" Daris had chastised him when a youth led her to Jali. "They think you're dead, you can escape now!"

But when Jali told her about his savior, her dark eyes glittered with excitement; they worked out the details of a plan. Jali returned to the dell to await the appointed eve, marking each passing day on a branch and each night creeping close to the labor camp where Daris smuggled him the food that kept him alive.

Jali wished he had Daris's knack for knowing just what to do, just as she'd known how best to plan for Khoti's return. Unbeknownst to the Minarians, Daris ruled the nine labor camps of the southern Lharan Mountains. Early in the Minarian conquest a ship's captain had abducted her for his own. While, for her sake, Jali detested the man who captured her, he understood the captain's desire. Merely looking into her dark Joffan eyes made his heart skip. From the first time she smiled that haunting smile of hers, looking up at him from beneath dark lashes, he'd been hers to command.

Her looks gave her power. It twisted him up watching her manipulate her captors with a subtle skill that brought them back for more. Her captain trained her well before a lost wager brought her here, her purpose never any other but to serve the guards' desires. Jali hated watching them leer at her as they rolled dice to see who would win her for the night as if she were some trinket they could buy with their winnings. But those services gained her favors, with which she helped others interred with her. Guards never shackled Daris to her pallet at night. She didn't leave, Jali knew, because of those who remained behind. She could stop an execution or beating, sneak food to those denied it and send word among siblings held in separate camps, her captors ignorant of how she maneuvered them. And now, through Jali, a troublemaker she used to avoid, she had found a way for all to escape with her.

Daris stood with Jali now. From the first narrow valley and stream they traversed, she had been lost. And when the wolvers howled she shivered. Jali moved closer, but didn't dare touch her. He had grown accustomed to the deceiving sounds in the mountains, had met all he could fear, and defeated it. But as the hours passed, and Khoti did not arrive, Jali sagged.

Daris lay a hand on his shoulder. "Maybe he just wanted to give you hope."

"He wouldn't have."

"How do you know?"

"I just do." He stared into the darkness. They risked too much staying in the open so long. Patrols might pass, and the full moon overhead threw a light like day in the valley bottoms. "Somethin' must've happened." He gazed at her. "What now? We don't know how to get to the forest, much less try to lead everyone. We got nothin' to feed 'em. We got no weapons, nothin'!" Jali sat hard on a fallen tree, dropping his head into his hands. "I'm so sorry, Daris. Who knows what you did to arrange all this. And I failed you."

"Why would you care what I've done?" she asked. Jali didn't answer. She took a deep breath. "Look, we had everyone set for two nights from now. We've got a lot of messages to deliver. If someone follows through and there's no one to lead them ..." She didn't need to finish; Jali knew the scenario. He continued to wait, his face buried in his hands. He knew she doubted his faith in Khoti. For all she knew, Khoti might have been some image Jali dreamt in his delirium. The clothing Jali wore, the tended wounds, all could be explained away without the tale of an avenging warrior come to save them. Even Jali himself began to wonder if it had all been in his imagination, that some vagabond fleeing the Minarians had taken pity on him.

When the moon sank behind the mountains, Daris sighed.

"I'm sorry, Jali. But no one's going to trouble themselves with us. I do have to be sure we get out word that the plans have changed. And what do we do with you? You can't live here anymore with winter coming and you without cloak or blanket. There's nothing I can do. You're too old to slip into a different camp. If you're seen they'll kill you on sight."

He didn't reply. At last, she disengaged herself from her patient pose leaning against a pine. She held her hand out to him. He looked up, finding in her expression something alien from the face she used to help the children she took under her charge. Without the moonlight her dark complexion had fallen into shadow, but that excited glitter in her eyes was gone

"I'm sorry I gave you false hope," he said, letting her pull him to his feet. With only an occasional backward glance, Jali led her back to the camp.

While Daris sent her frenzied messages ordering the other camps to halt their plans, Jali brooded. Waiting these two months so certain Khoti would return and Daris would know everything else that must be done, he never bothered to explore his freedom. Khoti told him if threatened he could seek safety in Tormor Wood. He knew Tormor Wood lay east of the mountains. But where?

He wandered from the dell, struggling ever eastward, finding the soft pine path would open suddenly into treacherous gorges and steep mountain faces. He had no plan but to point himself east. Maybe he could find Tormor Wood, and this Tedwa fellow Khoti spoke of could devise a new scheme for their rescue. But beneath the eaves of the mountain forest, he often turned himself hopelessly around as he sought a break in the trees to locate the sun. If the skies became overcast, or worse yet, if patrols forced him to travel in the dark, what then? The stars meant nothing to him but folk tales.

He walked for two days, learning only that climbing the steep valley sides and stepping over the debris of decades of windfall required more than the measly store of food Daris smuggled to him. The snow-covered peaks gave no sign of the eastern plains of which Khoti spoke, much less the leafy forest waiting there. Besides, he had no idea how to forage for unknown foods in a journey that might take him from the mountains far north or south of the great forest.

So, with an even heavier heart and empty belly, he turned around and headed back to the world Daris ruled, a place only the dead escaped.

As evening approached, eight of the labor camps nursed their sorrows at the cancellation of their plans. At the farthest outpost near the small lake at the headwaters of the Ymmenay River, the ninth labor camp – called Howl because of the way the wolvers' cries echoed among the peaks and valleys – finalized plans. The youths of Howl followed to the letter the only orders they had received. Euphoric, they felt certain that in the two days since the harvest moon rose, a warrior had arrived to lead them home. They peered out beyond the torch-lit ring of the compound, expecting to catch some glimpse of the savior who would guide them through the maze of valleys to safety.

They had no weapons. But they refined to the least detail the schemes Daris had relayed to them. They sharpened sticks to points as deadly as knives. They had secreted away food for several days into little bundles that could be swiftly rolled in their blankets. Each child prepared to act before guards fastened the shackles to pins by their bedrolls.

When darkness fell, the shifts working the mines changed. After the long trudge through the dusty shafts, the youths from the day shift fidgeted through their evening meal and went to their beds, clutching sharpened sticks to their chests. As the night shift marched to their work, a few pulled from the folds of their clothing bundles of tinder they deposited beside each mine brace they passed. Camp girls serving the Minarians hid stakes in the folds of their skirts as they went to the guards' beds. Children preparing meals set large fires beneath pots of boiling water. Others wandered among the youngest, giving them hope, making sure they understood exactly what they must do.

Kia Renali tucked her younger sister Rena in an unfamiliar bed, leaving Cydwyn, the oldest boy in their tent, to take Rena's, the first pallet in the row to be shackled at night.

As she waited for the appointed time, Kia taunted herself with her golden dream images. At eight, she still remembered the life four-year-old Rena had already mostly forgotten. Though sometimes Kia couldn't remember the particulars of which things she wished and what she knew had really existed, she knew she'd lived a better life in the cottage by the sea. Now she pulled out her favorite dream of a city glimmering in the distance, a white-washed town snuggling against an amethyst sea where the statue of Maura held out her hands to offer safety. That golden image always brought with it the aroma of bread baking and the comfortable scent of her father fresh with the ocean wind. Laughter filled the tiny house, her twin brother Bertal giggling at some clever prank, and the cry of gulls overhead punctuated the sleepy sound of waves lapping against the boardwalk. The Minarians hadn't yet dulled that dream with their lies. They told the daughters of Nali their parents sent them here for punishment. Kia didn't even have to close her eyes to recall her mother's body twisting in the wind, or the way they tossed Nalel aside. Because she did still remember life before their flight to the west, Kia often reminded Rena of what they had lost before her despair erased them. Her fa's stubborn streak in her allied her to the camp's troublemakers from the start. Kia didn't know why her father had never come for her, but she knew he had to be somewhere, waiting, and she and Rena would escape to find him and Bertal, and the four of them would live in that golden world on that distant sea.

So, as Kia tucked Rena beneath the thin blanket and double-checked the little bundle the younger girl would carry, she could barely contain her excitement. She could almost taste the bread baking in that far away oven.

Cydwyn clucked his tongue. The children scurried to their beds and ducked under their blankets, fingering the points of the stakes they held.

The tent flap opened. The thump of boots struck the wooden floor as the nightman held up his lantern to see all the beds occupied. As he began to fasten Cydwyn's shackle, Kia, in the next bed, moaned, clutching her stomach. She lurched up in bed.

The Minarian straightened, peering at Kia who continued to groan and cry in giant gasps. He held up his lantern to light her damp face and stepped around Cydwyn to approach her. As he bent to pull her hands from her belly, Cydwyn leaped up and stabbed his stake into the Minarian's lower back, twisting the weapon.

Kia and the others darted from their beds to help Cydwyn subdue the man who bellowed so loud the wolvers in the mountain peaks had to hear him. Kia stabbed upward and away with the strength of months stacking adanan bars and stoking forge fires. Her stake pierced the man's throat and ripped a chunk of flesh away. A splatter of blood cascaded down his neck and across the children stuffing blankets in his face to muffle his calls for help.

Kia froze. The blood from his wound covered her hands and reddened the stake she still held.

"C'mon!" Cydwyn hissed, yanking her arm so she almost fell in the blood slicking the floor.

Kia shook off his grasp, wrapping her bundle in her bloody blanket and grabbing Rena's hand. The youths scurried from the tent.

The night man's screams raised the alarm. Already the compound had turned chaotic. As Minarians rushed from their tents, youths posted at the cookfires threw mugs of boiling water while others tossed brands on the tents. The youths scattered as Minarians struggled to escape the burning tents.

The alarm propelled a dozen guards down the mine shaft where the glow of burning braces flared. Kia paused in her flight to look back at the mine where the twenty-five youths inside would now be faced by angry guards. They should have been out by now, helping the children in the compound. A puff of smoke exhaled from the shaft, then a rumble shook the ground and a billow of dust roiled from the mouth of the shaft, children and their guards buried together.

"C'mon, Kia!" Cydwyn hissed at her, pulling Rena's arm to get Kia's attention. They had only reached the shadowy edge of the compound when they should be meeting on the dark shores of Howl Lake already. The remaining Minarians recovered their wits before the children in the compound. Far out of range of the boiling water and sharpened stakes, they picked off the remaining youths with arrows, one by one. Counting on the pick-bearing youths trapped in the mine, those in the compound had no defense, and no way to reach the safety of the dark camp perimeter. At last Kia let Cydwyn drag her and Rena away.

In less than half an hour Howl had burned away to nothing. The mountain buried twenty-five youths within the mine along with fourteen Minarians. In the compound, a mere half-dozen Minarians from a squad of twenty counted the dead. Of the ninety-seven children of Howl, only thirty-five had escaped, most of them young and with no idea in which direction lay safety.

When Jali crept to the edge of Daris's camp a day-and-a-half later, Daris herself came bearing the stale biscuits and moldy cheese he needed to stay alive. A sharp wind whistled up the valley, tossing the tops of the pines with a mournful wail. A line of gray clouds crowded into the range. He shivered, wondering how long food would be enough to keep him alive.

She watched him silently as he stuffed a hard biscuit into his mouth to quench the growls of hunger.

"Word didn't get to Howl," she said as he washed down the biscuit from the rivulet running down the rock face behind them.

Jali turned to peer at her, his mouth dropping open. "So, they're all waitin' by Howl Lake for a man that hasn't come," he whispered.

"And likely about to starve." She gestured at the line of clouds. "The weather's turning. Can you find your way to Howl? You've got to do something, Jali."

Her gaze accused.

"I s'pose I have to," he mumbled, a knot in his stomach. Why hadn't Khoti kept his promise? He rubbed water-chilled hands together, trying to stop a shiver.

Daris pressed a bundle of food into his hands, barely enough to get him to Howl, much less back. From the waistband of her skirt, she pulled a tattered blanket. Jali stared at it, knowing another must have died. "North and west, that's all I know," she said. "If you find the big river, really big, that's the Ymmenay River, you're too far north. If you don't, you're too far south."

They both gazed at the rolling line of clouds moving at them. He'd lose direction without the sun. He merely nodded and pulled the tattered, sour-smelling blanket over his shoulders. He had to do something to fix the trouble he had caused.

Instinct told him little streams would lead him to the great river emptying the mountains. He scrambled along the sometimes marshy, often stony, valleys taking him in his intended direction. Now and then the mountains threw up huge scarps he couldn't descend, though the streams stumbled over them in a rumble of waterfall. He spent hours scrambling up valley sides to go around then descend again by clinging to pines that somehow grew straight up on these steep slopes. If nature hadn't set enough barricades, he had to skirt two of the camps, dodge several patrols plying the valleys and stay well clear of the paths the Minarians used to haul away their metals. The cold of early winter worked on his stamina, as did the growl of predators he knew stalked him each night.

He tried to ration the scraps of food Daris had given him, but already he felt light-headed with hunger as he expended his energy. He cursed the mountbucks he startled, remembering the savory venison Khoti gave him. He could no more bring down a mountbuck or even a groundrat with his bare hands than he could fight off a Minarian patrol.

He fought his way through the mountains for two days before he found the Ymmenay River. Here merely a large stream, it dropped from a falls hundreds of paces high. It took him another half day to find a way to the top of the falls to follow the infant river to its source at Howl Lake. He didn't dare think what he'd find.

It took all of the woodcraft his father taught him to read the small signs beside Howl Lake. From the cover of the forest he could see where horses had crisscrossed the length of shore. In a few places tiny footprints remained undisturbed. He tried to follow them, losing the trail when it passed deeper into the pines, the needles cushioning the ground from any mark. He glared at the ground, seeking the displaced needles scuffed into a pile here or there. He hoped he didn't follow the trail of some small animal digging for seeds or insects.

While peering at one of the minute little signs, he heard a twig snap. He straightened. A dour-faced boy his own age stood before him, stake in hand. The youth stood a protective step in front of a young girl bearing a stout branch. He stared; he knew her. He tried to recall the features of a child who might have gone to school with him or played in the streets of the Harbor.

"Kia!" he exclaimed when the name popped into his head. He couldn't believe he recognized her. Only a bit more than a year had passed, but her once-fleshy face had become pinched, her brown hair a matted tangle of sticks and mud. But she had Nali's eyes, and even his familiar dour expression. The boy beside her lowered his stake a little.

"Do you know him?" the boy asked in a wary tone that doubted coincidence. As if it couldn't be coincidence. At least five Harbor children had been in Jali's own camp at one time or another, and several Keeper children, minus one.

Kia, still clutching the branch in white-knuckled hands, took a step closer, peering up into Jali's face. "Maybe," she said in a trembling voice. "Cydwyn, remember my dream harbor –"

"Sihma Harbor," Jali said. "Remember? Your fa and mine are friends. You came to our inn on the boardwalk."

Kia nodded, brightening a little with a small, shy lift of one corner of her mouth. "Jali. You always teased me."

Jali grinned, but it faded fast. "I came to help. We tried to get word that the plan fell through. Where is everyone? I saw horse tracks all around the lake."

"Mostly dead," Cydwyn said, his expression a mask as he tucked the sharpened stake in his belt and eased the branch from Kia's fingers. "There's about three dozen as got away. Do you have food? Anything? We've got almost nothing left. The ones that made it were the youngest and it's hard to convince them not to eat it all."

"I don't know what to tell you. I'm here to lead you out. Not that I'm any expert, but I couldn't just leave you here waitin'. I got nothin' to hunt with. Sure, there's plenty of game, but no way to bring it down. It'll take about five days to get to the point as far east as I've been."

Cydwyn broke a twig from a branch, breaking it between his fingers again and again until it became tiny fragments. "Well, we got a little," he said. "Some fish, and Kia knows the safe mushrooms. Like I said, these are the youngest. All the older ones were set up in the compound. I only escaped 'cause I was s'posed to take out the nightman. Kia here's next oldest. Most are five or six."

A lump formed in Jali's throat, making it hard to breathe. The plan would have had the older youths carrying the youngsters when they tired and keeping them from wandering away. To lead so many little ones so far with only the three of them? Kia herself barely met a responsible age.

"Collect all you can," Jali said. "We'll set out when we've got food for five days."

When night fell, they used their blankets and the bits of string securing their bundles to fashion a net to drag the bottom of the lake, as often bringing up nothing as anything. As the night grew old, they collected the fish, shellfish and edible greens they thought might hold them five days. Kia searched the woods for late mushrooms and wild onions, her faint memories of working beside her father provided the expertise to clean and dry the fish.

They departed with the first streaks of dawn no more secure than before Jali arrived, but at least now they had a goal, symbolized by the small dark leaf pinned to Jali's collar.

Jali took them back the way he came because he remembered the route. Yet as he plodded along at a pace to match the shorter legs of the youngest children, he knew he attempted the impossible. Likely this plan wouldn't have worked even if Khoti arrived as scheduled.

Between their slow pace and the frequent stops for tired children, it took them several days more than anticipated. Their food would never have lasted if they hadn't come across an old bugledoe brought down by a pack of wolvers. They drove the predators off, sheer numbers and the racket they made, not any ability to harm the beasts, allowing them to steal the quarry. They had no knife with which to cut the age-toughened and horse-like animal into manageable chunks, but with sharpened stakes they crudely cut through the tough old hide and salvaged a large portion. Much remained for the pale-eyed wolvers circling and howling a stone's throw away. The beasts' whines wrung like the hunger in the children's bellies. When they went on, each child cradled a few pounds of meat while Jali searched ahead for a safe place to light a fire.

A ring of expectant faces watched in fascination as a few youths who barely remembered the things their parents had taught them fumbled through an ancient process to cure the meat to jerky. They had no salt or brine, but Jali knew the dried meat would be gone before it could spoil. The two older boys then rolled the lighter store of meat up in their blankets to prevent the rampant snitching that depleted their supplies. They guarded their treasure with more vigilance than a miser guarded his stells.

When Jali thought he could goad the children no further, nor take another day of keeping his eyes both on the trail and the stragglers that kept Cydwyn running in circles, Jali at last reached the sheltered little dell where he had awaited Khoti. He saw no sign anyone had passed this way since he and Daris had waited late into the night for nothing. Jali left a mark anyway, in the event some miracle brought Khoti in search of them. He remembered the small tattoo, slightly marred by some past injury, at the base of Khoti's neck. Using a sharp stone and a pointed stick to pick away at the bark, Jali carved the symbol on a tree, pointing east, and beneath it marked their number.

He left Cydwyn and Kia to dole out a little more of the jerky as he hurried to the camp to find Daris.

"Promise you'll go to the dell every day and watch for Khoti's return," he told her when she met him at the little rivulet outside camp.

"No great warrior is coming for us, Jali," she said, that glow missing from her cheeks, something vacant in her dark eyes.

"He'll come. He promised. I'm not leaving these mountains without your word you'll watch for him. All those young ones from Howl will freeze an' starve just 'cause you're too –"

"I'll do it," she retorted, then smiled at him with that haunting smile. He found something different in it. He didn't know what. Maybe she hadn't forgiven him for dashing her hopes like that. Maybe it just felt warmer.

"Daris, the plan wouldn't have worked anyway," he said.

She nodded as if she had realized it long ago and already carried the burden, her gaze locked on the carved wooden leaf Jali wore at his collar. A cold wind snapped her hair around her. Without thinking he brushed a hair from her face. She didn't react.

"He'll come," Jali promised.

She didn't look up at him as he retreated down the path to the dell to again goad on his ever-hungry, ever-weary charges.

When they crested a small pass at the shoulders of two low peaks a half day beyond the farthest point east Jali had traveled, he stopped in shock. The mountains continued, but in the distance he saw that they ended abruptly; only low barren hills marched away into the flatness of plains. On the very edge of the horizon he discerned the dark line of what must be Tormor Wood. He glanced at Kia and Cydwyn, wondering how long they would have waited if he'd gone just another half day more on his empty stomach. He hefted the fast-emptying bundle of jerky he carried on his back. He wouldn't think about it.

With the dark line set as a goal, they plunged down into the next valley, speeding their pace as if nearing home.

When at last they reached the last little foothill and gazed down onto the road that ran along the edge of the mountains, Jali found his euphoria premature. The dark line of forest stretched the length of road as far as they could see. In that vast tangle of wood he had to find one man.

They still had to cross the road and reach the cover of forest. Traffic on the road reminded Jali of market day in Sihmad Shal.

210

Carts laden with metals, farm and forest products rumbled by, as did the scattered traffic of locals and Minarian patrols.

They waited until dark, Jali, Cydwyn and Kia dividing their charges into pairs to dash across the road to throw themselves flat in the scrub and grasses of the opposite side until all had crossed. Several times they had to wait as a wagon lumbered by, or a lone horseman or patrol neared. As always, their hearts stopped when some child or other chattered or tripped or cried as a rider passed within a pace of them.

The sense that they made the last dash to safety sped them through the dense grass and shrubs east of the road. Chewing their jerky ration as they trotted, the children tripped over the stumps of trees, or became tangled among branches left behind when loggers harvested the forest edge long ago, leaving behind an obstacle course for short legs and tired feet.

When the deep shadows of the forest closed around them, many of the children expected a break, thinking they'd reached their only goal. Jali pushed them on, not really certain where he went but wanting to be far enough into the confines of the forest to avoid drawing Minarians to their light. Khoti had said he only needed to light a fire and the tribes of these parts would miraculously appear. Wandering deep into the tangle, they at last reached a sluggish stream where the children fell to the ground, rolling up in their grimy blankets as they chewed another piece of precious jerky. Jali gathered leaves and after a few attempts with the flint Cydwyn had purloined from the camp, managed to start a fire. The fire lulled the young ones to sleep with its sense of safety and soon only Jali and Cydwyn tended the blaze, awaiting another of Khoti's promised miracles.

Jali refused to dismiss everything Khoti had told him just because he missed their meeting. Anything could have delayed him, including death. A man like Khoti just wouldn't fill him up with dreams and send him back to die.

The first traces of morning already softened the forest shadows before Jali nudged Cydwyn from his doze beside him. Cydwyn looked up bleary eyed, then sat up quickly. A ring of faces peered at them from the cover of the trees. Arrows pointed at them; sinewy arms raised spears aloft. Jali remained calm, pointing at the leaf on his collar.

A man approached, his spear held out before him as he entered the small ring of light the dying fire threw. Squatting opposite Jali, he peered around him, then startled to discover sleeping children.

"What you want?" the man asked without challenge.

"Help," Jali said. "A warrior named Khoti sent me here to find Tedwa of the Tachi." He again pointed at the leaf pin.

The man's eyes closed to small slits as he measured Jali. "We are Tachi." He jabbed a thumb at himself. "I am Ledak. Tedwa is my uncle." He jabbed his spear toward Jali. "You know Khoti?"

Jali nodded, daring to hope Khoti might yet show up to lead Daris and the others to freedom. "He was s'posed to bring us here, but he never showed up." Jali gestured at the sleeping children, catching the glint of Kia's eyes staring back at him. "This is what's left of a labor camp of one hundred children."

Ledak scanned the campsite, his glance soft as he counted. "You came from where?"

"A camp at the headwaters of the Ymmenay River."

Ledak shook his head. He lowered his spear, letting it rest across his knees as he continued to squat before Jali. "Tedwa is far away. He expects Khoti's return. That he delays is no good sign." Ledak glanced again at the children then gave a curt gesture. His men lowered their weapons.

Cydwyn exhaled.

"Khoti promised help, not more burdens," Ledak grumbled.

Cydwyn dug into his pack to produce what made the children's bundles so heavy long after they'd eaten the food. He held up one of the metal bars smelted in the labor camps to be transported to smithies in the plains of Mershy.

Ledak took the bar, hefting it in his hands. "Adanan," he said in disbelief.

"And stellan," Cydwyn said, pulling another bar from his pack.

"There was s'posed to be more," Jali mumbled, suddenly feeling intensely weary. "To make weapons for the army he said you're buildin'." Guilt for every child that died at Howl reddened his face. He'd been hungry for this place so long. His victory tasted sour.

Kia untangled her blanket and came to stand beside Jali and Cydwyn. One grimy hand rested on Cydwyn's shoulder.

"What're you going to do to us?" she demanded, not in the plaintive voice of the child she appeared.

In a fluid motion, Ledak stood, staring down into Kia's unnerving gaze. "Wake them." He barked the order as if addressing soldiers. "We take you to Habdelion." With a sharp gesture, his men entered the camp, each hoisting the smallest of the sleeping children to their backs. Kia wouldn't let them touch

Rena. Cydwyn passed Kia his pack and carried the youngest child himself.

The children flourished on the two days' journey to Habdelion. The Tachi supplied them with fruits and game, and frequent rests between easy marches. Ledak couldn't ask them to be silent, their laughter carrying up into the trees as they cavorted and teased and questioned the Tachi about each strange sight they came upon.

Only Jali remained glum. Eight camps remained and all would suffer for Howl's rebellion. Jali's burden grew heavier with his every step, worming down into him where it sapped his great store of humor, a burden as heavy as all the adanan they bore.

Habdelion forced himself to look up from the bars of adanan and stellan at his feet to view the four bedraggled children before him. Emaciated, shackles still on their ankles and wearing eerily adult expressions, they made his gut ache. What had he done? Only a few days distant hundreds more labored at work that bent grown men. And he had done nothing. No wonder the king's words had carried such bitterness.

The youngest, Rena, still wore tear streaks on her face.

"Please forgive my lifemate's outburst," Habdelion mumbled to the children. They gazed back at him. His daughter, Habda, ushered a group of children past the window on their way to bathtubs set up in a glade beside the house. "Since the birth of my daughter her emotions have always been ... inappropriate for the situation."

Anlon had led the duchess away after she'd gone into a shrieking hysteria of laughter at the sight of the tattered children. Many of the youngsters cried, the eldest three staring at her with their stony gazes. Of all the random emotions in her repertoire, why couldn't she have at least chosen tears, or anger?

The red-headed leader, Jali, shrugged.

Kia's gaze haunted him most. She clung to the hand of little Rena, who generally seemed untroubled by anything that happened to her. That, too, terrified the duke.

"I had no idea."

"Khoti said the same," Jali said. "No one knows. The little ones get hauled off and no one even cares."

"We do care," Habdelion protested. "We did not know where you were. I hear of plantations near Shela, osfothye farms in the north, lumbering interests. All hearsay. We – we failed you."

"What're you going to do to us?" Kia demanded, echoing the question Ledak said she'd asked of the Tachi.

"Do to you?" Habdelion gave her a kind smile. "The question is more likely what we will do for you: find you food, shelter." Nothing changed in her challenging gaze. "Did you know your father is a very important man?" Habdelion nodded when her expression became wary. "Last I heard your father and brother were working hard to win back your home." He clapped his hands. A servant appeared. "Treat these two as due the offspring of heads of state," he said as the servant led Kia and Rena away. The gaze Kia threw back over her shoulder remained stony. He couldn't placate them with sweets and sweet talk. What had Shande lost?

Habdelion studied Jali and Cydwyn. "So, your father is no minor figure in Shande's future either," Habdelion said to Jali. Looking at them pricked something deep inside him. Were these children his conscience?

"He's a Harbor Gnat, nothin' spectacular." Jali reddened.

"There is modesty. So, after all, I am thrown into the politics of the north through the children of the king's supporters." He nodded at Cydwyn. "So, Cyd Lockman, what role does your father play in this war? A captain? An advisor?" Habdelion didn't mean his bitterness to carry into his words. The look Cydwyn threw him before gazing down at his feet stung like sand in the eyes.

"Fa worked the Etaleah locks up around Iyrafael. He died defendin' 'em. Mam, too." Cydwyn looked up as if to challenge a duke to find fault in that.

"So you bring me metals for the weapons I do not know how to use, sent by a man who promised to build me an army but sends me instead little burdens, and here I am, stuck. I cannot send you away when we have no place safe for you to go. All I can do is offer you the hospitality of my house until Shande's fortunes turn and you can go home to what is left." Habdelion studied rail thin and ragged youths. Jali appeared on the verge of collapsing. "As strong as you are, perhaps there is a service you might like to provide for your keep."

Both boys peered at him with suspicion, straightening – did Cydwyn touch a stake in his belt? – as if he had euphemistically described the labor camps. Habdelion held up a hand. "Khoti

214

was to build me an army to fight the Minarians. We will need apprentices, young men to serve soldiers."

Both boys nodded eagerly, their faces set with a brutal desire. Habdelion let out a long breath.

"But you say our champion is delayed."

"Champion?" Jali asked.

"Khoti did not share all his titles? I suppose in his way the marshal of Shande's armies is a modest man." Habdelion chuckled as Jali's blue eyes widened. "It is good you look nothing like a Minarian, Jali. In the dead of night, in a hostile land, you met the King's Champion, the Sword of Shande, and lived to complain about his punctuality. It is ridiculous to pin so many hopes on one man! Look what happened to you! Whatever the folly that is what we did. He promised to train us for battle. If he fails to show, we too will fail. When did you last see him?"

"The twelfth day of the full moon after the heat moon. He was s'posed to be back three weeks ago, on Evenday."

Habdelion stroked his chin as he calculated the distance to Sefresal. "Perhaps you missed him by a day or two."

Jali shook his head. "I was back again near two weeks later. No sign. Duke, what about the rest of the camps?"

Habdelion stared out the window into the dimness of the forest. "At least we can put these to good use," he nudged an adanan bar with his toe. "It would be nice if we knew what to do with them when we have them."

"Can't you do somethin' for 'em? It's not fair. They're probably being punished for what happened at Howl."

"Jali, it is not your fault he did not come."

"It isn't fair."

"We will do something. Maybe Khoti has already freed them. Think of that."

Habdelion turned back to the window, and motioned for a servant to find the boys a room. He didn't look up. What about the children still waiting? How many were thrown out for dead with each day that passed? What future could any land have without youth to give it spirit? He tried to picture how his own children might have dealt with the Lharan labor camps. He knew it ridiculous to consider. Habda was shawnsi, Anlon too old. If captured, they would be killed, likely the more merciful sentence.

But he would make warriors out of the survivors.

# 28: The Road to Tormor

A strangled cry ripped the silence of mountain autumn, startling birds up from trees an instant before something struck Khoti's arm with a tug and a sting. Khoti whipped around to discover an Eidhalt on the ledge above and behind them, clutching an arrow in his chest. Even as Khoti grabbed for his bow, the Eidhalt tumbled from the ledge. Khoti put a hand on his upper arm. The arrow only grazed him. Tre already ran to check the body, while Chati, bow drawn, surveyed the ledges around them for other enemies.

"Whose arrow slew him?" Khoti demanded as he dismounted to lead Fidra from the open trail.

"I'd say hers," Chati said, pointing to a ledge above and behind them. Khoti froze at the sight of Asteria replacing a second arrow in her quiver as she clambered down from a ledge to retrieve her horse. "Perhaps this proves her premonition?"

Khoti glared at him. "I'm already late. I don't need these delays!"

Asteria galloped to them on Clanna, a spirited gray among her father's favorites.

"What're you doing!" he demanded when she dropped to the ground before him.

"Hello to you, too. You are welcome. I am fine, thank you."

Chati snickered, turning to hide his face from Khoti's blistering gaze.

"I don't have time to haul you back to the Val. He'll hunt us –"

"Oh, you are so dramatic. He will not hunt us. There is a war to wage," she replied. "He will blame me."

"He'll accuse me of luring you."

"Why should you care! You are more than a Lharan officer now!"

"You'll be considered an unsuitable match for Anlon of Mershy." His tone burned caustic.

"I do not want him!"

"Well, that's where we're going." They glared at one another their breathing ragged.

Chati reddened, an awkward witness

"See, my premonition was correct again," she said. "You would be dead. See? I can take care of myself, Champion. I do not need a father or his officers to design my life for me. I am here to help. I can at least train your troops in archery."

"She's a mighty fine shot." Tre grinned as he returned from the body to offer Asteria her bloody arrow. She received it with barely veiled revulsion. "Clean through the heart. Couldn't have made a finer shot. And here her angle was tough, into the sun, him on higher ground and armored, from behind." Tre pantomimed the angle from which she had shot. "You have to be a confident archer to make a shot like that. Just beautiful."

"To accept your company's to condone it," Khoti said, ignoring Tre.

"You complain about my father clinging like an old fool to outdated traditions. You, Champion, are no better," Asteria said.

She looked down at the bloody arrow in her hand, her face paling. She swallowed hard, her nostrils flaring as if she could smell the blood on it.

"You would sell me to Anlon because my father ordered it, as if he had a right. And you who gave me gifts." Her voice trembled as she plucked at the hide tunic she wore. "You carried my father's words to my would-be captor, with whom I would be no more free than the Pladde. You who gave me a dagger to symbolize your protection would bring me such harm." She yanked the dagger from her belt, breaking the thongs securing the sheath at her waist, and tossed it at Khoti's feet.

Khoti stared at her, open mouthed, stung by her venom. Chati pushed past him, taking Asteria by the arm and guiding her to a jut of rock where she sat, head bowed as she took deep breaths.

"It's difficult, the first," Chati soothed, taking the bloody arrow from her grip to wipe it clean on a moss-covered rock before placing it in her quiver. "The first time I killed a man, I didn't have time to think about it. I still see it clear, that one, even though I've killed many times since. You know you had to do it but it's still worrying sometimes to think how much power you have. And you always wonder about 'em."

She nodded, still staring into her hands.

"I think she might be a finer shot than you, Khoti," Tre offered.

Khoti gave him a low, menacing growl. He stooped to tilt Asteria's face up.

"Will you be all right?" he demanded.

She jerked her head from his grasp and stared at him for response.

"I don't have time to take you home," he said, his words a hiss. He couldn't worry about her life as well as all the youths he'd already let down. And he'd had a bitter parting from Eithurdon, like a son spurning his fa, a fa rejecting his son. "So I'll take you to Habdelion. It'll give you an opportunity to get to know your future lifemate." Khoti's tone had turned scathing.

"I will decide how far I travel, and with whom," she said so softly he had to lean forward to hear her, could smell the freshness of the wind in her hair. "If Anlon strikes my interest, I will decide then if I will remain, or go on to some other place. You are not my master. If I had known to what dimensions your vanity had grown, I would not have had such misplaced respect for your abilities. Perhaps that is the difference in the nobles," she said, her tone so sour Tre and Chati turned away. "At least Lharan nobles are raised to be modest. Maybe you were given too many laurels, too much deference. You are not deserving of them if your character is so flawed."

Before Khoti could respond, his words locked in his throat, she rose and walked back to where she had left her mount. She swung up with ease. He had once worried how he could ever adjust to living within the walls of her world. Instead, her time in the crisp air of the Val, these days alone against the elements conquering her fears of avalanche, she had instead become a part of his world. The dignity with which she waited on Clanna, her hair bound in warrior braids – a slip of color in them wound up their length the way his mother would bind them – in the garb of a mountain woman, not a noble, what had he missed?

She turned to look at Chati and gave him a weak smile. The sunburst on her temple stood out bloody red with her anger, a presence at Khoti's back as they rode on that drove him to distraction.

Asteria felt the challenge of Khoti's world like a thrill in her heart. How had she ever withstood the confines of her father's halls? The wind sang through her. She could just ride on, make the world her own, ignore all these men who would own her. But alone in the world wasn't the answer either. To be rebuked like this by Khoti, on whom she looked with such awe ... and she had saved his life! Perhaps Anlon wouldn't seem so bad, now that she saw Khoti's darkest flaws. Perhaps she would reject them all.

As they moved along the path Khoti selected, she stared at his back. He wore a hide tunic she'd made him to replace the one shredded by the interrogator's lash. With regained strength, his muscles strained the seams in places. His hand reached up to touch the pendant she knew he wore on a chain, concealed beneath his clothes. For an instant the gesture made all the warm feelings for him return as a flush to her face. This time she forced them away. He embraced the flaw she'd always hated in her father's Guardsmen, that blind loyalty. The duke treated him no better than a stable boy and Khoti returned only for more. How many times had he begged her to leave him alone? Had his been a trifling interest and hers only awe of his gifts, that keen spirit that emanated from him? She blushed at the impetuousness that had driven her to chase after Khoti, to race from her father's good graces into Khoti's rigid wrath. After all, she had only her father and her uncle Steadon. Latra would have told her how to make Khoti come running to her. But Latra was gone.

If she hadn't followed, the Eidhalt would have shot dead the King's Champion. Had one man of prowess been worth her ruin?

As she stared at Khoti's back, oblivious to the world surrounding her, Tre and Chati flanked her with brotherly protectiveness. Each step took her farther from a world she knew and closer to a point of desperation. A moment's trembling took her as the sticky memory of the bloody arrow in her hand overrode her other thoughts. The faint metallic smell of blood clung to her senses. She knew Chati had returned the arrow to the quiver at her back, but the smell grew unbearable. Chati's hand on her arm steadied her. She nodded, reaching back to grab the soiled arrow. She nocked it, aimed. The arrow thunked into a tree high above and ahead of them, sending down a rain of needles. Khoti turned in his saddle. No one spoke. They continued on, leaving the arrow with its buff and pewter flights stained dark, quivering in the tree top.

Khoti didn't speak to her for days, leaving her to glower at his back. Chati and Tre taught her all she could absorb of the hand signs and scout craft that would keep her from blundering them all into danger. Khoti brooded.

His transformation when his mind turned to his labor amazed her. His single-minded intensity revealed a sharp temper when she moved too slow to seek cover, or if she caused any delay, or wandered from the path Khoti chose, risking their discovery by blundering into traps or onto loose slopes. She couldn't blame him when he cursed her. Any mistake she made could cost them their lives.

As the days passed, she began to let her instincts guide her to cover whenever she felt Khoti's tension rising, began to see many of the little things that alerted him. After several days of silence, Khoti nudged Fidra close and leaned over Clanna's neck, forcing her to look at him.

He smiled. "I'll make a scout of you yet," he said, handing her the dagger she'd thrown at his feet. He nudged Fidra to trot away, leaving her only more confused.

The harshness of early winter swept down on them as the wind blew the harvest moon color from those few leafy trees clinging to valley streams. A storm left behind a span of snow, though it melted the next day as the moist south wind brought a cold rain to wash it away.

For a month, from the time he had rushed back to the Val with Zopher, Khoti pushed from dawn until well after the last light left the sky, the northern Lharans a distant haze. Though he'd assured them they were near for several days, they looked around in surprise when he stopped in a little dell sheltered from the wind by tall pines that hid the protective little bowl.

As they picketed their horses and unpacked their gear to set camp, Khoti remained silent. When at last they settled around a small fire to fend off autumn chill, Khoti emitted a deep sigh.

"He was here. Jali's been gone a long time." Khoti pointed to the absence of wear on the place. "I guess I should've known that. It really did no good to come."

Asteria scanned the semi-circle of trees sheltering them from the valley, the wind blocked by the steep face of rock at their back. Her gaze fell on the scarred trunk of a pine near where they entered the haven. When she pointed out the tree, Khoti rushed to examine the signs, an ugly scowl growing on his face as he returned.

"He went for Tormor Wood, a party of thirty-six," he grumbled, slamming his fist against his thigh.

"Then it turned out all right –" Asteria began, but Khoti shook his head.

"We guessed there were a thousand here. He left with thirty-six. Something went wrong. There's supposedly a hundred in a camp. So how did he end up with so few? And for that matter, he'd have to lead them by ways he doesn't know, to a forest he's never been in, and hope he meets a headman who might or might not help him, and might or might not slit his throat." Khoti said nothing more.

He remained moody the rest of the afternoon giving them no idea what options he considered, whether they made camp for the night or would move on. With no plan, as night fell they made a cheerless camp, his sour mood weighing them all. They went to sleep with heavy hearts.

Asteria opened her eyes, the moon overhead lighting the small circle of dell. Khoti slept a pace away, Tre and Chati just beyond. The thing that awakened her moved among the trees, making the horses restless. A predator? A Minarian? She tensed, reaching for her dagger. A horse snorted, the sound loud in the quiet night. The movement among the trees stopped.

Asteria reached over and nudged Khoti, trying to conceal her movement from any observer. She felt the tension in his muscles. Whether the horse woke him or the same noise that roused her, she didn't know. His elbow bent back slowly as he searched for his sword. She pushed it closer, feeling the intensity in him as he grasped the hilts, threw back his blanket and dashed for some shadow among the trees only he could see.

Tre and Chati leaped up to follow, awake as well. She sat up, gripping the dagger. A small cry came from the shadows where the three disappeared. In a moment, Khoti dragged a young woman back to their cold fire. She scratched and bit at his wrist, trying to free her arm from his grip. When instead of skin she found the metal cuff, she stopped struggling and let him lead her into the clearing. Tre built up the fire. The young woman didn't resist as Khoti yanked her into the light to peer into her face.

Asteria sucked in a breath when she saw the youth in the face. The girl glanced at Asteria with a shy smile then turned on Khoti with an angry glint in her eyes.

"You're late."

Khoti took a step back, releasing her arm but placing one hand on his sword. "Then –"

"Khoti, right?" she demanded, waiting for his nod. "Jali couldn't wait no longer. He would've died for some cock-eyed dream of yours for being everyone's savior."

Asteria tucked her dagger in her belt and hurried to the girl, laying a hand on her arm. "Daris?" The girl nodded, wary. "He never forgot Jali or these camps. Khoti has many obligations. The Minarians captured a man whose information would have destroyed all the plans laid by many more than just Khoti. Such things cause delays. I know you feel he broke a promise. Do not condemn before you hear the excuse and apology." Asteria's voice soothed, calmed.

Daris studied her a moment, then turned away. "It wouldn't have been so bad, just dashed hopes, you know," Daris muttered. "But Jali and me are responsible for sixty-two dead. Sixty-two!" Daris trembled. "When he failed to show," she jabbed a thumb toward Khoti's stony face, "We canceled everything. Howl didn't get the word. Those that made it out were so young. I don't know how Jali got this far, but I doubt they all could've made it to that forest." Daris stood firm as Asteria placed an arm around the girl's shoulders.

"It is a tragedy," Asteria said. "Not your fault. We are here to help in any way we can."

"You're too late." Daris pulled away. "When they found out about Howl they tightened up everything."

Asteria studied her. For the first time she noticed a dark bruise on the girl's cheek and that bones pushing through her skin marred a dark beauty, as did an unhealed cut running from her cheek almost to her ear. Asteria reached for the cut, but Daris backed away.

"I don't need your pity."

Asteria sensed she did.

"We needed help."

"We're here now," Khoti said so softly Asteria turned to look on him. His gaze held none of the pain in his words.

"Don't you see? Before, I could get word to the other camps. I could ... help. When they found out about Howl they clamped down. Then they caught someone with a stake and the whole thing got blown open. They shut me down. I can't get away with anything. Now they know I just played the game." Daris gave Khoti a defiant stare. "So, what are you going to do? It's a wonder I even get out to come here, but I promised Jali for the fool he is. We can't break everything open in one night. They're ready for trouble and the beatings and the shortened rations have everybody just about dead. There's nothing you can do. Our one chance and you –"

Khoti grabbed her arm and yanked her close to face him. "So you enjoy it here? You want to stay?" he demanded.

Daris stared at him as if she looked on a madman. "Of course. It's better than the Shela Carnival."

"Tre, Chati, pack up. We're heading for Tormor Wood. They're happy here. Asteria, fetch the horses."

As they gathered their bedrolls, and Asteria went for the horses, Daris stared after them. They ignored her.

"What're you doing?" Daris cried, almost a shriek.

"Hold your tongue, child," Asteria said as she led Fidra into the circle of light. "You want the Minarians to hear?"

"How can you just leave?" Daris asked of Asteria, who didn't answer. Khoti kicked out the fire. The sparks shot skyward like bits of his temper.

"You refused us," Tre offered as he passed. "We didn't come all this way to play games. That's all you want to do. We're going where we're needed. Your folk weren't in our plans to begin with. We thought just to help –"

"But we need you," Daris pleaded. "You're playing games with me. You're pretending to leave to get me to beg you to stay."

"We are not pretending," Asteria said. "We want to help, but you will not cooperate. Gods, girl, The King's Champion and Sword of Shande builds armies. We are not accustomed to having those we help attack us. You are so busy railing at us about how we have failed you to give us any idea how we can help."

"Please don't go," Daris whispered. "They're killing us." She touched the cut on her cheek. "I used to be able to help the sick ones or stop a beating. Now, they make me work the mine. I don't know how to do anything but play the game. I don't even know how to deal with you people. I don't know how to ask. I don't even remember what the truth is. Just, please."

Khoti stared at Daris. At last, he slammed his bedroll to the ground and sat on a log pulled near the sputtering fire. He tossed a piece of wood in and stirred up the coals. "Why don't you start over. Tell us everything you know. I make no promises but that we'll try," Khoti said with an impatient sigh.

Daris let Asteria guide her to a place by the fire. The girl tore into the cured meat Asteria handed her, and the wine they offered loosened her tongue so that she finally answered their questions without challenge while the night grew old and the twice-rebuilt fire flushed her face with life.

They remained in the sheltered dell long enough to stock and cure as much game as they could pack on the horses. It would never be enough to feed hundreds of hungry children. This time the four northerners would ensure no Minarian survived to relay word of the attack. The youths still had their part to play. This time, the nightman would face a dagger, not a dull stick. And the attacker would know how to strike a killing blow.

They started at the most distant camp, a place cold and barren where even the trees appeared bent and worried.

"Thirty-to-one, Chati, some nasty odds," Khoti whispered as he smeared mud over the man's face.

Chati smiled, a lopsided slash in the dark, not unlike his uncle Konner's. "I never said I was going to take anyone on!"

"That's the point, don't," Tre countered with a tight grin.

Chati turned for their inspection. He had shed his weapons, except for a knife to be delivered to any youth he found at the little stream supplying the camp's water. As the most youthful of the three Guardsmen, Chati likely wouldn't draw attention.

As Chati faded into the blackness hovering about the boles of trees, Khoti made a silent plea to the spirits that this raid not result in the same staggering losses as Howl.

Inside of an hour, Chati returned, his message and dagger delivered. This had to work. He couldn't bear the weight of more innocent lives on his conscience. The hours until they could carry out their plan passed like days, weapons honed to the fineness of thread, each step gone over until Khoti's companions refused to respond to his drills any longer.

Finally, night settled over the camp. The time of the cat arrived, like so long ago when his fa stalked Tasch-el's captives.

Positioned near the backs of the Minarian tents, Khoti watched the furtive movements as Chati crouched on the side of the camp nearest the stream. Tre settled near the slope running from the camp down into a narrow valley at the mountain's feet. Asteria guarded the route to the horses, a dangerous position. She'd already smuggled the Minarian horses away to a forest clearing where their own mounts grazed, a safeguard against any Minarian getting past her and going for help. Khoti doubted many Minarians would make it that far.

The camp's youths went about their duties, each move calculated. Those assigned to the cooking built their fires large, putting on extra water to boil. Most still had their stakes, and bundles replenished with fresh food and more metal bars. Rather than hopeful, their expressions reflected apprehension. Everyone knew what had happened at Howl.

Khoti tensed when the night shift entered the mine and the day shift wearily exited. The miners went to the fires where they struck almost casual poses. Khoti held his breath when the nightman entered the first tent, then exhaled tension when the man did not reappear and the camp remained silent. A boy's head peeked around the tent flap to scan the few Minarians in the compound eating dinner, served by a girl they groped and pinched as she passed.

A knife pierced through the back of the tent and the captives slipped out to dash between Khoti and Chati to the assigned meeting place. Soon the boy exited the tent, going to the next where he cut the canvas, moving along the line of tents until all emptied.

Miners slipped from the mouth of the shaft, one by one, picks held behind their backs as they sped to the shadows beyond the ring of torches. A few crept within a pace of Khoti to circle around to the tents where a shift of guards slept. A sudden row began around the cookfire as several boys argued over a girl. It drowned out the sound of the picks smashing through canvas to strike the sleeping guards. The Minarians taking their meal shouted for quiet. When the argument showed no signs of ending several drew whips from their belts and stalked toward the cookfire. The youths turned on their captors.

Those around the fire tossed hot water in the faces of the lead guards as the day-shift miners turned against their captors with their sharpened stakes. The remaining Minarian diners ran for their bows; children from the other fires lobbed flaming brands at them. In the meantime, the youths with picks swung at any Minarian that appeared. One soldier burst from his tent, an arrow already nocked. It struck a girl stoking a fire, she fell, clutching her stomach. An arrow from the direction of the horses struck him in the back. His bellow as he writhed on the stony ground went unheard in the chaos. As other Minarians grabbed bows, they, too, mysteriously fell to arrows from the dark edges of the camp. One guard at last noticed the arrow in one of his fallen comrades. Calling a warning, he dashed with three others for the horses. As they ran, one fell to Tre, another to Chati. Asteria shot the third through the eye.

In the compound, the remaining four Minarians threw up their hands as the mine crashed in with a rumble that shook the ground beneath their feet. Tre ran to disarm the prisoners, sending two older boys to take up the enemy swords and point them at the Minarians' throats. Three youths fell injured. Two youths lay dead. Khoti ordered the dead buried in shallow graves at the edge of the compound according to the ways of their tribes. He stared after the bodies carried away, chewing on his dismay that any had fallen. How had Jali lived with the sixty-two from Howl?

While Chati and Asteria led the youths to the clearing where she'd left their horses, Tre and Khoti were left to deal with the remaining Minarians. They couldn't take chances. Killing unarmed men went against the Lharan code, but such codes were not made for wars against children.

When Khoti and Tre reached the clearing where all had gathered, Khoti froze. The youngest and injured perched atop Minarian horses among bundles of food and metal bars, looking down at him with their wide eyes. Older faces looked up to him. He counted one hundred and two, and seven camps to go. How would he feed so many, watch so many little feet, and keep them silent? When they at last reached the edge of the range, they must cross a road and open fields. Had he been wrong both times in his grand scheme? Perhaps he should have assigned others to meet his obligations to Jali, a squad of fifty, perhaps. How had Jali managed?

He felt a tug at his sleeve and turned to find a youth of perhaps fifteen. As tall as Khoti, the boy's expression might have been Khoti's on a face the rich brown of the southernmost tribes.

"What of the four who surrender?" the youth asked.

"Dead," Khoti stated.

The boy nodded. "If you have a spare bow, at the next camp I can assist," he stated.

Khoti studied the youth, taking in his size, his poise. "You know how to use it? Aren't you Shelan? What need did you have for weapons there?"

He bowed low. "Sedaik, son of Perouk. I am a man of Detarian, not a boy from Shela," he said easily.

Khoti peered at Sedaik.

"Since I became a man of my tribe, I passed many tests of marksmanship hunting with the poison arrows we use to bring down game." Sedaik studied Khoti with an unnerving gaze. "There is rumor from the forest. Things will change."

"Things'll change. That's why we're here –"

Sedaik shook his head. "In the last wagon, a Detarian child arrived. She spoke of a white-haired seer who came ashore at the mouth of the Detarian River. He held power in his hand that would blast the Minarians to ash. He told the headmen of the five tribes of Detarian, one of whom is the girl's father, about the many people already pledged to him. He mentioned you, named you his sword and champion. What such roles are?" He shrugged.

"So Arshal's made it to Detarian," Khoti said, daring to feel a glimmer of hope. "That's good news you give me, Sedaik."

"It is not for the news, Lord, that I say it," Sedaik said. "The girl said the seer asked Detarian's help. He claimed you aid the Tachi, who pledged to him. They are our neighbors and share the Akora River with us. But Detarian is a most southerly edge of Shande, often forgotten." Sedaik stared at Khoti with a gaze that seemed eerie in the spare light. "Help me. Train me as you would the Tachi so I can carry that knowledge to Detarian. Our people know archery, not Minarian warfare. Then we can fight beside our neighbors."

Khoti scratched the shadow of beard on his chin. Did Sedaik's captors consider him a troublemaker like Jali, a life close to death with each moment it considered rebellion? Did the Minarians know the dangers of assuming childhood based on age?

"Certainly, I can try to teach you what I know," Khoti said. "But what good does it do you if you have no weapons?"

Sedaik chuckled, startling Khoti. "Ah, but we might aid you, Lord. Arenh pledged your seer weapons for Detarian. Perhaps something can be worked out?"

Khoti grinned as they grasped each others' forearms in agreement.

"Maybe. If you stop calling me Lord. I'm not even close to nobility. Just ask the Lady Asteria." His smile faded when he glanced around at the silhouetted figures of the camp's survivors. His glance touched Asteria's pale face turned his way, blank. "First, we've got to get out of these mountains. And there's seven more camps. We'll set you up with a Minarian bow. Find out if there are others with any skill and we'll arm them as well. The more help, the fewer losses. Prove yourself and maybe we can talk about Detarian's future."

227

With that, Khoti made a small hand signal that launched them on their way. As they marched for the next camp, Khoti sensed Sedaik watching and imitating his every move. Sedaik practiced the hand signals Khoti used, and studied the way Khoti scouted his path, or read the stars or listened to the night. Sedaik even mimicked Khoti's walk, a footfall that made no sound and seldom even left a print. With pupils such as Sedaik, perhaps, after all, he could hope.

Khoti knew they lived the stuff of tales in their month-long escape from the labor camps of the Lharan Mountains. He imagined the storytellers of the Val trying to tell this tale as it happened, but the listeners claiming the teller exaggerated beyond belief.

As each camp fell the size of his host grew. He took to stalking ahead in search of danger, needing to escape their haunting gazes, the odd silence of their childhoods lost. Between camps, Khoti tested the mettle of youths who had already become adults, challenging them to feed the growing army of children and prove their prowess. Because of them, no Minarians survived and a growing herd of Minarian horses trailed behind them carrying the raw materials to forge weapons for Shande.

These war-hardened youths of a peaceful land looked at the world from stony gazes and vowed retaliation, performed ruthlessly in skirmishes. The Shande of old had died like the ashes of Tasch-el, leaving behind something bitter and dark. Even in the Val, the young learned things never before taught the youth of Shande, weaned on hatred and taught to kill.

Yet, they lived a paradox like his own. Like the healer-warrior, they had first known Terremar, a god of peace and forgiveness, not vengeance. Like him, these youths were a generation of opposition.

So, the storytellers of the Val would have an epic story with no need of embellishment. It would be a sad tale, Khoti decided, one that might one day be the marker that explained how the Shande of the future had grown from the Shande of now.

Finally, when he thought he couldn't swallow his bitterness any longer, Khoti led his army of more than eight hundred through the last gap of the Lharans and on into the barren foothills to the Mershy road. Staring out onto the plains, weatherworn and weary, Khoti couldn't help but compare his journey to Peshal's to Otayr, or Arshal's to the Val, or the evacuation of Sefresal and Eilime deep into the mountains, or even the many mountain tribes coming home to the Val. In these times people like Rathil Hostler moved from one home to another in search of a place to live without fear. Then came this army that followed him like a promise. It seemed Fyraer had already destroyed Terremar's peaceful creation.

Huddled in the cold shadows of winter, he waited for an overcast night to cross the Mershy road. A cold wind and freezing rain swirled around them as if throwing up a barricade to taunt them with their closeness to the end of their march. First the horses bearing the youngest, the injured, the food and the metals crossed the road and hurried ahead into the dark. Then groups of a dozen or more dashed across, spreading out through the wide tangle of lumbered forest. While Asteria, Tre and Chati brought up the rear to smooth and diffuse their trail and pull brush over the matted path through the grass, Khoti went on ahead, seeking the eaves of the forest, long overdue, but arriving as promised.

When, three days later, Khoti again came before Habdelion, he felt far older than the newly named King's Champion uncertain of his place in the world. Outside rose the din of Habdelion's household finding food and shelter for Khoti's charges. Falling into a chair a servant brought him and drinking deeply of the cool wine set beside him, Khoti felt as if he had finally reached the end of a journey, but recognized the mirage. He'd only arrived at the beginning.

"You traveled a hard road, Khoti," Habdelion said as he stared out at the children lining up for baths and hurrying to feast on Akoran fish chowder and fresh bread. "But you brought me an army, more than you promised."

"I'm sorry I couldn't warn you about the burden."

"Burden? Never. When Jali came with a few dozen small ones I thought, 'what will I do with this burden?' I was wrong. They are more a treasure than a burden."

"Duke, do you know how many of these 'treasures' I brought? Certainly, there's a number of older boys and girls –"

"More than ready to mete out their revenge. The little ones do small chores that balance the trouble. The older youths, Khoti, that's what our army needs. They help with provisioning, tend livestock, serve soldiers, prepare meals and pitch tents. Or they can do nothing." Habdelion splashed more wine in Khoti's cup as the silence of the room built against the racket of outside. "You are not so ready to argue with me," Habdelion said. "Something has you thinking more deeply than you should. Your

# M. Turville Heitz

mind is turned from battle, away from teaching my people how to carry out the king's wishes."

"I just spent weeks sheltering, feeding and guiding the future of Shande." Khoti sighed. "I have these memories of 'before' and 'after.' Before Tasch-el burned and Von died, I had an easy life, not a worry. I was nobody, a second son charged to watch livestock with a future mediating minor squabbles and collecting taxes. After Tasch-el burned, I have only images of blood and fire and a role that judges who lives and dies. Now I think 'before' is forever gone and there's only an 'after.' These children will never fit into the lives we knew. I doubt even we can. The little ones like Nali's youngest, who can't remember the names of their parents or villages, they are the ones who will shape Shande."

Habdelion stared at Khoti. "How do you find the time to take on so many burdens?"

Khoti looked up, startled by the tone of the question.

"You, the king, this fellow Nali, supposedly have gifts from the gods, missions to accomplish. Do you suggest the gods lack wisdom, that they have not thought of these questions and will abandon such prodigy to worse lives than we see now? Maybe the wrong was in the life of 'before.' They will have their peaceful villages and trivial concerns. But perhaps they will not be so ready to dismiss the early warnings of trouble. When the first signs came from Minaria, no one listened. I remember Eithur bemoaning the intractability of the Minarian apprentices. I had Shelans complaining of beatings and rapes and kidnapping. Did we listen? We were too ready to believe nothing untoward could ever happen here. I sat here thinking only of myself while labor camps operated only a few days distant. Would you have acted so quickly if your village had not been attacked? Or, like the rest of us, would you have instead said, pity those poor people affected but it is not my problem? These young people will not be lulled into acting only when they feel a personal threat. They will act out of compassion, knowing what others face even if they themselves are safe."

Khoti inclined his head to acknowledge Habdelion's point. "So, what made you accept Arshal's charge, if you weren't personally at risk?"

Habdelion snorted. "Guilt. Nothing noble. Here is my king telling me how the royal family has been decimated. The queen my sister, Esthen and Peshal my nephews, Resala my niece. So there, it is a thing that affects my family."

Habdelion splashed more wine in Khoti's cup. He felt light-headed, the duke swimming in the glare from the window.

"So, you bring me a hundred horses, an army of apprentices, the metals for my weapons, the expertise to train my army, a daughter to join my house. And all I have to do is supply the men? It seems unfair. What did you leave Eithur?"

"Not much. He has his army. Yet his second officer abandons him for another and couldn't control his wayward daughter. That he won't forgive." Khoti sighed. "I took two of his Guardsmen, and high-tailed it to warmer climes at the onset of winter. I'm a pretty untrustworthy fellow. So, I better make it worthwhile."

Khoti stood, feeling the flush of unwelcome anger to think of Asteria beside Anlon. He didn't think he could witness them together. How could he let his mind wander from important things? He'd fought beside her as a comrade; she'd earned the mark of a Tawnkat, yet she would again be cloaked in her titles.

Taking his leave, Khoti followed a servant to a room adjacent to where Asteria already slept. For the first time in two months he would sleep beyond reach of her, unable to hear her soft breath. He paced the narrow room, feeling caged. His stomach took a queasy twist as he wondered where Chati and Tre slept. He couldn't remember the last time he'd been completely alone with himself. He stood beside the wall, trying to hear Asteria's breathing, wishing he could just sleep at the foot of her bed. Instead, with the stiffness of one testing a funeral platform, he lay on the bed and accepted the war in his head.

# 29: A Challenge in the Air

Ytri dropped, pushing himself into a snowdrift. He clicked his tongue against his teeth to send the furtive shapes behind him darting to cover. A sentry trudged by in his circuit of the Sefresal wall.

Fat snowflakes obscured Sefresal and rapidly covered their tracks in older drifts piled hip deep. A calm wind kept it mild, and quiet. In the swirl of flakes, they moved unseen. The lanterns and torches of Sefresal sent an eerie yellow glow skyward, resolution lost. Below, the base of the wall drew deep black shadows, like some inky pit into which they would descend.

As the labored passage of the sentry faded, Ytri released his breath in a puff of mist. He pushed himself to his feet and shook off the coat of snow covering him. With another click of tongue against teeth, a sound not unlike the shift of stone, the snow around him erupted with figures.

"When did they start posting sentries?" Geleg whispered close to Ytri's ear.

"Tonight." Ytri stared after the sentry.

"They're nervous. That or someone talked."

The rest of his force closed around them, muttering their fears under their breaths.

"There's no way to warn Kefta or Efen," Ytri said. "Just everybody be extra alert, extra careful."

Ytri scanned the bowl of an ancient cirque on the mountain side in which Sefresal nestled, the city's east-facing gate opening on foothills containing the Dodfrenyen Sea. Though they approached from the slopes above the pass they still couldn't see the rooftops over the lofty walls first built for protection in the time of the gods' Great War. Battlements peered over the treeless perimeter around the wall and towers watched the corners where the city walls met the edge of the mountain basin.

Ytri nodded at his men. Somewhere on the south side of the basin, hidden in the softly falling snow, Kefta and his squads also stalked Sefresal. During the last week, fifty Guardsmen had slipped into town to hide in the homes of those known to be faithful. Even with the hundred approaching the walls from the outside, and those secreted within, retaking the city would be a challenge. They couldn't let a single Minarian escape to bring reinforcements to a city now quartering more than five hundred Minarians.

Zopher's men, posted at all the thoroughfares outside of the city, the rampart and the postern doors they hoped to open to enter the city, would prevent any Minarians from slipping by. But Ytri still wished Khoti executed so bold of a plan. This action suited him more than Kefta. As the elite of the Guard stalked the walls of Sefresal, the Val's women and youths established and secured a supply line for a siege, and Eithurdon readied two hundred cavalry and more than eight hundred foot soldiers to march down the pass. They wanted to win the city with one hundred and fifty Guardsmen. If they failed, they wouldn't have sacrificed Eithurdon's entire army, only his best.

Ytri scanned his men, his gaze pausing on one figure, standing erect and apart with a challenging stance. At least he had one Tawnkat of renown in his squad. He smiled when Amhese caught his eye. Sword at her side, bow slung at her back and hair pulled in tight warrior braids over her ears, she fit the picture of the soldier he had in mind. Not just Tsevon passed along the warrior spirit to Khoti. She quickly dealt with the grumbling of men hesitant to be led by someone's mother. While no longer young, and no match in strength for many of the Guardsmen, no one doubted her skill. They didn't have Khoti, but if any could mirror his gaze it was Amhese.

The moment Ytri awaited arrived. At a swipe of his hand, the Guardsmen fanned out, dodging snow-covered boulders as they dashed to the deep shadows at the base of the wall. The light footfalls of sentries ranging the battlement carried down to them. The Guardsmen moved silently in the shadows, with, they hoped, surprise on their side.

Hugging the cold stone of the wall, Geleg crept to a postern door overlooked by one of the four towers. No light fell on the entrance. Ytri grit his teeth as Geleg pushed on the stone that would release the inside lock. The door slid open easily. A face appeared in the darkness beyond. Geleg reared back, one hand reaching for his sword. The face grinned.

"You were almost a dead man, Efen," Geleg growled.

Efen motioned for them to enter. "Rast is on the other side," he whispered as fifty Guardsmen filed along the wall to slip inside. Efen pointed down a short passageway that led to the inside of the city. "All the interior passages are closed off. You'll have but one entry." He shrugged at Ytri's frown. They had hoped the postern door still opened onto a myriad of passages within the wall so they could assault the city from a number of places at once. Perhaps some astute Minarian recognized the flaw in security. Fresh masonry blocked their intended route.

"Improvise," Ytri whispered as each squad leader passed, Geleg taking the lead.

When they came to the low stone door opening onto the square, Geleg halted the nine men of his squad. "Same objective, just a different route," he whispered to each. They gripped the hilts of their swords, their free hands tensed to unsling bows at the first sign of trouble.

Geleg peered through the door onto the torch-lit square beyond. He pulled a chunk of charred wood from his pocket, smearing it over his face and hands as the men around him followed suit. He then slipped through the door, darting from shadow to shadow, his squad quietly following as they made for stairs up to the battlement.

Amhese and her squad followed Geleg's at first then continued past the stairs to the battlement to reach the armory. The next squad moved on to huddle near the Guard barracks, which now housed Minarian officers. Ytri took his squad the other direction, followed by the last squad, to circle around to approach Eithurdon's Halls. They moved with the certainty that Kefta's Guardsmen crept on their targets on the other side of the city, and with the determination of exiles returning home.

Amhese crouched in the snowy alley within the shadow of the armory wall. She prodded those of her squad who leaned against it. They had to be ready to spring if someone raised an alarm. She gazed at the lamp-lit window of the house across the alley from the armory, hearing only the sound of her squad's tense breathing as the flakes of snow settled on them.

At last, the lamp in the house next to the armory winked out. She jabbed a gloved finger at two of her squad, who darted to the shadow beneath the house window. She led the rest along the side of the building to where it fronted on the square. The bright glow of light bounding back from the low clouds lit the square, and light glowing from an armory window fell on the space leading to the large double doors into the armory. Clinging to the wall shadow, Amhese sidled up to the corner of the window. It opened into the armorer's tiny office where a taper burned low in a lamp, the room empty. Voices vibrated against thin Jashiho glass.

With a glance, she singled out Mitte, Kefta's red-headed younger brother, who crouched beside her. With a grin, Mitte dashed across the lighted space before the doors and slowly pulled, hiding behind the open door. The voices ceased. Boots thumped as the armorer investigated, commenting that some prankster disrupted his game.

When the armorer stuck his head out the door, Mitte jabbed with his sword, pushing through the entry with the armorer still impaled on his blade. Amhese and the rest of the squad pressed in from behind and on into the armory as Mitte tugged his sword from the armorer and slammed the door behind them.

Three men tried to rise from a little table, wine and dice telling their story. Their gazes locked on Amhese as she approached with more shock than if Ghyldus himself had burst into their game. Before they could regain their wits, she'd unsheathed her sword and struck the nearest dead, his neck spewing blood onto the worn stone floor. In another moment, her soldiers had sent the other two Minarians to join their comrades. Pats of congratulations struck her back as her squad raced to the tasks for which she'd trained them.

Within minutes her men formed a brigade to hand the contents of the armory through a window to the two Guardsmen outside who passed the goods through the window into the darkened little house. There, thirty men waited to take up arms again as Guardsmen, roles they hadn't held since Sefresal fell. When each man was laden with as many weapons as he could carry, they slipped from the dark house to some other dwelling where small groups of Sefresal's faithful gathered. If all went as planned, when Amhese's squad emptied the armory, they would have another seven hundred armed Guardsmen within the walls, each soldier carrying at least one weapon of choice.

As they passed the last weapon into the little house, Amhese nodded. Her men put out the lamps and hid near the windows and doors. When the Minarians came, they would be ready.

While Minarian blood stained the floor of the armory, some sixth sense, some current in the air, unsettled Minarians throughout Sefresal. Though no sound carried through the still air, their bodies tensed, the hair prickling up on the backs of their necks. Peering into the falling snow, sentries found only phantoms that leapt from snowflake to snowflake, the uncommon silence of the wind only giving a keener edge to their apprehension. A sentry might turn at some movement caught in the corner of his eye to find only empty darkness. He might whip around at a half-heard footfall or creak of door to find nothing.

Even in barracks and dining halls something oppressive, some challenge in the air made men feel hunted, stalked, by shadows with no substance. A more eerie silence had never before fallen on Sefresal, as if even the spirits of the mountains hushed the constant winds.

As Kefta's men joined Ytri's, and the re-armed residents of Sefresal encircled barrack and hall, the foreboding grew to such a point that Minarian soldiers fell silent, their own breaths disturbing some message of warning. Thus, when with a shattering roar the city erupted, the Minarians stood ready.

As hundreds of Shandean voices rose up to echo Kefta's bellow, Geleg and his men bolted for their targets, trying to catch the sentries before they could react. Minarians on the battlements had felt the odd silence of Sefresal the strongest, the fleeting phantom shadows raising the hair on their necks.

When Geleg swung his sword at a sentry, he didn't expect the solidness of the parry. The man's strength forced him back. All around him over the din from the streets below, he heard the clank of metal on metal and metal on stone as the rest of his squad met stiff resistance.

He'd had a little over three months to mend from the injuries he'd received when Minarians captured Zopher. His shoulder hadn't completely recovered.  His foe threw the history of Minarian warfare into each blow, targeting Geleg's weaknesses. Geleg swiftly tired. Sweat dripped in his eyes and slicked his hands. When he tried to back out of range to wipe the snowflakes from his lashes so he could see, he slipped in the slushy snow on top of the wall.

As he stumbled toward the lip of the parapet, the sentry lunged, pinning Geleg against the edge. Geleg's feet slipped out from beneath him. The glint of torchlight lit the man's sword as it rose above him. He had an instant's thought of Khoti, that he wasted the life Khoti had bled to give him. As if his friend sent some call through the blood they shared, Geleg jerked aside just as the blade came down. A splinter of metal peeled from the Minarian's sword where it struck the stone. Geleg jabbed his elbow into the Minarian's ribs. The sentry slipped to his knees in the slush. As he tried to regain his feet, his sword lashed out, only grazing Geleg's arm. Geleg stabbed, forcing the blade through the chain mail tunic the man wore. The sentry gasped, but the mail kept Geleg's sword from penetrating far. Struggling to one knee, the sentry launched at Geleg. Both fell, Geleg beneath his attacker with the wind knocked from him. The wound slowed the Minarian and his hands, slicked with Geleg's blood, lost their grip. At last, Geleg pulled away and thrust his sword into the man's neck.

Geleg left his foe gasping and gagging. All around, his squad still fought similar tough battles. The men who carried Zopher away might have been oafish but not these reinforcements. The medallions glinting on their chests seemed to give them some supernatural strength that weakened their opponents and the eerie oppression of this night made Geleg wonder if the enemy god could now see beyond the bounds of Minaria.

Amhese's swift success was not repeated. All that night the little skirmishes continued until the overwhelming tide of Guardsmen forced the Minarians to retreat. Small clusters of the enemy darted through the many doors into Eithurdon's Hall. In the close confines of the isolated duels, archers could find no mark. With the loss of surprise, the odds had evened, despite the Shandeans' numeric superiority. The Minarians had the experience. At least one hundred Minarian archers lined the stout walls of Eithurdon's Hall, sniping at Shandeans who drew too close, but otherwise ineffectual. The Shandeans had more than two hundred soldiers equipped only with bow. Those with no bow or sword could strike only by deceit, from behind with daggers, an open target to the Minarian archers. The casualties, too, were even. The streets of Sefresal ran with blood.

Geleg, Ytri and Kefta fought together again as they rooted the Minarians from the barracks and sent them retreating through the alleys. More than ever, they missed Toban's sour humor and Khoti's brutal grin. As blood from their wounds splattered in their eyes, their men falling beside them, they prayed all the battles to regain Shande wouldn't be such a contest.

When dawn filtered through the thick overcast skies of the browning moon, and the snow abated to flurries that melted into the bloody streets, at last came a lull. More than three hundred

Minarians had holed up in Eithurdon's Hall. Among two hundred enemy dead, lay almost three hundred Shandeans. No Guardsman stood unscathed with more than one hundred bearing serious if not fatal wounds. As they looked on the besieged hall, not a few wondered just who would win when Minarian messengers failed to return and reinforcements marched on them.

Kefta knew every room, passage and secret of Eithurdon's Hall. The Minarians may have stored away a year's worth of rations in the maze of cellars. They could hole up in myriad nooks and crannies or slip out numerous doors.

"We got all the uniforms. And I selected the men who look the most Minarian," Ytri said, startling Kefta from his survey of Eithurdon's Hall. Ytri adjusted the rag wrapped around his head to staunch the blood leaking from a nasty gash on his scalp. "We're in position: some on the wall, some manning the gates."

Kefta nodded as if to some tempo within his head. This hall had been so much of his life. He served there as a page, then Guard apprentice assigned to serve the duke, then a cadet Guardsman, before making full rank, and finally Captain of the Guard. In this time of war they made apprenticeships short and skipped the difficult role of cadet altogether. Kefta had made a life of it. His family might live in the Val now but his heart remained in Eithurdon's Hall, and he never realized how much so until now.

"You need rest," Ytri stated.

Kefta turned to look at Ytri, startled.

Ytri pointed at the deep wound on Kefta's leg. "You're pushing yourself. Take a rest."

Kefta scowled. "No time, maybe later." He turned his back on the hall. "Your report. How many did you lose?"

"Not many," Ytri admitted, his words guarded. "Mostly among the insiders. Shows what a little training'll do. Of fifty, I could call up thirty-eight on a moment's notice. Another seven wounded bad. Only five dead. That's better than you did." The line of his mouth hardened. "But I lost Amhese. Mitte says she took five with her. Wounds, just a lot of them, no one great blow felled her. Gods, Kefta, we could use an army of mountain women. I think someone's mother was the best warrior of the lot." Ytri's tone had grown soft. "They destroyed his entire house, every last one."

Everything felt so silent. Ytri nodded at him, leaving to wander among his squads, checking wounds. Kefta scanned the churned and bloody snow, including his own bloody footsteps. A bitter wind swirled in from the northeast, picking up and blowing away muted conversations as townsfolk ventured from hiding to view the damage. Every so often someone strayed too near the hall and the whistle and strike of an arrow might break the silence. He encouraged taunting as long as the enemy wasted their arrows. Otherwise, on this morning of victory, Sefresal lay as quiet as the dead. A wagon load of arms rolled in from the Staph-el mine, and Zopher's men wandered in from their posts. He didn't dare move, the throb in his leg still for the moment; he merely stood in the bloody snow and stared about him. This small victory cost dear. The Minarians still occupied Eithurdon's Hall, and they had a long campaign ahead.

# PART 3. TRAITORS

# 30: Hothur's Choice

"The fools attacked Shiad," Konner blustered, staring up at Eithurdon as they stood in the pass surrounded by the duke's troops.

"What does it mean?" The duke scanned the curious faces within hearing. He felt so weary already. Sleep eluded him each night as the horrors that might face his daughter played out in his mind. His hand went to the pouch where he kept the tattered slip of parchment on which she'd penned her parting note.

"Means they can't supply the Pladde no more. Means they won't be shipping us grain no more. Means our northeast flank's exposed," Konner said, staring up at Eithurdon. "Here we got a war raging, and Ghyldus, idiot that he is, attacks Shiad! If he keeps this up, no one's going to support the king. They'll all be too busy looking to their own houses. Maybe that's his plan."

Eithurdon signed for his men to rest. Horsemen dismounted, soldiers flopped into the snow, exhausted by the labor of trudging through deep snow bearing heavy packs. The supply line had strung out ahead of them, but fresh snow and the wind had already buried that path. Eithurdon pointed at the snow shoes on Konner's feet. He grimaced. He should have realized they'd need such a thing if they intended to launch a war in mountain winter.

"Well, it is too late to change anything," Eithurdon mumbled at last, leaning against his mount to shield him from the harsh wind. "We already control most of the city, the mines. We cannot give up just because our flank's exposed. We should be able to make do if we take back what the Minarians collected –"

"That's fine for the Lharans, for Kishma," Konner said. "But then we won't be able to send our surplus on to folks in Mershy, Joffa and Kalilia if we've got to supply the Pladde. Nali only had one ship. Habdelion's probably got nothing. The Pladde lose, we'll have Minarians in our faces faster than you can shout 'Ghyldus.' We'll have weaponless armies and nothing to feed them. And we got no way of telling the king what's happened."

"Why would Ghyldus attack Shiad now?" Eithurdon mused. "The reinforcements certainly mean he heard of the resistance. I would think Resala would try to stop this action."

"How much control do you really think she'd have, Eithur? She might've delivered the warnings, but once done, the mission's complete. It's Ghyldus's call now. He likely knows what we've got, or even more. Maybe he dragged everything from poor Latra. He's probably warned all his people that we're on the attack."

Eithurdon shook his head. "He can tell his men nothing and give them only vague warnings. He cannot claim to be omnipotent and openly fear a mortal man. It will be something else that he devises. We must warn Mershy. With our extra troops left here to guard the Shiad border, and diverting supplies to the Pladde, there will be nothing left for Habdelion."

Konner nodded. "The messenger can also bear that other news as come up the pass."

Eithurdon glanced at Konner, daring him to say the name he had made taboo in his presence. Yet, mountain headman, and King's Champion, the man seemed to be implied daily, named or not.

Konner grinned. "It sure shows that even our older women can outfight a bunch of dandy shawnsi. If you got problems breaking that siege, duke, I'll just send down a dozen of my old folk to mop things up for you."

Eithurdon grimaced. Konner's jibe struck too close to the truth. "Just see what you can do about the Pladde." With a motion of his hand, the duke's men climbed to their feet for the long march to Sefresal.

The duke urged his mount through the deep snow. He'd hoped his homecoming would be grand, that he'd sweep in and take his ancestral seat with a flourish and a clear call on his horn. Not with Minarians besieged in his hall. Already Kefta's

241

men had foiled attempted sorties, and one Minarian had almost escaped, caught outside the gate by Zopher himself. When Minarian dispatch riders arrived, the duke and other shawnsi would be forced to hide. It would probably be Geleg who would sit in his hall, dispatching his messages. With that scarred face of his, the dark hair, Geleg looked like a Minarian warrior with a decade of hard campaigns behind him. As Konner trekked over the snow back to the Val, Eithurdon led his weary men home.

Zopher sauntered to meet Kefta, noting the fever in the captain's eyes. "You should have that wound tended," Zopher said, peering at the swelling that bulged from thigh to ankle.

"It was tended. Man thinks I'm going to let him saw it off. I'd beg Khoti or Konner for their medicine first."

"You'll die –"

"What good's a warrior without his leg?" Kefta's face blazed red beneath his russet beard. "I'm treating it. It's grown no worse. When the duke comes, I'll take leave and see it tended." Kefta shrugged. "They're not taking it off. My fa became half a man when he lost his arm."

"If that's how he thought himself, certainly he'd –"

"Geleg thinks he recognized a man. I thought you might verify." Kefta pointed at a window by the oak doors of the hall where a face peered out, holding a flag of parlay.

"Hothur."

"Then you treat with him. I'm not in the mood." Kefta started to pivot away, but instead motioned impatiently for a man to support him to the armory where he had set up his command.

"What would I say?" Zopher protested.

"Whatever you want," Kefta said. "They're the ones besieged. Knowing them, their terms are likely laughable."

With an indifferent shrug, Zopher called for a man to unfurl the duke's flag of parlay, and strode to a point just out of reach of the archers on the roof of Eithurdon's Hall. The tall doors nudged open. Only Hothur paced down the steps and across the snowy yard to meet him.

Hothur sprouted a rueful smile when he reached Zopher. "Some innocent." He held out his hands in the motion of truce.

"Why bother, Hothur? You know we'll accept nothing less than surrender."

Hothur nodded toward the hall where faces peered from around the doors and out the upper windows. "They think you will be convinced by the utter wisdom of Ghyldus's prophetic words, and naturally the threat of his wrath. What a lot of fools I am thrown in with." Hothur's tone rang so caustic Zopher almost winced. "I rose from nothing to Captain in the Third Northwest Corps, proud fighters. We were a nation of unparalleled warriors. Look at us now: the corrupted tools of some despot's revenge. We once were wise enough to know when to retreat. This Ghyldus convinces these fools that with just the shake of those medallions they can drive you from Sefresal. He convinces them to ignore their eyes, to imagine Shandeans weak-willed and defenseless. He makes them forget how to look with their minds. They cannot even comprehend that his mission to destroy your king implies weakness. They believe it is to destroy the heart of demonism. And those fools give him the larder."

Hothur took a deep breath then pulled out a sheet of parchment. "I am ordered to read you this dogmatic missive that will compel you to lay down your arms for the greater glory of Ghyldus. What idiocy!" Hothur's disillusion stood out stark in the man's pale face. "Instead, I will let you read it and laugh among yourselves. It turns my stomach. I give instead a word of advice. We have about three hundred and fifty inside. As you know, we have water. We stored most of the food in the buildings you hold. We have perhaps a month of supplies with severe rationing. Our archers depleted their stores and collect your arrows now. These fools trust in Ghyldus's benevolence so much they will not ration, but fritter it away to the refrain, 'Ghyldus will guide us.'" Hothur shook his head. The man appeared near tears. "It sickens me, don Saran, to see such groundless, blind faith." Hothur dropped his hands to his sides. "I have delivered my message. I will return now with your answer."

Zopher stood for a moment so dumbfounded the words would not come. "You don't need to go back, Hothur," Zopher said at last when Hothur moved to leave. "We promised to treat you well when we defeated you, and certainly I owe you my life. If you return, I can't protect you when at last we break the siege. In such a battle, there's no time to determine which of the enemy is honorable. You don't want to die for such foolishness, Hothur! We'll accept your individual surrender and merely detain you until you're no threat to our plans."

Hothur cast a glance over his shoulder at Eithurdon's Hall and then scanned the many armed Shandeans standing watch.

"You kept your promises. Now you must trust me. You're a wise man, Hothur. You see how Ghyldus hurts Minaria. We won't ask you to help us, just not hurt us. For that, you go on knowing you were not a party to this crime. While I don't choose to die, if I did so today, I would at least be comforted knowing I died for something in which I believe. Can you say that?"

Hothur stared at Zopher. His shoulders sagged, his eyes grown moist. Again, he looked over his shoulder at Eithurdon's Halls. He scanned the square full of Shandeans. He shut his eyes and bit his lip, hands forming fists at his side.

"Do you know?" Hothur whispered, his eyes still pressed shut. "Shawnsi are no longer the only targets. New orders say we are to assemble midwives, herb masters, craftsmen and blacksmiths and execute them. It removes the community leaders. The people must turn to us for their medicine and services. We are told to demand more work, take all property and produce, and keep the people hungry. Then the people must rely on us completely for their existence. When a man works from dawn to dusk with nothing to eat he soon grows too weak to think of anything but surviving."

Hothur opened his eyes to stare into Zopher's stunned gaze. "No one questions this policy. They merely take the orders, digest them and see them as the word of Ghyldus. They do not see this as debasement of a proud people, both yours and mine, to parasites. My people have become a disease. All they can do is follow the orders of the largest parasite of us all."

Hothur took a deep breath and held it. Slowly he exhaled as he let the flag of parlay flutter from his fingers to fall in the slush of the yard. He straightened, standing as erect as he could under the burden he wore like a shroud.

"I am your prisoner," he whispered.

Zopher didn't smile. He understood the weight of the decision, had seen it fought out in the Minarian's face. As if the submission had shed some burden, Hothur laughed.

"Imagine their faces," he said as he fell in step with Zopher who led Hothur to the armory to be presented to Kefta. "A captain, an honored warrior, forsaking the Great God of Ea." Hothur's chuckle held menace. "I hope your king fries him." The faces peering from the windows of Eithurdon's Hall opened mouths wide with amazement.

# 31: Tormor Wood

Far from Khoti's home where the snows of the dark moon settled over the northern Lharans, Tormor Wood dripped in a damp wind from the Sea of Simiriel and days on end of drizzle, darkening the already murky forest. Beneath the trees the air hung humid and stale despite the cool wind above, coils of mist lingering around the branches of trees.

In a clearing in the midst of the forest, far from Minarian haunts, the four northerners worked from the moment the dim light found the clearing until dark, training Habdelion's army. A city of tents huddled among the trees beside the clearing, like mushrooms growing in the damp wind, while soldiers drilled to the beat of the forges turning out swords for Shande.

Khoti sweltered in the humid clearing as he watched Anlon repeat the exercise he'd just demonstrated for the seventh time. Anlon jabbed at a straw-filled dummy with a newly forged sword Anlon refused to carry with the respect owed a weapon. Already Anlon blamed Khoti for the tiny cut he'd received when the blade bounded back at him from the dummy.

"A man has bones and armor, not straw protecting him," Khoti chastised. "You tickle it as if you're cutting butter. Hack like it's a tree!"

Anlon glowered at him and continued to cut butter. With such basic skills, Khoti wanted him working with sticks, but Anlon refused, Khoti forced to yield to the whims of his host's son.

Beyond Anlon, Chati drilled Tachi and Habdelion's household in swordplay and Asteria trained apprentices in archery while Tre trained them with daggers. Other soldiers churned the clearing on the backs of Minarian horses, battling dummies or swinging at each other with rag-wrapped sticks. Khoti worked with Anlon alone.

Khoti pulled a long face as Anlon again mounted Fidra.

Anlon wrenched Fidra's head to the side. Khoti hated every moment that he submitted his fine mount to this indignity. They just didn't have enough horses to go around. As Anlon stabbed his sword at the dummy, he again jerked Fidra's mouth. She reared, hanging in mid-air a moment as Anlon toppled from her back, then trotted a few feet away. Anlon jumped up, shouting curses at the horse. Khoti chuckled as Fidra trotted just out of Anlon's reach, her reins trailing along the ground. Anlon scrambled along, trying to grab the reins. Each time he neared, Fidra tossed her head, snapping the reins out of his reach. As she trotted beyond his reach again, he slapped her rump with the flat of his sword.

Khoti's fists clenched at his side.

"Fidra!" he called. She trotted up to him, nuzzling her head against his shoulder, leaving a smear of blood from the bruised corners of her mouth.

Anlon stalked up to him, scowling. Khoti pointed to her injured mouth. "What kind of idiot are you? A horse won't work for you if you don't treat it with respect –"

"What she needs is to know who is boss," Anlon returned, ripping the reins from Khoti's hands.

Khoti grabbed Anlon's arm in a grip Anlon couldn't shake. "It's like this, Anlon. Fidra's mine. You treat her with respect or I'll beat that lesson into you."

"You cannot talk to me that way! I will rule Mershy one day. You are only the leader of armies that do not exist. You are nothing but some goatherder that is –"

"That's King's Champion, perfectly capable of beating you senseless without working up a sweat." Khoti felt his warrior blood rising in him as he stared at Anlon. "Now I see why Han stuck me with you. He wants a man for a son. Well, I'm no nursemaid. I don't care if you ever learn. You're not riding in this army until you've proven yourself."

"And just who are you to say what I can and cannot do in my father's army? It is his, not yours. Who do you think you are? Where did you grow such an ego! You are but some ruffian that steals away lords' daughters and turns them into camp followers. A real trustworthy type you are. Probably sell us to the Minarians as easily as –"

Before Khoti could stop himself, he'd bruised his knuckles on Anlon's face. The son of the Duke of Mershy stared up at Khoti with an expression of utter shock. He blinked several times, as if trying to clear his vision, then stroked his jaw as a knot grew.

Khoti bent, grasping Anlon by the collar, reminded of Tait as he peered into Anlon's face.

"I've dealt with your kind before, Anlon. Those men are dead. Every last one."

Khoti swung the reins up over Fidra's saddle. He clicked his tongue against his teeth. Fidra turned and trotted away from her master. With another click, she stopped. As he continued to click instructions, Fidra displayed her paces for the startled Anlon who lay on the ground, leaning on one elbow and still exploring the bruise on his chin. At last, Fidra trotted back to Khoti, who stroked her nose in praise. She quivered at his touch, her lips tugging at his shirt as if to calm him.

"Creatures respond to respect and good treatment," Khoti said. "You haven't learned respect yet." Khoti stared down at Anlon, who studied the grassy glade as if he hadn't heard a word. "Stand up!" Khoti barked the order.

Anlon jumped to his feet, the haughty expression on his face mysteriously gone.

"I'll teach you respect," Khoti affected a fighting stance, raising his fists.

Anlon stood back, shaking his head. "It is not a fair fight!"

"No? I thought you were more of a man than I, as if class were the marker. Would you rather daggers?" Khoti drew his knife so swiftly Anlon didn't see it until it flashed by his eyes, nicking his cheek. "Or do you prefer swords?" Khoti laid his hand on the hilt of his blade.

Anlon took another step back. "You have lost your mind!"

"Then what is it? You think I'm incapable of training you, but you won't fight me bare-knuckle, with daggers, with sword. Or do you think a fairer fight's if you're armed and I'm not." Khoti kicked Anlon's sword to him. "Go ahead, try me."

"You are pretty sure of yourself."

"He's earned it," Tre said from behind Khoti, who took a step back. The warrior in him chafed his idleness.

"Oh, you call reinforcements. Some fair fight."

"Sure, a fair fight, one armed, one not. I came to see some blood. Most likely yours," Tre said with a grin. "It's been a while since I've seen a good fight, at least a couple weeks. I only waste my energy killing Minarians. How many battles you fought? How many of the enemy in your tally?" Tre looked Anlon up and down. "Tell you the truth. I came to protect you. Khoti gets carried away sometimes. So tell me. How much battle you seen?"

"I never said I was some soldier."

"You're not any soldier, little Lord," Tre laughed. "What do you suppose we're doing here? We're experienced, even the Lady Asteria's fought for Shande. So, why don't you just let us help you so we can get on with it?" Tre turned back to his charges.

"Thanks, Tre," Khoti called. "I've never been the diplomat." Tre strode on, grinning and shaking his head. Khoti turned to Anlon. "Well?"

"I am not looking to fight you."

"Then do as I say. If you see battle, and let that rampant stupidity of yours loose, I don't want to explain to Han why you're the one soldier we couldn't train."

When Anlon approached Fidra, this time he patted her neck, and mumbled a few words before mounting. Khoti couldn't get rid of the echo of Asteria's accusations, that his ego exceeded him. Was that why he and the duke's son were like a spark to fuel? Maybe jealousy was part of it, for both of them. Asteria chose the life of a warrior over life with Anlon. What a blow for a man like Anlon to face rejection from someone soiled by her reputation.

Khoti smiled to himself as Anlon hacked the straw dummy as if attacking a tree. Maybe Anlon needed time, as Khoti had, to learn the futility of defiance in a chain of command. The hours passed almost unnoted beneath the overcast sky as noon gave way to the growing gloom of evening in the forest.

The clouds overhead thinned and late afternoon sun peeked through for a buttery moment before Khoti called an end to the day's training. As Khoti supervised Anlon's proper care for his equipment, he paused in his scrutiny to wave at Tedwa's approach. He grinned when he recognized the man with Tedwa as Kefta's brother Mitte, who had been one of Khoti's scouts. The two hugged, grasping arms in the greeting of men happy just to see the other remained alive. He noted Anlon's odd expression at witnessing the greeting, almost a jealousy of the special knowledge Mitte and Khoti shared. Khoti grinned more broadly.

"What news brings you that the Tachi let you enter a free man and they bound me up like a bale of fleece?"

"'Twas hard, mind you, to convince them I was no Minarian spy," Mitte said with a grin, pulling at a strand of flaming red hair. "I so look the part."

"Khoti had a mean look," Tedwa said with a sage nod.

Mitte's smile faded fast. "I came with news, some good, some bad. When I left, we had a little over three hundred Minarians besieged in Eithurdon's Hall. An old friend of yours surrendered." Mitte gestured at the brassy cuff on Khoti's arm.

"Hothur!" Khoti supposed he should have expected it.

"To Zopher! If you want to see a strange friendship ... but then again, Hothur's told us things that has Zopher racing off to his private battles. You're to watch your borders! Hothur says Ghyldus learned the king is here and his warriors are a terror seeking him."

Khoti scowled. He slammed his fist against his thigh so hard he felt a bruise rise. "I shouldn't have left him! It's what he feared. And Zopher! He's a fool if he thinks he can help her." Khoti peered at Mitte. "Did Eithur send any message for me?"

Mitte squirmed. "Only ... to the Headman of the Independent Lharan Tribes the Duke of Lharan sends ... sympathies."

"Sympathies?"

Mitte cleared his throat. "You know Amhese led a squad under Ytri in the attack on Sefresal? I served under her with honor."

Khoti turned away to stare across the clearing to where the soldiers stowed their gear and cooled the horses as shadows crept out from beneath the trees. Suddenly he felt drained and alone.

"Our squad took the armory in minutes, the most successful assault. When the battles broke the enemy rushed for the armory. She took five with her." Mitte fell silent, awkward.

"Was she given to the spirits?" Khoti asked, his voice raspy. He wished Asteria stood near this one time that he needed to reach out to her.

"Kefta accompanied her to the Val. Konner saw to the rites. I really am sorry, Khoti."

Khoti shrugged, a muscle working in his jaw. "That's the choice she made. That's the way of things, you outlive parents. She would've hated wasting away as an elder." He took a deep breath. "There's more?"

Mitte more easily recounted the rest of the events in the mountains, and the news Hothur volunteered.

Khoti turned to Tedwa as Mitte finished. "Han will need to know about Sefresal and Shiad," Khoti mumbled. Tedwa nodded, grasping Khoti's arm a moment before leading Mitte toward Habdelion's rambling shack.

Khoti turned back to his chores to find Anlon staring at him.

"I am sorry for you," Anlon muttered, reddening. "I guess you come from a warrior family. That is why you know what you do."

Khoti would have laughed but the grief was too keen in his throat. "If shepherds and miners are warriors. Now I can say my entire family has been erased by the Minarians." Khoti peered at Anlon, his gaze narrowing to that brutal battle stare that sent his enemy fleeing. "You wonder why I know what I do? When we've lost a few men in battle, some of your friends, maybe a relative, you'll understand. It's getting closer to you, Anlon. You'd best be prepared." Khoti slapped Fidra on the rump, sending her out into the clearing to graze as he carried her saddle into the creeping shadows of evening under the eaves of Tormor Wood.

As the clank of the forges continued and the weary chatter of soldiers heading to their tents greeted him, he clung to the knowledge that now he built warriors for Shande that would mete out his revenge.

A few days later, as the cold moon chased the dark moon, Khoti followed Anlon into the forest, far from the perimeter of Tachi that watched Habdelion's haunts. They walked on the animal trails as the Tachi did, Anlon refusing to say where they headed, but that he wanted to show Khoti something and see if the champion would see it without Anlon pointing to it.

The farther they went, the more a sense warned Khoti to be wary. Some undercurrent of danger hung in the air. What could threaten them so deep within the wood? Anlon seemed so eager to prove himself Khoti didn't want to thwart the enthusiasm. If Anlon hadn't finally stopped in a small clearing an hour from camp, Khoti would have called a halt to the game.

"Look around, see if you can figure it," Anlon challenged with a smile.

"If it's important enough for you to drag me from other things to come out here –"

"Oh, then, just look at the ground, the tracks," Anlon grumbled. "You have no sense of fun about you."

"Looking for animal sign is a sense of fun?"

"It is the competition! It is not just animal tracks." He pointed at a patch of bare ground.

Khoti crouched to peer at a horseshoe print left in the moist soils of the damp clearing. They were at least a half-day old. "It's not Shandean," Khoti admitted. "Good spot, Anlon. What were you doing out here? What were Minarians doing this far in –"

He froze, hearing a sound unnatural to the wood he had come to know. He signed for Anlon to take cover in deep grass on the edge of the clearing where the canopy threw long shadows. Khoti crouched behind the still live branches of a fallen tree.

Soon, he clearly heard voices, then words, and a horse's snort. Likely one of the scouting parties Tre trained, he thought. He didn't hear the musical cadence of the Tachi, nor the lilt of Habdelion's household.

"You go on ahead and tell them we hear the shawnsi seer is in Shela now," a voice said. A Minarian accent. "We will take care of Verdaen and send for troops to destroy this so-called army," the voice continued.

The shapes of four horsemen flitted among the trees. Khoti craned his neck to spy Anlon crouched in the tall grass. He signed for Anlon to follow his cue. Khoti couldn't let them carry this news from Tormor Wood! As they neared, he recognized the fluttering horsetails of the Eidhalt on their helms. His mouth went dry. He doubted Anlon could defeat an Eidhalt and these Eidhalt had come for battle. Besides their swords, they carried long spears and clubs bobbed at their hips. Beneath their cloaks, breastplates peeked, not the mesh or leather armor most Minarian soldiers wore. Large medallions glinted on their chests, their capes fluttering back behind them though no wind reached beneath the canopy. Even their horses wore bright trappings, red gems set in their bridles. He had never faced such heavily armed men before, and certainly not on foot without strong support beside him. They appeared far more capable than any Eidhalt he'd ever encountered. Khoti doubted just the two of them could stop them. But he had to try.

He eased himself closer to the path they followed, and observed as Anlon did the same. Signing more instructions, he crouched low, wishing he had his bow.

When the lead rider passed Khoti and rode abreast of Anlon, Anlon leapt from hiding to knock the Minarian from his horse. In the same instant, Khoti knocked the last rider from his mount and swiftly slit the man's throat with his dagger. The second rider rode at Anlon, his spear pointed at Anlon's chest. Anlon leapt aside and fell still in the long grass as the man he'd unhorsed regained his mount.

Khoti grabbed the spear from the horse of the man he slew and turned to face the oncoming Minarians. He had no skill with this kind of weapon nor the strength to resist a blow from a horsed rider. As the first man bore down on him, a grim smile on his face, Khoti knelt, then sprung aside last moment, using his propulsion and the weight of the heavy spear to knock his enemy's weapon aside and strike the man's mount from under him.

The two mounted Eidhalt circled around and came at him, discarding their spears and drawing swords to better maneuver in the tiny glade. They rode at him from both sides, hemming him in as the man he'd unhorsed captured the loose beast of the dead Eidhalt. Khoti's breath quickened as he fended them off, first one, then the other as they came at him. He had to stop them! The familiar fury rose in his limbs.

"Verdaen!" one called when Khoti's cuff flashed in the sunlight. They wanted him dead. He could see it in their faces.

Too pressured fending off the combined blows of the two horsemen, he didn't see his danger as the third Minarian approached. Last minute, he rolled beneath one of the horses, dodging shifting hooves and slashing upward as he went. When the horse stumbled, he wielded his sword two-handed at the unbalanced rider. His blade came against the man's breastplate, sliding up to cut the base of the rider's chin, not a fatal wound.

The air shifted behind him. He whirled too late. A blade slashed across his back, but his move averted a deadly blow. He ducked around the side of a horse, stabbing it to bring the rider down as he spun away.

Blood pulsed down his back, sweat running in his eyes as his breath came in ragged gasps. He bent beneath their combined blows, sure and powerful, their armor turning his weapon. He sensed a man behind him as he engaged another in front. Knocking the sword from his opponent's grasp, he lunged. His blade slid into the man's neck and glanced off bone. In a fluid motion, he spun, bringing his bloody sword up to parry the other's blow before the first fell. From the corner of his eye he saw the mounted man, holding out his medallion, lips moving.

Suddenly, massive talons descended out of the air at Khoti. Attached to a foul-smelling dark mass, like a conjuration hastily formed so that only its weapons emerged, it gripped him in the shoulder, the stench almost toppling him as his eyes watered and his throat closed. Giant wings extended from some elusive mass, beating him until his head throbbed. He tried to duck out of the way, expecting each moment that the other man's blade would fall on him, or that the horseman would now stab him. Again, Khoti caught movement from the corner of his eye. He ducked aside, slashing at the creature as the talons tried to rend his shoulder. It exploded in a fury of sparks that swirled skyward. The man raised his medallion again, but suddenly sped away, his horse kicking up sod behind him. Khoti turned to find the remaining Minarian impaled on Tedwa's spear.

Khoti sank to his knees, leaning heavily on his thighs and gasping. Anlon jumped up from the grass, unscathed, and clapped.

"Such a lesson by the best!" Anlon crowed. "You still needed help!"

Khoti didn't think; the warrior in him leapt at Anlon, bloody dagger drawn. Anlon crumpled beneath Khoti's solid weight, his eyes bulging as Khoti pressed the dagger to Anlon's throat.

"The game isn't so funny now, is it!" Khoti hissed in Anlon's face, a tawnkat's angry threat. "How many will die for your entertainment! Is the one escaping going for reinforcements? Or do they race to Ghyldus to report the king's location? You make me sick!"

Khoti felt Tedwa's firm grip on the shoulder the creature had clawed and let the Tachi pull him from Anlon's chest. Khoti could only gasp with the rage that filled him, his perilous cat's eyes trained on Anlon.

"Cross me again, Anlon," Khoti threatened as Tedwa continued to restrain him.

Anlon sucked for air, still lying on his back in the glade as Tedwa towed Khoti to a patch of sun.

"Your timing, Tedwa. I owe you," Khoti mumbled as the Tachi peeled away Khoti's shirt, the bloody fabric clinging.

"I hear horses pass. See Minarian tracks. I follow. My curiosity is fortunate." He peered at the talon wounds which stung, but had done no serious damage. "Their magic has teeth." He plucked a feather from Khoti's hair and held it out to the sun, where it withered to white ash.

Khoti winced when Tedwa pulled apart the sword wound on his back, then shivered to think of the strange creature.

"Not serious," Tedwa muttered, studying the crisscross of scars on Khoti's back. "Just one more mark from Minarians."

Khoti felt Anlon's gaze on him, and cast a glance over his shoulder. Anlon's mouth hung open as he stared at Khoti's marked back. Khoti yanked his shirt on.

"We'll have to be ready for trouble from the one that escaped." Khoti slammed his fist into the turf, churned and bloodied by the dying horses. "Arshal's out there somewhere trailed by such Eidhalt and I'm here doing nothing for him! If they send an army of magical creatures at him, can he escape? And there's someone among us who told them where to look!"

"You do for the king. He is nothing without an army," Tedwa stated. He stood, offering his hand to Khoti and pulled him to his feet.

"I failed. The man that escaped –"

"You expect much from yourself," Tedwa stated. "Odds uneven. Better armed, mounted, armored, with magic. You expected too much."

As they headed back to Habdelion's shack, Khoti threw a glance at Anlon trailing them. "I expected too much." Khoti growled as they trudged along the path he and Anlon had followed.

"You watch him," Asteria warned him later as she bathed and wrapped the gash on his back. "I sense trouble."

Khoti waved the warning away, his anger fading. They sat outside his tent on logs around the fire, their friends already gathering as they did each night to tell stories of their different worlds. "He's just got some learning to do."

Heat rushed into his face as her fingers made his skin tingle. Khoti twisted to look up at her. She gave him a curious smile as he turned away. He remembered her disgust with him, her disillusionment conveyed with such bitterness. His skin clenched and he shivered.

"Is something wrong?" she asked, leaning over his shoulder to look at him.

"You tickled me."

"I did not," she said. He thought he caught a private smile on her face as she turned to fashion a bandage for the cut.

"I think Anlon thought it all a game," Khoti said. "He's so competitive. I almost killed him." Khoti gave Chati a sour smile, holding up his thumb and forefinger to measure a tiny distance. "I doubt something like this will happen again. Right now, he's probably realizing the danger we're in. Remember, we were out there because he saw those tracks. All four would've escaped –"

"And just what was he doing out there to find the tracks, I'd like to know," Chati grumbled as he fed kindling to the fire.

Khoti stared at him. "You think –"

"I don't know what to think." Chati shrugged. "It just all seems so ... convenient. But I wasn't there."

"No, you weren't. I'd have given everything to have had you and Tre there." Khoti glanced up at Asteria. "And a good archer. None would've escaped." He winced a little as she bound the wound tight. "Han's son knows what they do to shawnsi –"

"He's not shawnsi," Tre said. "He's got his own plans. He said he'd rule Mershy, Minarians or not."

"It's not just shawnsi," Cydwyn mumbled. He peered into the darkness toward Habdelion's shack. "He knows that. He can't ignore eight hundred of us. I don't trust him."

"He's blind to some things, all right," Tre said, nudging Asteria as he brushed by to get more wood for the fire. She reached out to swat him but he'd ducked beyond her reach.

Khoti stared into the flames. Anlon might be selfish and foolish, but he didn't seem so ruthless as to turn against his family. Khoti looked up at Asteria. "Do you really believe the son of a duke would betray his father?"

Asteria helped him on with a lightweight tunic suited to the warm forest, before she spoke.

"Look at the doubts people have," she said quietly. "Han and Zel refused their king. Han relented, but he is shawnsi. The threat is to his existence. Anlon may have been raised in a shawnsi house, but he is not shawnsi. The extermination of my people might trouble him little, if he is that callous. He cautioned Han against listening to King Arshal, claiming the Minarians would relent in time and allow normalcy to return. He is eager to declare Habda flawed because of her mother's illness. I think he is more concerned about becoming duke, or ruling this province without the title, than he is about Shande."

Khoti stabbed a stick into the ground, his face a scowl. "I just don't believe it."

"You believed it of Tait," Tre reminded him.

Khoti inclined his head. "Anlon's got more to lose supporting the Minarians. I just think he's impetuous, immature. I've done stupid things –"

"Not like that," Chati said. "You never risked anyone's life but your own to prove a point."

"I'm still not ready to think that of him. We can keep an eye on him. I'm sure it was an accident. It's his forest. He's entitled to wander in it where he wishes. And it's natural the Minarians would leave the forest by the same route they came in."

"Just watch yourself," Asteria warned. "They know you are here, now."

Khoti shook his head. "They seem to know a lot. I wonder just how much."

Whatever they knew, Ghyldus knew. Khoti's dismay at his failure clung to him like the damp of Tormor.

# 32: Wrecked

As a dark moon squall whipped the Sea of Simiriel into a fury, the King of Shande stared into the black clouds rolling at him from the southwest and berated himself for a fool. He had spent months alone in this little boat and aside from the first few days each moment passed more unbearable than the last. His great adventure dissolved into pure drudgery and discomfort. Certainly, the vision that convinced him to take this route had been crafted by Ghyldus, or even Fyraer. His early successes only made his failure so much greater.

He lost his way in the maze of islands off the mouths of the Detarian and Akora rivers, wasting weeks trying to find his way around reefs and bays that drew him into an almost land-locked trap. At last, running low on fresh water, food and patience, he let the wind and current take him, hoping it would lead him out to sea. Instead, he blew days backward to the Detarian river delta. It took another week to convince the Detarian tribes that the King of Shande truly stood before them and needed supplies and repairs so he could continue his journey. In a month at sea, he traveled no farther than a week of easy riding on horseback.

At last set on a course for Shela, guided by Detarian boatmen in their long canoes, Arshal rowed through the arid heat of the waning moon's last days. When the Detarians left him, alone again on a quiet sea with no breath to push him, he rowed until his arms and shoulders went numb. Callouses deepened on his hands until they were so thick he could barely make a fist and his shoulder muscles strained against the sleeves of his tunic. Burned and weary he made Shela in the middle days of the harvest moon only to languish trying to make any contact.

He spent weeks cajoling anyone to listen to him, many doubting that a solitary figure so weather-worn and calloused could be the King of Shande. His subjects even threatened to reveal him to the Eidhalt seeking him if he didn't leave the port immediately. While they watched in awe as he made each display of the stone's power more convincing, more draining, they would not help him. They lived in ruin already, their lot perhaps the worst in all of Shande because they dared fight the occupation with deadly poisoned arrows and darts. He asked just too much to stand there asking for help without an army to back him up.

Now he spent another lonely month and a half at sea with nothing to show for it, no support, no subjects willing to gamble on the white-haired seer with the magic stone in his hand.

Arshal brooded in the cramped boat, staring out at the Shandean shoreline in search of places he might find food, water, a friendly face, or hide from passing ships. He found nothing. Only a half day inland from the lush, rain-soaked coast, loomed a desert so vast he doubted he had the courage to face it. He would have to, eventually, to reach Euzzeldir.

And now another storm.

Arshal unstepped the little mast and hung it in its brackets as the first blast of cold air churned the shallow sea into a rough chop. He clung to the rudder as waves buffeted the little boat as if fighting for dominance over the craft. At last, settling into a decided course, the chop grew to swells looming larger and larger as the wind built around him.

The sky opened. Rain slanted at him as he fought to keep the little boat on course, uncertain in the giant swells and lowered sky where the shoreline now lay or the submerged reefs or islands that dotted this treacherous sea. Lightning struck, ever closer. Thunder deafened him. He had ridden out many squalls in this long voyage, but none compared to this. The Straits of Saraihi lay days ahead yet, but with this wind he feared he would be driven far east of where he hoped to land on the Shikoran shore near the seat of King Wyeff Shikora. He wanted to appeal again for foreign aid before seeking Euzzeldir, far lands seeming less likely than his own subjects to dismiss him. Shikora could outfit him to face the Jashiho Desert, and with a promise from Shikora, Arshal might sway the intimidating Joffan prince.

Arshal peered ahead into the gray curtain of rain. He could discern nothing but the white crests of waves all around him, no shore, no horizon. For all he knew he could be blown through the straits and into the Far Sea, not even seeing the treacherous straits in this closed world. He set the oars in the water and pushed backward, locking his rudder to the side, hoping to bob in circles. He had no sense of distance in the murky darkness. When each lightning flash split the sky, he saw only the march of waves. When rain began to fill his little boat, he could no longer hold the oars steady. Cupped hands bailed as the boat sank lower and lower in the water. Waves threatened to pour over the side as the little craft grew sluggish and resistant.

An icy blast of wind crashed from above, almost overturning him. Just when he thought he had leaned far enough to balance the craft, a large wave threw the boat on its side. Arshal clung to the wales, fighting to stay aboard, only to upset the balance when another wave crashed against the craft, overturning it.

Sputtering up from beneath the boat he managed to stay with it, coughing water as he struggled to grip the keel. His grip weakened as each successive wave sought to right the vessel again. Long minutes in the cool water sapped his strength as he fought the press of water from above and below. At last, he scrambled atop the overturned boat. When he took in his predicament, he saw, just out of reach, an oar taking its own course away from him. The mast floated beside him, sail so sodden he couldn't lift it without losing his balance. Despite his attempt to hold onto it with one leg pressed against the boat's side, it, too, took a course of its own. With his water supply, if still lashed to the boat, likely spoiled, and his food certainly wet and worthless, survival appeared bleak. He had only his cloak, the sword always at his side, the small pouch on his belt, and an overturned and unnavigable boat.

When the squall line passed, the wind died to a series of sturdy gusts, the rain a steady downpour that kept the world hidden from him. The swells still loomed large, but the rough chop went the way of the wind. He didn't know how long the storm continued its slow pace overhead, but when the skies at last cleared to a few fleeting tatters, stars shone overhead and the moon tinged the thin clouds silver. As he calculated his position, he felt only utter defeat. He drifted northeast, but from what point he couldn't tell. If near the Shandean coastline, he should be able to spy it in the spare light of the moon. He saw nothing but waves.

As Arshal stared over the sea, he could only think that as western Shande went ahead with his plans, counting on him, he failed. When Eithur and Han struck, they would be alone. He should have listened to his council instead of sketchy osfothye dreams and visions. Why hold a council if only to ignore it when voices argued against a fool's mission? How could so much stock be placed in one man, and that one man take so many risks? Certainly, history would name him a fool. Here he held the gods' gift in the palm of his hand, and he risked all of Shande to do things his way. Though more dangerous, he could have tried the cross-country journey with scouts for guides. He should have let Khoti accompany him overland, as his champion suggested. Wasn't that the purpose of the office he'd bestowed? Then, Arshal knew the Eidhalt searched Shande for him. Often in his lonely and frustrating dreams at sea, he saw their illusory beasts flicker to life at Ghyldus's behest. He and Nali had trusted the visions in the past to succeed. What if the intended path wouldn't have cost both of them their families? Visions could be wrong. What if they meant to caution them from the very paths they took? If he hadn't limited himself to the stone, maybe he could have called a current to sweep him to shore. For all he knew, the currents in this part of the sea flowed back west to the Sea of Tebez. His stone could only light the way.

As the long night passed, and then the day to follow, Arshal floated, out of sight of land, without food or water. He couldn't sleep for fear he'd lose his grip on the craft. He couldn't even tell if the boat moved, as nothing about the scene changed from hour to hour. Once, he tried to slip into now calmer waters and right the boat, clinging to it and attempting to push it over at the same time. He only tired himself out and swallowed enough salt water to make him sick and even more parched.

He decided he'd selected a terrible way to die: of thirst in the midst of a sea. He remembered Khoti's tale of scavengers swirling overhead and slinking in the shadows nearby as he lay near death, how he'd felt so lonely and helpless it overwhelmed him. Arshal pictured himself lying on the bottom of the Sea of Simiriel, the fish and shellfish eating his remains, his mission ended as the gem in his palm glittered between bones of a lifeless hand.

By the color of the water, he thought perhaps the sea grew deeper beneath him. Did he close on the deep rift of the Straits of Saraihi, or float over the great basin off north central Shikora, far from any known cities?

Sometime the next night, while Arshal struggled against sleep, the winds picked up.

His mind conjured up the consequences of his failure as he wandered in the realm of the feverish, his tongue grown thick in his mouth and his eyes dry. The emaciated faces of starving

Shelans turned accusing gazes on him, their backs bloody with the lash. They peered at him from the darkness where the stars should have glinted overhead.

He dreamt of the tumbling rivers from which Khoti drew fleshy fish. Before his eyes, white froth shone in the moonlight in the midst of the Val's dark lake. Waves reared larger, their crests purling with whitecaps. On the other side of the lake, instead of the Val's mountains, a dark line of shore drew closer. A thunder, at first like a waterfall, but then like surf, roared over the tiny lake.

He opened his eyes to find his dream around him. His little craft rose on a wave to lurch forward and slam into a rocky headland his shaky reason told him had to be Pali Point on the Shandean shore. The boat splintered to pieces. Numb, Arshal barely had the presence to crawl beyond water's reach and cling to the fine sand beyond the rocks, feeling instead of solid ground, the roll of the sea beneath him.

When he awoke, at first, he thought he'd been blinded by some blow when he'd smashed into the shore. After rubbing the cake of salt and sand from his eyes, day blazed back at him. Tongue thick in his mouth, his mind felt fogged by thirst. Every muscle in his body ached, each certainly bruised when he struck the rocks.

He forced himself to his feet. Stumbling and staggering at first, he caromed off the rocks, off trees, dropping to his knees and rising again before he had a sense of purpose. He let his instinct save him.

He staggered up the beach into the shade of a dense forest fed by rich rains from the sea. The cool shadows eased the fever in him. He let his feet carry him along the slope of the land to a small, marshy water hole covered by a thin scum of algae, the stale water replenished by recent rain. Dozens of animal tracks told his hazy reason he could drink from the water. He gulped it down, only to be sick, then gulped again. He continued to drink, after a while allowing himself only small sips to ease his parched throat.

At last, he sat back and tried to take stock of himself: bruised and weary, and sick from dehydration that would leave him weak long after he drank his fill. He had no food, and certainly didn't know what he could eat in such a forest. He knew this must be Pali Point. The lushness and the jut of rocks aiming back to the southwest matched the maps he had carried, memorized in his boredom of long days at sea, and now lost with the splinters of his boat. Shikora's border with the Sea of Simiriel stretched barren, brown and fringed by low mountains, Simiriel's rain seldom falling there. If Shande, if Pali Point, then he had reached Joffa. The forest would end in savanna to the north, falling from a plateau to the barren Jashiho Desert, a place forgotten by Simiriel. The hardiest of Shande's diverse peoples made the most isolated spot in Shande their home, overseen by Prince Euzzeldir. Arshal had no choice now but to seek the man who sent messengers home with jeers and laughter and to try to salvage something of his misguided mission.

Stiff from the long stint at sea, Arshal only moved a short distance north before nightfall. Each step away from the little puddle of water made him more nervous than the last. He had no way to carry water and no idea if he'd encounter more. It would only grow more arid the farther north he went. The village of Hainad that he sought, if it still existed under Minarian rule, could be anywhere. Only one road led to Hainad, a place where the perfect blend of sands fed the production of fine crystal and glass. If too far east, he would find no road. If he reached the road, he might be many days' journey too far west. A few deep wells dotted the length of road, but set the distance apart of a rider, not a man crawling toward his death.

Ignoring everything but the moment's need to survive, Arshal again let his instincts lead him, not only north, but to the few ponds and the little streams draining rainfall back to the sea. He watched for animal trails and followed them to water.

Food was another matter. After noting birds tearing the berries from a tree, he gorged himself on the bitter fruit. He felt sick the entire night that followed. The next morning, he picked as many of the berries as he could roll in his cloak. It might be all he had to sate the incessant growling of his stomach. He lived off the berries for two days before he ran out. That night he stumbled upon some sort of groundrat and without thinking, blinded it with the stone, stunning the creature long enough to stab it with his sword. His tinder worthless from his lengthy dip in the sea, he found dry puffs of seed and with his flint sparked a small fire, crudely cleaned the animal with his sword and spitted it, at last dining on what seemed a feast. While no food of choice, tasting of the bitter nuts and insects on which the creature foraged, it kept him on his feet another day.

Arshal imagined a picture of himself aimlessly padding through the dense forest, white-haired and sun-burned, head to the ground in search of tracks, with no knowledge of what he sought and ignorant of what predators lurked here. He must look a mad man. Though in some parts of the coastlands small tribes congregated and lived off this forest's bounty, he felt as inept here as he had in the mountains. He didn't even know what things to be afraid of, and what not. For all he knew, he passed a bounty of plants to feed him. Since he saw nothing eating them, he didn't dare taste them.

He did shy from the plethora of snakes hanging from the trees, or sidling through the undergrowth and even poking their heads out of little ponds to stare at him, their tongues darting with a message of menace. He lived in terror of discovering too late which were poisonous and which merely bluffing. The forest seethed with them. Some lazed in the sun on fallen logs, only a span long. Some, as thick as his arm and twice his length, coiled up trees or stretched along a branch. Insects, too, kept him wary. He feared some beetle or spider might fell him with a curious bite. From the tracks he found, he knew some cousin of Khoti's patron cat wandered these forests and the thought of it left him at times too terrified to close his eyes.

As the days passed the landscape changed. The air turned arid, the water holes fewer and farther. Animal trails became more random. In time the undergrowth grew sparse, the trees sturdier, their roots anchoring them deep into the ground as leaves reached for dew to sustain them. He discovered a plant with ewer-shaped leaves that held several cups of water. As water sources grew scarce, he relied more and more on the few drops he allowed himself from this guarded treasure tied to his belt, its long leaves folding over to seal the ewer's mouth.

He continued to watch for small animals to blind and kill, always afraid he might expend too much if he did more than flash a little light in their eyes. While difficult to clean and not much of a meal, at times the forest's variety of mice and a few small birds that crossed his path had to suffice. Any time he came upon a tree bearing nuts or fruit he waited to witness animals eating from it, or searched the ground for signs that creatures dined there. This vigilance paid off as he came to recognize a few bushes that no animal came near, and the trees and shrubs with the sweetest and most palatable offerings.

After a week of such travel, in the first days of the cold moon, Arshal at last reached the open savannah fringing the Jashiho desert. He knew he'd ambled a far piece more than he'd traveled, often turning himself around within the forest as he followed trails to water. The journey from Pali Point to Hainad might in real distance equal the three or four days' walk from Sefresal to Eilime. But before the Minarians came, prosperous inns sheltered travelers along a plain road with wells, not this struggle just to lift legs over undergrowth or find ten berries in a day's foraging.

Now he faced the most difficult trek, his route unlikely to take him near potable water. He retraced his steps an hour or so to the last muddy pond he had found. It spread from a small spring surrounded by a rim of lime, evaporating before it could form a stream. He filled the half dozen ewer plants he had collected, attaching each to his belt so it wouldn't slip out or tear from bouncing against his leg or each other. His cloak held a few nuts and fruits he'd found. Now he added juicy tubers he saw several animals digging for. The root grew abundantly near this pond and he spent several hours collecting this prized staple that could both quench thirst and fill an empty belly. Just the few he nibbled on while he dug kept him on his feet all day.

Returning to the savannah he walked down the long stepped plain toward desert. The open savannah held dense scrub and grasses that grasped at his feet; and in the open beneath the sun, the heat baked him to exhaustion. When the grass gave way to rock and gravel, the footing bruised his feet even through sturdy boots. The sun parched him each day, the nights near freezing.

When rock and stone at last gave way to coarse sand, he waded into it as if through a river. He labored each step to climb the windward side of dunes, the sand slipping from beneath his feet, each dune larger than the last. When he descended the leeward side he slid, almost falling, risking the destruction of his delicate water plants. Sometimes the sand sucked at his legs, like sinks in a river bottom. Or the wind would whip up and blast his face raw and burn his eyes as the fine grains filled his nose and mouth with grit. He feared resting, when the shifting sands might bury him, the heat parch him or the cold freeze him.

Already weakened by his uncertain diet, and only allowing himself half an ewer plant's store each day – not nearly enough to replenish the amount he shed in labor or breathing – Arshal's pace slowed further as he grew light headed and disoriented. Even the treasured roots couldn't keep him on his feet. When he squinted out at the endless stretch of dunes, he dismayed ever finding Hainad, no more than one small grain in all this sand.

When he emptied the water plants one by one, he filled the ewers with the last of his roots, fearing sunsickness if he didn't put on the heavy cloak, despite the heat. His steps grew confused and the ache of thirst more unbearable.

He wandered a week into the Jashiho, ten days from the edge of the forest that now loomed inviting in his memory, before emptying the last of the water plants. He tried to ration the roots, but most had lost their flavor and grown tough in the arid desert. To chew them now only made his mouth drier. He stumbled often or fell. Each time he rose, it took more will and effort to move on. When he hadn't relieved himself for more than a day, he knew death stalked him.

Then the wind came up again. Though clouds rolled overhead, promising rain but not delivering, he gained little relief from the cooler temperatures as the sand abraded any exposed skin and dust filled his throat. As the sand storm raged, he didn't dare stop, but continued on, bent and parched, seeking to face away from the wind. The wind lost direction at the base of each dune, circling him like dervish wolvers.

When he crested the largest dune he'd yet to climb, gasping through the thick film of sand scratching his throat, he stepped out blindly and lost his footing. He fell on his side, scrambling for a hold on the shifting, steep, lee side of the dune. The sand allowed no grip and he slid faster. He came to a jolting halt on the hard, wind-swept base of the dune, leg bent beneath him. From the way it had twisted, and the stabbing pain shooting up into his hip, he knew he'd broken it.

Arshal cried out his frustration, but only got a mouthful of sand. He had ruined everything. He would die here – starve, die of thirst, be buried by sand – but certainly die.

He tried to straighten his leg. The pain made him cry out again, the sweat breaking out on his face wasting more precious liquid. He used his sword to pull him up, his leg dragging useless behind him when he tried to stand. Dizziness and nausea settled on him, the swirl of sand becoming dark before his eyes, each grain a flash of light. He took a hopping step, using his sword to hold him up. After a few tentative paces, the jolts sending a fire through his leg, he again fell in a sprawl.

He lay there a long time, only a pace up the next dune, the sand sifting around him with a ghostly sound. He had to give up. Just accept it and stop torturing himself. As he thought it, he sobbed, dry-eyed. He imagined Shande's people suffering an eternity of slavery because of his failure.

"How could you let me be such a fool?" he shouted, his words carried away into the shift of sand. "Why have you let me fail? They'll suffer because of me!"

No answer came but the sand hissing over the crest of the dune. If he died, would he remain some lonely spirit never allowed to pass completely from life to death as Khoti's people believed? Unfulfilled, unaccomplished, would he wander forever, witness to the consequences of his lost mission?

He screamed, a bellow that tore his sand-scarred throat so that he tasted blood when he coughed.

"Terremar!" he shouted into the gray sky. The stone in the palm of his hand barely glowed, only a dark and murky surface like the luminescence of moonlight behind thick clouds. He knew he fell toward that room inside him where he might lock away the pain. He couldn't allow it. He might never escape that place, merely wander from room to room for eternity.

The sand settling over him collected in his clothing, weighting him. Already it caked the bloody wound where his bone pushed through his skin. He wished for Khoti, could almost see the penetrating emerald eyes staring at him, feel the fingers probing the wound, the breath of spirit Khoti mastered. He opened his eyes, half expecting to see Khoti bent over his leg. He found only sand and the overcast skies above. His journey had come to an end.

He felt a sudden desperate need to move, to make one last effort. What if just over this dune Hainad waited and he died almost within sight of it? He rolled onto his stomach and crawled, using his sword and his good leg to propel him up the slope. With each movement forward the world faded before his eyes. He had to expend his last energies in some attempt to save himself. The effort made him choke more desperately for water, for anything that could sate his thirst. He paused, reaching for a root, but the water plants were gone, blown away or covered by sand. No food or water, a mangled leg, death loomed certain before him.

That realization made him dig more desperately for purchase. He continued to edge up the dune, much smaller than the one he had fallen down. As he reached the crest, he almost wept at the sight below. Not Hainad, not the road, he found only more sand. As far as he could see, no people, no well, nothing but sand.

He eased himself down the slope, wondering how he could be so stupid as to kill himself trying to reach only one more dune.

He laughed at his idiocy. When he laughed, he knew he had lost his senses.

When at last he reached bottom, he lay in a stupor, waking long enough to cut his hand on the edge of his sword to suck at the blood to give his tongue the moisture it craved. As the last hours of daylight passed, the wind finally dying as dusk fell, Arshal lay in wait for anything that might pass. When darkness closed, and no sound could be heard but the sift of sand slipping by his ears and again collecting in his clothes, and as the chill fell over the desert with the sojourn of the sun, Arshal at last crawled inside the little room in his head, to die.

# 33: Detarian

A figure detached itself from the shadows, approaching the glimmer of red in the darkness beneath the forest canopy.

"There is much I could tell you," he gasped, gaze locked on the two rubies glowing from the medallion. All his certainty, all his rehearsed words, the fabric of all his plans fled at the sight of the talisman.

"Tell me now," a shadowy figure replied. The red gems seemed to flare and a hand clamped his arm.

Eyes accustomed to the deep nights beneath the canopy, the man studied the black-garbed Minarian, the arsenal of the Eidhalt glimmering in the faint starlight touching them.

"If I tell all you will kill me." He dragged his gaze from the medallion. "A request in return. I gave you good information once. It is your fault you failed to take advantage of it."

The Minarian spat into the darkness, releasing his grip. "What you ask, if reasonable, will be considered. You are hardly in a position to negotiate." Something flashed in the darkness, then the edge of a knife against skin, a cat's scratch.

The man held his ground. "What I can give you, and what you can give me in return, yes, there is a position for negotiation."

After a long moment, the Eidhalt gripped his arm again, knife against his back propelling him even deeper into darkness.

Anlon's expression revealed how much he disapproved of the banter between Asteria and Khoti. She trimmed Khoti's tawny hair while the champion shaved, sharp knife scraping his skin.

"I want to go along," Anlon stated.

"No," Khoti replied, determined not to let Anlon's persistence annoy him.

Khoti could see through the open flap to the tent Asteria shared with Daris, Kia and Rena, to where Kia listed to herself which of Asteria's gear she'd packed, while Rena tried to climb into Khoti's lap. Kia had taken to Asteria, determined to beat out all the older youths who wanted the honor of attending her. Wherever Kia went, Rena followed. It felt like a family here. At night, Khoti could hear in the next tent Daris and Asteria giggling over how Asteria's presence, a fallen woman – unchaperoned and dressed like a soldier – scandalized Habda and her mother. Even Khoti chuckled silently at the thought: what Habda didn't know about the gentle children she'd welcomed into her home. Jali, who hung about wherever Daris lingered, had become Khoti's attendant and shared his tent, his sleeping voice a soft snore. On the other side of Asteria's tent Chati, Tre and Cydwyn spoke in low voices late into the night, and when asleep they seemed to breathe as one. Cydwyn, ever protective of Nali's daughters, had become Tre's attendant, with Chati recruiting Daris to a similar job. Khoti may have lost his blood family, but these warriors were home.

"Why bother to cut your hair, shave?" Anlon asked, drawing Khoti's thoughts from the way Rena smiled up at him.

"My folk always keep the hair short," Khoti said. Asteria's fingers brushed against his neck as she trimmed. "The wind, you know, is constant. Hair gets in the way. Lhatans braided theirs, but Taschian and Staphian men find short convenient. Beards, however, are customary." He looked up at Asteria. "But –"

"Khoti looks awful in a beard," Asteria volunteered. "It is that Staphian blood in him. His beard grows darker than his hair, and in no orderly fashion. It makes him look vicious. Not at all like himself." Asteria poked Khoti in the side.

Anlon took a deep breath. "Why will you not let me come along?"

"Do I need to remind you that you've yet to prove yourself capable –"

"How can I prove myself without the opportunity?"

"You had the opportunity."

When Anlon again tried to protest, Khoti rose, almost dumping Rena from his lap. He wiped his face with a cloth, throwing it at the stump of log upon which he'd sat. Asteria trying to snip off the last long strand of hair.

"Don't push me," Khoti warned.

Khoti sheathed his knife and tossed his cloak over his shoulders. Kia hauled Asteria's pack from her tent. Jali had already saddled Fidra and Clanna and secured Khoti's pack to the saddle. He held the horses as he spoke with Sedaik, who stood tall and serious beside his own mount.

"You've improved, Anlon," Khoti conceded. "But you need to practice more with Chati and Tre to get used to working as part of a unit. It'll be just Asteria and Sedaik with me –"

"Sedaik is just a boy. And Asteria is shawnsi –"

"Sedaik's a man of Detarian," A slash of Khoti's cuffed hand silenced Anlon's protest. "I won't hear more!"

Khoti went to Fidra to double check Jali's work. He hated starting a journey on a sour note. Seeing that Jali had packed everything exactly as he liked, he rewarded the youth with a grin, roughing up his unruly red hair.

Khoti wished he didn't have to leave the pleasant world of Han's forest. Certainly, they had their labors creating an army. But the hardy Tachi, with their warrior spirit, made such work exciting. He had even discarded his earlier distaste of the forest, the mild winter a pleasant change.

Most, he'd miss the way his warrior family gathered by the fire each night, often visited by Tedwa and Han. Their fire circle came alive with laughter and the various talents each possessed. Tedwa proved a dynamic storyteller, regaling them with versions of history not told in Khoti's part of the world, which Tre countered with the chanted tales of the north. Han and Khoti challenged one another on their flutes, Chati piping in with a rich baritone voice and a vast repertoire of Shandean songs. Jali, Daris and Asteria mimicked characters in the tales told by Tedwa and Tre until the little camp's occupants held their sides, wiping tears of laughter from their eyes.

So as Khoti mounted Fidra, he felt a little sorry for himself when he thought of the rich banter he would miss and the comforting nights of ease. As he rode from the clearing on this morning of the first day of the cold moon, he felt invigorated by all the Shandean successes. Eithurdon had regained his halls, the Tawnkats their mines, and certainly the king's journey had proven a success. After all, they rode now to collect the riches Arenh sent for them, hoping King Azren would not recant his promise when he heard of the attack on Shiad.

Once reaching the edge of Tormor Wood, the trio rode at a lope through rich prairie that replenished their mounts with each nightly camp. The terrain remained free of the marshes dotting Kishma, and even the prairie stretched less tangled and tall. Avoiding the road and villages Sedaik knew, they sped south to the hilly and hot region near the headwaters of the Detarian River, where they hoped Arenh's caravan awaited. They traveled light, their camps merely bedrolls thrown in lush meadows. Sedaik quickly picked up the quirks of Khoti's traveling style and mimicked his precautions. Thus, the entire route they never lay eyes on a soul, Shandean or Minarian, their pace such that they reached Detarian in only a week.

Khoti had never seen a world remotely like Detarian. It fell to Sedaik to lead them through terrain grown swampy and steamy despite winter passing elsewhere and choose camps at sites least likely to be infested with snakes and poisonous insects. Sedaik knew the fresh water from stale by the lay of the land, which plants would blister the skin if touched, and which routes would only become more of a tangle if they took them.

In Khoti's world, the easiest paths followed valleys and streams. Here Sedaik kept to the ridges, the valleys a choked and damp tangle of fens and uncrossable streams. Sedaik pointed out a plant distilled to make the syrupy liquor of Mershy and another that made sturdy furnishings, others now cultivated on plantations near Shela. He casually identified the abundant plants from which Detarians culled poison for their arrows and stunning powders, or that had healing properties such as the one Khoti knew to be in Konner's salve. Khoti carefully collected ingredients to augment the medicine purse his father once carried. For many plants they asked about, Sedaik could only shrug, having never seen its like before.

Khoti could barely take it all in, his lungs sucking in the steamy aroma. Everything grew a lush green, overlaid by brightly hued flowers and birds that spanned the spectrum of color. The symphony of bird and insect, the rush of waterfalls into green-shaded pools, the forest's sense of fullness and growth made his memories of home seem barren and dead.

When at last they crested a ridge and came down into a broad plain to meet the caravan, Khoti could only grin foolishly. He scanned a herd of five hundred horses, many of them mares that would foal come spring. His amazement grew in him, a knot that took his breath away as a teamster led him from wagon to wagon, the teamster flipping back the canvas to show him the gleaming contents: swords, knives, maces, battle axes, pikes, bows and arrows, shields and the tack to outfit the horses. Some wagons held sacks of grain, dried beef and cured seafood. One even held the accoutrements of light cavalry, with short, light-weight spears similar to but lighter than the light lances some

Eidhalt carried. Khoti's throat tightened when he saw the image of a lion trampling flames, eagle clinging to its back emblazoned on each shield, a special touch only a true friend would trouble to provide.

"We'd better get to work. It'll take a long time to load all this gear on the horses," Khoti said when they'd reached the last wagon. The teamsters only laughed, parting to let through a sturdy Arenhian dressed in light armor, a sword at his side.

"These wagons double as the camp wagons of an army," the man said. "And they are yours." Khoti's jaw went slack. The man grinned. "And there is more. King Azren sends me, Ernik of Ar-Tebez. I am to fight for Shande in your armies, as the representative of Arenh. I will train your best in the art of the mounted charge."

If so many hadn't stood there watching him, Khoti might have wept. Instead, he prodded Sedaik. "Go! Get Detarian teamsters before I wake from this dream!"

As the Arenhian teamsters left for home, Khoti and Asteria waited with Ernik for Sedaik's return. Khoti took a closer look at their bounty, growing ever more amazed.

"Even if I were king, I don't think I could ask so much of another country," Khoti confessed to Ernik as he examined the fine workmanship in the weapons.

"King Azren is a wise king," Ernik said, demonstrating how to hold one of the light spears. "When he heard that Minarians attacked Shiad, he ordered more wagons and horses for Shande."

"He knows?"

"We expect trouble on our borders soon."

"But Shiad stopped supplying arms to the Pladde the moment the Minarians attacked," Asteria said. "Why would King Azren not behave the same?"

"King Keyen is not as wise," Ernik said with a grin. "This assault on Shiad only proves what your king told us. More than ever, King Azren believes all our futures will be determined here. He saw the gods in your ruler. He is a scholar of that history. Thus, King Arshaldon's warnings, his mention of Fyraer, it has King Azren weighing choices." Ernik handed Asteria a spear, and demonstrated how to position it as he spoke. "King Azren must always think first of his people. To think of your people, to help Shande, is the concern of Arenh, now, as clearly as guarding our border with Minaria. If King Arshaldon fails, all of Ea will fail with him."

As the middle days of the cold moon passed, Ernik, Khoti, Asteria and Sedaik, joined by several dozen Detarians, at last hauled the gifts of King Azren's hope into the heart of the Rainforest of Detarian. Their hopes rested on a king long silent. Certainly, they imagined, by now he must be resting in the King of Otayr's halls preparing for his triumphant return home.

When from the dark shadows of Detarian a burly, dark-skinned man stepped forward to grasp Sedaik to his chest, then push the young Detarian back to view him, Khoti, Asteria and Ernik stood by in awkward silence. Khoti felt a pang, reminded of his own fa meeting him fresh from the burning of Tasch-el. Sedaik had that same wooden expression Khoti had worn, that of one unsure how to respond to an embrace so uncharacteristic of the parent.

"I gave you to the dead," Sedaik's father, Perouk said as he peered into his son's face.

"You were premature. We must convene the headmen."

Perouk stood back, as if from a blow. Khoti could still see the rage simmering in Sedaik, the youth having erupted in an anger more like Khoti's on discovering the Detarian headmen had made no promise to the king.

Recovering, Perouk gestured at Khoti. "Of course, this man brings you safely home. He must be honored before the tribes –"

"Certainly Khoti deserves honor. Many Detarians should thank him." Sedaik nodded toward his mentor. "His business is otherwise. He is the man of whom the king spoke, his champion."

Perouk stared at Sedaik. Khoti could see the questions the man wanted to ask as he glanced from Khoti, to Ernik, to Asteria, especially taking note of the mark on Asteria's temple. Perouk merely nodded and strode away to call the council.

Several hours passed into nightfall before a man found Khoti and Asteria at their fire beside the wagons and bade them follow him. They left Ernik with a shrug as the silent man led them to a low meeting hall in the center of the small village beside the Detarian River. This village held ceremonial and historical significance to the peoples of Detarian. Though the headmen served tribes as far away as the Akora and Shela, they ruled from this distant spot where their forbears had agreed to an ancient peace. Now Sedaik would have them contemplate an ancient war.

Near the front of the hall, Khoti and Asteria stood ill at ease beside Sedaik, the rest of the villagers milling about behind them. Khoti could feel their wary gazes on them, their northern features discussed at length as if the two modeled costumes for sale. With the arrival of the five headmen, each attired in the colors and dress of his particular tribe, the attention ended. The leaders' stern faces dominated the hall as a heavy silence fell, broken only by the sucking sounds of torches burning in wall brackets, the acrid smoke coiling up and out of a hole in the center of the hall's roof.

"Sedaik of Perouk," one of the headmen called out. Sedaik stepped forward, his stature erect, his features proud and taut. Khoti knew Sedaik's strength and skills as a warrior. Now he saw a new side of the young man. After bringing the color to Khoti's face with his praise, Sedaik demonstrated a mastery of the tale, of the politic of his world, as he meshed the dramatic and tragic of his story to manipulate emotions and facts to prove his point: to convince Detarian to fight for Shande. The gathering gasped at the point in his tale when he wanted them to gasp; they cried when he wanted them to cry. He named each Detarian child who entered the camps, each who died, and those who now trained to apprentice the armies of Shande.

"We are not just Detarians," Sedaik said as he paced before the headmen. "We are Shandeans, five tribes, not one of which is called Detarian. Like Shande, we are many tribes going by one name. So, as we think of ourselves individually by our tribe, and as we look at our five peoples as Detarian, we must also view the whole as Shandean. Shande calls for help. What of Detarians still detained in Shela? How many Detarian children languish in other labor camps, marked for life by their treatment?"

Sedaik glared at the stony faces of the headmen. He paused then and yanked the laces at his neck, letting his tunic fall open to his waist to reveal scars from a lashing criss-crossing his back. As his audience turned their gazes to the floor, Sedaik continued his pacing, not covering the markers of his internment. Khoti thought that perhaps he now began to understand Sedaik. Asteria's hand gripped Khoti's cuff-ringed wrist.

Sedaik scanned his audience. "Oh so many years we have disdained the Tachi for choosing not to join with us to end our tribes' petty bickering and warfare. Even the Tachi we spurn for their self-interest have sworn to King Arshaldon. They look on the children of Detarian, children beaten and mangled by Minarians, shrieking at the shadows in the night, and they feel compassion. Do we feel none for our own or others'?"

The silence in the hall had become palpable. Khoti found even he had become caught up in Sedaik's words.

"You view me as a man of this tribe. To the Minarians I am a child. This is how they treat children: the labor, the beatings, the young girls and boys to serve their urges." Sedaik took a deep breath. "All Shande is represented. All are destroyed. Tossed in pits lined with garbage and tailings, their spirits gone up into the air as a stench, like the howls of the wolvers. Lost. You can hide here now. But one day the Minarians will come."

Sedaik pulled up his shirt. Nodding to the council, he took a step back and bowed his head to await their judgment. Khoti felt the heat of Sedaik's passion radiating from him, heard the young man's labored breathing, saw the pulse of blood in his temple. Instead of making a cowed servant to Minaria, in Sedaik the Minarians had built a warrior.

One of the headmen pointed at Asteria. "It is your people they seek. Have you comment on their claims they come to Shande only to root out shawnsi? Is it true your people are the root of this nation's woes?"

Asteria kept her restraining hand on Khoti's wrist. "If their battle is solely with shawnsi, why would they inter your children?" Asteria asked.

"They say it is to teach them how wrongly your people have treated them."

"You believe this?" Asteria asked calmly. "Would not such teaching be a more appropriate role for parents or derna than conquering warriors? Do you condone then the killing of innocents because their parents have not taught them to hate shawnsi? And if it is shawnsi they want, why have they attacked Shiad and Arenh? Ask Ernik how many Arenhians are shawnsi. It is an excuse to conquer Ea. Why should you give to a foreign ruler more than was ever asked of you by your own people?"

"I am not shawnsi," the headman retorted. "You are not 'my people.' My people are shal tribesmen."

"As are mine," Asteria retorted. A little of that bitterness she could spew so effectively crept into her tone. "My mother of Lharan, a grandmother part Shelan, part Joffan, a grandfather half Kalilian. I am Shande, more so than you. In me runs the blood of every province."

"And this king?" The man challenged.

"The blood of Tachi and Shela from his mother, the tribes of Kishma and Kalilia from his father," Khoti replied. "What's your point?"

When the headman started to retort, another silenced him with an imperious wave, leaning to whisper in the man's ear.

"Sedaik?" The questioner asked in a more subdued tone.

Khoti realized not all the headmen agreed with the questioner. As if to prove Khoti's assessment, Sedaik addressed not the interrogator, but the others as he outlined the plans he and Khoti had drawn. The meeting hall buzzed with exclamation.

"All this to risk our people's lives to help some king who lives weeks away. What do we need of kings? We have this council and our own interests." The recalcitrant headman challenged.

Before Sedaik could respond, the villagers made their own desires known, a chant begun by a few younger men grew into a chorus carried by all, the interrogator forced to back down as the other four headmen voted for Sedaik's plan.

They lived in a time of war, a time when traitors betrayed kings. When the chanters pressed out into the dusty road to encircle the Arenhian wagons, Khoti spoke in Sedaik's ear. The young man's eyes widened a moment, but then with set jaw, he nodded. Sedaik motioned to Perouk. Later, when villagers discovered the body of the recalcitrant headman in the Detarian River, the council of headmen ruled he had failed to navigate one of the river's many rapids. Khoti could not regret such decisions. He already knew the face of treachery.

# 34: Anlon's Choice

Only a few days later, Khoti left Sedaik in Detarian with half the horses and the skills to train his people. When called, Sedaik – voted officer by his Detarian peers – would have mounted archers under his command. Detarian didn't need Arenhian arms other than bows, the arrows to which they touched poisons, and shields. Ernik and his bounty moved on to Tormor.

It took weeks to transport all the goods, wagons and horses through trackless Detarian to the Akora River, then build keeled barges both sturdy and large enough to transport twenty horses each, plus supplies. Khoti and Asteria chose the smallest barge to lead his flotilla upriver to attract the least attention. The other vessels proved so cumbersome it took fifteen Detarians to maneuver them against the sluggish pull of the Akora as they at last left Detarian behind and crept near Tormor Wood.

"Hey!" a call rang out from the west bank of the Akora River, startling a flock of birds, which protested the intrusion as they vacated the leafy canopy of Tormor Wood.

Detarians poling the barge Khoti and Asteria rode upon with a dozen horses and a canvas-covered arsenal halted the craft mid-stream. Khoti kept his gaze down, bobbing his head at the caller. Asteria tensed, her face hidden beneath the broad visor of a Shelan farmer's hat, her fingers digging into the wood of the raft.

Khoti edged his bow and sword out of sight, but within easy reach. As if sensing the danger, Fidra shifted, blocking Asteria from the three Minarians hailing them from shore. Khoti perspired. Dark river mud he had caked in his hair to darken it moistened beneath the orange scarf wrapped around his head. Detarian women, laughing and teasing, had painted his face with a root tint to mute his fair features, the dye now dripping from his chin in droplets of sweat. Asteria edged closer to her bow. He didn't look up at the Minarians, but maintained his subservient posture.

The Detarian boatmen called back easily, assuring the Minarians their barge's freight augmented a post upstream expecting replacements.

The Minarians waved them on then returned to their post on the streambank, staring at the continuation of forest on the other side of the river. The barge rounded a narrow curve and touched the bank. Khoti, Asteria and four of the boatmen grabbed up their bows and leapt ashore to stalk downstream. By the time the Minarians realized they had fallen under attack, the skirmish ended. Khoti rolled the three dead Minarians into the river, where the following barges would add them to the tally. As vanguard, Khoti was merciless.

Khoti glanced at Asteria as they returned to the river. She listed many reasons for joining him on this journey to Detarian: fear her father would abduct her, that something would happen to Khoti if he left her sight, and that Anlon would continue pestering her with his tendency to pop up out of nowhere with an unnerving stare and nothing to say. Perhaps even more than Chati and Tre she suited him as a comrade-in-arms, mastering the skills he'd taught her and reading his moods and unspoken intents. It didn't ease him. He agonized over her safety each time she raised her bow. He couldn't close his eyes at night until he heard the regular breaths of her slumber, and he feared she had thrown away her life among her own people to save him. Often when he looked at her, saw the sunburst on her temple, his stomach constricted into a knot. If the Minarians ever captured her – He drove the evil thoughts away. Imagining Asteria in a plight like Resala's might make it come true.

Midway through the first moon and closing on Evenday, they finally brought all the barges ashore an hour's ride downriver from the lumber yards closest to Habdelion's ancestral seat. Tedwa himself greeted them, alerted by the Tachi scouts Tre and Chati had dispatched along the river. As barges bumped against the muddy bank and discharged horses and gear to supply the army, Tachi scurried to conceal all traces of their arrival.

It proved no minor interest that brought Tedwa to greet them.

"They are too curious," Tedwa muttered, gesturing toward the lumbering village. "They just about found Han's house." Tedwa smiled a thin grin of menace. "But we made them think different. Nine dead. Some got away. You build a good army. Even Anlon killed his first man. Now they look for their missing men. They come sneaking around. We lost good Tachi and a few of Han's men. Now we must ensure it will not happen again."

Khoti thought of the Eidhalt who had escaped him. "There must be a hundred Minarians in the lumber yard, if not more. Not all the Shandeans working for them can be trusted."

Tedwa grinned. "We work like Tawnkats. This is forest, not mountain. But the same idea." Tedwa didn't elaborate, motioning for them to follow him on a different trail than the Tachi whisking away the Detarians and their cargo.

Tedwa chuckled as he led them, looking back at Khoti and Asteria now and then to chuckle louder, the pair growing uncomfortable at his scrutiny. At last, Tedwa stopped by a small stream and motioned for Khoti to come close and pointed into the water. When Khoti bent to look, the Tachi headman gave him a light push so that Khoti fell face first into the tepid water.

"What the –?" Khoti sputtered as Tedwa held his stomach and chuckled soundlessly.

"You lousy-looking Detarian. Your skin all streaky, your hair dirty. Detarians look better than that."

Khoti grinned back, standing in the waist deep water to rinse his face and hair, feeling better as the water swept away the days of hot travel.

"Now your turn," Tedwa said, reaching for Asteria.

"Oh no," she cried, backing away. She giggled as she gingerly stepped into the water. She splashed Khoti. He dunked her, the Shelan hat almost floating away.

At last, settling on the bank, Khoti wound the Detarian scarf into a band across his forehead that would keep the sweat of the day's heat from dripping in his eyes. He watched as Asteria wound her dark hair into braids as his mother had taught her, and tucked them beneath the hat. He chided himself for noticing the way the wet mountbuckskin clung to her. He wouldn't think such things of Chati and Tre, yet he tried to convince himself he felt for her only the kinship of a comrade.

When they continued on, Tedwa led them toward the lumber camp, not calling a halt until they'd reached a point so close they could hear the saws and axes of the yard clearly.

Tedwa lifted branches from a man-width hole in the ground, then looked up at Khoti and gave him his broad smile. The roots of the forest still trailed from its edges and no trace of the dirt from the excavation remained. The hole fit naturally into the landscape. Tedwa dropped into the opening. He looked up at

Khoti from a depth greater than Tedwa's height and then some, motioning for them to follow him.

Khoti found himself in a small room dug beneath the surface of the forest, from which a narrow tunnel proceeded toward the lumbering town, so tight they had to crawl. A span of mud made up the floor of the room, with supplies stacked atop slats laid over the muck and a short ladder to aid in escape. Khoti grinned when he recognized Chati and Tre's addition: pottery jars with wicks trailing from them in readiness.

"You make us bathe, then take us in a mud hole," Asteria grumbled, pulling her feet from the sucking floor.

Tedwa grinned and put his finger to his lips. Handing her pottery jars, he showed them how to loop the handles around their belts. Then he dropped to hands and knees and led them through the tiny tunnel, the pottery jars now and then banging together and their bows snagging on the low, root-encrusted ceiling supported by a few rough-hewn timbers. After they'd crawled along in the dark for what felt like half an hour, they came to a wide space where the three could crouch side by side. Tedwa motioned them to silence, pushing his ear against the brush-covered opening above.

Khoti hefted the two pottery jars in his hand while Tedwa explained his plan in sign. When the sun fell low enough to spread deep shadows throughout the forest and night had descended here if it hadn't anywhere else, Tedwa lifted the brush away from the mouth of his tunnel, sticking his head out a moment to ensure no Minarians watched. Khoti realized they had crawled well inside the Minarian sentries' perimeter. Tedwa made a clicking noise that mimicked a local bird, and waited as similar calls came back from various points around him. Khoti and Asteria recognized the order. She struck the flint and lit the wicks on the jars. Tedwa clicked his tongue. Throughout the camp, figures erupted from tunnels, springing forward to lob their jars at anything flammable and as quickly nocking arrows.

Tachi arrows seldom missed an intended target. Khoti heard the steps of someone rushing at them. About to draw his sword, he realized Shandean laborers dashed for the tunnels. The faithful knew where to go, the rest made targets.

In a few moments flames had engulfed the lumber yard, dead sprawled throughout the camp. Khoti had thrown his jars, but never saw a target for his arrows. He glanced at Asteria, knowing from the stony look on her face that she, at least, had found something to shoot. He wanted to reach out to her. Instead, he clenched his fist.

As Tachi swept through the area to ensure no enemy lived to detail the attack, they again returned to their tunnels, carefully concealing the openings. If the Minarians returned, the tunnels might again be used.

Khoti stared at the flames reaching up into the growing darkness. Tedwa strode up to him, measured Khoti's store of arrows, then Asteria's.

"The lady is a warrior. Why are you here?" Tedwa teased.

"'Parently she read the plan better than I did," Khoti admitted, face red.

"We look out for this one," Tedwa said, tugging a braid that had come free from her hat. He laughed loudly as he covered his tunnel with brush and swept away their footprints. In a few moments, silence reigned as the Tachi disappeared into the forest, only the pop and hiss of flames breaking the still night.

Only a day later, Khoti dozed, sprawled in the lush grass of the clearing. A short way distant Asteria and Kia chattered around the campfire. Fidra grazed just beyond and already Jali and Cydwyn pulled logs near the fire for the homecoming celebration.

One of Khoti's eyes opened a slit when his senses told him someone neared. As the shadow loomed over him, he leapt up, one hand already on his dagger. He halted mid-motion when Anlon grinned back at him.

"Don't ever sneak up on me." Khoti sank back into the grass. The fog of sleep disappeared with that first sense of danger. Now he sighed, waiting for his lifebeat to slow.

"I was not sneaking. How else should I approach?" Anlon asked, squatting beside Khoti and pulling idly at the lush grass. "Would you have me yell from a distance?"

"It's safer that way," Khoti admitted with a lopsided smile. Anlon continued to tear at the grass at his feet. Khoti cleared his throat. "I hear you saw battle."

Anlon shrugged, ripping up another hunk of grass.

"You're being modest, Anlon, something new."

Anlon didn't speak, but continued to tug at the grass until he had cleared a small circle of bare earth. Khoti grabbed Anlon's arm, forcing the young man to look at him.

"You will only laugh," Anlon said.

"How do you know unless you say it? If it's a serious concern I'd have no right to laugh, no matter what it is."

Anlon studied Khoti as chatter drifted to them from the little camp and an occasional round of laughter. Khoti leaned on his elbow, at ease as cool evening drifted down from the canopy.

"Why do men die for you? How do you make them follow you?"

Khoti leaned back, lacing his hands behind his head as he looked up at the crosshatch of branch and leaf high above them. Far distant he caught a hint of starlight. The low branches glowed as Jali's fire blazed out from the campsite.

"I don't know. I guess I don't ask of them anything I wouldn't do myself," Khoti mused. "And I suppose it's recognizing, overcoming, and using fear. And knowing who works best at what task, and those who work best together. And, maybe being both close and keeping a distance with all but a few special friends. If I'm a good commander, I never have to use rank to force anything."

Anlon remained silent, staring at the grass in his hands.

"Now, tell me what's really troubling you. I doubt it's fear or your rock-headed way with orders."

Anlon looked away, his fingers still nibbling the blades of grass rimming the bare space he'd made. "I cut a man down. His blood all over me. I could only look at it and hate the horror I had done." He looked up at Khoti. "Despite Habda, I was trained to be duke. I was always taught I must deal justly, rule firmly, but always seek a compromise to avoid a battle. He had no chance to beg mercy." Anlon shrugged. "I feel like such a fool."

"It's not like that," Khoti said, remembering his arrogant words to Arshal. "Times come when compromise won't work, and someone's wrong. This is one of those times. Though a second son, I was raised to be able to serve as headman in my brother's stead, at the minimum to be his Second. In my world that meant learning to be rigid so you can lead people equally stubborn. Anlon, you need to learn to ignore compromise, just as I had to learn when to back down." Khoti smiled up at the canopy, imagining Tsevon's response to his assessment.

Anlon peered at Khoti with an unnerving lack of expression. Then he reddened a little and looked away. "You know, I rode into that battle, though merely a skirmish, with only the thought that I had to prove something to you. Instead, I think I should have been trying to prove it to me." Anlon shrugged, peered at him again then looked away. "I may not be experienced, but next time you go into action I would like to accompany you. Even if it is just a skirmish. I –" Anlon took a deep breath, studying Khoti from the corner of his eye for a reaction. "I just would."

"We'll see," Khoti mumbled, not seeing Anlon, but himself running from a burning barn. He'd been trying to prove something ever since. He turned and gave Anlon a warm smile. "Why don't you join us at our fire tonight? There's lots of tales to hear, lots of things to learn just by knowin' other people. I've learned there are many tribes besides mine and at my fire tonight will be all of Shande. In such friendships lies Shande's future." Khoti lay a hand on Anlon's shoulder, using the other man for leverage to rise, and then strode away, leaving Anlon in the shadows of nightfall, staring after him.

When Khoti and Habdelion winded their flutes – a lively song that brought Chati, Tre and Asteria out to teach the others the dance, Daris chiding them for their graceless movements, Jali and Cydwyn pouring wine, Tedwa chuckling in that silent way he had – Anlon at last approached the fire. When the light fell on his face, no one made a ceremony of his arrival. They greeted him heartily as Jali rolled another log near for him to sit on.

The celebration gave way to late night, Anlon listening in fascination to all they said and sung. Wine, the warmth of the fire and closeness of those gathered, brought a flush to his face as at last he learned lessons that could not be taught.

They did not sink in.

He had committed himself. He had things to do. Overcome fear and use it to best advantage, as Khoti had said, but always keep in mind the lessons learned to become a duke.

His duty was the ancestral seat.

When the revellers drifted off to their tents, passing into untroubled slumber, and Anlon had learned what he needed, he slipped away. He took a horse, and riding hard on trails he'd walked his entire life, he soon neared the eaves of the forest.

It would be late in the day before they missed him, and several, likely, before they grew concerned. By then he would be well on the way to claiming the title, Duke of Mershy, by compromise, ensuring no rabble from the north could take it away.

# 35: Verdred

In the middle days of the cold moon, when heavy snow and icy winds closed down the northern Lharans, Zopher at last donned his huntsman's gear and trudged to the Val to speak one last time with Konner. He didn't listen to the Tawnkat's warnings that he could do no good in Minaria, any more than when Hothur tried to dissuade him. He turned over to Konner the network he and Khoti built, and walked one last time through the caverns, drawing in the scents, the sounds, absorbing a place in which he had dwelt what seemed a lifetime, echoes chasing through passages, the high chatter of birds nesting in the common. The people who mattered most had gone. The Val had become an empty place despite the hundreds who lived there.

He rode west in search of Aibak and the Shiadin war with Minaria. He'd spent months honing his skills, his mission consuming him more with each day he trained. His need to find Resala – to redeem himself for failing to rescue her – filled his first and last thoughts each day, his nightmares and the drift of each daydream. Even when he had absorbed all that he could learn from Hothur, he wanted more, needed to know his enemy completely. Though he hoped to enter Minaria in the garb of an Eidhalt warrior – the helm covering the shawnsi mark on his temple and hiding his shawnsi features – he knew it would take more than a likeness to succeed.

"They will discover you when you do not kill Shandeans," Hothur had told him. "When they do not recognize you or know your name, when you do not honor Ghyldus's orders. They will see your gray eyes and mark you as no Hogde."

"And what of yours, hazel brown."

"The mark of my shame," Hothur replied in the soft voice of the confessor. "A man one quarter Pladde could not become an

Eidhalt. The people who killed my Pladde grandfather, and banished my fourteen-year-old Hogde grandmother for loving a man of inferior race, would not make a gray-eyed man an Eidhalt."

"Then I'll wear my helmet low so they can't see my eyes."

"Not enough. You may be a master huntsman and accomplished swordsman, but can you make them believe you have the skills of a lancer, or the brutality of the interrogator? Will you wear their medallion? Will not this spy of Shande instead become prisoner of Minaria and tell all he knows? Is Shande's safety worth such a risk for a mission of the heart, no matter how worthy the goal?"

"It won't be for Resala alone." Zopher had touched the necklace around his neck, the promise that had kept him safe through the battle for Sihmad Shal. In his pocket lay a brilliant blue sapphire, his promise to her. "How better to spy on Ghyldus, or learn enemy movements and plans," he'd boasted, not even wondering how he would send such information on to those who would need it most.

Yet, he conceded he could learn more. Thus, as Shiad's mountain fighters skirmished along the Minarian border, Zopher don Saran fought beside Aibak, honing his battle skills on matches with higher stakes than merely fencing in the streets of Sefresal. Now when he took to the field, he watched his enemy with eyes opened by Hothur's teaching. The enemy rewarded him with its predictability. As the days passed – each one a new skirmish that took him on horsed charges through frozen valleys, or stalking across glaciers, or scrambling down frozen waterfalls – Zopher learned to carry long Shiadin spears and shoot their strange darts, bear their heavy broadswords and maces and wear restrictive breastplates and the heavy helms like a second skin.

As the last moon in the dark heart of winter came to a close, Zopher at last donned the dark cloak, breeches and helm of an Eidhalt warrior and equipped his horse in Eidhalt trappings. Aibak drew his sword when he spied don Saran standing outside his tent then gripped the shawnsi's arms in parting.

"I will see you in battle again, Zopher," Aibak promised. "And we will look on defeated Minaria, the glory of our victory dripping from our swords."

Zopher mounted his horse and raised his sword in salute. "When you next see me on the field of battle, you will see me victorious," he declared. The boast felt empty even as he uttered it. As he took his leave to descend into Minaria, fitting more closely the dour and brutal disguise he had assumed, he wondered if history would write up Zopher don Saran as one of the war's greatest fools.

As he rode southwest through barren lands, rumors came to him from the mouths of passing messengers who imparted their tale to him when he assured them he made for Lagdche and could carry the news, speeding them on to other duties.

"Tell Verdred, the mountains are in turmoil, Verdaen's work," said one Eidhalt who lost in battle the special medallion that would have relayed his tale to his master. "He builds armies in Mershy, and destroys Eidhalt forces. We last hear the shawnsi seer walked Shela. We sent our best to destroy him."

Each messenger Zopher encountered in the eastern plains of Minaria asked the shadowy Eidhalt to deliver words to the great Verdred, Ghyldus's Champion, so they could rush back to the aid of their fellows and not face that Dread Warrior. Yet, while they might escape Verdred, they didn't escape the Spy of Shande. Zopher left in his wake a trail of dead.

The last moon passed and the early days of the first moon hinted of spring and coming Evenday before he reached the more habitable lands of Minaria. At last, a week and a half into the first moon, he found the great reservoir outside of Lagdche, rebuilt and filled following Halieri's Flood. The runoff from a rare squall trickled into the great barren lake as the squall line rumbled away to the northwest over the sea, leaving Lagdche clean and damp below him as the parched earth around the reservoir gasped, the moisture gone in a moment.

When he stood atop the high levee to peer down onto Lagdche below, he had no doubt where Ghyldus's Halls stood. Veiled in a protective fog, what had been Mol Azezial's palace now loomed a fortress. Hothur told him sorcery locked its doors and only those Ghyldus recognized could pass through. He claimed Ghyldus held such power his vision encompassed this entire land, the Great God of Ea capable of knowing the mind of all who entered his world. Did Ghyldus already know Zopher don Saran stood here, stark against the sky as the reservoir stretched out behind him, his approach watched for weeks? Or did one dark figure in Eidhalt garb appear too inconsequential to matter?

The sun blazed out suddenly as the storm clouds cleared, the rays soon sending a mist of steam coiling skyward. Sunlight glimmered from the chop of the reservoir behind him as a cool salt wind that reminded him of Sihma Harbor threw welcome dampness in his face. Somewhere in that city below, he'd find Resala.

Ghyldus brooded on his throne. Some flaw existed in the fabric of his web. Something stepping lightly as it neared the heart of his realm jiggled a strand. What could threaten him? Had Resala grown stronger? Had she learned the properties of her art and found, at last, skills that might threaten him? She claimed no powers. Ghyldus knew better. How else could she so tenaciously resist his enchantment? He could not see into her mind, nor read her intent. When she stood near, something confused him, his enchantments muddled. He couldn't define this power she wove about herself. If his command had no power over her, perhaps truly this brother of hers might be a creature of concern.

Yet, as vigilant as she believed herself, as slyly as she wove her spells, Ghyldus knew himself greater. Hadn't he already drawn many things from her she wouldn't want revealed? He learned her brother quested for a power not strong in him yet. He knew his Visionary had been struck down before this king knew the power, grew into it or developed it. This king wandered the world alone, vulnerable, as he must to gain the strength, knowledge and following of an exiled martyr, and to hide until he learned to defend himself. How characteristic of those gods the Shandeans revered to demand sacrifices and silly rituals from adherents. They wanted the tool to prove itself worthy of the power they could easily bestow with a thought. Likely they demanded he master the elements before earning their power. If they truly wanted to build a weapon of this king, they could just make him. Why worry whether the vessel they used could withstand the powers and temptations of their gift? If the tool grew too strong, they could merely destroy it after it served their needs.

One bit of news Ghyldus learned from the Shandean princess made him chuckle long hours after she'd returned to her own bed. This king, either through his own foolishness or the bad counsel of some other fool, limited himself to a stone like Dynfearn's. Such rich irony! Only Ghyldus and Dynfearn's gods witnessed that Shandean king's demise. Dynfearn's stone weakened him, enabled his downfall and destruction. Now the upstart king had only one weapon to challenge Ghyldus's arsenal.

Though this Dyndevas king had his weaknesses, Ghyldus couldn't allow him to learn all the properties of his power, nor let him find a seer to teach him, nor permit him to gather the world to his banner. Ghyldus must see the upstart king utterly destroyed in view of the recalcitrant rabble challenging him. And he must accomplish it soon.

Did Ghyldus sense the King of Shande now? Was that who jiggled his web? He looked around his shadowy hall. The gallery trembled as his gaze touched them. Verdred stood at stony attention. Something trod on the enchanter's web. Had this king foiled Ghyldus's search and came now to seek him? Or did Resala cause his foreboding?

He closed his eyes, envisioning a silhouette against a sparkle of waves and tatter of storm wrack. Verdred, the shape appeared, but Verdred stood at the door of his hall. The Shandean King's Champion had come, perhaps, the man Minarian soldiers named Verdaen. As the idea struck him, Ghyldus knew he'd struck truth. No warrior of Shande could be as fierce and skilled as legend made Verdaen. Likely, tales enlarged the exploits of a man little better than his fellows. If Verdaen had come, certainly the warrior heard the laurels of his people and deemed himself strong enough to face a god.

Ghyldus laughed, an evil sound. He liked the way it brought his gallery to attention. He chuckled, twisting the sound into something of menace and power as his petty attendants paled.

"Verdred," he called. "You deserve some sport for your loyalty. A creature of Shande stands atop my reservoir contemplating entrance to my halls. A warrior enlarged by his own ego? I give him to you to destroy."

With a bow, Verdred departed. Ghyldus grinned. Now he would watch the battle through Verdred's eyes, witness himself victorious and the Shandean legend crushed. But a nervous messenger hung at his door and with him arrived Resala to rob her lord of concentration and foil his view of what tiptoed over his web. He scowled at the woman, who gazed back at him with an infuriating air of innocence. As her hand came to rest on his shoulder, he sat back to hear the messenger's tale, content he would at least glean the story later from Verdred's vacant mind.

"Terremar, what have I set myself," Zopher muttered as he looked upon the menace below. He knew he gazed upon Verdred. Ghyldus's Malice, some called him. The warrior moved like a shadow across the ground, his horse as black as his garb, as dark as the heavy lance he held before him. Though the creature's face hid in the shadow of helm and hood, Zopher still sensed the assurance, the brutality in the warrior. Why had he talked himself into this? What fool stood so open a target on his enemy's field?

Zopher raised his spear. Verdred's horse charged up the hill, nostrils flaring, teeth bared and eager. The medallion flashed red on the dark mailed chest. Zopher drove his mount down the side of the reservoir, the greater speed behind him. When the two met, both spears turned on heavy breastplates, both riders toppling to the hard-baked ground.

The blow sucked the wind from Zopher's lungs. Already Verdred stalked him with drawn sword and a club. Hothur's warnings taunted Zopher's thoughts as he faced Malice. But Zopher had a mission, a purpose he'd driven into his mind like a spike, more firmly anchored than even his identity. It eased his doubts, made all but his goal fade from view. He'd come for Resala.

Verdred held sword in one hand, a massive club in the other. With a mighty swing, the club crashed into the side of Zopher's head. The helm Zopher wore turned the blow but left flickers of light before his eyes like dapples of sun on the reservoir. A pounding ache echoed Zopher's lifebeat as medallion-eyes blinded him.

Zopher swung, unable to focus on his assailant. His blade turned from Verdred's armor. Verdred pressed his attack, alternately striking with the club to send Zopher staggering, and swiping at him with sword to keep the shawnsi constantly on the defensive, unable to do more than parry as they moved up the slope to the top of the levee. Zopher stumbled forward, his sword smashing the mighty warrior in the face. A spurt of blood erupted from Verdred's exposed jaw. Verdred's counter blow ripped across Zopher's chest, snapping the straps on the breastplate and exposing Zopher's left shoulder.

Staggering again, Zopher stabbed as Verdred closed on him, blade driving into the mesh tunic protecting Verdred's abdomen. The sword stuck there, gripped by the mesh. Verdred continued to swipe at Zopher as if the weapon protruding from his armor troubled him no more than some insect deviling his ears. Ducking, beneath a blow that fell on his back, Zopher drove his wedged blade deeper into Verdred and twisted it with all his strength.

Verdred's jaw hung broken, bloody and useless from his face, blood flowing over the dark mail glinting in the westering sun. Gaze riveted on the red-eyed medallion, Zopher continued to twist and wrench the sword lodged in Verdred's body, driving it ever deeper. Verdred's mouth gaped silently, his sword hacking Zopher's back and shoulder.

Still gripping his sword, Zopher tugged his dagger free of its sheath to stab it into the hole between Verdred's helm and breastplate. Just then, Verdred twisted his club around and smashed it against Zopher's skull so hard it drove the helm from Zopher's head. Zopher reeled. Both men toppled into the murky reservoir, Zopher still clinging to the sword in Verdred's middle.

When the familiar malign shape returned to its station at the door, something felt different. Ghyldus peered at his champion. The stance had changed, the shoulders bowed in weariness. Had he faced Verdaen? Verdred had destroyed many men for his master and always came away victorious, unscathed, showing no outward sign of exertion. Something in Verdred's reaction, as if he looked upon his master for the first time, though the medallion glinted brightly on his chest, again brought him that strange sense of danger.

The shadowy head turned slightly to look on the princess behind the throne. Ghyldus looked over his shoulder at her, finding her gaze locked on the horrible champion whose countenance and nature so often appeared to terrify her. Her spell had ruined his fun. Again, she drew his victim's gaze to her where his sorcery had no power to intervene.

"He is mine," Ghyldus growled. "Why would you take him from me?" he demanded of her. She shook her head in innocence, but continued to hold his champion's gaze. Now the god could not read the tale of battle, but only ask a mute man questions he could not answer, perform the ruse of an omnipotent god for his gallery while his mistress controlled his servants.

"You defeated this warrior," Ghyldus stated.

Verdred inclined his head.

Ghyldus peered at the trickle of blood running from beneath Verdred's helm, noted the rents in his champion's cloak.

"Verdaen?" he asked eagerly as Resala gripped the back of the massive chair with white knuckles.

Verdred rose black-gloved hands in a gesture of doubt. Then, if such a thing could cross the face of Malice, Verdred smiled, a grisly grin revealing bloody teeth. With only his teeth visible within the shadow of hood and helm, a ghostly visage, Verdred brought his hands together, twisting as if wringing cloth then snapped them apart, as if breaking a twig.

Ghyldus laughed. It was a vicious chuckle. "Likely Verdaen if he touched a sword to you." With a sign, Ghyldus propelled Verdred into the dark alcove by the door, from where his Malice peered at Resala.

Ghyldus still sensed that hint of danger, as if some menace had passed through his web, the cords not sticky enough to hold it, perhaps the strands parting to let it through. Verdred stared back with loyal awe, had responded to a silent command. Ghyldus's spell still held. If Verdred ever escaped it through Resala's meddling, what violent wild thing would be unleashed! Verdred could not assail him, no one could, but his loyal Minarian servants would die. Was Resala the menace he sensed? The feeling of imminent danger had abated since Verdred's return, testimony that indeed a Shandean warrior had stood atop his reservoir. Resala grew into her abilities, he guessed. The time had come to stop it.

His gaze darted from one to the other: a war of loyalty. He could not recall to whom he owed the greater fealty, couldn't make up his mind which took precedence. In His presence, the medallion burned on his chest. What powerful god! What great master he served! His heart swelled beneath His praise. He wanted to speak and tell all to his mighty sovereign, but his Lord didn't expect that; he knew the first instant he'd gazed into the ruby glistening on his Lord's omnipotent brow. Mute, he knew that of himself. The blows that had dinted his helm made his head throb as he beheld the godly face, and he felt his master's desires creeping into his battle-weary mind.

A small voice within him warned him to be wary. The godly face held a strange gleam, something not right about it. And he had another purpose here. He was Verdred because his Lord named him thus. But first something else: protector of his god and protector of his god's mistress. His gaze drifted then to the beautiful face that hung, suspended it seemed, above his master's shoulder. He fell into eyes so dark and blue, so deep and penetrating, they appeared almost the color of amethyst, a shade similar to the waters he'd seen in a distant harbor somewhere ... Sihma Harbor.

His heart pounded his danger. He sensed the enchantment creeping into his mind, the sheer exhaustion of battle leaving him unable to stop it. He felt Ghyldus's gaze, the intent probing of the seer seeking his tale, sifting through the mind it touched. Her gaze, the stronger, held his and his Lord gave up as she pounded hard on the anchoring spike he had driven.

He must remember his purpose and use it to protect him from this unexpected assault. Resala. His thoughts called the name. Suddenly he remembered where he stood, why he fought like a demon in the deep water of the reservoir and survived to strip his dead foe. He entered these halls someone else, but he had gazed on that omnipotent face and its bright gem. Now he had become Verdred, because that is how his Lord named him. Once he'd been someone else.

He put his hand to his throat where a gold chain hung, concealed beneath his cloak. In his pocket a gem rested. Not the rubies of his trappings, but a sapphire, royal blue and brilliant. He'd become Minaria's Dread Warrior, but not Ghyldus's Malice. His purpose here stood behind the throne. Resala. He must keep the name, the image of her, always in the front of his thoughts. He glanced at Ghyldus, knowing the vanity to think one could smite a god. How dangerous to hold any thought secret within Ghyldus's realm! How long could he hide his gray eyes and shawnsi face?

As he held Resala's gaze, answering his Lord as his Lord expected, in sign, he felt her strength entering him. If she stood here as Ghyldus's courtesan – in fine satins and jewels, her hand resting on Ghyldus's shoulder – didn't this mean she had already fallen under the spell of this great god? Yet to look into her gaze, to feel how his Lord's intents had turned at her will, clearly she fought the god with some enchantment of her own. She endured this willingly? The thought lay like cold steel against his neck.

When he backed into the shadows of the doorway, because his Lord's motion expected that, he knew she worked toward a goal. He could tell it in the way her gaze locked on him, in the expression in her eyes – a gaze the person he once was knew intimately – an expression of resignation, of revulsion, of mourning for the friend she certainly must think had died for her. He saw ice and venom in her unlike anything he had known. If, as it seemed, she could protect him from detection, he could protect her and find a way to help her. Perhaps he had not sacrificed himself to the god in vain, if he could just evade Ghyldus's gaze, if he could just retain that part of him that remembered why he stood here, even if he knew nothing of himself but Verdred.

# 36: Rebel Heart

"Send me a servant. I want to bathe."

Resala looked down her nose at the guard pacing her as she entered her rooms, her prison of fine furnishings, seductive gowns, perfumed water and flowers.

With a crisp salute, he hurried to call the Pladde handmaiden assigned to Ghyldus's haughty mistress.

Resala stared out the little window overlooking the sea as she waited for the soft knock that would herald Teshet's arrival. Far out, breakers preceded a first moon storm rushing toward land. What truly happened in the world? She knew the rumors, and knew not to trust them. Ghyldus had gleaned too much from her and now pursued Arshal too ardently, too soon. If they had truly found Khoti's mangled remains in the reservoir, then Arshal wandered the world unprotected. Time passed so slowly!

The door closed behind Teshet. Resala gave her a tender smile, a gesture seldom seen on the lips of the imperious mistress to the ruler of Ea.

"You wish to bathe, my lady?" Teshet called loud enough for the guard to hear as she went to the deep tub set out in the middle of the room.

"Why do you think you were called?" Resala demanded loudly, as Teshet helped her step out of her gown.

"Second bath today, Lady, you will soon have an old woman's skin," Teshet whispered as she brushed Resala's hair and bound it above her shoulders.

"I will never be clean," Resala muttered as Teshet poured into the tub the warm water servants brought, and tested the temperature. Resala stepped in, sinking into the comforting water with a sigh.

Teshet took a corner of her apron and wiped Resala's cheek. "If your eyes are red, he will know he hurts you."

Resala nodded and forced the emotions away. How long could she maintain the subterfuge? She teetered on the edge of a precipice. Each day new assaults from Ghyldus threatened to topple her. Eventually, Ghyldus would realize he could toss her aside without raising speculation and tear the fabric of her plan.

"Did you get it?" Resala breathed.

"It is powerful medicine," Teshet warned. "It will make you sick for days."

"I refuse to mother a demon meant to destroy all I believe in." Resala fought down tears.

Teshet pulled a sour-smelling, grimy pouch from her skirt and poured the contents into a vial on Resala's dressing table, adding crushed herbs to hide the stench. Resala watched her, seeing both the assuredness of a young woman living in dangerous times, and the tender heart of a friend. Teshet gave Resala her only sense of comfort. When the serving girl named herself in those first days, Resala had clung to the girl as if she held a tree in a flood, remembering the bold tales of Amhese and Tsevon like some tenuous link to her own world. The girl's uncle Jeret had sent Teshet back to serve the enemy. Teshet served as the rebel Pladde ear in the heart of the enemy camp. Her role might be less debasing than Resala's, but no less dangerous.

"Take it tonight," Teshet whispered as she tucked the empty pouch in her skirt pocket. "I will let out that you did not appear well today and have the other girls watch over you as well, in the event you fall too ill."

Resala smiled. "You almost burned me, fool!" she screeched, almost wrecking the ruse with a giggle.

"Lady, I do not know what more we can do."

"Eithur sent no weapons?"

"He sends, but not enough. They come in marked wagons headed for Lagdche. Our people must attack the wagons to get the weapons. Now the shipments are guarded, and they take vengeance on the innocents in the area, not only for the raids, but the flawed weapons they discover. We become so disorganized the Hogde could crush us soon."

"You can't give up, Teshet!" Resala's eyes went wide with sudden fear. "Please don't make all I do here worthless," she begged. "If you give up now, it'll only be worse for having dared rebel." Resala chewed her lip a moment. "I'll write a letter and beg Eithur to find some other way of sending arms to you. A letter from me might assure them that –"

"They know you are alive here." Teshet winced at Resala's expression.

"Alive? Hardly. What they know surely shames them."

"I think they will understand your sacrifice," Teshet said, stroking Resala's hair.

Resala threw a sharp glance at Teshet. Sacrifice. She had not expected her augured name to mean mistress to a crude despot. "They'll never know, Teshet. I won't return home to face any of them."

"Do not talk foolish. There is your brother and the man to whom you were betrothed."

"My brother won't want Ghyldus's courtesan near him. Zopher certainly won't want such a disgrace for a lifemate."

"Lady, they would honor you." Teshet's tone carried more respect than Resala deserved. "You give more than a warrior's blood. It is not lost honor, but greater because you placed importance on something larger than yourself. Your mission seems fruitless because the seed has only sprouted. When the fruit is ripe, it will be Princess Resala your country will thank and honor. If don Saran is worthy of you, he will not hold this against you."

Resala gave her a weak smile. "So much wisdom from one so young. Amhese wisely chose to spare you. My head says you're right. Inside, I ache at this disgrace. Likely, Ghyldus will defeat him and all for nothing."

Teshet bit back her reply. She helped Resala from the bath, wrapping her in a thick robe and seating her on the bed to comb out her hair. The gentleness of Teshet's ministrations soothed and eased the burden of hatred with which Resala bound herself.

After braiding Resala's hair for the night, Teshet took Resala's hand, squeezing it. "Do you have any message for my uncle?"

Resala considered a moment. The calm Teshet had brought her fled. "There must be a major attack, disrupting," she said, accepting a slip of parchment and ink from Teshet's deep pocket. "Ghyldus intends to assault Arenh. I'll try to convince him it's premature. I need some trigger to prove it. If he continues like this, he'll end any foreign support for Arshal. We can't let that happen, Teshet. It's too soon. He could move on Arshal before he's ready for him."

Teshet tucked the letter in her shift, nodded, and left Resala alone again to brood, pacing her luxurious prison with nothing but hatred and despair in her heart as she unstopped the vial and drank the bitter stuff that would help her thwart Ghyldus's designs.

Rising from her bed more than a week later, still shaky and pale from long days of an illness that sapped her strength, Resala paced to the door, wrenching it open to glare, red-eyed, at the guard.

"Send Teshet, she ruined my favorite dress!" Resala commanded, turning away and slamming the door as she raced to the basin to be sick again, the low clouds clinging to the western horizon as dark as her mood.

When the guard pushed the girl into the room, and the door closed behind her with a slam, Resala railed at her for fifteen minutes, while Teshet read the instructions Resala had written on scraps of parchment Teshet smuggled to her.

"Tonight?" Teshet whispered, laying the back of her hand against Resala's pale forehead.

"High-level meeting. Officers traveling with only a few soldiers. It'd be such a blow!" Though so sick she didn't know how she kept her feet, much less her stomach, Resala had convinced Ghyldus to be wary. She had laughed at him and claimed he fell into their trap by spreading his troops thin to assault other countries. He still needed to see his danger to reconsider his plans.

"So little time," Teshet muttered. "But I will tell my uncle." Teshet peered at the princess. "The medicine has poisoned you, Lady –" she began, but Resala ignored her.

She hugged the girl as she flung a few more curses for the guard's benefit. As she sent Teshet on her way, Resala wondered if she needlessly risked Pladde lives for her plans. If only she could do something herself, not have to live vicariously on Teshet's tales. The worry comforted her fever as she crawled back into her bed.

Rumbling wheels and the clop of horse hooves against the rock-hard dirt triggered a tensing that sent currents through the still night. Bow strings tautened; arms strained as eyes peered for targets. Two dozen bowmen hid along the road that wound up from the harbor to Ghyldus's fortress. Buildings that bustled with trade each day sent out long shadows into the greening moon night, hiding archers in doorways and the dark mouths of alleys.

When all four carriages came into range, a signal loosed bowstrings. Some of the coachmen dropped soundlessly. Others cried out their warning.

The lead coachman snapped his whip, goading the team to a wild gallop that sent the carriage careening up the road, a man's startled face peering from the window. An arrow flew at the space where the face had appeared as the carriage sped away, the soldier on its roof struggling to keep his balance to shoot.

The second carriage tried to follow the first. The coachman sagged to one side clutching a wound while a soldier on the roof sought a target. The third carriage stopped in the street, the coachman dead against the brake as the last tried to pass. One soldier dashed from the carriage, shoving the dead coachman aside. Arrows whizzed around him. He yelped when one struck, but freed the brake and whipped up the team as the soldier on the roof distinguished targets in the shadows.

As the third carriage at last moved, the fourth fought to keep from tangling with it as that coachman, the fear of death in his eyes as blood poured from him, tried to control his team.

When the carriages had clattered from sight, five Pladde archers lay dead, the shadows not enough to conceal them from soldiers on the carriage roofs, three others injured. Only one dead coachman lay in the street, two more wounded. They would only learn later that the arrows they aimed through the carriage windows resulted in only a few minor wounds to Ghyldus's officers. If their purpose had been to deliver a blow against the country's leadership, the raid failed. But word soon came that Ghyldus had placed on hold all other plans until this annoying Pladde rebellion ended.

That night a petitioner arrived, dusty and weatherworn from his journey, to appeal to the Great God of Ea for privileges in exchange for information. Ghyldus chuckled. As if he felt inclined to grant dispensations for information he could take with the power of his gaze?

Verdred shoved the petitioner. The man sprawled before the Mover of Ea. The surly twist of his face, mouth ready to hurl an insult at the ungracious servant treating him so harshly, froze as his gaze fell upon the powerful figure gracing the throne.

Wind-whipped auburn hair hung in the petitioner's eyes, but not enough to hide him from Ghyldus's penetrating stare.

"So, Anlon, heir of Habdelion, comes begging," Ghyldus said.

Anlon choked, as if the words he had prepared to say suddenly fled. Ghyldus enjoyed that effect he had on petitioners. Let them stutter and stammer as they tried to find a way to beg for graces. Prettified speeches meant nothing to him.

"I would give you information," Anlon gasped. His gaze shifted slightly and Ghyldus knew the man now saw Resala. Most people hoped to keep their minds to themselves. This Anlon wanted to divulge all that he knew, selectively, as if he could manipulate the God of Ea. Anlon tried to rise from where he'd sprawled. Ghyldus glanced at Verdred, who moved closer to the petitioner and laid his black-gloved hands on Anlon's shoulders, holding him on his knees on the rough stone floor.

"I can take it at will," Ghyldus replied, letting his most menacing chuckle coil about the young man. "And you expect a gift in return. As if I must treat with some dirty Shandean and give him rule in a country I have duly conquered. I would instead present such honored roles to the faithful who serve me. What a presumptuous lot are the brats of Shande."

"I only hoped to rule in my father's place, to protect my people from King Arshaldon's dangerous plans." Anlon stared up from his knees, beseeching. "I was wrong to ask for position ahead of your faithful. Gladly I would become your humble servant."

Ghyldus glanced over his shoulder at Resala. Again, she meddled. He could not read this mind though the man resisted not at all. She looked back at him, innocently.

"What is it you must say that I should appreciate the service," Ghyldus demanded.

"The King's Champion gathers armies in Mershy and Detarian, armed by Arenh," Anlon stated boldly. "Then, they aim to march on Shela and retake it. The champion emptied the labor camps in the mountains, stealing metals and servants for his warriors. Spies work in Sihmad Shal and Sefresal, preparing for the king's call. All of this is part of …" Anlon stammered as he stared at a place above Ghyldus's shoulder. "Arshal's plans … to … to unite the country … to unite … when the star is … to –" Anlon stuttered to a halt, his gaze locked on Resala's.

"To do what!" Ghyldus demanded.

Anlon wavered a moment, but Resala's gaze held him.

"You, be gone from my hall!" Ghyldus roared at Resala. "I am tired of your meddling in these affairs."

Resala blinked as if she tried to fathom his meaning. When she abandoned Anlon, he lunged upward against Verdred's grip with his eagerness to speak. The move came so sudden and unexpected Verdred's hands closed on the man's throat.

"Verdred!" Ghyldus bellowed when he realized how his champion had interpreted the move. His shout came too late. Anlon lay prostrate on the floor, his neck broken. Ghyldus glared at his champion, the man's head hung in shame. Ghyldus could not fault him, of all creatures. He had bred his champion to protect his master. He had killed many a petitioner whose reactions threatened. Likely, the champion's dim wit placed Anlon as merely one more in a long line of petitioners with evil intent.

Ghyldus reached up to touch Resala's hand on his shoulder, held it tightly, the pressure enough, he hoped, to impress her. The joints in her fingers cracked. "You are beginning to anger me, dear one. You will outlive your usefulness soon."

Now she stared at Verdred again, ignoring him with the infuriating way she had about her.

"So, Resala, what is the king's plan this dead man fears?"

She continued to gaze at Verdred, then, as if finding something he said remotely of interest to her, she dared turn and look into his eyes, as if to flaunt his inability to enchant her with his very glance.

She smiled. "Why, to destroy you, Lord," she said with feigned innocence. "Of what other plan could Anlon know?"

Ghyldus released her hand. From where did she derive this incredible power to flaunt him? Shadows still clung beneath her eyes from the illness she hadn't yet shaken. She appeared thin and pale, yet in the dimness of his lofty stone hall that delicacy made her even more beautiful. A lavender gown accented the color of her eyes, making the fall of fair hair appear bright against the shadows. He glanced at Verdred who appeared ready to spring to the aid of his master if Resala's power proved strong enough to harm him.

"So, Verdred, you desire to get your hands on this Dyndevas neck as well," he laughed. Resala continued to gaze into the God of Ea's eyes, undaunted, her expression open and innocent, yet somehow like a stone barrier he couldn't pass.

Verdred's hand went to his throat. Ghyldus emitted a raucous laugh.

"See, dear one, Verdred awaits the day I present you to him to do as he will. He, too, is tired of your groundless threats."

"Groundless?" Resala mumbled, returning to her scrutiny of Verdred. "Hardly."

"Verdred, send me a courier. I will no longer play your game, dear one. I have grown bored with it. We will prepare a fleet this moment to sail to Shela and put down this resistance. Your Anlon did not wish to reveal it, but clearly the rotten body that fouled the reservoir was not Verdaen. That one leads this resistance." He studied Resala as her gaze followed Verdred's exit. "Our troops were to strike Arenh, but it appears Shande still does not learn. Let the rebels in Sihmad Shal and Sefresal grow bold. We will deal with them in time. Your brother's plans are ash, dear one."

"And the rebellion here will sweep you before it," Resala muttered with little conviction.

"It will take little to put down this so-called champion's rabble, leaving plenty of troops in Lagdche to end these Pladde skirmishes. Your vain hopes for your brother are wasted. He will be the king of nothing."

Resala stared at him a moment. She hesitated. He saw it. A moment's questioning? Or did she merely think better of some insult she would fling? How could he not read her! For a nagging moment he wondered if she had grown so strong that Verdred's assault on Anlon had been no accident, but her manipulation of his own tools. He felt certain now, something jiggled his web. He would jiggle back and see what he could shake loose.

With his eyes hidden in shadow, Verdred knew the rest of him melted into the dim alcove of a meandering corridor. Teshet left the rooms he had secretly watched for these long weeks. As the young woman hurried past him to the task assigned by her mistress, she remained ignorant of her danger, the hard gaze on her and the shadow that slipped behind to follow her.

Keeping a distance that made him one of many shadows, an art at which he'd grown adept, Verdred trailed Teshet to the edge of the city, and then beyond to a mean village of low huts that baked in the heat of day, and now steamed with the cool damp of night. Nothing like the abodes many Hogde kept in Lagdche, these huts of mud and straw with their dirt floors and dirt-packed roofs encompassed an area scarcely larger than the foyer of a Hogde home.

He waited while she at last threw a glance over her shoulder before slipping into an unassuming shack at the end of the row lining the main path. A brief square of light framed her, revealing a crude table and several figures crowding the hut, before the door closed. Light continued to filter out around chinks in the wall and the hides hanging over windows.

He crept up and listened a moment beneath the hide-covered window cut in the mud wall. He smiled to himself, his hunch proven. Teshet's mistress worked with the Pladde. When he learned all he sought to know, he shoved his shoulder into the door, pulling the brackets holding the bar from the wall. The door banged open, the bar clattering to the floor at their feet.

The half-dozen figures within jumped up. He smiled again, holding out a placating hand.

"I deliver a message," he said, voice rough from long silence.

The burly man who likely belonged to the voice of Jeret peered at him. His hand was on Teshet's shoulder prepared to thrust her behind him for protection.

"Are you the Healing Warrior sprung from Tawnkats?" Jeret asked, ignoring Teshet's shaking head.

"They call me Verdred."

Faces paled, eyes widened as men jumped to grab their weapons and Jeret thrust Teshet behind him.

"You'd be dead already if I meant harm to you. I was another before I became Verdred. I took the original, live on his laurels, though taking him at all's laurel and tale enough."

Teshet peered at the face that so mesmerized her mistress. "Verdred is mute. It is a surety of fidelity. Yet you speak, and not with the voice of Minaria, but more in the dialect of –"

"The princess?" He pulled off his helm, which had remained on his head for long weeks. He knew what they would see. The red mark of the helm on his face, a dark bruise that still gathered at the base of his neck, a scar along his hairline that disappeared in unkempt brown hair too light in color for the Hogde and so long it hung down his back. They might note the three parallel white lines across his forehead, and the hint of another scar behind his ear. Perhaps they'd even see the tiny mountain tattoo on his neck that he had once borne with pride. Surely, they could see that beneath dark brows, stone-colored eyes peered, and within them the hint of lost gods, proving this no Hogde warrior. Above all, they would see the sunburst on his temple.

"Shawnsi, and yet you turn to Ghyldus," Jeret muttered.

"Shawnsi," Verdred tested the name. "If I'd turned away, would I stand here? Things must be learned. It's a task I appoint myself. No one must know of this, no one!" His hand rested on the sword at his side.

Jeret straightened. "Then why reveal yourself to us? Who are you?"

"I'm Verdred, come to speak to the handmaiden, Teshet." He looked down at the helm in his hand, feeling naked. "You must not tell your mistress," he warned in a softer tone. "I'm here to protect her, but she must not know this. I have a token, for hope. I see it die in her. She must remain strong to do those things she plans."

He looked up at Jeret's hiss of breath.

"Yes, I heard you speaking. You should be more careful."

He returned his attention to Teshet. "She learned a power from him. For me to go undiscovered she must be present when I'm there."

"She says that of you," Teshet muttered. "That in you she sees all that is most revolting about Ghyldus. It hardens her resolve and protects her from the enchantment."

"She finds me so revolting?" He inclined his head then yanked the chain from his neck, breaking the clasp, and dropped it into Teshet's palm.

"She will wonder where the chain comes from, what it means."

"She'll recognize it," he said.

"Then she will know you."

"She must not."

Jeret took a step forward. "So what is your purpose? We hear all we need from the princess, and she is protected by Ghyldus's own designs. What can you accomplish here?"

"I'll know when I've accomplished it. Don't be certain her position is unassailable, nor that she's as resolved and unaffected as she appears. Likely she doesn't intend to survive to return to Shande. She must be protected from herself and from him. There are those who would give information to Ghyldus that it's best he does not get. Much comes through me. There is much I know, and have learned, that she hides from him. There are things I might yet accomplish."

"How do you know all this?" Teshet asked, incredulous. She shook her head at her uncle. "I cannot imagine the Lady knowing anyone as cruel as him well enough to know how she feels about her plight."

"I know her well, Teshet. It's her nature."

With that, he once again donned his helm and turned to leave.

"What is your name?" Jeret called. "She might take hope knowing you came to her."

"She mustn't know! Would it serve her to know those for whom she cares witness her suffering? Already he knows much of her mind she wouldn't wish. She could reveal me if she knew me."

"Why should we trust you," a man demanded. "For all we know you have been enchanted."

"I have," he admitted. "As for trust, it's late to be asking that."

He whirled and slipped into the shadows of Minaria, leaving Teshet gripping the chain that had hung around his neck since the eve of war.

"Zopher refuses me," Resala murmured as she examined the chain Teshet presented.

"No," Teshet whispered, flushing. "It came from Verdred."

"Verdred! Then it was Zopher, not Khoti, he slew." Stricken, she stared at the chain as she fought back a sob.

"You never said Zopher was so fell a warrior he could wound Verdred."

Teshet turned away, busying herself rearranging the scents and powders on the princess's dressing table so Resala wouldn't see through her lie.

"I didn't think so, but he may have changed. He could change like the wind, fit the role most suited to the moment, become that person, huntsman or aristocrat, friend or enemy, idiot or scholar." She sighed. "Back in Sihmad Shal he played aristocrat to woo me, then the wounded heart to leave me, then the fawning child to win me back again." Her voice wistful and sad, Resala held the chain close to her eyes to inspect each link, several of which had bent.

"Maybe it was a token the warrior, whoever he was, sent."

"Then still a refusal," Resala replied.

Teshet stared into a tin of powder. "My uncle recommends you always be present when news comes to Ghyldus."

"Why?"

"When you are present Ghyldus cannot read Verdred's mind."

"I know, at least Ghyldus makes this claim. How would Jeret know? How do you come by this?"

"I cannot tell you. You must just trust me. The less you know the better. Always be present when there are petitioners, when Verdred is in the hall. And accept the chain as a token of hope, not refusal."

She could feel Resala's eyes boring into her, but she wouldn't look. She couldn't lie to Resala, couldn't keep much of anything from the princess. She found it difficult to resist doing anything Resala told her.

"Why hide this from me, Teshet? It's obviously something to do with me, that I have a right –"

"It is to protect you, Lady. If you knew, you would be in danger."

"But Verdred!"

"Receives all messages, which Ghyldus gleans from his mind. If you are there the message cannot be delivered. So what Verdred learns is worthless. He can sign, but much remains unrevealed. If you are not there, and Ghyldus delves deep enough, he may find many things, dangerous things, never before known because of your presence. Trust me, please."

Resala stared into space, her fingers stroking the chain in the palm of her hand.

"I'll never see Zopher again. Even if he lives, the shame I must bring him."

"It is not a refusal."

"It wouldn't be Zopher's nature to abandon me with a cold gesture," she admitted. "So, it's meant to be hope, then. What hope? That someone cared enough to slip the smallest of tokens to me so I wouldn't become despondent? But Verdred?" She shivered with her familiar revulsion.

"There are many things in the world we cannot know," Teshet whispered. "Take your hope where you can find it, Lady."

Resala nodded. "I'll accept the challenge."

Teshet grasped her mistress's hand for assurance then slipped away, leaving the lonely woman alone to plot her enemy's moves.

# 37: Pranks

As Evenday and the first day of spring arrived and departed with none of the fanfare of the past, Nali ticked off the days with growing concern. He'd worked beneath Sihmad Shal for nine months now, recruiting little more than one hundred men each month. Certainly, a thousand well-trained and angry Gnats exceeded the three dozen they'd been when he arrived. It seemed pittance.

"What we need's something big to draw attention, show people these reprisals are nothing to fear," Nali growled as he paced the storeroom they had made their command post.

Jan gave him a weary glance as Nali began the same tired debate. Each time the Gnats struck, the Minarians countered with reprisals against the innocents of the city or Harbor. Even when Aron fed lies to the enemy and drew them into a trap, the people only saw the punishment, not the mastery of the feat.

"Any grand ideas?" Jan mumbled irritably. "All they'll do is string up a few more folk, or throw 'em in the lock-up. They'll always find enough room for a couple more in that hole."

"It's got to be daring," Nali replied as if he didn't hear Jan's sarcasm. "To prove the Minarians aren't as strong as they appear. Gods, Jan, we have tens of thousands of Shandeans up there," he waved vaguely at the ceiling. "Not to mention the Harbor, the countryside. They have twenty-five hundred. We outnumber them at least ten to one! What better odds can you get?"

"Many's the man who's lost on a sure bet and won on the long shot," Pedr said as he leaned his stool back against the wall, stretching his legs out with a creak.

Nali glared at him. Pedr's caution, his unflappable patience could irritate a man to death. As Pedr tapped his pockets in search of his pipe, Nali jumped up with an exasperated grumble, tossing a record book on a rickety table with a crack that made Jan startle. If they could just get out of this cramped tunnel, do more, prove themselves with something grand, it might lift the morale of the young men they had shut up in this dark dank world but for a few night forays.

"And you forget," Pedr continued, ignoring Nali's pacing and Jan's fingers rapping the table. "They wear armor, carry weapons, congregate in fortified towers –"

"Tell me something I don't know," Nali interrupted. "And we're armed, assembled –"

"But when it comes down to it, they outnumber us, Nali," Jan returned. "We can't count on those lazy do-nothings up there," he waved at the ceiling, implying the Shandeans too cowed to help. "So it's our thousand against their twenty-five hundred. The odds look skewed to me."

"Are you lookin' to give up?" Nali challenged in a menacing undertone. "Are we just gonna consign ourselves to misery and abandon Arshal 'cause folk up there are blind to the truth?" Nali jabbed his thumb at the spot to which Jan had pointed.

"Settle down, Nali," Pedr said, letting his stool slam onto the stone as he leaned forward. "We said nothin' of givin' up. We just need somethin' to show the people what we can do. What that is, I don't know. It does have to be daring, and it does have to be noticed. And," he leaned back on his stool again. "It should be somethin' that'll make folk laugh at 'em."

Nali's scowl faded then grew into a cold smile. Slapping the heel of his hand against his thigh, he sat on a crate, holding his side to suppress the desire to chuckle.

"You onto somethin', Nali?" Jan asked. "Or are you finally losin' your wits?"

"I don't think I've seen even a smile since he's been back, maybe he's cracked."

Nali continued to laugh silently, unable to stop now that his frustrations had found a release. The idea presented itself like a clear note.

"Remember what Jali and those other boys did?" Nali asked, trying to regain his breath.

"My boy did a lot of things, Nali. You gotta be more specific. He's always a trial," Jan said with a quizzical smile.

"That's the point, Jan. Pranks, a lot of little pranks," Nali said, his words tumbling out faster as the idea took shape. "Nothing humiliates a person more than when they're the butt-end of a good prank. Remember what they did to give a certain

306

lighthouse pilot his come-uppance, what was it, three years ago? Remember how Aron was hasselin' the fishers? Always made us wait inside the breakwater 'til they'd brought in all the big ships so a man couldn't get out 'til near midday."

"Aye," Jan said at last, a grin breaking his face. "Now that was a good joke, one of the best. Had to punish Jali for it, 'specially after Aron straightened up again and minded himself, but had to give the boy a pat on the back for being involved." The twinkle left Jan's eyes and his face fell. He shook his head. "But them's pranks, Nali. You don't fight a war with pranks."

"If we can't show the people that the Minarians can be humiliated, they'll continue to be terrified. Remember how we kept obeying Aron because he was authority appointed by decree? Once he'd been put down, he lost respect. It humanized him. Once the people realize the Minarians aren't immune, don't have some magic power from that demon they worship, then maybe we'll get some help. It wouldn't hurt to learn to laugh at them."

"It wouldn't hurt to try," Jan agreed.

"But if there's more reprisals, it still won't work," Pedr warned.

"Maybe, maybe not," Jan mused. "As much as we punish pranksters, they keep on doing it. A lot of times folk get punished for some prank they didn't have a part in and keep mum."

"But when you punish a boy for doing somethin', you don't go killin' him or tossin' him in a lock-up," Pedr replied.

"We'll see," Nali said with a cold smile.

He felt it, knew it. And he had an idea.

When the palace above grew quiet, its occupants asleep or dozing at their posts, a handful of shadows slipped up from the storerooms to exit in the back of the reception hall behind the tattered royal blue curtain. Silently, they padded behind Nali as he led them through the dark corridors he'd walked as King's Counselor.

A noise sent them flat against a wall, backs pressed into the stone as if it could swallow them. When the footsteps receded and they released a collective breath, Nali signed for one of the men to check the juncture of two passages. The man crouched as the footsteps returned. He edged to the end of the wall, holding to the shadow between two torch brackets.

The sentry stopped in the intersection of the two hallways, peering toward Nali's group as if sensing a presence in the darkness ahead. At last, shrugging to himself, the sentry turned to peer the other way. He pulled out a pipe, lighting it from one of the candles flickering in a wall bracket. While distracted and blinded by the bright flame near his eyes, the Gnat crept up behind him. The sentry didn't see his danger until a thin wire pressed against his neck. Nali had trained the Gnats in some of Khoti and Zopher's most proficient techniques. The Gnat held both ends of the wire in one hand, throwing his other arm over the man's face to muffle his choking gasps with the crook of his arm. Moments later, the sentry's body went limp. Dropping the body, the Gnat shrugged toward the shadows where his companions hid.

With a swift sign, Nali dispatched two men to carry the body back through the hidden door where men would strip him of clothes and weapons and eventually drop him in the Rigannon.

Down to three, Nali moved more cautiously. Apparently the Minarians felt their position precarious if they needed to station so many watchmen in the corridors. The Gnats couldn't take the time to deal with each they encountered and skirted around several sentries.

Finally, they reached the obscure doorway leading up to the Window of the Sun. Nali eased it open, then closed it behind them, leaving one Gnat on guard. Not knowing if anyone occupied or used the high tower, they stepped lightly. But when they reached the little door at the top of the long winding stairway, they found it open, and no one inside.

"If it stays this easy we could just take over the whole palace," Nali said under his breath.

"Why don't we?" the man remaining with him asked with a grin, as if the idea had never surfaced before.

"Soon."

Nali hurried to the narrow door leading to the conical tower roof. The cramped and dusty stairway seldom saw use. After fumbling in the dark to find his way and trying not to sneeze as the dust puffed up into the air, Nali at last reached the top. He climbed up on the little stool beneath a hatch in the roof. Tugging on the rope, he lowered the Minarian flag and pulled a treasured strip of cloth from inside his belt: A royal pennant as wide as a man at its large end and longer than he stood tall, embossed in white with the Dyndevas coat of arms. He handed it to his companion, who reached out and clipped it onto the rope in place of the black, orange and red Minarian pennant. With a grin, Nali hauled on the rope, hoisting the flag of Shande over the city once again.

"That ought to get folks talking," Nali whispered as they giggled like schoolboys, almost bursting before reaching the safety of Peshal's Tunnel.

Morning had aged several hours before most people noted that instead of the Minarian pennants, royal blue flags flew from the five towers of the palace. Not a few Harbor folk held forth that they knew where the idea came from. They recalled how a crudely-lettered and demeaning pennant rose over the pilot's own lighthouse while he slept and flew there near all day without his notice. The folk knew the Harbor spirit had reawakened in Sihmad Shal. They didn't know who, or how, but they bet on Gnats. As a few who had heard rumors began to compare notes with those who knew nothing, the city filled with chatter and chuckling, a thing largely lacking for well over a year. When Minarians passed, before they noted the change, they met amused smiles and on occasion even defiant grins.

It took the Minarians a while to notice. They didn't awake each day hoping they had only dreamed that conqueror's flags hung over the city. The Minarians might never have noticed if a red-faced Aron Keeper hadn't eventually pointed it out.

For two days the royal blue pennants snapped on the towers, and during that time a wave of pranks had the city squares full of chatter. A dozen Minarian wagons mysteriously lost wheels while rolling down the Sijway during a formal processional, dumping even the governor from his regal perch. With Esthen's memory in the back of pranksters' minds, horses reared, unseating their riders, to shed blankets stuck full of pins. Sails unfurled on the merchant flotilla, only to display huge rents in the canvases. Warehouse walls inexplicably collapsed.

The morale of Sihmad Shal blossomed as the enemy fell prey to an evil humor. The trickle of new recruits grew to a torrent. Before the Minarians could decide on reprisals for these seemingly harmless pranks, the damage had been done. Despite past actions against spies, traitors and soldiers and the sabotage of property and goods, the people would recall harmless pranks as the Gnat's greatest coup. In the week before the reprisals began, the Gnats doubled.

When one morning at the close of the first moon the city awoke to find three bodies swaying from the gallows in the market square, instead of cowing the Shandeans, it only brought more recruits in search of the covert resistance. Nothing pointed out injustice and oppression better than such vicious reprisals for such victimless acts.

As Nali sat in his storeroom command post logging the assignments for his new recruits, he wondered why it had taken so long to remember what it would take to jar people from their passivity. They had needed to laugh. The glimmer of a chance made his heart pound. Soon they could move beyond victimless games. Soon, they would be ready for war. They awaited only the king.

# 38: Return to Eilime

The thunder of hooves on the Staph-el road echoed against the walls, tensing sentries pacing in their Minarian uniforms as the warmth of the greening moon wafted up from the plains. Eithurdon paused to stare up at Ytri who manned the gate command.

"What is it?" Eithurdon shouted, ready to call the alarm that would send shawnsi and children out of sight.

Ytri called for the gatekeeper to swing open the gates a crack for Davin to ride through.

Ytri had reached the ground before the Tawnkat had passed through the gate. "Trouble?" Ytri demanded as the duke drew near.

Davin held up a letter sealed with Resala's mark.

Ytri's eyebrows rose as he glanced at the duke.

"I need a response," Davin said. "There's a Pladde messenger at the mine. All those Minarian uniforms are making him nervous."

"Come," Eithurdon said, signing for his senior staff to join them at the small house that served as the duke's command.

Davin turned about him as he tried to keep up with the duke. On first look Sefresal appeared little changed from the occupation. Well-fed townsfolk performed tasks more suited to a free city than one occupied. Hogde faces didn't match the Minarian uniforms and mail. The dungeons of Eithurdon's Halls had returned to storerooms and the armory again stored the weaponry of an army. When needed, Geleg took the seat in Eithurdon's reception hall, using few words with messengers. On occasion a child's face appeared in a window before a parent pulled him or her away. Visitors might note the number of people congregating around a small house owned by the Sefresal branch of the Hostler family. Rathil and his wife had moved back

311

to serve their duke, but the people came there to find Eithurdon holding court in the Hostlers' tiny kitchen.

After reading the letter, Eithurdon let Resala's note flutter from his fingers.

"They only assume it was Khoti," Davin said.

Eithurdon looked up, startled at the name. "More likely Zopher. Such a waste of a good man!" He stared out the window. "We must devise another supply route to the Pladde," he said, tapping a finger on the note without looking. "Without them, Ghyldus will send more reinforcements." Eithurdon began pacing. "We have sat here too long," he announced. "Having our city back is not enough. It is time to move on."

"So soon?" Geleg gasped.

"We control several mines, the city."

"We've defenses here. How can we hold anything we reclaim?" Geleg challenged.

"Just the way we planned last year in the Val. Gods, it has been over a year!" Eithurdon turned a stunned gaze on them. "Look at what little we have done in all this time." Eithurdon leaned on the table, staring at Geleg. "When is the next courier due?"

"Two weeks."

"Then we move now –"

"Now!" Kefta stood, balancing on a leg that, though intact, remained useless and numb beneath him. "How can we?"

"When the Guard has been called in the past they have always moved with immediacy."

"Not with fifteen hundred in one day!"

"Have you lost your stomach for battle, Captain? Perhaps there are others, better suited, for command."

Kefta stood as straight as he could. "Are you relieving me because I challenge this plan?"

Eithurdon turned away. "We must move, quickly. There is much to do to be ready when the courier arrives. Two weeks. That is not much time."

"After he leaves, we have another two weeks before another arrives," Kefta protested.

"And by then, we will be in the blossom moon. We just do not have the time! I have been idle too long." Eithurdon shook his head. "We still have the Pladde to supply. We need more men, now! Look how long it has taken to train what we have into any semblance of an army. That is the whole point of using all this time wisely." Eithurdon leaned on his fists, peering across the table at his officers.

"My scouts will be ready at dawn," Ytri declared.

"And you?" Eithurdon asked, turning to Kefta.

"Am I still your captain?"

"Who else? I would not drive another of my officers away. I know of no other who can lead as you, Kefta."

"As half a man?"

"Half a man? Such self-pity. Did they damage your head in battle? It is what is in your head that makes you captain. Your sword makes you a warrior. Stay on your horse and no one will note the difference." Eithurdon laid a hand on Kefta's shoulder. "Have them ready at dawn."

As his men filed away, Eithurdon sank into his chair, head in hands. As much as the admission hurt, he needed Khoti, needed the special brew the gods had mixed in an uncultured mountain man. Guard morale, even among tried veterans, slipped. They needed Khoti's spirit to inspire them, his humor to give them perspective, and his recklessness to overcome their fears. Eithurdon doubted he could ever again face this man he loved and hated in the same breath. Now, he could only look forward to recouping his honor in heroic death on the battlefield. Let Steadon rebuild this broken House of Lharan with the young offspring hiding in the Val. Eithurdon would return now the gift Khoti had given him.

When Eithurdon rode away with twelve hundred Guardsmen at the end of the first week of the greening moon, leaving behind four hundred Guardsmen and aged militiamen under Steadon to defend Sefresal, he never expected much trouble subduing the little port town at the head of the Eilime River. After all, fifty Tawnkats controlled two mines with other hardy mountain tribesmen filtering into the Val from throughout the region. They seemed so strong now. It made him doubt their vulnerability.

Eithurdon wanted a ruse of occupation in Eilime much as he had in Sefresal. From there, they would branch out, recruiting the people of Kishma to train and serve in his army.

But the enemy had established policies in Eilime to put down resistance. Scouts often mentioned that life there had grown difficult. Eithurdon didn't know what to expect.

Moving through open country without drawing attention, especially, when so many bore shawnsi features, had stomachs in knots. Ytri's scouts fanned out around the host, ready to hunt down any witness. They found none. They moved through a seeming silent countryside. The enemy in Eilime feared nothing.

When Eithurdon stopped on the little hill overlooking the town, he at first thought the Minarians had prepared for them. Only now and again did some Minarian lazily cross an empty street from one building to the next. Fishing boats bobbed on the chop of the Dodfrenyen Sea. No one wandered the little village.

"What are those long buildings there?" Eithurdon pointed toward the river, gesturing at crude warehouses built along the marshy banks of the river.

"One's a fish processing plant," Ytri told him. "There's another for wool and other farm products. Another stores Lharan goods for shipment downriver. That one there houses soldiers, barracks for laborers, others full of little workshops for everything from woodwork to sewing."

"Where are all the people?"

Ytri gave Eithurdon an odd stare. "In the barracks. In the warehouses."

"Everyone?"

Ytri nodded. "As far's we know all the houses in town are either used by the Minarians or vacant. The people live in the barracks."

"Why?"

Ytri shrugged.

Eithurdon's eyes narrowed. "Fetch Hothur. I will go no nearer until I know what I face."

Ytri went in search of Hothur among the remaining men of the original Guard, his Minarian gear concealed beneath a buff and pewter cloak. He had proven himself first when his advice helped break the siege of Eithurdon's Halls. Oddly, on his counsel the Shandeans executed the comrades who worshipped Ghyldus. He warned such zealots could still do harm. The few dozen men he knew had no love of Ghyldism became prisoners of war, held in conditions better than any imagined. On Hothur's guidance, too, the Tawnkats forged light mesh tunics to which Shandeans could grow accustomed. If Ghyldus came he would bring his best. But the enemy would not decimate the Guardsmen as they had in the past. Hothur could no longer be numbered among the enemy.

When Hothur peered down on the town of Eilime, he paled. "This is not a good thing," Hothur muttered, staring at the ground as Eithurdon waited for his assessment. "I advised you of the orders we received. The people are in those barracks, under guard, and likely being worked and starved to death. You will find no help there."

Eithurdon leaned back in his saddle. "How do we approach this?"

"If alarmed, they will kill the laborers," Hothur whispered.

"How many guards?" Ytri asked.

"If there has been no resistance, probably only a few to each building, more in the warehouses."

"If scouts secured the buildings, then a signal could send the army into the town," Kefta suggested.

Eithurdon still stared down at the ghostly streets. "Do it." His face reddened as he pondered the consequences of his long delay in Sefresal. "Take Hothur." He glanced at the Minarian. "If you have your Minarian cloak with you, it might be useful."

Hothur sprouted a grim smile. "I wore it for just such a purpose," he said, pulling back the buff and pewter cloak to reveal the black clothing and captain's markers.

"Hothur," Eithurdon called as the Minarian turned to follow Ytri and Kefta. "You do not have to do this. These are your people, some even your friends. I cannot ask this of you."

"You never asked me," Hothur stated. "Your folk have killed their own people. There are times when such things must be done." With a stiff nod, Hothur hurried after Kefta and Ytri.

When night fell over Eilime the boats drifted in to deposit their catch, but after the fishers filed into the processing house, they never reappeared.

Ytri's scouts crept among the clapboard warehouses, oppressed by the absolute silence of the place. A bell clanged, startling the men. From within the buildings came a shuffle of feet on planks as laborers moved to their beds and others went to their work. Then all fell silent again.

"How could they give in?" Ytri muttered.

"Hunger is an equalizer," Hothur replied in a thin voice. "Strong and weak are one when they starve, when they labor to death, when their families are threatened, but no leader emerges because the leaders have all been cut down in front of them. Death is the greatest equalizer of all. I imagine it is not far from these people."

Hothur tucked the buff and pewter cloak into a tight roll beneath his mail. He gave Ytri a rueful smile. "It does not comfort me to wear my captain's insignia again. I like riding beside the Lharan Guard."

Ytri gave his arm a reassuring squeeze. "The only problem's you prove the enemy human."

"The worst curse of a warrior is thinking that way, thinking at all." He stared ahead at the barracks. "They could have chosen anything they wished to believe in. But they chose to embrace a faith in hatred. Such people are no longer men of my tribe, but merely tools of a demon, to be destroyed lest their disease spread to others."

With that, Hothur strode to the largest barracks. After opening the door a crack to peer inside, he glanced back toward Ytri, holding up four fingers. He stepped in, looking around him at the many sleeping forms and the startled guards lazing at a table near one end.

Hothur gave them a companionable smile. "I have a treat," he called as the men rose to greet him. "I come from Lagdche to commend you for fine work here. We hear good things about this operation." The men grinned with anticipation for any reward from Lagdche.

"Step outside, it smells terrible in here. I will have to get your names, rank, outfit, all that paperwork, and I cannot stomach this odor," he said, curling his lip at the haggard forms sleeping there.

They nudged each other as they followed Hothur out the little door. When the five stood in a small circle in the yard, Hothur nodded as he lauded their accomplishments. Several of Ytri's men crept up behind the four Minarian soldiers. On one signal, Ytri's scouts clapped hands over Minarian mouths and stabbed, remaining firm until the men fell limp.

Hothur searched the bodies, finding the keys to unchain the sleeping laborers from their beds. "I do not think they will trust me." He handed the keys to Ytri.

Ytri grinned, sending a man to free the captives and lead them to the waiting army.

In this manner, they emptied three barracks without incident. It seemed so simple. Yet, they still had to get into the warehouses where more guards stood watch.

When Hothur entered a building reeking of smoked fish and entrails, a curt challenge greeted him in a familiar voice. "Hothur, what brings you from Sefresal," growled his one-time superior, Kubel. Of all people, he would have to find Kubel standing defensively near the door.

"Merely to examine your progress. We have not had your success, Kubel," Hothur drawled, willing himself calm.

"I hear nothing changed in Sefresal," Kubel sneered, "that your laborers even look to enjoy themselves. My friends do not reply to messages. Likely they are too busy socializing with the labor."

Hothur's lip curled. "I think our commander has a weak stomach. We could use such leadership as yours." Hothur peered beyond Kubel. "A tour, perhaps?"

"Of a fish processing plant?" Kubel returned. "Hardly seems what mining interests should care about, unless you fancy cured and pickled rock." Kubel maintained his posture.

"I am sent to inspect –"

"At midnight?"

"Why else would I be here?" Hothur returned. "It is a surprise inspection. And it is how long it took me to arrive."

Kubel peered at Hothur then glanced out the door. "Rumor says you fear some Shandean king. Perhaps you turn coward."

Hothur straightened. "I reported things that should be reported, Kubel, any matter of security. As for cowardice, test me." Hothur's hand went to his side.

Kubel took a step back then held his hands out to apologize for the affront.

Hothur shrugged, smiling again. "I brought gifts from Sefresal. The finest Saran osfothye and Shiadin liquor." Hothur touched his fingers to his lips with a look of bliss. "Wondrous stuff. Join me, bring your friends."

Kubel grinned. "Bring it in! Not much of the quality stuff goes out into a wilderness of insects and mud as we suffer."

"I need help. Full keg of liquor, three men to lift one. And a bale of osfothye."

Kubel's eyes lit. "A whole keg! Bale!" With a brusque command, he called seven of his men to retrieve the trove.

As they clambered out the door, Kubel's eyes narrowed and his hand went to the hilt of his sword. "Where is your wagon?" Kubel demanded.

"I could not drive cargo over such soft turf."

Kubel peered at Hothur. He shook his head. "I do not believe you. What are you up to, Hothur? Why would you bring a wagon of gifts to inspect a fish processing plant when there are no fisheries in the mountains?"

At that moment, Ytri's men struck. Kubel shook off his attacker and instead pulled his dagger. He lunged for Hothur, who fell back from the blow and stumbled in the marshy turf. He whipped out his sword, but Kubel straddled him, blade drawn and pressed to Hothur's neck.

"Traitor!" Kubel hissed as he kicked Hothur's sword arm away. Suddenly he arched, his sword falling from his hand to strike Hothur's neck. Kubel collapsed on top of Hothur as Ytri tugged free his bloody blade.

"I am very pleased to see you," Hothur muttered as Ytri helped him to his feet. He rubbed at the trickle of blood on his neck. Ytri eyed a dagger sticking from Hothur's side.

"Your wound –" he began.

Startled, Hothur looked down. Laughing, he withdrew the dagger, not flinching. He smiled when he pulled away his cloak to reveal a rent in his mail. The dagger had fouled in the buff and pewter cloak rolled up beneath it. Only the tip of the dagger had pierced his skin.

"A sign the colors of your house will be the victor." Hothur laughed.

Ytri shook his head. "Do we dare try again?"

"We have to. An army on the hill waits to take the town. There will be dead Shandeans if we do not."

"But you're bleeding –"

"Then I will claim a revolt has broken out in one of the sheds." Hothur smiled. "Only a few more to go, we are doing just fine." He stepped over Kubel, who stared up at him with dead and accusing eyes, and moved on to the next warehouse.

Dawn grew in the sky by the time Ytri gave the signal. With the remaining people of Eilime out of the way, and the guards in the warehouses dispatched already, Eithurdon swept in to little resistance. As Ytri struck down the commander of the town garrison in the only fight of any merit, the blank-eyed folk of Eilime trudged home to somehow pick up their lives and continue.

Days passed before Eithurdon's army found a single person capable of beginning the difficult training the Guard required, and even longer before the recruit could work at it long.

"How can we build an army with ghosts?" Eithurdon muttered as Kefta tried to establish some organization among the hundreds of captives stumbling into their camp.

Eilimean laborers remained haggard and listless from long captivity. Sixteen-hour workdays on a few mouthfuls of food had already sped the demise of many of the older folk. Their captors had beaten the will to resist from many, some unable to even communicate their needs clearly in those initial days.

Those who came forward to repay their saviors with service threw themselves into training with a will that belied the condition of their bodies. Others pointed out the traitors, Banen, the man who had betrayed Nali, among them.

He wondered how they would prepare for the Imperial Minarian Courier's twice monthly inspection and report. How would they ask Eilime's people to re-enter the warehouses and barracks and carry on the ruse of captivity? Then they searched through the piles of Minarian paperwork, a record that detailed the occupation in measurable terms that made Eithurdon choke.

"Oh, this is a nasty bit to find," Hothur muttered as he sorted papers in the former office of the commander. Cringing, he set a ledger on the table in front of Eithurdon as Ytri peered over his shoulder.

"'Executions and relocations,'" Eithurdon read, scanning the list. He tapped his finger on the page. "Here. Family Nalisson, Olna hung for treason, infant died of nature." He glanced over his shoulder at Ytri. "Of nature, what rot. Here, two girls transported to a Lharan labor camp." Eithurdon looked up at Hothur. "Did you know about these?"

Hothur looked away. "You heard my reasons for surrender."

"Maybe Khoti rescued them," Ytri offered.

"If they still live," Hothur said softly.

"And we did nothing!" Eithurdon ran his hand through his hair. "All those months! What did it take to free Eilime? We could have stopped all this suffering."

Hothur's shoulders sagged. "The infants of Shande are made into warriors with blood on their hands, too young to understand." He looked up at Eithurdon. "What have we done?"

"We are as much at fault. We let you do it."

As Eithurdon turned his attention back to the papers, he wondered whether he had any better claim to honor for executing the practitioners of Ghyldism than the Minarians had for killing the shawnsi. He couldn't let himself think such thoughts. He pulled out another journal listing executions under the heading of undesirables. Midwives, herbmasters, craftsmen, historians – anyone with a skill that leant itself to authority or respect in the community – all gone, all recorded to prove to Ghyldus their success. The conquerors had stolen even Shande's knowledge.

Eithurdon wanted to ask Hothur if other cities knew such executions. Hothur couldn't tell him. The man's shoulders sagged more with each day he witnessed what his people had done.

Eithurdon realized now, he had over promised the strength and number of the Lharan army that raced to the king's itinerary. Too many Eilimeans had died, with more broken beyond any hope of serving their duke. He prayed King Arshal had the support of foreign nations and far provinces more populous than Kishma. When Arshal finally faced Ghyldus in Sihmad Shal, he would need far more than the measly few thousand Eithurdon could muster.

# 39: Keeper

The thump of the rocking chair running off the edge of the rug on the backside of each swing made Aron's knife rattle on the platter sitting on the floor beside the chair. He ignored it, didn't hear the rattle. He heard and saw other things, recalling his decades of life. His lifemate craned her head around the doorway. He kept his eyes locked on the pattern of the rug as his body thrust the rocker back and forth at a furious clip, the very ends of each rocker carrying the full weight of the chair for less than a beat before throwing the weight forward again.

"I'm taking to Dlan these extra loaves Laria sent. There's a family there with sick ones," she said.

He didn't turn, didn't respond, though he couldn't stop his lip from curling slightly at mention at the shame of his life. Didn't he see the cast of Laria's eyes when her keeper let her visit? She threw her hatred at him like shards of broken glass. Though always quiet, she'd never been so mute, so haunting. Hadn't he seen the bruises she shrugged away? Hadn't he noticed the way she now puffed out, swelling with more than just her maturity? Into what torture had he sold his eldest? Into what torture had he sold them all? Had Libria truly fallen while playing? A sure-footed girl, the second of ten, he'd raised her to be responsible and she always seemed confident. They hadn't even returned her belongings. Even the smallest memento might have soothed a father, a favorite scarf, a special stone.

The things he did for Nali, Pedr and Jan could not erase the sins he committed against his flesh and blood. He might redeem a little of the trouble he'd made for the Gnats, but how could he ever live to face any of his children again?

His gaze briefly left the cords of the braid rug, the chair slowing its furious rock. The house fell silent. Closed against the noises of the city, the shades and shutters hid the occupants

321

from view. He lived among lush furnishings, the appointments rich. For the noble who once lived here it may have felt comfortable. Not for the grizzled pilot. Not for Aron Keeper.

They asked him who could possibly get into the palace, so close to the governor, to raise pennants on the tower. They asked him how he knew so many things when everyone labeled him a traitor. They asked him how he evaded Gnat justice unless he worked with them. They asked him how he knew things so obviously close inside the circle of Gnat doings. He lied, as he always did, uncertain anymore where truth hid. He lied to himself about his children; about Laria's role; about Libria's death; about his rights to comfort when his lifelong friends lived in squalor, hand-to-mouth, smuggling crusts of food to children hidden away in dark cellars and false walls. He lied to his keepers, telling them he paid for the information, told them he listened well, that his lifemate picked things up in her good works. Lies. The key to survival. He told lies to gain this comfortable house for children who never lived in it. He told lies to gain his daughter a position in which she served as a toy for Loch Asmodiel and Adesia. He lied to return to the fold of the Gnats. He repeated their lies. He was a lie.

He heard a slight noise outside. He didn't look up, but rocked harder. The platter and knife again rattled. The door crashed open. He didn't raise his head. He rocked furiously as they gathered around him, one stooping to gather up the dish and throw it against the wall. He refused to look at them, acknowledge them as they grabbed his arms and the chair flew from him with a crash against a cabinet filled with a noble's trinkets crafted of various hues of Jashiho glass. The tinkle of shattered crystal, like fine chimes in a soft breeze, rained from the shelves. A little more fell with each thump of his assailants' feet.

They threw him on his stomach. A knee crunched into his spine, thrusting the air from his lungs, his elbows brought up and tied behind him. They bound his hands as he squirmed, crying for mercy, for forgiveness for whatever angered his keepers. They secured his feet with a cord that went around his neck. He could hear the squeal of muscles, the scrape and pop of bone dislocating, tendons unraveling. They covered his eyes and gagged him. They pummeled his ears with Ghyldus's wisdoms, reminded him of Ghyldus's compassion, of the good things Ghyldus had done, and maligned him for his ingratitude. Wasn't Laria honored by the governor? Weren't his children educated at the governor's expense? Hadn't he and his lifemate moved from mean station to luxury? Aron cried into the gag as they demanded he return to their fold. For all the things done for him, hadn't he been selfish to hold back knowledge for his own gain? What had he been before? The governor took nothing and made it something. He owed everything, his life, his fealty, his soul to the governor and Ghyldus.

Aron couldn't speak through the gag, couldn't appeal with his eyes. It grew silent. Had they left? The silence came so sudden out of the blackness of his pain, out of the cacophony of his terror, his muffled sobs. Where had they gone? A blow caught him in the face, boot scraping against cheek. It remained silent but for his whimpers. He tried to cry out but the gag muffled him as he choked on the blood from a broken nose. Out of the silence, the darkness, the unknown, kicks found his ribs, his spine, the backs of knees and balls of bared feet.

Suddenly the silence shattered with the prophetic words of Ghyldus next to his ears, spread upon him like a promise as the beating continued. Each kick: fire. Each word: a promise of peace, comfort and healing. Days, it seemed, the darkness erupted in stabs of pain, white lights shooting before darkened eyes. When he thought the pain could get no worse, the fear no more real, his hold on life no more tenuous, the words in his ears no more shrill, they whipped him over onto his back and yanked out the gag and ripped the blindfold from his eyes. A blazing medallion filled his gaze with its searing glare.

"Who!"

He gasped, gagged, squirmed. He couldn't! Snakes slithered across him, their scaly bodies coiling about his limbs as heads rose to flick tongues in his face. Rats scratched in his clothing, searching for the flesh, their yellow teeth tasting the air. Giant spiders paced up his neck and sent curious forelegs onto his cheek.

"Who!"

"Reve Pedr the Drayman," he blurted, his heart faltering at the betrayal of a friend for whom he truly cared, hating himself, wanting to die.

A kindly smile. The snakes, the rats, the spiders, gone, back inside the medallion from where they had sprung.

"Is that all?" The bonds loosened. A cool compress wiped his face then rested on a feverish forehead. Water touched his lips. The rope around his neck jerked. "Is that all?"

He thought of Nali and Jan, the fire in them, the strength in them, the survival of a people in them. He shook his head.

"Where?"

His eyes closed. A sob. A secret sworn, or a lie? It was a secret sworn. They wouldn't have lied to him about that, it had been too casual, too much like friends talking, not tools working.

"Where!" the face pressed close to his ear again. The light of the medallion fell on him, glowing through his closed lids.

"A house by the river, west bank." The words tumbled from his mouth, the directions. The look of the place. Tel's farm. Pedr's wife and grown children would meet there with all the Gnat leaders to celebrate their successes and plot their next moves.

Suddenly he felt comforted. They gave him food, bathed and pampered him. They propped pillows about him and massaged ointments into strained limbs. Exhausted, he could only let them treat him as he heard a voice assuring him Laria would rest easier now. What had he bellowed before Pedr's name escaped him? Praise Ghyldus, God of Ea? His stomach flopped like a fish on the bank. He could have made no greater denunciation. He might as well be dead. Only Ghyldus would have him now.

THE END BOOK II

# Cast of Characters

## In order of mention

*Khoti of Tasch-el* – Surviving younger son of Tsevon and Amhese; Tawnkat leader; Lieutenant in the Lharan Guard; aide to Eithurdon; healer; aspiring suitor of Asteria; named Verdaen by his enemy; favorite mount: Fidra.

*Chati the Cooper's son* – Taschian. Konner's nephew. Former attendant to Khoti; Lharan Guardsman; Tawnkat.

*Asteria* – Shawnsi. Daughter of Eithurdon; friend of Khoti.

*Eithurdon* – Shawnsi. Duke of Lharan and provincial leader in exile of Kishma; brother of Steadon; father of Asteria; nephew of King Ebon.

*Tait of Eilime* – Mayor of Eilime; King's Council; aspiring suitor of Asteria.

*King Arshaldon Dyndevas* – Shawnsi. Eldest son of Ebon and Sala; King in Exile of Shande.

*King Ebon Dyndevas* – Shawnsi. King of Shande; lifemate Sala; children: Arshaldon, Esthenshaldon, Peshaldon, Resala; dies in the mountains.

*Konner* – Taschian Constable and Second to Tsevon; Tawnkat; healer.

*Aibak* – Shiadin border guard and ally to the Val.

*King Keyen* – King of Shiad.

*Prince Peshaldon Dyndevas* – Shawnsi. Youngest son of Ebon and Sala.

*Zopher don Saran* – Shawnsi. Son of Baron Sipheron don Saran. Suitor of Resala's and friend of Arshal. Scout.

*Cree* – Advisor to the king; Arshal's tutor; Visionary; also known as Idenai.

*Esthen* -- Prince Esthenshaldon Dyndevas. Shawnsi. Second son of King Ebon and Queen Sala. A revered commander who falls in the defense of Sihmad Shal.

*Amhese* – Staphian. Lifemate of Tsevon and mother of Von (who dies in Tasch-el) and Khoti; assassinated Mol Azezial.

*Tsevon of Tasch-el* – Headman of Tasch-el and the Independent Lharan Tribes; Tawnkat leader; healer; sparked the Pladde rebellion.

*Latra* – Taschian. Culture keeper; kinswoman of Tsevon and Khoti.

*Geleg* – Member of the original Lharan Guard, scout and friend of Khoti.

*Nali Drulson* – Fugitive from Sihma Harbor who uses aliases Nali Bertalson and Jani Hostler; derna of the First Degree (scholar); Harbor Gnat commander; King's Counselor; children: Bertal, Kia, Rena; lifemate Olna and son Nalel killed in Eilime.

*Bertal Nalisson* – Sihma Harbor. Son of Nali and Olna. Twin of Kia.

*Rathil Hostler* – Eilimean farmer who takes in the Drulsons/Bertalsons; former Lharan Guardsman; lifemate Atnil.

*Mol Azezial* – Minarian king assassinated by Amhese.

*Toban* – Member of the original Lharan Guard; scout and friend of Khoti.

*Ytri* – Member of the original Lharan Guard; scout and friend of Khoti.

*Princess Resala Dyndevas* – Shawnsi. Daughter and youngest child of Ebon and Sala; betrothed to Zopher.

*Kefta Salman* – Captain of the Lharan Guard and friend of Khoti.

*Von* – Khoti's older brother who died in raid on Tasch-el.

*Steadon Dodfrenyen* – Shawnsi. Younger brother of Eithurdon; nephew of King Ebon.

*Hothur* – Minarian Captain in charge of Sefresal's dungeon.

*Anlon of Mershy* – Adopted Dasireian son of Habdelion; potential suitor of Asteria.

*Queen Sala* – Shawnsi. Lifemate of Ebon. Mother of Arshal, Esthen, Peshal and Resala. Sister of Habdelion of Mershy; dies in the Val.

*Tre the Imager* – Taschian. Khoti's former attendant; Lharan Guardsman; Tawnkat.

*Prince Euzzeldir* – Shawnsi. Joffan provincial leader titled as a former line to the throne.

*Jan the Innkeeper* – Owner of Sihma Harbor's Old Scow Inn; lifemate is Cookie; son Jali; Harbor Gnat leader.

*Tel* – Sihma Harbor farmer; Olna's cousin; Harbor Gnat.

*Pedr the Drayman* – Former Reve (officer of the peace) of Sihma Harbor; Harbor Gnat leader.

*Aron Keeper* – Former lighthouse Keeper of Sihma Harbor; informant/traitor.

*Verdred* – "Dread warrior" King's Champion of Minaria; Ghyldus's Malice.

*Loch Asmodiel* – Governor of the Minarian Protectorate of Shande. Lifemate Adesia.

*Cookie* – Lifemate of Jan the Innkeeper and mother of Jali; Gnat cook.

*Rollynd* – Life-long friend of Nali.

*Tedwa* – Tachi leader; uncle to Ledak.

*Habdelion* – Shawnsi. Provincial leader and Duke of Mershy; brother of Queen Sala. Children: Habda, Anlon.

*Mitte Salman* – Younger brother of Kefta. Lharan Guardsman and scout.

*King Azren* – Arenhian king, derna.

*Jali Janson* – Son of Jan the Innkeeper and Cookie.

*Libria Keeper* – Second oldest child of Aron Keeper.

*Daris* – Joffan labor camp internee.

*Ahrwesz* – Taschian. Lifemate of Latra; Tawnkat; Cousin to Khoti.

*Segan* – Taschian. Tawnkat.

*Davin* – Taschian. Tawnkat.

*Teckhan* – Taschian. Tawnkat.

*Velder* – Tawnkat.

*Gelter* – Tawnkat.

*Kia Renali* – Daughter of Nali and Olna; Twin of Bertal; labor camp internee.

*Rena Renali* – Youngest daughter of Nali and Olna; labor camp internee.

*Cydwyn Lockman* – Kalilian from Etaleah. Labor camp internee.

*Ledak* – Tachi. Nephew of Tedwa.

*Habda* – Shawnsi. Daughter of Habdelion.

*Sedaik son of Perouk* – Detarian. Labor camp internee; protégé of Khoti.

*Efen* – Lharan Guardsman.

*Rast* – Lharan Guardsman.

*Ernik of Ar-Tebez* – King Azren's representative to Shande.

*Perouk* – Detarian. Father of Sedaik.

*Teshet* – Pladde servant rescued by Amhese; niece of Jeret; part of Pladde resistance.

*Jeret* – Pladde resistance leader; uncle to Teshet.

*Kubel* – Minarian captain in Eilime.

*Laria Keeper* – Eldest daughter of Aron Keeper; servant to Adesia and Loch Asmodiel.

*Adesia* – Lifemate of Loch Asmodiel; "Matriarch" of Shande.

# TERMS

*Taschian/Staphian/Lhatan* – Shal tribes of the Lharan Mountains.

*Shawnsi* – descendants of unions between the gods and shals prior to the Great War. Shawnsi are largely identified by a small star-shaped birthmark on their temple.

*Second* – The second in command to a Lharan tribal headman.

*Pladde* – Labor/lower caste of Minaria.

*Tawnkat* – Lharan tribal resistance fighters and "soldiers" under Tsevon and Khoti.

*Dynfearn the Lost* – Historic shawnsi leader of renown from the Great War.

*Derna* – Scholars qualified to serve as advisors and cast auguries; recipients of Certificates Dernailye after many years of study; level of "degree" (first, second, etc.) suggests initial ranking of skill; singular or plural term.

*Visionary* – Term said to be reserved for the gods who remained behind after One called them home, but also a name given to the highest ranking derna.

*Verdaen* – "Demon warrior" a name Minarians apply to Khoti.

*Shal* – the people of Ea who survived the Great War; creations of Terremar and his children.

*Eidhalt* – elite warriors of Minaria.

*Hogde* – Ruling/higher caste of Minaria.

*Osfothye* – A plant with multiple medicinal, food and ritual purposes.

*Lierye* – The official history/documentation of the land of Shande.

*Reve* – Royal appointee who serves a town leader and constable.

*Harbor Gnats/Gnats* – Nickname for Harbor militia.

*King's Champion* – Elite warrior in service to and representing a king in battle.

*Sword of Shande* – Commander of the armies of Shande.

*Independent Lharan Tribes* – Federation of northern Lharan shal tribes.

*Tachi* – Shal tribe of Tormor Wood.

*Stellan* – A silvery metal softer than adanan mined in the mountains; often edges weaponry or is used for decorative purposes.

*Adanan* – An extremely hard metal mined in the Lharans.

# DEITIES

*One* – The ultimate energy and fate (intent) of all that exists.

*Ghyldus* – Lesser god who aids Minaria after the Great War; known for enchantments; source of Ghyldism; acolyte if Fyraer.

*Kedtair* – Son of Terremar whose star rises every ninth year to create chaos as a sign from the gods; can mark those who will be good or evil if born during the month it's overhead.

*Terremar* – One of two "offspring" of One.

*Fyraer* – One of two "offspring" of One; banished.

*Maura* – Daughter of Terremar who rules the sea; creations include water, and the Merien.

*Idenai* – A lesser god who remained behind to become the Visionary Cree.

## About the Author

A former journalist, editor, and farmer, M. Turville Heitz's short fiction appeared in anthologies and magazines before she took a break to collect a PhD and teach science and technical communications to undergrads. Her novel Black River was published in 2024 under the Mystique Press imprint of Crossroad Press. She lives on a defunct farm near Madison, Wisconsin where she coddles chickens and is kept by cats. She can be found on social media at MegT.bsky.social

https://Oaklandhillsfarm.com

## Other Novels by M. Turville Heitz

Black River
Specters from a Dream (Book I of The Enchanter's Web)
The Rising of Kedtair (Book III of The Enchanter's Web)